POISON IN THE BLOOD

Glory is Poison Book 1

KATY L. WOOD

www.Katy-L-Wood.com

contact@Katy-L-Wood.com

Educators, librarians, and others interested in arranging an appearance by Katy L. Wood at their event should contact her at the above provided e-mail.

Summary: Dustin Lockwood sets out on a cross-continental adventure through a post-post-apocalyptic world ravaged by plagues, wars, and vampires with his younger brother Russell to rescue their sister Shae ten years after she was kidnapped, desperate to ignore every sign that things might go wrong.

Hardback ISBN: 979-8-9861137-1-5
Paperback ISBN: 979-8-9861137-3-9
EBook ISBN: 979-8-9861137-2-2

First Edition 2020

Let's go on an adventure.

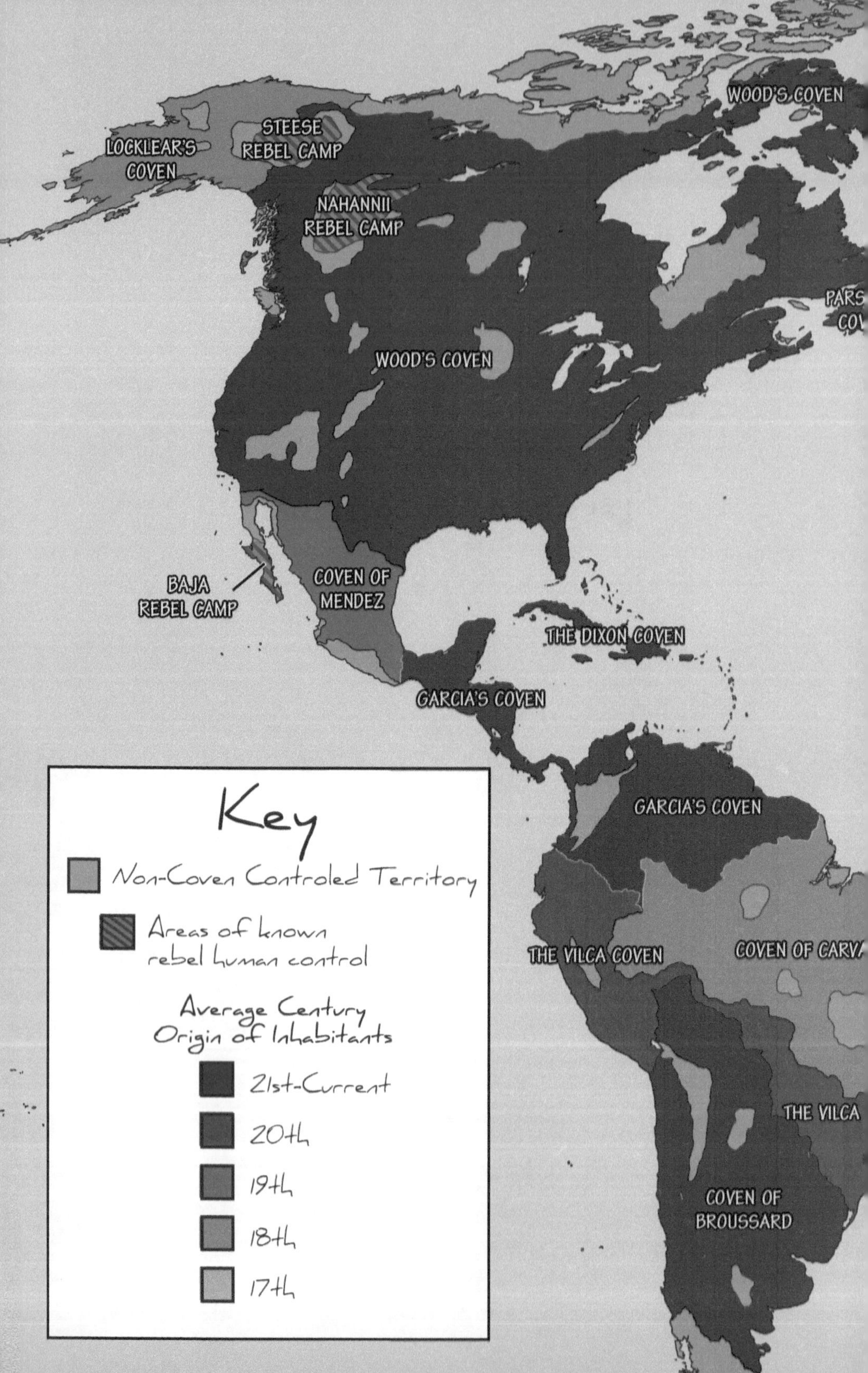
WOOD'S COVEN
LOCKLEAR'S COVEN
STEESE REBEL CAMP
NAHANNII REBEL CAMP
PARS COV
WOOD'S COVEN
BAJA REBEL CAMP
COVEN OF MENDEZ
THE DIXON COVEN
GARCIA'S COVEN
GARCIA'S COVEN
THE VILCA COVEN
COVEN OF CARVA
THE VILCA
COVEN OF BROUSSARD
Key
Non-Coven Controled Territory
Areas of known rebel human control
Average Century Origin of Inhabitants
21st-Current
20th
19th
18th
17th

JENSEN'S COVEN
COVEN OF THORIRSSON
PERM REBEL CAMP
VOLKOV'S COVEN
VOLKOV'S COVEN
RIDDLESDALE'S COVEN
MONTPELLIER REBEL CAMP
COVEN OF RODRIGUEZ
COVEN OF D'CRUZ
DEMIR COVEN
TAHAN COVEN
T.C.
COVEN OF RODRIGUEZ
COVEN OF D'CRUZ
NIGER REBEL CAMP
CHAD REBEL CAMP
COVEN OF SLEIMAN
KOLINGBA COVEN
COVEN OF AFOLAYAN
KOLINGBA COVEN
HU REF
RIO GRANDE DO NORTE REBEL CAMP
THE COVEN OF ROHAN-ZELLERS
KGALAGADI REBEL CAMP
MADAGASCAR REBEL CAMP
THE PRETORIUS COVEN

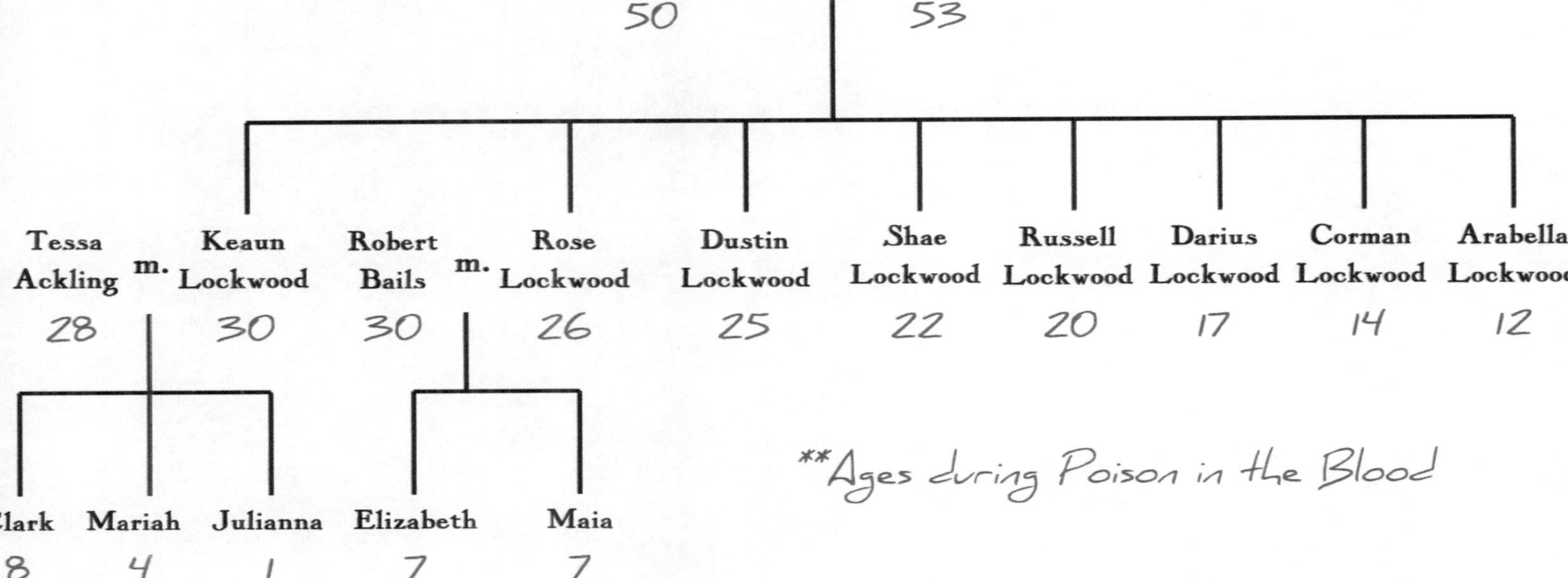

Isabella
Lockwood ne McAllen
50
m.
Christian
Lockwood
53
Tessa
Ackling
28
m.
Keaun
Lockwood
30
Robert
Bails
30
m.
Rose
Lockwood
26
Dustin
Lockwood
25
Shae
Lockwood
22
Russell
Lockwood
20
Darius
Lockwood
17
Corman
Lockwood
14
Arabella
Lockwood
12
Clark
8
Mariah
4
Julianna
1
Elizabeth
7
Maia
7
**Ages during Poison in the Blood

Prologue

"I get why you're doing this, but does it have to be him? He just... looks like a slimeball," Shae's girlfriend Helen said, face screwed up in distaste as she studied at the cracked laptop screen over Shae's shoulder.

"Him being a slimeball is why I picked him," Shae told her. On the screen was the profile of a local talent agent, the last standing of the twenty or so Shae had been considering ever since she'd started this plan.

Helen made a dissatisfied noise.

"Or I could not do this, and we could stay stuck in this place forever," Shae responded, standing up and throwing her arms wide to make her point. Both her hands smacked into the opposite walls of their "apartment." It was a single room, four-and-a-half feet wide, twelve-feet long, and seven-feet high. A twin bed was crammed at one end, supported by milk crates filed with their clothes. There was a tiny desk, a hot plate, and a mini-fridge. Helen's books were scattered in haphazard stacks across the floor and Shae's good dresses hung from the ceiling.

There were ten other such apartments on their floor, the sixth floor of fifteen, and each floor shared a single bathroom with two toilets and one shower stall.

"Keep it down!" The neighbor to Shae's left growled, voice clear through the thin wall. Shae gestured in its direction to further make her point.

"Okay, I'm not saying you're wrong. Living in The Park sucks, but we're right on the edge of London and we both work in the city, anyway. We're barely ever here," Helen replied.

Shae threw her hands out a little harder this time, causing dust to rain from the ceiling while she stared at Helen, making sure exasperation was clear on her face.

Their neighbor shouted again, threatening to call the super and have them kicked out. Shae didn't much care if he made that call. Their super was Turned and Shae had bought him off with a small jar of her blood before. Not that Helen ever needed to know about that. It would upset her. Partially that upset would be over Shae bribing someone official, but it would also launch Helen into a rant about the unfair distribution of blood to the Turned and the rising costs of blood infused foods.

"I just… I worry about you getting famous," Helen sighed. "Being an actor can be dangerous. Putting yourself out there like that, in front of the Turned, especially with who you really are…."

Shae came over and leaned down in front of Helen where she sat on the edge of their bed, cradling Helen's face between her hands. Helen was a beautiful woman, maybe not by the standards of the post Plague War world, but beautiful to Shae. Bright blue eyes, blond hair, tall and lithe frame. Her naturally tan skin kept people from noticing her now, but Shae liked it. Liked the contrast with her own intentionally pale skin. Meeting Helen a year ago had been an unexpected sidetrack in Shae's plans, but it had turned out to be a good one.

"I love you, Helen," Shae said, leaning in for a quick kiss. "But I can't keep living like this. I have a way to get everything I want, something I've been after for nine years since I ran away from my family, and I will not waste that."

"What about your adoptive parents, Barbra and Devon?" Helen tried. "I know you don't talk to them, but—"

Shae cut her off, gently, "Barbra and Devon are good people, but they have their own lives to take care of."

Helen sighed, giving in with a slight nod. "Go get famous then."

Shae smiled and kissed her again, deeper this time, before pulling away. "It'll be fine, Helen. Besides, it's the anniversary of the declaration of the Plague Wars today. They say it's a lucky day."

"I've never understood how the declaration of the wars that nearly ended the world could lead to luck," Helen returned. "Besides, it isn't even a major anniversary.

"Oh, come on, the wars didn't nearly end the world. Just. Shook it up a bit," Shae said, straightening up and starting to gather her things.

"Four billion people died, and almost a billion of those left got turned against their will!"

Shae blew out a breath, aware that she'd stumbled into one of Helen's interests that she could go on about for hours. Actually, Shae realized she'd stumbled into two of them. The wars and the turning process.

"Well," Shae said, scrambling to head off the lecture, "maybe people consider it lucky because we survived after all that."

Helen had a knowing smile as she watched Shae. "You don't want to listen to me going into this again, do you?"

Shae smiled sheepishly and nodded. "I'm just not into that stuff the way you are. And you were talking about the wars all day yesterday."

"I was lesson planning! Half my students don't even know what year the wars started!"

"Does it matter?" Shae asked. "It was three centuries ago."

"Three-and-a-half, Shae. 2029. They started in 2029."

Shae was edging towards the door. "Fascinating, really. But I'm… ah… gonna be late."

"You're leaving three hours early," Helen pointed out.

"Late!" Shae said, grabbing her purse as she smiled at Helen, who was laughing. She could still hear Helen's laughter once the door was closed. Yeah, Helen had been a good sidetrack.

Shae'd spent all her money on this new dress—a slinky corseted number with a late Victorian cut to the shoulders and a hint of bustle, the fabric all black with a touch of red shimmer, and the skirts slit up to her thigh—so that meant walking to Mr. Buckholt's office. She didn't mind. The whole point of today was getting noticed, maybe even starting a rumor or two among those who were really paying attention.

Most of the people she passed only spared her a glance before going back to shuffling along the dirty Park streets. Some asked her for money, holding out little cups in her direction. She had no money to give, not yet, but she did give them each a sympathetic smile. They likely hadn't asked for their lives anymore than she'd asked for her real parents to destroy hers, and it was because of her parents she knew what it was like to live on the streets, even if it had only been for a year. Leaving them, and her siblings, behind had been the right choice. If she'd followed them to the all-human settlements in northern Canada her life would've been miserable forever, rather than just for a handful of years.

Within a few blocks she was out of The Park and into the edges of the industrial side of London, though that didn't improve things much. Really, the only difference was that now she was among the poor Turned rather than the poor humans, and the poor Turned took a little more notice of her walking in their midst. Their pale, grayish faces lifted, following her progress down the street, instincts to feed warring with the knowledge of laws against feeding directly from humans.

London, and the coven that controlled it along with most of the northwestern parts of Europe, were technically one of the richest covens in the world when it came to blood. They had a healthy balance of humans and Turned, unlike many other covens. But even the richest countries always had poorer citizens, and that was who Shae walked among now. She had sympathy for them as well, but didn't show it. An unfriendly beggar could stab her, but an unfriendly Turned could drain her dry in five minutes, laws be damned. She wasn't famous yet, so her death wouldn't be worth anything. Just another footnote in the paper and the whole point of today was to be worth a hell of a lot more than that.

"Derringer, Anastasia," the front desk attendant droned. Shae had been listening to her call out names for the last two hours and not once had the woman looked up from her phone.

"That's me," Shae said.

"You've got five minutes," the attendant told her, waving at a door to the side of the front desk.

At eye level on the door was a gaudy gold plaque proclaiming the office belonged to "Evan Buckholts: Renowned Talent Agent." Renowned was one word for it, but underhanded and greedy were more accurate. That was why Shae had picked him. She went through the door and into the office beyond, sweeping the whole room with her eyes. The walls contained lots of photos of a portly man with an arm around the shoulders of famous English actors, both ones he represented and others he didn't. Jeremiah Doven, Ricardo McHill, Ariane Cordova, Jaysie O'Halligan. No family photos. Nothing personal at all that she could see.

Shae turned to face the portly man in question where he was sitting behind an oak desk that was far too big for his office, leaving little room for anything else. He had scant hair to speak of and there was a beady quality to his eyes. The photos on the walls had clearly been altered to improve his appearance. Somewhat.

Time to get things rolling.

"My name isn't Anastasia Derringer," Shae said.

"Get out. I don't work with people who lie their way into my office," Mr. Buckholts replied, waving her away.

"It's Shae Lockwood," Shae said, hands on her hips, accenting her corseted waist. This dress was the most expensive she'd ever owned as an adult. Hopefully it would be worth it.

Mr. Buckholts' hand froze mid-wave, his little eyes narrowing as he studied Shae. She'd been planning this day for over six months and she knew she looked the part, looked like her mother had twelve years ago, the last time anyone who mattered had seen Isabella Lockwood. Shae's caramel brown hair was cut to her shoulders and pressed straight, light brown eyes framed with just a dusting of deep red eyeshadow, matching lipstick, a splatter of freckles across excessively pale skin, veins tracing along her arms and neck.

"Can't be," Mr. Buckholts muttered, lowering his hand but still looking intently at Shae. "The Lockwood family vanished twelve years ago, all nine of 'em—ten if you count that Isabella was pregnant—ran from Mendez Coven after their oldest son murdered the politician's kid. Rumor had it they stayed in the Baja Rebel Camp for a couple years, then went north. Haven't been seen or heard of since. Probably died in the Sonoran desert...." He seemed to be talking more to himself at this point, and Shae didn't interrupt. "Can't be...."

"You'll find that I can be," Shae stated, producing a folder from her large purse and placing it in front of him on the desk.

Settling herself into a chair, she watched as he opened it. The first thing in there was a glossy, full-page portrait glamor shot of Isabella at a press event for her movie *Oranges in the Ashes,* the last movie she'd ever made. Shae had found the photo on an old gossip website and printed it at a local shop. Mr. Buckholts lifted the photo up and held it in front of him, eyes dancing between the paper and Shae's face. For once Shae was glad she looked so much like her mother. Ever since she'd ran away nine years ago, she'd hid the resemblance, kept her head down, dyed her hair darker, contoured her face, waited. But now, well, twelve years was enough time for the world to have forgotten the sting of murder accusations lobbied at her brother, forgotten the sting of her parents betraying everything they'd stood for to protect him. And she was an adult now, not a kid being dragged along on an adventure she'd never asked for. There'd be sympathy for her if she played this right. Sympathy, and adoration.

Mr. Buckholts face split into a leering grin and he set the photo back down, reaching out a thick finger to press a button on his desk phone. "Cancel the rest of my appointments for today."

Shae allowed herself a modest smile. "Thank you."

"I'll need more proof, before any contract is signed," he returned.

"Of course," Shae nodded, pulling out a little glass vial and her pocketknife. Mr. Buckholts eyebrows crawled up his forehead as Shae slit the tip of her left pointer finger open and squeezed several drops of blood into the vial before screwing the lid back on. "A DNA test should suffice, I think? I know my parent's DNA will still be on file with Mendez Coven."

"Drawing blood like that is dangerous in this part of town," Mr. Buckholts said, but he took the vial. "Lots of poor, hungry vampires around."

Shae shrugged, pressing her bleeding finger between her lips. "If I were worried about the Turned wanting my blood I wouldn't be trying to become an actress, now would I?"

He eyed her appraisingly for several long minutes and Shae let him, lounging in the chair.

"I met the Lockwoods once," he said after a while. "Isabella and Christian Lockwood were quite the duo.

Lots of rumors about them, especially after the murder."

"They were famous actors in a part of the world that never quite clawed its way back to being civilized after the Plague Wars," Shae said simply. "Of course there were rumors."

"If what you're telling me turns out to be true, we're going to have to play this carefully," he said.

"That's a given."

He contemplated her for several minutes. "What do you want from me, Ms. Lockwood?"

Shae grinned at the use of her true name. She had him. "I want you to make me more famous than my parents ever were."

1: Lunch with Ariane

Shae Lockwood looked like a faded version of the photograph of her mother she'd used to gain her fame nearly two years ago; the same eyes, the same smile, the same oval face, but all of it bleached of color. She had only a slight dusting of the Lockwood freckles now, barely visible on skin she kept so pale her veins were as clear as roads on a map. Her hair, grown out to chest-length and allowed to stay its natural lighter brown was swept to one side, crafted waves spilling over her right shoulder. The only true color to her was what she added herself. Today it was a deep red dress cut in a mid-Victorian inspired style with subtle dull gold embroidery in a pattern that accented her curves. A petticoat helped the skirts flow out around her and sweep along when she walked. Black stilettos with a red iridescent sheen and a few bits of ruby jewelry mimicking bloody slashes at her throat and wrists completed the look. It was not a look her mother ever would have worn. Isabella had favored tight, expensive jeans and silk blouses and, while she'd been pale, she'd never pushed it as far as Shae did.

There was still enough left of Isabella in Shae's features for people to comment on her resemblance to her long missing mother, however. Comments that had started as whispers once her agent started getting her small parts, then grown steadily over the last two years as her parts got bigger and bigger, until finally, just recently, there had been a tearful official reveal. She was indeed, as everyone had been speculating, a Lockwood. It went exactly as Shae and her agent had planned.

Her hansom-cab lurched to a stop in front of a cute little bistro, earning an annoyed honk from the regular taxi behind them and pulling Shae back into the present. Outside stood a cluster of reporters being monitored by a Turned police officer. It was easy to spot who among the photographers was Turned and who was human. The Turned photographers didn't have to jostle for position, knowing that neither they nor anything they wore or held would show up on the cameras. Meanwhile, the few human photographers had been forced to the back where they'd be out of the way.

The officer monitoring them was leaning against an artificially distressed column at the entrance, arms crossed and only glancing at the crowd when their energy revved up at Shae's arrival. Shae's newest friend and current co-star, Ariane Cordova, was waiting for her at the edge of the sidewalk, standing with his best side to the cameras, two large Turned security guards hovering at his back.

"Shae-Shae, looking as radiant as ever," he said, his voice low and mouth twisted into the slightest smirk beneath his sleepy eyes.

Where Shae was a faded photograph, Ariane was one that hadn't been exposed quite long enough in a dim room. It was hard to find his edges, but once you did you realized they were rather sharp. His skin was far too deep a shade of brown to naturally show his veins, no matter how much he avoided the sun, forcing him to get vein tattoos and implants to appeal to his Turned audience. But aside from those limited modifications, hardly even worth considering modification in today's world, he was a blank canvass. Shaved head, fake earrings, no other tattoos or scars. At any moment he could slip into being something else because he was already nothing at all.

"Nice top hat," Shae snickered from the seat of the cab.

Ariane rolled his eyes and offered her his arm to help her out. "Says the woman wearing a dress that involves a petticoat."

"It's in fashion. The Riddlesdale Coven *loves* its Victorian throwbacks."

And they did, especially in their actors. To be an actor in the post Plague War world was to be elite and beloved. Turned could not be captured on film or audio in any manner, meaning humans were the only ones capable of making most permanent forms of entertainment now. The only ones who could make movies, audiobooks, radio shows, any of it. There was value and adoration there. But that love could be snapped away if an actor wasn't careful, and Shae worked very hard to be careful. It had taken over a decade and abandoning her family to get this far. She would not ruin it with the wrong dress.

They paused, arms still locked, to entertain the small cluster of photographers that swarmed forward, stopped only by the glares of Ariane and Shae's combined security. Inside the restaurant was a lunch meeting, one they were late for, with their co-stars and other people involved in the movie the two of them had stared in. It was some ridiculous survival movie about a plane crash called *The Odds of Two*. More specifically, the meeting was about the month long press tour they were about to embark on. Late or not, though, there was no reason not to spend a few minutes outside entertaining the tabloids.

Shae waved and gave a slight smirk and a playful tilt to her hips. She knew exactly what angle she needed to set them at to get the open-fronted style of her skirts to drape just right to show off her legs. The dress may have been inspired by five-hundred-year-old Victorian styles, but it had modern influences in the amount of skin it showed off. Ariane merely inclined his head to show off his neck, directing focus to the snaking faux varicose vein implant winding up the right side.

"What was it like filming in the Maldives?!" A Turned photographer with a video camera shouted.

"Filming in the Maldives was a bit too sunny for my taste," Shae chuckled, repeating the question in her answer so it would be on the recording.

"Great setting for a plane crash, though, and the

locals were delightful," Ariane added, giving the camera a mischievous wink.

"Do you miss your family, Shae?" Another photographer shouted.

Shae arranged her face in the properly remorseful expression and lied. "I miss my family every day."

It had been over a decade since she'd left them behind, living on the streets for a year before being adopted under a false name to avoid their mistakes, and in those years she'd felt a lot of things about her choice. Most of those feelings could be summed up as anger towards her parents for putting her and her siblings in the position that they did. The family had had everything they could've ever wanted until the murder, and then her parents tucked tail and ran, destroying it all.

"What do you think of visiting Wood's Coven for this tour with so much unrest there due to the blood shortages?" A human at the back of the crowd asked.

Ariane shrugged. "A little unrest keeps life interesting."

"Anastasia, Anastasia! Ms. Derringer! Over here!" One photographer shouted.

"Come now," Shae said, her smile hardening a touch for a fraction of a second. "My name is Shae Lockwood. It has been two months now since the story of my real identity broke, and two weeks since I proved that I am one of the missing Lockwoods with that silly little DNA test. No need to call me Anastasia Derringer anymore."

With that she and Ariane turned and strode into the restaurant, letting the door swing shut behind them and cut off any further questions. Their security remained outside, and Shae assumed they'd be splitting up to cover all the entrances as usual.

"Enjoying being London's newest movie star?" Ariane asked. He tossed his top hat onto the floor now that they were inside. Unlike Shae, who wore the height of fashion to tempt her fans with the blood running under her skin, Ariane didn't care in the slightest about fashion trends. An actor since he was fourteen, nearly eleven years now, he'd already managed to permanently ensnare the public eye enough to keep his ego satisfied. He still wore fashionable things, they just weren't *in fashion* things unless his publicist forced him into it.

"As soon as our movie is out, I'll be famous in more than London," Shae said. "That's the whole point of all this."

She leaned over to look in a mirror hanging on the wall of the restaurant lobby, pulling a tube of lipstick out from where she'd tucked it in her corset and under her breast, using it to touch up the maroonish color of her lips. Ariane was watching over her shoulder, making no attempts to hide it. They'd only known one another for about a year, since Shae had auditioned to star alongside him, but Shae had decided the man was worth getting to know. She had no interest in a relationship. Her girlfriend Helen was perfect, but that didn't mean a connection with Ariane wouldn't be useful. He knew this industry, knew this world, better than she did. Until recently she'd only ever existed on the fringes of it. Her childhood didn't count, as her parents kept her well clear of their work.

"You certainly raise a lot of questions that pique the average person's interest," Ariane commented. "The daughter of Isabelle and Christian Lockwood, two of the most famous actors in the world until they turned against their coven and vanished all those years ago. The only one of their eight children to ever be seen again. Keaun, Rose, Dustin, *you*, Russell, Darius, Corman, their unborn daughter, all gone with Isabella and Christian in one night. Not that anyone ever saw much of any of you in the first place. Always secreted away in that compound on the coast of Mexico."

Shae met Ariane's eyes in their shared reflection, forcing away the shiver that Ariane saying her siblings' names sent down her spine, especially Dustin's. Plenty of people had asked her about them since the reveal of her identity—mostly about where they were—but none of those questions had been as direct as Ariane's plain statement. She tucked her tube of lipstick back in its place, rolling her lips to even out the color as she did. "My parents didn't want us in the public eye. They felt it was safer that way."

"Safer from what?" Ariane purred. "The dangerous little vampires that swarmed the world following the plagues, getting high off all that sick-blood? Your parents' whole lives revolved around entertaining the Turned, just like yours now does."

Shae moved to look him straight on, hit with the realization that this was the first time they'd talked since the DNA test results had been published. His interest was unexpected, as was his knowledge of her family. Though, to be fair, if anyone would seem intimately familiar with the details of her past, it made sense it would be him. He was from the same coven she'd grown up in before her parents fled, The Coven of Mendez, after all. Still. Something seemed to be hiding under his questions that Shae couldn't pin down.

"We would have made for quite tasty snacks for the Turned, and even better bargaining chips," Shae said eventually. "My parents *were* loved. Perhaps a little too loved."

"And yet here you are. Rising from the ashes after living under an assumed name for ten years, surfacing again with a daring story of familial kidnap and miraculous escape after they all died, all at twelve-years-old. Quite the story."

"The press is rather fond of my story."

"As am I," Ariane said. "I just happen to be aware that it is a *story*."

Shae shrugged and gave him a little smile. "The truth doesn't matter, nor does anyone's belief, as long as people are interested."

Ariane barked out a laugh, breaking the tension that had been welling up. "And that, Shae-Shae, is why you are such an interesting creature."

They slid into the last available seats at the far end of the table. Everyone else already had drinks and appetizers. The scent of fried cheese mingled with the scent of salsa mingled with the scent of half a dozen soups. Shae found the contrasting odors annoying and resolved to purchase something that would overwhelm everything else. Something fishy.

Picking up the menu, she started scanning it for options. It was all the usual small restaurant fare; burgers and chips, soups, salads, a few pastas. Each option listed the standard ingredients, then the options for human blood additions and substitutions. A ketchup blood sauce, bloody marinara, and other such things. It seemed like every day they came out with new ways to mix blood into food. Had to keep the Turned fed somehow, and adding it to the food had proven to work better than just providing pure blood to be purchased at donation centers. Easier to distribute. Infused food and pure blood from the centers were the only way the Turned could *legally* get blood, anyway, as feeding straight from humans was outlawed.

The director of their movie, Nadia, stood up at the head of the table and clapped her hands for attention. She was an older woman, somewhere in her sixties, and highly respected in the film industry. She had never worked with Shae's parents back in the height of their fame, however. This had been a disappointment. Working with one of her parents' former directors would've gotten the press in even more of a tizzy.

"Well, now that the last of us have arrived," Nadia said, shooting a pointed look at Ariane and Shae.

"Can't help the traffic, Love," Ariane said.

There were some hushed laughs and murmurs from other members of the party insinuating that it wasn't traffic that had kept he and Shae. Neither bothered to correct their cast and crew mates.

Before Nadia continued a mousy waitress, a human boy no more than eighteen, asked Ariane for his order. The boy looked star-struck, taking several tries to get Ariane's order of a margarita written correctly. To save time, Shae asked him to bring her the same for now.

"Drinking before noon, how naughty," Shae quipped.

"I prefer to think of it as drinking after midnight," Ariane returned. "And did I not hear you order the same thing?"

"Our little secret," Shae said sweetly. "Helen must never know. She already thinks you're a terrible influence."

"She's your girlfriend, not your mother. It's not as if you and I are having some saucy tryst together, much as we may encourage the odd rumor here and there." He reached over and tucked an errant strand of hair delicately behind Shae's ear, both of them aware of the tabloid camera outside the window behind them. The photographer had crammed himself between an ornate bush and the window, a very uncomfortable looking position. It had been worth it, though, for him to get that photo. Shae wondered what headline would be plastered over it tomorrow.

"If everyone could please turn their attention back to

our reason for being here," Nadia said pointedly.

Satisfied that she had everyone's focus, she ran over the plans for the press tour. Technically, it was her sister running the tour. That was how the two of them worked; one making the movies, one marketing them to the world. However, that sister, Elaina, was sick with the flu and legally confined to her home until it passed. Wouldn't want any Turned getting tempted by her sick-blood for a quick high. That had been what kicked off the Plague Wars three centuries ago, after all. Good old Ebola had been bad enough, but when the Turned, still a thing of myth back then, discovered that the blood of Ebola victims gave them an enjoyable high, things had gotten dicey. One domino after another fell, plagues led to Turned losing control led to attempts at extermination led to wars led to half the world dead. People were a little more careful about getting sick after that.

"So," Nadia said, "we leave in one week, as planned. However, there have been some last-minute changes. We will still tour across Wood's Coven, most of the tour going through the United States. As you all know, we had rented a private plane to escort us from stop to stop and we were going to stay in local hotels. However, due to the North American Fuel Worker Strikes having doubled over the last month, that is no longer a financially feasible option. We just can't afford the jet fuel. Thankfully, Ariane's father has graciously offered the use of his private electric train for the duration of the tour, so long as we add a few stops in his coven, The Coven of Mendez.

In the end this should work out better for all of us. We'll have a lot more room, won't have to constantly pack and unpack, and we can make a few more stops along the way, aside from the ones in Mendez."

"What sort of man is your father to have a private train that he can lend out for his son's movie tour?" Shae asked, her suspicions from earlier beginning to build once more. No one in Mendez could afford a private train. No one good, anyway.

As much as Ariane and Shae had grown to like one another over the months since they met, she hadn't gotten to know much of the particulars of his past, nor had they discussed hers. Ariane had never spoken of his family, and Shae had never spoken of hers beyond dropping the necessary hints for the revelation of her true identity. All Shae knew of Ariane's father was that he was some sort of politician in Mendez Coven, the overseers of much of Central America. Mendez had brought together Mexico, Guatemala, Belize, El Salvador, Honduras, and Nicaragua to help end the wars, much like the United Kingdom and parts of northern Europe had been brought together to form what was now Riddlesdale Coven. Each country within a coven was technically still self ruled, but the covens helped handle the Turned populations within them. Shae also knew that Mendez was one of the poorest covens in the world, both in money and blood. A private train given away for a month was a lot of wealth for a man who lived in such a place.

The rest of the table's occupants looked interested too.

It was a mark of how good Ariane was at manipulating the press that no one else seemed to know his background either.

Ariane tilted his head at Shae's question, a calculating look in his eyes. She got the strangest sense he was waiting for her to notice something. After a beat of silence he answered; "My *step*father is a senator in the coven. One of the highest rated human politicians there, though he has applied to be Turned. He's responsible for lovely bills like making it illegal to be in same-sex relationships and requiring all women to have at least two children by the age of fifty in an attempt to bolster the blood supply." His voice was heavy with disdain. "He uses the train for political transport since Mendez Coven doesn't have a good air transport system in place. Not that they could afford the fuel if they did."

A memory niggled at the back of Shae's mind, awakened by Ariane's comments. She couldn't make it form into anything solid, though. Perhaps she had just seen the man on TV when she'd lived in Mexico as a child. It seemed the most likely answer as she'd almost never left the family compound there until the family fled. The only people outside her family that she'd known were the servants.

"Is that really the sort of man we want to have sponsoring our tour?" The head costume designer asked. She was a Turned woman who looked nineteen but, if Shae remembered correctly, was closer to one-hundred-and-fifty. Those on either side of her, humans, had set their chairs a few extra inches away.

Ariane shrugged. "He's well liked by most people, technically. He keeps the limited blood supply for the Turned steadier than it ever was before he was elected, even if his methods for doing so are rather reprehensible."

"What does he get out of offering us his train?" Shae wondered. She couldn't shake the feeling that there was something else she wasn't quite remembering right, and it was starting to annoy her.

Nadia had moved on to the finer points of the tour, leaving Ariane and Shae to talk in lower tones.

"Who knows. More 'I'm pretending to be a good person' points, I suppose. Though, perhaps he wants to torment me by giving us the ability to make more stops. He and I have never gotten along."

"Oh, the adoring fans aren't that bad, and they must be appeased," Shae replied absently, still puzzling over what she couldn't recall. The memory was floating right at the edge of her mental grasp, taunting her like an itch she couldn't reach.

"No one will be appeased when I've been stuck on a train for a month."

Shae shrugged. "Just bring plenty of your little distractions. I imagine LSD would be quite fun on a train while zipping through the countryside."

A slow smirk wound its way across his lips. "True. And I could always pick up one or two of those adoring fans to distract me as well."

"Now you're seeing the benefits."

The waiter returned and set down their drinks. He looked like he'd overheard the last bit of their conversation and rather liked the idea of being one of those fans, something Shae found adorably amusing. Ariane would sleep with people and Turned of any gender, but she knew he'd never go for someone so meek.

"No picking up fans for you, though," Ariane said once the waiter left. "Not with Helen coming along on the tour."

"And why would I need a fan when I've got Helen? She provides plenty of distractions."

"Oh, please do explain, I love hearing the wild details about your sex life," he said with only a hint of sarcasm.

"Alright," Nadia said a little louder. "Before Shae and Ariane continue down a road of conversation none of the rest of us want to listen to, I'm calling this meeting over. We've covered everything pertinent. Shae, Ariane, given that you've ignored the majority of what I've said, would it be worth my time to type up everything and send it to you, or would you ignore that as well?"

"We'd ignore that as well," Ariane said.

She rolled her eyes, too used to the two of them by now to bother being mad. "Make sure you're packed and ready to leave in a week. I'll send someone to collect you."

She dismissed everyone, though most stayed at the table to order full meals. Shae was still intent on something fishy, reaching for her menu again only to be stopped by Ariane's hand on her elbow pulling her up from the table.

"Come on, there are much better places to spend a Friday afternoon," Ariane whispered in her ear.

"Will those places get me in trouble with Helen?" Shae asked as they maneuvered outside, Ariane not bothering to retrieve his jacket and hat.

"Most definitely."

"Delightful."

"Delightful, hmm?"

"As you said, we're going to be on a train for a month. I want to have some fun before we go. Helen will live with it."

Ariane grinned. "Such a delightful creature."

"Glad you think so, because this will have to wait for tonight," Shae told him, stopping just outside the door. "I have to pick Helen up from work. There's a surprise at home that I've been planning for a month. But I'll join you tonight, I promise."

Ariane put on an exaggerated pout. "You know I am terribly impatient."

"It's only clubbing," Shae assumed with a laugh. "Besides, the clubs won't be interesting until sundown."

"Perhaps it's not clubbing that I'm interested in," Ariane returned. "There's a conversation the two of us need to have."

Shae stilled, reminded once more that she felt as if she was missing something crucial, and now she sensed Ariane knew what it was, that he was playing with her.

"But, if you do have to go pick up Helen," Ariane said over her confusion, "you should be going. Meet me at the corner of Fifth and Downing at ten?"

Shae agreed with a slow nod as the cameras and their personal security swarmed them, switching to a smile as Ariane bent to kiss her cheek. More titillation for the tabloids she was happy to provide, even if her mind wasn't on them anymore.

2: The Attack

Dustin Lockwood took in the little town he visited so often, set right on the border between the Nahanni Settlement for Humanity and the surrounding Wood's Coven, stomach sinking as he surveyed everything. The military supply shop that had been on the south end of town smoldered, walls folded in on themselves and charred black, a faded and dinged up firetruck spraying the remains of the structure with a lethargic jet of water. Six bodies lay on the opposite sidewalk, eerily cheery yellow tarps covering them and weighed down with broken bricks. Four other bodies dotted the sidewalks along the length of the street, all covered in the same tarps. A soft breeze carried the gut churning scent of burnt flesh towards him and he tried to focus on something, anything, else.

Closer to Dustin, the town inn loomed up, one of the tallest and oldest buildings in town. It had technically been here since before the Plague Wars, but the amount of renovations raised the question of if it was still the original building despite every piece having been replaced one by one over the years. The Yukon winter, several months passed now, had not been kind to it this year. It would need a new roof before winter came again. Though, after this battle, that was the least of its problems. All the windows on the first floor, which housed a bar, were broken. Windows were hard to get out here in the middle of the wilderness with the coven on all sides. A lot of things were hard to get, but it was worth it to not be under the rule of the vampires.

Dustin mounted the steps to the raised sidewalk in front of the inn, taking it slow and noting with interest that the glass was broken outward, shards glimmering against the warped wooden planks of the walkway. His heavy elk-skin and tire-sole boots cracked the glass further, the sound grating in the silence.

"Hello?" Dustin called through one of the broken windows. He knew better than to just walk in the front door of this place right after an attack.

"Lockwood?" A smokey old voice sounded. Dustin let himself relax a little at the familiar tone.

"Yeah, it's me," Dustin replied, opening the door and stepping into the dim bar.

It didn't look much better inside than it had outside. The pool table was overturned, worn green felt facing the windows and rifles still propped along the back. Balls were scattered everywhere, drinking glasses decorated the floor with more broken glass, and a newspaper had gone to pieces where it seemed to have fallen off the bar.

The room smelled of the drinks that had been spilled, their sharp scents mixing with used gunpowder and old wood. A few shocked looking patrons sat at one end of the counter nursing drinks with shaking hands.

The innkeeper, Ramona, stepped around the bar, holding a shotgun longer than she was tall. It wasn't that it was a particularly long gun, it was just that Ramona was somewhere around ninety-years-old and had never been all that tall even before age shrunk her. She always gave Dustin free drinks and told him the best times to get out of the settlement unnoticed based on the patrol schedules, since it happened to be illegal for him to leave at all. She wasn't supposed to have the patrol schedules, but she knew them anyway.

Ramona, as usual, looked unfazed by whatever had occurred. Thick glasses settled tightly on the bridge of her nose, silver hair braided out of the way, faded plaid button-up shirt tucked in to prevent it snagging on anything as she worked the bar.

"You picked a hell of a time to come home," Ramona remarked.

"I'm sorry," Dustin told her. And he meant it. He might have been able to make a difference. Might have saved at least a few lives. "What happened?"

"One of the cults from the starving towns attacked around dawn."

The starving towns. Dustin hated that term. It was accurate, it just didn't seem quite right. It wasn't enough.

Nahanni was isolated in northern Canada, Yukon

Territory, surrounded on all sides by area claimed by Wood's Coven. The isolation had allowed it to become possibly the biggest all human settlement left in the world, though that isolation made it hard to say for sure. It had been built up out of the ashes of the Plague Wars by people who didn't trust the covens when they appeared suddenly with an offer to help end the violence. The offer had been simple: help build a system to feed the vampires without anyone having to die, and they would help humanity reign in the swarms of new vampires that had been accidentally created by uncontrolled feeding during the plagues. Maybe it had started well, Dustin didn't know, but it hadn't lasted. Those who'd seen the failure of the new system coming never bowed to it, isolating themselves in ever-shrinking pockets all over the world.

There were a handful of small coven towns within a hundred of the Nahanni border, and they were all struggling. It seemed the ruling coven of the area, Wood's Coven, had been failing to supply them with the blood they needed to survive. Dustin had heard rumors this was causing cults to form around various figures promising as much blood as the citizens could eat. Problem was, that blood came from Nahanni residents. The laws against feeding directly on humans didn't apply outside the coven that made those laws, the cult leaders would assure, so no punishment could be given.

"The military didn't... help?" Dustin tried. He wasn't particularly fond of their military for a lot of reasons, but they had to have done *something*.

Ramona laughed once, the sharp sound startling the patrons at the bar. "Oh, there were a few clouts in town when the attack started, and a few more happened to wander in halfway through. Didn't get here until after the shop blew, though. Quite the light show, all those explosives going off. We handled most of it ourselves, as we usually do."

"You seem to have done a lot of the handling," Dustin pointed out, gesturing at the destroyed room.

"Oh, they sure tried to come in. We didn't let them, though," Ramona replied, affectionately patting her shotgun. She pointed a thumb over her shoulder at the other occupants of the bar. "Had a bit of help too, though I must emphasize that it was only a bit. Not the best shots, those three."

Dustin felt a small smile quirk his lips at Ramona's grumbling. "Well, I'm glad you're alright."

"I am indeed."

"Let me help you clean up in here," Dustin offered, moving to take off his pack, the tin pot and cup hanging on one side clanging together lightly as he moved.

She held up a hand to stop him, glancing over at the patrons at the end of the bar. They'd gone back to sipping their drinks without paying Dustin and Ramona any mind.

Her voice was low as she spoke, "I appreciate the offer, kid, but it might be best you head out."

Dustin frowned. "No one saw me cross the border.

Nothing illegal about living rough within Nahanni itself."

"All true, however... that little brother of yours, the soldier one, he's in town."

"Russ?" Dustin said, heart leaping into his throat. Images of Russ torn to bits or burned to ashes clawed through his mind, ripped the breath out of his lungs. He couldn't lose another sibling.

"He's fine," Ramona assured. "I saw him right before you showed up. Came in to check for bodies. Amazing how much you Lockwood boys look alike."

The tension left Dustin so quickly he felt his knees almost give out. A steadying hand on a crooked table kept him standing.

"*But*," Ramona pressed on, "he might be a bit more suspicious about seeing you here. I know damn well your family doesn't know what you get up to."

"Neither do you," Dustin said without thinking.

Silence stretched between them for a painful amount of time.

"I know you leave," she said. "That's enough. Back door's unlocked."

Dustin dropped his shoulders and nodded, taking a step in that direction. The sound of the front door scraping along the floor broke the quiet before he made it to the hallway. He stopped, staring at the cracked mirror behind the bar, eyes locked on the equally frozen reflection of his little brother standing in the doorway.

Dustin had only been away from home for two months, but Russ had been deployed for six. It was the longest they'd ever gone without seeing one another. Russ hadn't changed much and while there certainly was a resemblance between them like Ramona said, it was only a genetic one. They had the same soft brown eyes, the same wide nose and slightly thin mouth, the same thick eyebrows, but their lives had led the rest of their appearances in different directions. Dustin, who went south frequently, was absolutely covered in freckles, while Russ only had a smattering of them on the most prominent parts of his face. Russ' hair, a few shades lighter brown than Dustin's, was buzzed, and he was clean-shaven. Dustin's hair was currently down to just below his chin, the top layer pulled back in a ponytail to keep it out of his face, and his full beard was nearing in on an inch long, the longest he'd ever let it get.

Despite being in a battle only hours earlier, Russ didn't look all that geared up. He had on military issue pants with protective plates built in to prevent vamp bites, which was something. His shirt, though, was a regular long-sleeved shirt meant to go under their armored jackets. It would be nothing more than tissue-paper when it came to a vamp bite. At least Dustin's toughened buckskin jacket would slow a bite down.

As they'd stared one another down without moving, Ramona had busied herself pouring two generous glasses of whiskey. "Sort your shit, boys," she declared before vanishing into a back room.

Russ seemed startled by Ramona, watching the door she'd gone through with wide eyes. Sometimes Dustin forgot how strange people found such a brash yet tiny old lady. He turned to face his little brother.

"So… you're here," Russ said, finally stepping all the way inside and closing the door behind himself.

"Yeah. I was swinging by to visit Ramona, she's a friend, and I saw the town had been attacked. From the smoke, I mean."

Dustin saw the other patrons glancing furtively at them, curious as to the tension in the room.

"Are you coming home?" Russ asked.

"Of course," Dustin said. "I never leave for too long, you know that."

Russ hummed noncommittally, eying the glasses of whiskey Ramona had set out. One glass was missing a rather large portion of its rim.

"I *am*, Russ. I was on my way there, I swear. This was just a stop on the way."

Russ stared at his brother for a moment before softening, shoulders dropping and lips curling up slightly.

"I missed you, Dustin."

"I missed you too, Russ. I didn't think about how my being gone worked out with your deploy—"

An earsplitting shriek tore through the shattered windows, interrupting any further apologies. Russ spun and darted out the door, pulling a pistol from a holster under his left arm. Dustin cursed and ripped at the straps of his pack, letting it smash to the floor as he followed, drawing his own pistol from his right hip to cover him.

Out on the street stood six vampires, ranged in a

half-circle across the road. At the center of the arc was a tall woman, crisp blond hair cut to her shoulders. She had on nice jeans, a deep purple shirt, and a dark black suit jacket that had been nice as well, but one arm was badly singed. One of her hands, sharp nails painted pink, twisted tightly in the hair of a young boy, the other clenching one of his shoulders.

A human boy.

No more than ten-years-old and flushed with life, a clear contrast to the woman who held him. She was the blue-grayish sort of pale the vampires got when they hadn't fed. All the vampires were. Another woman, Dustin assumed she was the boy's mother due to their similar features, was sobbing in the arms of a Nahanni soldier who was holding her back from running to her child and getting killed. The boy himself, however, was furiously stomping at the vampire woman's shoes and pulling at her fingers. Even starving, she was strong enough to not care about his attempts at escape. Dustin admired the kid's effort, though.

"We weren't finished eating," the woman said. Her voice was crisp and authoritative. "So let's make a deal—"

"Fine," Dustin interrupted before she could name her terms.

Russ, still a few feet in front of him, startled and glanced back, eyes going wide when he saw Dustin standing there. Russ opened his mouth to say something, probably to the effect of "shut up" or "go back inside" if his face was anything to go by. Dustin pressed on before he could speak.

"You want blood, right? Six of you, eight pints in me. Let the boy go."

"Dustin—" Russ' tone was frantic.

Dustin wished he had time to explain his ruse to his brother. He didn't, though, so he continued to ignore him and plowed on, lowering his pistol and taking a few steps forward.

"A kid won't feed all of you."

The vampires all surveyed him, stances shifting in his direction, but Dustin kept his focus on the one holding the boy. Her gaze was intent, assessing, as her followers shuffled around her. Their fingers clenched and unclenched, jaws hanging open and lips pulled back, fangs slid out over their regular teeth and dripping saliva. They looked so inhuman Dustin guessed they hadn't had a good meal in days. Before she could make a decision one of her pack let out a frustrated growl and in a flash of movement he had ripped the boy from her grasp and sunk his teeth into the child's throat.

Dustin dove past Russ and into the fray, ignoring the risk, ignoring the screaming. He had to get the boy, get them off the boy. The other vampires, scenting the blood, piled on as well, creating a mess of flailing limbs and guttural noises. Dustin couldn't even see the boy. Abandoning his pistol, he slid a hunting knife from his boot and grabbed the blond hair of the leading vampire, yanking her head back and sliding the knife across her throat. He finished with a quick and practiced twist of the knife that slipped it between two vertebrae and sliced her spinal cord. The body went limp, still tangled with the others. But it was enough. The others knew there was a threat now.

A cacophony of screams and hisses descended on Dustin as all five still standing vampires turned their attention to him, taking him to the ground. He felt two of them gnawing at his limbs and knew he only had a minute or less before they made it through the toughened leather and hit skin. There was just enough room for him to wrench his knife around and bring it to the throat of one creature gnawing on his left arm, sawing awkwardly upward into the flesh of her neck until she gagged and released, scrabbling at the blade with slick fingers. She had nowhere to go, though, tangled together with everyone else, and Dustin finished her off the same way he'd done with the previous creature.

He was distantly aware of shouts and possibly even shots as he brought his knife to the next biting vampire. This one was ready for him, rearing back out of range. Whatever. Dustin didn't care what order the vampires died in, he just cared about the fact that if they were on him they were off the boy. Kicking out at another vampire he managed to push it back enough that whoever was shooting got a clear shot, the vampire's head exploding from a high caliber round. The three remaining vampires slowed their attack, glancing at their fallen friends, and Dustin felt something yank at his shoulders, dragging him backwards out of the pile.

"WHAT THE FUCK?! WHAT THE FUCKING FUCK WAS THAT?!" Russ shouted. One of his hands stayed firmly on Dustin's shoulder, preventing him from standing as he took shots at the remaining vampires, all three of whom had run off into the woods.

"The kid," Dustin demanded, spinning around in a desperate search for the boy.

He found him splayed out on the ground several feet away, unmoving. His mother knelt next to him, rocking and screaming his name, as the other soldier checked for signs of life. The soldier tried a few times with a few different pulse points before shaking his head and dropping his hands.

"Landen! Landen! Landen!" His mother screamed, pulling his limp little body to her chest and rocking him.

Dustin felt himself going numb as he watched the scene, memorizing more detail than he wanted but unable to look away. The limpness of Landen's arms, the gory mess that was his throat, his blood soaking into his mother's gauzy white hijab as she clutched him to her, no longer able to form words.

Russ broke the moment, hauling Dustin to his feet.

"You—you," Russ spluttered, running his eyes over Dustin, pistol still raised slightly in the direction of the woods. Dustin realized Russ was shaking, eyes wide with fear. "You just fucking dove in there. You should've been... They could've...."

"I'm—I'm fine, Russ," Dustin said, wishing his voice was steadier. "They didn't make it through my jacket."

Russ shook his head, eyes still wide. The look of fear and confusion set Dustin's nerves on edge. Russ was looking at Dustin like he didn't know who he was.

Ramona broke the moment as she walked silently through all of them and knelt by the mother's side, reaching out a arthritic hand to rest on her back.

"Bring him into the inn, Sabiha, we'll make sure he's warm," Ramona said, tone gentle.

"He's, he's only eight," Sabiha hiccupped, puffy red eyes turning up to Ramona. "He has a soccer tournament this weekend."

Ramona nodded. "Great sport. I've got a few soccer books at the bar we can put with him, alright? Let's bring him inside."

Sabiha nodded shakily and scooped Landen up, cradling him to her chest as she followed Ramona inside. Dustin, Russ, and the other soldier waited, staring at the empty doorway until Ramona reappeared, alone. She stood in silence, surveying the scene. The three injured vampires sprawled awkwardly on the ground, none showing signs of healing yet, though the second one whose throat and spinal cord Dustin had slit was scowling and baring her teeth at them. The other soldier had a high-powered rifle slung across his back and he walked over to shoot her in the forehead, tears in the corners of his eyes.

"You're going to die pulling stunts like that, Dustin Lockwood," Ramona said eventually.

"I had to try," Dustin returned.

Ramona grimaced but gave one curt nod. Behind her the few people who had been at the bar warily poked their heads out of the shattered windows. Other citizens wandered into the street to stare, peering tentatively at the scene without coming close. A few had followed Sabiha into the inn, but most were watching Dustin and Russ. Dustin winced, trying to avoid their questioning faces and wishing there hadn't been witnesses to the fight. Too late now, though.

Ramona shuffled out into the street, kicking at a fallen vampire once she was close enough. The vampire's hand twitched towards her foot and she shot the hand with her ever-present shotgun.

"It was still a fool move, Lockwood," Ramona muttered. "And if anyone knows how badly hostage situations with vamps can go, it is me."

Dustin had no idea what she was referring to. Based on the haunted look in her eyes, he wasn't sure he wanted to.

He dropped his eyes, giving a small nod. "Point taken."

"You got a lot of fight, though," Ramona admitted, "for a kid raised in the covens."

An uneasy silence settled over their little group. The Lockwood family having only been in Nahanni for about nine years was an awkward topic for everyone aside from Ramona. She had no qualms about diving into awkward topics. Leaving a coven was not an easy thing to do as a single person, and for parents to escape with their eight children was unheard of. Well. Seven children. Dustin and

Russ' parents had pulled it off, though, escaping Mendez Coven despite their worldwide fame. But trust was a hard-won thing in Nahanni. It would take a lot longer than nine years for the Lockwood family to find complete acceptance here, if they ever could.

"We weren't raised in the covens," Russ mumbled. "We were raised on the run. Same as so many people that didn't have the luck to be born in a settlement."

"There isn't time for this," Dustin interrupted. "Those three other vampires ran into the settlement, not back to the coven."

"They could be miles away by now," the other soldier pointed out. Dustin felt like he should know the man's name. He was sure they'd met before, if only in passing.

"Vampires may be fast, even when starving, and better coordinated than humans, but our forests are a mess on this side of the settlement," Dustin said. "They haven't burned since the wars. There's deadfall and brush everywhere that will slow them down. They may not have gotten far at all. Call in a chopper if you can. The thermal sensors can't see them, but one is wearing a bright red jacket. It will stand out."

The man and Russ glanced at one another uneasily.

"There's no chopper," Russ said. "We've only got six and the other five are up north doing water drops on a fire that's threatening the geothermal energy plant. They left one for us, but a bolt failed on one of the blades last week. It's grounded until we can make a replacement."

Curse their cobbled together military, Dustin thought.

Everything they had was ancient Plague War equipment or bits and pieces stolen from the coven over the years. He picked his pistol back up from where it had fallen in the fight, holstering it slowly to give himself time to think.

"The border road has a northern turnoff about three miles out of town," Dustin said, stringing together a new plan. "It goes north six miles and then there's a turn west back this way. If we hurry, we might be able to cut them off. Ramona, can you get these ones beheaded and burned?"

Ramona nodded, and Dustin turned to Russ expectantly. Russ stared at him for a short moment, then groaned.

"Fuck it, alright. Mike, you're with us," he said to the other soldier. "We'll radio for backup on the way."

🌲

They climbed into a military truck parked on the north end of town. Russ and Mike took the two front seats while Dustin climbed into the high-set bed. Two benches ran the length of each side, providing seats for up to ten soldiers. The metal shell encasing the back had a few badly welded patch jobs, light filtering in along parts of the edges. Dustin crouched behind the front seats, open to the back, as Russ threw the truck into gear and sped through town, turning so fast and hard they drifted around the corner onto the border road. Mike radioed in their plan, frowning at the poor signal as he did.

"You've been fucking lying to us," Russ shouted over the roar of the truck once Mike finished.

"Says who?" Dustin asked. He'd maneuvered to kneel so he could look through the windshield and see where they were going, eyes roving the forest around them for any sign of their targets.

Mike, for his part, seemed very intent on not involving himself in a fight between the two Lockwood brothers, and was studying the forest even more intently than Dustin.

"You didn't learn to fight like that in the damn Nahanni woods," Russ said. Clearly, he'd gone from freaked out to mad and Dustin wasn't sure that was any better, so he didn't answer.

"I swear, if you've been leaving the settlement," Russ hissed. When Dustin didn't rebuke this statement Russ went a bit pale. Apparently he hadn't believed Dustin had been leaving, not enough to keep from being shocked that it was the truth. "You... you could be killed! Dammit, Dustin! If the covens knew there was a Lockwood in their territory they'd destroy you! Not to mention what *our* government would do if they found out! You'd be labeled a damn traitor, *especially* with our family history! They barely trust us as it is!"

Dustin thought about lying. Before today it would've been easy. Even though he usually just lied by omission, he could've come up with a story. But now Russ was suspicious and had very good reasons to be.

"I was in Colorado..." Dustin said slowly, still unsure how to proceed.

"Colo—*Why*?" Russ ground out.

"I've been trying… trying to find Shae," Dustin said, just loud enough for Russ to catch his voice over the roar of the truck.

Shae.

Speaking her name forced the images of Landen's battered body back into his mind, except Landen's face was replaced with Shae's the last time Dustin had seen her. He gulped in some air, shaking his head in a physical attempt to rid himself of the mental picture. He'd seen more than enough like it in his nightmares.

She'd been missing for a decade now. Abducted from their ramshackle camp when the family was on the run. Of his seven siblings, Dustin had been closest to Shae. She was a few years younger than him, a couple years older than Russ, and the only family member who hadn't made it to Nahanni when they'd fled the accusations of murder levied at their oldest sibling, Keaun. All Dustin had left of her was memories and one old snapshot from when she was ten-years-old. And all the terrible imaginings of what might have happened to her.

Russ stiffened. "She… she's gone, Dustin. Probably dead…."

Dustin's first instinct was to snap at Russ. Shae was not dead. She couldn't be, no matter how often his nightmares told him she was. She was alive, somewhere, and just needed someone to help her get home. But there was something in his little brother's face, something in the tense set of his shoulders…. He was lying.

Before Dustin could follow up on his second instinct, which was to figure out what the hell Russ was lying about, Russ slammed on the breaks, nearly sending Dustin flying into the front seats. Regaining his balance, Dustin looked through the windshield to see that five new vampires were standing in the road twenty yards ahead. Instinctively he twisted around and saw that the three who fled from town were now behind them, along with four others.

"Fuck, fuck, fuck," Russ hissed.

They had nowhere to go. To their left rose thick forests, to their right a steep drop-off that led to a river a-hundred-and-fifty feet below the road. Beyond the river was empty wilderness that turned into coven territory in less than a mile.

"I can handle this," Dustin said. He even sort of believed the statement, despite twelve vampires out in the open being more than he'd ever handled alone.

He'd already moved to jump out of the truck and do just that when Russ snapped, "No you can't, sit down and shut up."

Dustin didn't have time to object as Russ floored it straight at the vamps standing in a line across the narrow road in front of them, didn't have time to warn him that this was probably a much worse idea than Dustin's.

3: New Apartment

Shae watched Ariane shrink into the distance, swallowed by reporters as her new cab, this one a closed carriage, pulled away. It would take fifteen minutes to get to Helen's school where she taught year fours from, so that was all the time Shae allowed herself right now to think about the puzzle Ariane presented.

What she knew for sure was very little, but it had to be connected to her childhood somehow. It was the only point of overlap between them. Even then, there wasn't much overlap. Shae and her siblings had grown up in a walled compound on the western coast of Mexico. Only Keaun and Rose, the oldest of her siblings, had ever been allowed to leave, and even then it was under heavy supervision of security. Back then her parents had told Shae and her siblings it was because they were royalty and that was just how royalty lived. Shae supposed it had been a decent enough lie, as it wasn't that much of one. Their family was coveted and beloved, rich in a country of the starving. That wasn't so different from royalty, and a much better thing to tell children than if they went outside they risked being kidnapped and repeatedly drained for their blood which would sell for thousands on the black market.

Even now Shae was constantly surrounded by security, more than the average actor since her true identity had been revealed. An ever-present bit of background noise that she didn't pay much mind to. One had climbed up on the front of the cab with the cabbie and there'd be one outside Helen's school as well, ready to shadow her if she ever left the gated grounds during the day.

All her security were Turned. Faster, stronger, and unable to get in the way of any cameras swarming her as no part of them would show up in the photos. It was one of the most enduring mysteries of the Turned, their lack of recordability. Science had begun to explain many of their other aspects—their lack of aging, their need for human blood to function, their heightened abilities, their varying reactions to sunlight depending on their age—but no one had ever come up with a viable theory as to why they couldn't be recorded, let alone why that extended to the things they wore and held. There had been, and continued to be, plenty of tests over the last century and Helen, ever obsessed with the biological mechanisms of the Turned, rattled on about every one of them ad nauseam.

Shae never knew much about the Turned when she was growing up. Her parents had explained them as being another aspect of humanity, different from humans but still people. They'd always made it clear to the kids, though, that the Turned were dangerous. Now, as an adult, Shae couldn't quite remember how they'd done that. What had they said that convinced Shae and her siblings the Turned were to be respected but never interacted with?

But it wasn't just careful descriptions of the Turned that her parents gave her. Growing up the compound meant Shae had been cut off, learning only what her parents wanted her to. Her every want was catered to: fancy food, the best toys, interesting home-school lessons on whatever schedule she liked, maids to do the cleaning and cooking. But she'd never known anything of the politics of the country and coven she lived in, let alone anything about any of its senators, and never cared to ask. What child would? As much as she pulled at the loose strings of memory, there didn't seem to be one that lead to anything relating to Malcom nor Ariane.

The carriage clattered to a stop in front of the old pre-war brick building where Helen worked, easily finding parking right in front as most parents who sent their kids here couldn't afford their own transportation. Shae lounged in her seat, knowing Helen wouldn't leave until her entire class had been picked up from the summer day-camp she was helping run. Shae could have used that time to continue thinking about Ariane, but something about watching the children get picked up always fascinated her.

There were six gates, one for each year at the school, and the students of each year lined up behind the gates. The parents lined up on the street side and the head teacher of each year stood at the front of their line, letting the children out to their parents one by one. It was orderly, but in a sort of disturbing way. Like the children were cattle being parceled out.

Having never been to a real school herself, Shae had been fascinated by Helen's work ever since they'd met. It was an example of what life was supposed to be like for children. Schedules and homework and parents there to pick you up at the end of the day instead of traveling the world to film movies.

"Lost in thought?"

Shae smiled at the sight of Helen's face in the window. She was her usual prim-and-proper self; light blond hair in a high and tight bun, not a hair out-of-place even after a day of wrangling children. Her simple black-rimmed glasses were settled perfectly on the bridge of her nose, sky-blue eyes softening at Shae.

"Just about you. Ready to go?"

Helen nodded and pulled open the door of the cab, tossing her purse in first before climbing in and sitting across from Shae, her lavender and vanilla perfume filling the closed space. Shae bought her that perfume. Helen melted into the seat once she sat, slouching down and letting her head hang back.

"Long day?" Shae asked.

"One of my students this summer has a fondness

for biting things. Up until today it was inanimate things. Books, his desk, pens and pencils. Then, today, he apparently decided inanimate things weren't good enough and he bit three other students. Three—stop laughing, An—Shae."

"I'm sorry," Shae gasped, wiping a tear from her eye, "but, I just, your tone!"

Helen stuck out her tongue and Shae leaned across the gap between them to give Helen a quick apology kiss, the seat cushion creaking beneath her as she settled back into place.

"So, what is the punishment for biting three people when you're nine-years-old?" Shae asked.

"Therapy and constant observation so he can't bite anyone else. Wait, wasn't that our turn?" Helen leaned over to look out the window, a frown on her face.

"It used to be our turn."

Helen looked at Shae with narrowed eyes. "Used to?"

Shae just smiled.

"I'll cook your favorite for dinner if you tell me where we're going," Helen tried.

"A very, very tempting offer as your tamales are dangerously good, but I have been working on this surprise far too long to give it up that easily."

Helen thought for a moment. "How long do I have to continue negotiating?"

"Ten minutes."

"Tamales for the whole week?"

"They're better when they're an occasional thing.

Builds up anticipation."

"Tamales tonight, and I'll go to your next press thingy with you?"

Shae whistled in surprise. Helen loathed press events. Too many jealous people mad that Shae was taken, too many pointed questions about the personal aspects of their relationship. Shae was perfectly fine with handling those things while Helen liked to pretend they didn't exist.

"Technically, you're already going to my next 'press thingy' by coming on the tour with me. Next?"

Helen pouted and stayed silent for a bit, a look of concentration on her face. "Tamales tonight and... I'll wear a dress to your next press thingy?"

"You hate dresses. You always look miserable in them. Not worth it to have a miserable girlfriend with me."

"Yeah, that's fair."

"Tamales tonight and—"

"Too late, we're here!" Shae interrupted.

Helen looked out the window again and frowned at the little bookshop they'd stopped in front of. It was on one of the quieter upper class streets of London, large bay-windows filled with posters about new releases and events. Shae had only been inside once, pleased by the picture-perfect maze of uneven shelves and cluttered books placed on every available surface. The shop's resident tabby lounged in one window, watching traffic rumble by.

"I feel like the bookshop isn't actually it..." Helen said.

"Nope. It's just a nice bonus given your love of books

and inability to live in a library. Come on."

Shae unlatched the door and let it swing open, sliding elegantly out and turning around to hold out a hand for Helen. Together, with Shae in the lead, they walked to a narrow door set on the far right side of the three story building. Shae produced a key from her corset and opened the door, pulling Helen into the little alcove on the other side. Helen looked around dubiously as they ascended the stairs and came to another door, which Shae unlocked but didn't open.

"Ready?" Shae grinned, hand poised on the doorknob.

"I still don't know what I'm supposed to be ready *for*."

Shae rolled her eyes and flung the door open with a flourish of her arm.

"Welcome to our new apartment!"

Helen's eyes widened as she stepped inside, her jaw dropping once she looked around. It was nicer than anywhere they had ever lived. When they'd met they'd both been living in The Park, but after Shae had gotten her first movie role, a smallish secondary role still under the name of Anastasia, they'd moved into a little studio just outside The Park. It had barely been any bigger but did have a cramped bathroom and a slightly larger cooking area with a real, though half-sized, stove.

Now, though, they could finally afford a place worth living. This apartment was two floors, the first with an open plan livingroom and kitchen area. The kitchen was huge and contained a full-sized everything; fridge, oven, stove, double sink, dishwasher. Even a little island with a bar on one side. The wall opposite the kitchen was floor to ceiling bookshelves Shae had already stocked with Helen's books and new ones she purchased to fill some of the space. Along the wall facing the street were two bay windows matching the ones in the bookshop, a large fireplace between them. An arrangement of cushy chairs and a long couch were settled in front of it, their legs sinking into the plush carpet. At the back of the room and to their right was one door leading to a modest bathroom, two others to closets.

"When… when did you do all this?" Helen asked, stepping into the kitchen and running her fingers over the whiteish quartz countertops.

"Been looking for a place for a few months but couldn't find the right one. This place came on the market two weeks ago and I bought it immediately. Ordered the new furniture a few days ago and had all our stuff moved in today while you were at work."

"Are you sure we can afford a place like this, An— Shae?" Helen asked. "I mean, it's huge! And these appliances are state-of-the-art."

Shae wanted to point out they weren't state-of-the-art; Riddelsdale Coven, which controlled most of northwestern Europe, was a bit behind on the times. All of its major ruling figures had been born in the late 1800s, and they were very set in some of their ways which affected just about everything in some manner. Though, Helen had grown up in a coven run by even older Turned and had only recently started to move up in class with Shae here in London, so Shae supposed they did seem state-of-the-art to her.

"I've been in three movies now, my real identity is out there, and I have three more movies lined up. This place is a conservative estimate of what we can now afford."

Helen shook her head but smiled, continuing to explore the kitchen. It had everything she could ever want, and Shae had made sure the fridge and pantry were fully stocked with fresh food. Helen poked through everything before shifting her attention to the bookshelves. She contemplated them from a distance for a moment before turning back to Shae.

"Show me the rest?"

"Of course."

Shae toed her boots off and slid them over against the wall to retrieve when she was wearing something that was easier to bend down in. They accessed the second floor via a door opposite the entrance, leading to a staircase that went behind the bookshelves. There was no door at the top, the empty doorway opening on a beautiful master-suite. A king-sized bed sat between the bay-windows, the bedding Helen's favorite navy blue color. At the back were three doors; the first an extra large closet, the second a small laundry closet, and the third the master-bathroom.

"This bathroom is bigger than our first apartment," Helen announced once she stepped inside. "And the tub is bigger than our bed was."

"Calling that hovel an apartment is very generous,"

Shae replied, following her into the bathroom. "Unlace me?"

Helen did, expertly working the laces on Shae's dress and corset until Shae could shimmy out.

"Any chance I could convince you to make those tamales now? I didn't get to have lunch," Shae asked as she carefully secured the dress on a hanger and hung it from a towel rack.

"I thought you had a lunch meeting at that little bistro downtown?"

"I did, but once it was over Ariane told me he wanted to speak to me about something, so I left with him, and then I came to pick you up from work, so no lunch."

Helen frowned, watching Shae redress in black leggings and a red, silky long-sleeved shirt. "I still don't like him, An—Shae."

"Why do you keep almost calling me Anastasia?" Shae asked. "When your friend Sean changed their name last year, you never had this much trouble. And you've known my real name for ages now, even if we never used it until I went public with everything."

Helen shrugged, casting her eyes down to the floor. "I guess... it isn't that you've changed your name. I think I'd be fine if you just changed your name. But sometimes... it's like you've changed more than your name. Like there's two different people. There's the sweet theater girl I met almost three years ago, and then there's this suave actress who everyone is clamoring over."

"Oh."

Shae didn't really know what to do with this answer.

She was the person she had always been; the one who did what she need to get by.

"So... um... tamales?" Shae said, not sure what else to say in response.

Helen sighed, leading the way back downstairs.

As they wandered back through the bedroom, Helen's eyes dancing over everything, Shae caught sight of the framed picture on her nightstand and stilled. The picture was one of only two things she had held onto from her childhood. It was the last picture of her family before they ran from Mendez, and the only time they had all left the compound. Her parents had taken them to a private beach for some celebration Shae couldn't remember. In the photo they stood behind their children, both looking like regal masters of their world. Shae and her siblings were staggered in front of their parents, all smiling ear-to-ear and holding dripping popsicles.

Shae stepped over and picked up the frame, studying the picture closer, brushing her thumb across the faces of people she hadn't seen in so long. Her younger siblings didn't evoke much memory as they'd mostly been annoying toddlers when she'd left. Rose, her only older sister, was smirking and had put up bunny-ears behind Dustin's head, which brought up scattered memories of many little pranks over the years. Dustin, though... he elicited plenty of memories. They'd always been close. Really close. Almost close enough for Shae to trust him. She hadn't, though.

Her oldest brother, Keaun, was on the farthest right

side and around his shoulders was a tanned arm of someone who had been left out of the photo. It hadn't been cut, so Shae never thought much of it, figuring the photographer accidentally left the other person out. Or intentionally left them out, as they weren't a Lockwood. The other person had never been a concern to her. She didn't even remember paying them any attention that day.

Until recently the photo had been tucked in a folder and never bothered with. Shae hadn't even meant to keep it when she left. It had just been folded up in the pocket of her hoodie. Something made her hold on to it over the years, keeping it hidden. When people had been asking for proof of her identity, she'd offered the photo as part of proving it, turning it over to the authorities for an age progression to be done on her childhood face. It had been returned last week, and now it was out, sitting prominently in their bedroom due to Helen's insistence, bringing up memories, memories of that person who had been cut out of the photo....

"Helen, I have to go."

4: Post Attack

Running vampires over pissed them off more than anything else. Not that it wouldn't piss a human off, but it would also generally kill a human. If you hit a vampire you'd end up with a damaged vehicle and an angry blood-thirsty monster even more intent on ripping out your throat than it had been before.

"Fucking listen to me next time, Russell!" Dustin snapped. "I could have handled it!"

Beneath them the truck was making a very concerning grinding sound, coughing black smoke from under the hood. It was still trundling forward, though it was losing speed as it did, and not caring how much Russ cussed at it and slammed his foot down on the gas and clutch. Mike, meanwhile, rolled down his window and looked like he was contemplating hanging out of the moving vehicle with his rifle. Dustin admired the thought while doubting Mike's ability to do it safely.

"Stay in your seat!" Dustin shouted over the much louder grinding noise that had started up, now accompanied by a strange thwapping noise.

He spun on his heel and made for the back of the truck, knife at the ready, intending to jump out the back to deal with the vampires face to face. A loud ripping sound from beneath his feet pulled him up short. There was the second problem with running vampires over; if there was enough room they tended to grab on to the undercarriage. They had the strength to tear the vehicle to pieces and the healing abilities to not worry about a little road rash.

The truck gave a magnificent shudder and started careening to the right. Russ screamed a new set of curses, attempting to wrestle back control of the vehicle. It seemed the steering wheel no longer served its intended function. Dustin scrambled back towards his little brother, wrapping his arms tightly around Russ' seat and Russ' chest, trying to hold him in place as the truck vaulted over the edge of the road and down towards the river below.

Dustin tucked his head in, keeping his arms tight around his brother, and pushed down the spinning sensation that went through his organs as the car flipped onto its top. The roll cage kept it mostly in shape, but not quite enough. Glass shattered and choking dust filled the cabin as the truck slid upside down towards the river, metal shrieking and tearing around them. He'd been forced to let go of Russ once they were upside down and now crouched on the ceiling, one hand thrown up to grip the bench above him, riding out the rest of the crash.

When the truck stopped, Dustin let the relief that they hadn't gone into the water overwhelm him for a moment, but only one.

"Russ?" He said, forcing a quiet calm into his voice. If Russ was hurt Dustin didn't want him to panic. Neither did he want the remaining vampires to hear them.

"Fucking vamps," Russ said with a growl that turned into a cough. Dustin could just make him out in the haze of dust filling the car. Being in the shadow of the mountain they'd crashed down wasn't helping either.

"Are you hurt?"

"Left arm's broken, but I'm alright," Russ said after a moment. He was still hanging by his seatbelt.

Dustin wiggled his way into the front compartment over a torn open section of the roof and helped support Russ' weight as Russ cut his seatbelt to release himself. He fell in an awkward heap in Dustin's lap, letting out a hiss of pain as his arm was jostled. Before they could move to help Mike, who was unconscious and still upside-down, both froze at the sound of distant voices. They were too far away to make out words, only an unfriendly tone.

"Get Mike down, then stay put until I get back," Dustin whispered.

"What the fuck do you mean stay put until you get back?" Russ hissed. "Where the hell are you going? You can't handle however many are left on your own!"

Russ moved to grab Dustin with his good arm, but Dustin grabbed his wrist first. "*Listen to me. Right now.* Your friend is hurt, probably badly. You are hurt.

I am not. Either I handle this or we die. If you go out there they will grab you, and they will use you. Do you understand me?" Even through the dimly lit dust Dustin could see the fear in his little brother's face. He released Russ' wrist and gently squeezed his shoulder, giving him a reassuring smile. "Have I ever not come home?"

Russ hesitated, then nodded his consent for Dustin to go. Dustin wasn't sure where his knife had gone in the crash, but he still had his pistol with a full magazine. Hopefully that would be enough. He slid down the roof of the truck, avoiding the jagged edges of the holes and glad that the truck had landed in such a way that exiting through the back would give him cover to asses the situation.

Inch by inch he peered up over the edge of the undercarriage and up to the road, about eighty yards above where the truck had stopped. There were at least eight or nine vampires standing at the edge, somewhat silhouetted in the setting sun.

"Fuck," Dustin grumbled to himself. Their forms would've made great targets up on an exposed ridge like that if not for the darkening forest behind them. Dustin could barely tell what was vampire and what was trees. He'd have to lure them in closer to stand a chance of hitting them. There was no other option. He couldn't let them turn back to the town.

He lined up his pistol, aiming to incapacitate if he could but mostly to piss them off. Exhale. Trigger pull. One vampire crumpled, screeching and clutching at its shoulder, and Dustin couldn't help the slight thrill of satisfaction that raced through him. Several of them hesitated before turning and running away, the others racing down the slope, leaping from foothold to foothold on the torn up earth. They weren't particularly good at it, stumbling frequently, only their heightened senses and speed catching them before they fell.

Dustin steadied his aim using the bumper, keeping the truck for cover. His chances of shooting them as they ran were slim, but he still tried and managed to get one. Its body kept tumbling, making no attempts to stop itself. It had been a good shot. The second vampire reached the truck and leaped onto the torn metal, fangs bared. Dustin fired up into its chin, sending it toppling backwards as the third vaulted the vehicle. It overshot and landed on the ground several feet behind Dustin, forcing him to turn his back to the last two. His pistol sounded once, a bullet slamming into the vaulter's left cheek, before Dustin was knocked forward by something slamming into his back. Spinning with the momentum, Dustin rolled and brought his gun back up, firing straight into the chest of the vampire that had tackled him. It stumbled and coughed, not needing to breathe but still thrown off by the hole through its lung.

Unsure where the final vampire had gone, Dustin fired another shot into the head of the one clutching its chest, then for good measure did the same to the one he'd hit in the cheek. Standing, he turned around, pistol raised as he searched for the last creature. It, a woman, was standing at the head of the truck, illuminated by the somehow still functioning headlights, her bright red jacket glowing in the light. She looked almost human, if not for the pallor of her skin.

"I'm sorry about the boy," the vampire said, a note of seemingly true sadness in her voice. She looked like she'd died in her early thirties, maybe late twenties if the world had been unkind to her, which it likely had. Her black hair had a tracery of silver in it that glinted in the light, and the beginnings of deep lines were etched around her eyes.

Dustin kept his pistol trained on her. "I'm sorry for what happened to you."

Exhale. Trigger pull.

"How's Mike?" Dustin asked, going around the truck and crouching to peer through the shattered windshield.

Russ had gotten Mike down and had him laying on the roof of the truck with his head in Russ' lap. Dustin sucked in a worried breath when he saw the blood coating half of Mike's face.

Russ, bent awkwardly in the confined space, looked at Dustin with wide eyes. "You... you just killed six vamps on your own. With a *pistol*. And they had the *high ground*. And we just *fell down a fucking mountain*."

"I didn't kill them, I took them down. I need to behead them and burn them to kill them, you know that," Dustin said.

"You still took out six vamps on your own, not to mention the ones back in town!" Russ spluttered. "None of our guys can fight like that."

Dustin sighed, relegating himself to the fact that he would need to calm Russ down before any further progress on the situation could be made. "Look, if they were soldiers themselves I probably couldn't have done it. But they weren't. They were untrained civilians who went looking for food where they shouldn't have. My only advantage was training, that's it. Yes, it is different from Nahanni military training, but it isn't some magical skills or anything. Just. Training."

"From *where*?" Russ pressed.

Dustin hesitated. Telling Russ everything could be dangerous. Russ would never even consider telling the military, Dustin was sure of that, but he was also sure Russ *would* tell their mother. Isabella Lockwood was a fierce woman and Dustin loved her immensely, but their relationship hadn't been the best since Shae disappeared. She would be furious at Dustin for what he'd done over the last seven years. Protectively furious, but furious none the less.

"We need to treat Mike," Dustin said at last.

"From *where*, Dustin?" Russ insisted.

"Help me slide him out here into the light," Dustin said.

"*Dustin.*"

When Dustin didn't respond Russ gave in and started helping carefully maneuver Mike out into the light. It was hard work with Russ unable to use his left arm and both of them trying to keep Mike's head and neck stable. Mike started to grunt in pain, which Dustin took as a good sign. If he was conscious enough to be in pain and making noise about it then he was in a better state than Dustin had first assumed. After a lot of slow and gentle tugs and pushes they got Mike into the light enough to get a good look at his face. Not much could be seen through the blood coating the left side, however.

"What are the chances of a med kit in the truck?" Dustin asked.

"Should be one in the glove compartment," Russ said. There was a tinge of pain in his voice that worried Dustin, however head injuries took precedence.

Dustin went around the passenger side and reached in through the empty window, rooting around until he found the latch for the glove compartment. He let the contents fall, scattering across the roof. A bunch of papers tumbled out along with a heavy black flashlight that clanged loudly as it hit, and the promised med kit. The thing was disappointingly small, but it would have to do. He took the kit back around to the front, along with the flashlight.

The kit was even more disappointing when opened. Several regular sized bandages in brittle, yellowed packaging, a couple tiny packets of antiseptic ointment, some tweezers, a few sealed gauze pads, and not much else. Dustin grabbed one of the gauze pads and tore it open, using the sterile cloth to dab away the blood on Mike's face, attempting to uncover the actual wound.

Once he found it both he and Russ hissed in unison. A jagged gash ran from Mike's hairline at his left temple, across his eye, and down to the bottom of his cheek. There was still a small piece of glass embedded in his eyebrow. Dustin didn't say it out loud for fear of scaring Mike if he was awake enough to hear them, but he didn't think Mike would ever see out of his left eye again. One glance at his little brother's ridged form told Dustin that Russ was probably thinking the same thing.

Dustin turned back to the med kit, surveying the contents once more, checking every pocket as he tried to figure out what to do. Field medicine for cuts and scrapes, even serious gashes and knife wounds, was something Dustin knew how to handle, even with limited or no actual medical supplies. But he'd never seen an injury that went across an eye like this.

Russ, seeming to sense his hesitance, leaned over to whisper in his ear; "His life is more important than his eye. We've got to stop the bleeding and hope the doctors can fix the rest when we get him to the hospital."

Dustin nodded and pulled out the three remaining gauze pads, strategically layering them over the length of the wound, using the band-aids like tape to secure the pads in place. Once a sterile layer was established, Dustin went and tore off a strip from the red jacket of the last vampire. He helped Russ get pressure on the wound using the cloth and his good hand, while avoiding the area where there was still glass in the cut.

"Alright, let me see your arm," Dustin said. He'd caught

a few glances at it as they'd worked on Mike and while he was relieved that it wasn't an open fracture it still didn't look good, the skin turning a mottled purple color and a chunk of bone creating a lump under the skin about two inches from his wrist.

Russ gingerly held out his left arm, wincing as he did. "The adrenaline is starting to wear off, so it hurts like hell. Feel free to cut off the whole arm because that might feel better."

Dustin managed a small chuckle as he examined the break.

"I promise you it would not feel better," Dustin told him. The radius was displaced a significant amount, though the ulna seemed to still be in place. "Two options here. We can leave it be until backup gets here, since Mike did radio in, even if it wasn't the best signal. However, because it's displaced, if it doesn't get set soon there could be complications."

"What's option two, then?" Russ asked warily.

"You let me set it now and get a brace on it."

"Option two is gonna hurt, isn't it?"

"Yes."

"Have you set bones before?"

"Yes."

Russ still looked hesitant.

"Russell, I need to get these vamps decapitated before they start to heal. Option one or option two?"

"Fine," Russ gritted his teeth. "Two. But only because I like this arm."

"You're right handed," Dustin pointed out.

"I still like my left one!"

Dustin shook his head and placed both hands on his brother's arm, instructing him to let up his pressure on Mike's face so he didn't hurt him when he undoubtedly flinched from what was about to happen. Without further warning Dustin quickly set the pieces of Russ' bone back into place as best as he could. Russ let out a yelp and glared at his brother through watering eyes.

Dustin shrugged. "Warning you would have made it worse."

"Big brothers are mean."

Dustin rolled his eyes and left to find some sticks the right size and strength to make a splint, using more strips of cloth torn from the vampires' clothing to secure them in place.

Mike was starting to mumble more but still wasn't anywhere near coherent.

"Is the radio still in the truck?" Russ asked once Dustin finished.

Dustin wasn't sure about the radio, so he grabbed the flashlight to check, disappointed to find a gaping hole where the device should have been.

"What can I do?" Russ asked when Dustin told him it was gone. "Mike's bleeding has stopped, so tell me how I can help."

He looked desperate to do something other than sit there, and Dustin felt another pang of guilt in his gut. Lying by omission to the family hadn't been that bad.

No one got hurt that way. Dustin got to do what he needed to do to find Shae, and the family got to think he was safe inside the settlement even if he wasn't home with them. But now, straight up lying to Russ, seeing his little brother look at him like he might not trust him anymore, that hurt.

"Get a fire going," Dustin said, not sure what else to offer. "It'll be the best way for someone to find us. It's too dry to safely make a whole pyre, but at least make it big enough to burn the heads." Dustin tossed Russ a lighter out of his pocket.

Russ nodded and moved to do as told. Dustin wondered at his brother's sudden shift to listening without question, but didn't press it. Grabbing the red-jacketed woman, he hauled her over to the wreak. She'd started to twitch, old blood sloughing out of her head in fat dollops. Dustin wondered how long she'd had to suffer being a monster before he'd shot her tonight. Without his knife his options for beheading her were limited, but a piece of the siding of the truck had peeled away, leaving a sharp and accessible edge at about knee height. Taking a fistful of her hair with one hand and getting a firm grip on her shoulder with the other, he dragged her neck along the edge.

It was slow and messy work, but seven years of hunting both animals and vampires made it manageable, though still a bit sickening. Russ eyed him warily the whole time as he stoked the fire to life, not commenting. The silence worried Dustin more than the endless questions and disbelief had.

Any other day, this would have been a victory worthy of beer and old records and dancing. But what had he really accomplished? There were still three vampires loose in the settlement, and now Russ knew just enough of the truth to be wary. None of it felt victorious, and the brutal work of beheading without proper tools wasn't helping.

Once the red jacket woman was dealt with, Dustin circled around to the back to grab the next vampire; a gangly man seemingly in his forties in an old canvass jacket. Before he grabbed the body Dustin was brought up short by a gleam of metal several yards down the hill, nearly at the edge of the river. Hoping it was the radio, he made his way down to it, flashlight in hand, only to be disappointed by the sight of nothing but an ammo box with a crushed newspaper pinned under it.

He was halfway through turning to go back up the hill when his mind caught up with what he was seeing. On the paper a bold headline proclaimed "*ODDS OF TWO: WOOD'S COVEN PRESS TOUR.*" Underneath the headline was a photo, staring up at the darkening sky. The woman in the photo looked so much like Dustin's mother that he believed it was her until he knelt down and looked closer, catching the date in the top corner. The paper was only a few weeks old, in perfect condition aside from being a bit crumpled, and it was a coven paper. It had to have come from their truck. There was no other way it would be this intact out here.

Dustin pulled the paper out, flattening the pages and shining the flashlight on it to read. Looking at it now, in good light, Dustin saw that it wasn't his mother in the photo. The woman here was certainly related to Isabella, but there were marked differences. Thicker lips, a slightly rounder face. A face that was still familiar, even if it had been ten years since he had seen it, and it had belonged to a pre-teen then, not a young woman.

Shae.

It had to be Shae. There was no one else it could be. Their mother had no other family; she'd been orphaned at four-years-old in a fire.

Dustin studied the photo, drinking in every detail, every bit of vindicating proof that his sister was alive like he had always believed. She was wearing a burgundy Victorianesque dress that showed off quite a bit of skin, her hair twisted up into an elegant knot on the side of her head. A dark red rose was woven into the knot. Standing next to her in a suit without a jacket was a black man with heavy eyes and a smile that had something wicked about it. Beneath the photo was a caption that said the people in the picture were "Ariane Cordova and Shae Lockwood—formally known as Anastasia Derringer—at a London press event for their new movie *Odds of Two*."

Anastasia Derringer? Dustin struggled to figure out what this meant, only to be interrupted by a shout from Russ asking what he was doing. Keeping the paper held close Dustin marched back to Russ and held it out without a word. Russ stilled, glancing between the paper and Dustin, not offering any explanation.

"Should I start with the fact that, apparently, I'm not the only one leaving the settlement illegally? Or the fact that *you knew our sister was alive*?" Dustin said.

Russ remained silent for a few long seconds before answering; "First of all, *I am a soldier*, Dustin. I am *allowed* to leave the settlement when needed. But there's a strict protocol for it and only soldiers can go. You aren't a soldier. Not a Nahanni soldier, anyway. You leaving is an entirely different thing than me leaving with permission and backup." Dustin didn't like the stiff tone that Russ' voice had taken on. It didn't feel like talking to his little brother anymore. It felt like talking to a soldier.

"And Shae?"

Russ swallowed heavily and looked away, his posture slumping. "I only found the paper a couple days ago. Some coven trucker got stupid and came too close to the border to save time, so we stopped him and took his cargo. The paper was in the bunk of the cab. I took it before anyone else in my unit saw it, and I hid it."

"Have you told anyone? Called mom or Rose or... or something?"

"I hadn't... decided what to tell them yet."

"Hadn't... *hadn't decided*? Russ, she is our *sister*! Our sister who got *kidnapped* ten years ago *by vampires*! What you do is tell the family that she's alive and needs our help!"

Russ smacked the paper that Dustin was still holding between them with the back of his good hand. "Does that look like someone who needs our help, Dustin? She's a freaking actress about to go on some huge cross-country press tour for a shit movie that's only getting any attention because she's one of Mom and Dad's missing kids! She's not turned, she's clearly not being held against her will, she's clearly not unhappy. Hell, she's apparently been living under an assumed name! And not just any assumed name. A freaking missing princess from four-hundred years ago and an old pistol brand? Seriously?"

Dustin spluttered, scrounging around in his mind for a comeback to this. "She's... she's still our sister, Russ. I don't care what happened to her. She's our sister and we need to bring her home."

Russ' answer was interrupted by the sound of a motor up on the road. He and Dustin both listened as it came closer, stopped, and the sound of two doors opening echoed out above them. Two flashlight beams shot down the slope, blindingly bright.

"Damn, Lockwood. You've had a hell of a day." The voice was gruff, but Dustin saw Russ relax a little at the sound of it.

"You have no idea, Sir," Russ shouted back. "We need a med-evac. Mike's hurt bad. Head injury."

"You and the other guy?"

"I've got a broken arm. My brother is fine."

"Brother, huh? Which one?"

Russ hesitated before answering. "Dustin. We've got six vamp bodies down here that need dealt with as well, Sir."

The soldier standing next to the man Dustin assumed to be Russ' commanding officer let out an impressed whistle. "You've got three up here on the road too, ya know. Three back in town, and we bagged one on our way here. Might've set a new record for single day vamp kills."

"Guess it was just that sort of day, Johnny, but based on what we saw there's still two unaccounted for if your counts is good. Radio it in and come get us, would you?"

"Alright, alright, don't get your panties in a twist," Johnny said. "Give us a minute to rig a backboard. Down in a few."

With that the silhouettes of Johnny and Russ' C.O. vanished.

"There's no point in hiding that I did what I did today, Russ," Dustin said lowly. "Half the town saw me do it."

"If they ask, I'll answer," Russ said, his voice still tense. "Otherwise, I'm not saying anything. You should know all about that."

"I don't think you have as much room to judge as you seem to think you do," Dustin returned.

They stared at one another in tense silence for a long time. Finally, Dustin folded up the paper and tucked it in the back of his waistband and under his shirt. "We tell no one about this until it's just the family," he said. "Not a word around the military. Once we're home, we'll figure it out."

Russ nodded, refusing to make eye contact with Dustin as they waited for help to reach them.

5: Let the Games Begin

Shae slipped out of the apartment and went straight into the bookstore, exiting out the back of it when the owner wasn't looking to lose her security. Helen had been confused at her abrupt departure, but Shae hadn't had time to explain what was going on. She needed to get to Ariane's and, though she'd never been there before, she knew where it was. Downtown, three streets over from where they'd had lunch, and in the Dale high rise building. Fifteenth floor, apartment C. She'd seen the address on some paperwork he'd been filling out on set months ago.

Once she was a couple blocks from her apartment she hailed a cab, a regular old car, and gave the cabbie the address. In the back she drummed her fingers across her knee, excited but wary of what was about to happen when she got to Ariane's apartment. Now that she remembered what their connection was, she wasn't surprised the memories hadn't come easier. The connection wasn't with her; it was with Keaun. With the murder he had been accused of.

The high rise loomed up in front of them and Shae exited the cab, leaving a large cash tip. She stood on the sidewalk with her head tilted back to look at the building. Even though it was still only mid-afternoon, this side of the structure and the whole street below it was shadowed. People walking by on the sidewalk winced as they reentered the light and stumbled as they came into the shadows.

A Turned doorman was at the door, his uniform a crisp white. Shae could practically smell the starch from here. She watched him for a few moments, debating how to get past him without an invitation into the building. The problem with uniforms was that they made it very hard to read people, hard to find an angle to work. The man had to know that a movie-star as famous as Ariane lived in his building, though, and there was no way he didn't know who she was.

She walked up, smiling sweetly.

"Evening, Miss," he said in a professional, clipped tone.

"Evening, Jayden," Shae read off his gold name-tag. "Just visiting Ariane. Need to go over some scripts with him. Some silly last minute reshoots before we head out on the press tour. Apparently the sound got corrupted in the take of a scene they wanted to use for the final cut."

The doorman looked her up and down, then nodded. "They never did get the computers fixed quite right after the wars, did they? Amazing we can keep anything from getting corrupted these days."

"Isn't it?"

He stepped aside and pulled the door open, bowing her in.

She thanked him and went straight for the elevators, selecting Ariane's floor and enjoying the sensation of getting whisked up so quickly. The elevator opened up on a white hallway with six doors, three on either side, and red carpet accented with swirls of a darker maroon. Ariane's was the last one on the left and she strode down to it, rapping her knuckles on the black door.

After a moment the door opened to reveal Ariane on the other side in ratty gray sweats and a loose black t-shirt full of holes. Shae had never seen him look so casual, and it was rather off-putting. Like a poison frog stripped of all its warning colors. He quirked an eyebrow at her and leaned against the frame with his arms crossed rather than inviting her in.

"I was not aware I had told you where I lived."

"I wasn't aware Clayton had a brother," Shae returned.

Ariane's contemplatively distrusting look flipped to that of a wolf in a butcher shop and he waved her inside, shutting the door behind her.

The apartment was not what she expected. She wasn't sure what she *had* expected, but this wasn't it. Expensive looking paintings adorned the walls, statues stood on pedestals in little nooks, and everything else was gleaming glass and shiny white surfaces. Even the couch was white leather. The two outer walls were solid glass, bathing the large room in sunlight. A warm, spicy smell drifted out of the kitchen, separated from the livingroom by a long bar. Ariane had gone back to the stove, stirring a large pot there as he watched Shae examining everything.

"Want some doro wat? It's Ethiopian. My mother's recipe," Ariane said.

"So cooking is what will get you to finally talk about your family?"

Shae began slowly walking along the walls, examining the art as she went. She saw Ariane shrug out of the corner of her eye.

"It's just a recipe. Some old thing passed down the generations and more of a suggestion than a set of rules. I'm personally fond of adding a little wine to it, which my mother would kill me for."

Shae stopped at one painting of a couple on a staircase. The woman was in front in a satiny pink dress, a large white fur shawl draped elegantly around her shoulders. The man was behind her and up several steps in a slim black suit that wasn't really there at all, merely implied by the gesture of his form against the black background, a cigarette dangling between his fingers. Both stared down over the intricate railing, looks of superiority on their faces.

Ariane came up behind her, stopping shoulder to shoulder to look at the painting as well.

"This is an advertisement painted in 1932," he said. "But it has always appealed to me. I commissioned this reproduction a few years ago."

"It suits you," Shae replied.

"It suits us both, I think."

"Oh?"

"Not a couple, but presented so as the casual viewer might assume they are. Willing to put on a show to get what they want—"

"Manipulative," Shae interjected. When Ariane raised his eyebrows she continued, "you could have just told me you are Clayton's brother."

"I could have, but the problem was not in you knowing it, it was in you remembering it. If you remembered then you truly are Shae Lockwood. If you didn't, then you would have just been a girl pulling a very convincing scam. Delightful either way, but only one of those things interests me, and it is not the scammer."

"Was the DNA test not enough for you?"

"The world runs on blood now. A DNA test means nothing to someone who is determined enough. Perhaps you paid someone to fake the results. Perhaps you somehow purchased a vial of Lockwood blood on the black market; there are rumors of a few floating around still. Perhaps they just got it wrong."

Shae knew he was right. It was why she hadn't relied entirely on the DNA test when she and her agent had been plotting how to reveal her identity ever since he'd signed her two years ago. The Lockwood family photo had been key as well, just large enough for an age progression to be done on her childhood face, and the only known photo of Shae as a child.

"And what about the truth of my identity interests you? My older brother is accused of *killing* yours. They were best friends until the day Clayton died."

"*Exactly*. And nobody knows. Your identity is out there, yes, but no one has picked up on the fact that you are acting in a movie with and, as far as the tabloids are concerned, sleeping with the younger brother of the boy your older brother is accused of killing."

Ariane was as tightly wound as a spring, and Shae felt herself winding up as well, possibilities flying through her mind. Ways to turn this to her advantage, ways to keep climbing the ladder. Revealing her true identity had done a lot to help her fame, but she knew it could be wiped away in a moment by a bigger, juicier story of some sort. The revelation hadn't been the end of her journey, it was a midway point. There was a long way yet to go. Neither of them had taken their eyes off the painting as Shae thought it all through.

She let out a slow breath. "Okay. No more beating around in the dark. Clearly we both want something from this conversation, so let's lay it all out."

Ten minutes later they were seated on opposite ends of Ariane's four person glass-topped table, bowls of wot and glasses of wine in front of each of them.

"You first," Shae said.

"It would help to know exactly what you remember."

"Not much more than I've already said. Keaun was

friends with Clayton and I vaguely remember seeing Clayton at the gates to the house a few times when he'd come to pick Keaun up, and he was there the day we all went to the beach, but I don't think I ever interacted with him beyond introductions. He was just my oldest brother's best friend. However, I do *not* remember any mention of him having a younger brother."

Ariane nodded and put down his spoon, took a swig of wine, and started in on his side of the story. "Clayton was my step-brother. His mother died in labor with him and his father, Malcom, married my mother about fourteen years later when I was six. My mother was, at the time, an ambassador from Ethiopia in the Kolingba coven, which was how they met at some political function. When they got married it was a conflict of interest and my mother left her ambassador position and moved us in with Malcom. We didn't stay long, though, as Malcom got my mother a new traveling ambassador position with the Mendez government. My mother always took me with her as her position changed to different places in the world.

"Now, as to Clayton. He was indeed best friends with Keaun, but I have about as much knowledge of Keaun as you seem to have of Clayton. I was never home to meet him and, apparently, they didn't spend much time at home anyway. Always out on Clayton's boat, and that's what killed him in the end. The fuel tank blew when they were docked and the boat sunk. That's where the story gets messy. Clayton was killed by shrapnel which caused him to bleed out, that much I know. Your brother was blamed because he was supposed to be in the boat as well, but turned back at the last moment and no one knows why. They say he rigged the tank to blow to kill Clayton over some fight they'd had, making an excuse to send their security away beforehand. That's the story Malcom tells, anyway."

"And you don't believe him?"

"Not in the slightest. Do *you* believe your brother killed mine?"

"All I know," Shae told him, "is that after the explosion at the docks the cops brought Keaun home and he locked himself in his room. He never spoke about what happened, didn't speak at all for a long time. Three days after the cops brought him home they showed up again with a warrant to arrest him, saying he'd killed Clayton. Somehow our parents got the cops out of the house and the family was on the run that night. Took a boat across the gulf to the Baja rebel camp. We stayed there for about two years until my parents decided it was still too close to Mendez and decided to head north through the Rockies to get to the camps up in northern Canada. I escaped during our journey north, lived on the street for about a year with my head down, then went to a shelter and eventually got adopted with no one questioning where I'd come from."

Ariane nodded. "After Clayton died, my mother and I came straight home and I spent a lot of time listening at doors, trying to figure out what was going on. All anyone would tell me was that Clayton was dead, nothing more.

Most of what I learned came from the local papers that I took from one of the maids, but one night, about three weeks later, I heard my mother and Malcom talking in his office. Malcom was going on and on, shouting about how he was a failure and a disgrace, saying he messed everything up by trusting the wrong people, that it was his fault the wrong person died. My mother was trying to comfort him, saying there was still time to fix things, to capture your family before they got too far, to turn things back around."

Shae eyed Ariane across the table, feeling like she knew what he was getting at but not quite believing it. "If you are implying that Malcom killed his own son when he meant to kill my brother, then we need to switch to whiskey for the rest of this conversation."

Ariane wordlessly got up and slid a whiskey bottle out of a rack on the back wall of the kitchen, retrieving two glasses from a cupboard. He set the glasses down, clinking them against the table-top, and poured a generous portion into each before sitting back down.

"Damn." Shae shot back some of the whiskey, delighted at the expensive taste of it.

Ariane lounged back in his chair, swirling his whiskey glass between sips. "I have never been able to confirm it, but I believe Malcom saw your family as a threat; they were very liberal and actively campaigned against many of his harsher policies. When Clayton and Keaun became friends, I think he saw an opportunity to take your family down a bit by taking out their oldest son."

"Except he somehow killed his own son instead."

Ariane tilted his glass towards her and pointed, giving a small nod. "And there lies the biggest mystery, and why I am so interested in you being you."

"I don't follow," Shae admitted.

"I want answers. True answers. If one of the most important and ruthless politicians in the world were to be found to have *murdered* his own son, well, wouldn't that be interesting?"

It would, but Shae still wasn't quite sure why it mattered. This was all in the past, thirteen years ago. The answers would certainly be intriguing, maybe even useful to her, but could also be catastrophic if they drew any attention to the rest of her family. Shae didn't know where they were for sure, just where they'd been headed ten years earlier. When she'd revealed her identity she had very intentionally said that nearly her entire family had died on the road of some unknown sickness. It was the biggest falsehood she'd laid, and the one that worried her the most. If it unraveled so did everything else. She almost regretted letting Helen talk her into it.

Every other aspect of her story was set solidly in fact, or at least solidly enough that she was the only one who could dispute it. She'd left because she was afraid to die of their sickness. She'd used a false name because her parents had terrified her into believing that she'd be killed by Mendez Coven if she didn't. She'd revealed her identity now because as she'd grown up she had realized her parents had been wrong to make her think that.

Those were the tent-poles of her story. It was a wild one, sure, but it was set firmly in her control as long as her family remained dead in the eyes of the world.

And why did Ariane want to know about all of this? That was equally intriguing. He hated Malcom, Shae got that, but why not wash his hands of him and move on? Ariane himself admitted that he hadn't been home enough to know Clayton well. So what was he in this for?

"Tell you what," Shae said slowly, "if you help me I'll help you."

"And what do you need help with, Shae-Shae?"

"Depends on what my help gets for you."

Ariane nodded. "Fair."

He held his glass across to her and they clinked their drinks together, each downing the rest of theirs.

"Which leads us to: what help do you want from *me*?" Shae asked, holding out her glass for Ariane to refill.

He grabbed the bottle and tilted it over her cup. "Simple, I want you to keep doing what you're doing, but with an awareness of what's going on. I haven't spoken to Malcom since the conformation of your identity, but there is no doubt in my mind he is aware. He never stopped blaming your family, never gave up on getting what he sees as justice."

"So?"

"So why help us out on this tour? He certainly didn't do it for me, I've made it clear I want nothing to do with him."

Shae eyed him over the rim of her glass as she took a slow sip. "You think he's using it to get to me?"

"I think... that there are a lot of ways for him to make something happen to you while on his train, on a determined and known path through lots of abandoned territory, but still have himself come out of it looking good."

Shae could see that his expression had become guarded and idly wondered if Ariane might be the one to make something happen just so he could blame it on his father.

"Why do you hate him so much?" Shae asked.

"That's my business."

"Not if I'm going to be your bait."

He stared at her in silence, his only movement slow breathing.

"Are we allies or opponents?" Shae asked into the quiet, voice soft but with a hint of venom.

"Both, I suspect," Ariane answered.

"You will tell me why you hate him, eventually."

"Maybe. Will you help me now, without that answer?"

"I don't know how I could say no, considering you just want me to carry on as normal," Shae pointed out.

His lips quirked into a sliver of a smile. "Is that a yes, then?"

Shae rolled her eyes to the ceiling. "Oh, I suppose we could have a bit of fun at Malcom's expense."

They passed the rest of the afternoon and much of the evening drinking and pulling on the threads of their pasts. Shae remained guarded about certain things, and it was clear to her that Ariane was doing the same. Both were angling for control of this new game they had started, and by the end of the evening it was still unclear who had it.

Shae took a cab home, waving lazily at her annoyed security guard when she arrived. It took a few tries to get the key in the lock and, once inside, she nearly tripped over the rug on the other side of the door. Helen seemed to have been going through her bookshelves and reordering them to her liking. There were piles of books all across the floor and Helen was in the middle of them, hair in a looser bun, wearing one of Shae's t-shirts along with her own pink pajama pants with cats on them. Her cat, Mr. Pouty, was clambering all over the stacks, meowing delightedly. Shae still had scratches from wrangling the creature into a carrier for the move earlier in the day, having not trusted the movers to do it.

"Hello, Helen, Darling," Shae said sweetly.

Helen glanced up at her and frowned, both hands hovering in the air with books.

"You're drunk…" Helen observed.

"Possibly," Shae admitted. "Probably. Ariane had a very good bottle of whiskey that he was kind enough to share."

Helen took a deep breath through her nose, a familiar sign that she was holding in her anger. "This is why I don't like that man."

"You've hardly spent any time around him," Shae pointed out. "Probably not more than half-an-hour all together.

"That limited amount has been more than enough."

"I love you?" Shae tried.

"Don't frame that as a question," Helen returned. She'd set her books down and was picking her way over across the messy floor. When she reached Shae, she hooked an arm around her waist and started leading her towards the stairs to the bedroom.

"Are you mad at me?" Shae asked.

"Yes. But I refuse to argue with you when you're drunk. That won't solve anything. We'll have this discussion when you're sober."

"I *do* love you, though," Shae said as Helen helped her up the stairs. She didn't honestly need the help, she wasn't *that* drunk, but she figured it would be a bad idea to debate her level of drunkenness at the moment so she didn't say anything.

"I know, Shae," Helen said as they reached the top of the stairs. She leaned over and gave her a quick kiss on the cheek. "But you've been making some stupid decisions lately."

"Oh, I don't know. Ariane might not be as useless as you think he is."

Helen didn't answer, just deposited Shae on the bed and went to the dresser in the closet and dug around until she found some pajamas for her.

"Change, drink some water, and get some sleep. We'll talk about Ariane tomorrow."

6: At the Hospital

The ride to the hospital in Watson Lake, the biggest town in Nahanni, took hours, during which Mike floated in and out of consciousness. Russ and Johnny did their best to keep him distracted from his facial injury, glad that he seemed cognizant if still a little dazed. Dustin watched all of them from the back corner of the covered truckbed they were riding in. Russ winced every time they went over a bump while doing his best to answer the questions his C.O. asked him from the driver's seat.

"How'd you and your brother meet up?"

"He just happened to be in town, Sir."

"Some people are saying he did most of the killing of the attacking vamps in town during the second wave."

"Dustin is good with a pistol, Sir, and a knife. He took a risk to save a child, though, unfortunately, it didn't work."

"And what about once your truck rolled off the cliff?"

"I didn't see much of what happened once we went over, Sir. I was still in the truck. Couldn't get out until the fight was over."

The officer glanced at Dustin in the rearview mirror and Dustin shrugged. "Like Russ said, I'm good with a pistol. They didn't all come at me at once and they were civilians, not anybody with training."

"Where'd you learn to be so good with a pistol?"

"I live rough a lot, mostly to hunt. I trade the meat and pelts in the market to help support my family. The Yukon has its fair share of dangerous creatures beyond the vamps. It was either get good at shooting or die."

The officer nodded and went silent. Dustin was wary of the man, and shocked that Russ was apparently working under him. As soon as they'd been pulled up the hill Dustin had recognized the soldier. Anthony Stedly, one of the leading generals in the Nahanni military. He had been the biggest opponent of the Lockwoods being allowed into the settlement. There wasn't a worse person to have found them. The paper... Dustin could feel it pressing against his spine where he leaned against the rough plastic coating of the bed. He was glad the sound of the truck hid any crinkling sound the paper might make when he moved. If he got caught with a coven paper, one he'd clearly hidden, there'd be no getting out of the situation. Not to mention the fact it was a paper focused on Shae, the biggest reason Anthony and others hadn't trusted the Lockwoods when they arrived. What the hell had Russ been thinking, just carrying it around?

They pulled up at the hospital and Dustin was the first out of the truck, helping the nurses slide Mike's backboard out onto a waiting stretcher, then forcing a stubborn Russ into a creaky wheelchair another nurse had waiting. They were taken inside and Mike was wheeled behind a curtain followed by most of the nurses. Two stayed behind with Russ, moving him to a curtained off bed of his own.

Dustin situated himself in a corner out of the way, eying the medical instruments ranged along a counter at the back. He'd never been in the Watson Lake hospital before, but he heard it was the most up to date medical facility in the settlement. Nahanni was completely, intentionally, isolated from the surrounding coven. They didn't speak to them, they didn't negotiate with them, they didn't trade with them. But they did steal from them. Not much, as, despite being in the Yukon, Nahanni could provide most of what people needed for a comfortable if rustic life. There were some things, though, that Nahanni couldn't create on their own. Medicines and advanced medical equipment were rather high on that list, and everyone knew the military made it a priority to take those things from the coven. Sometimes they came from unaware truckers like the one who'd had the paper about Shae, other times they came from places that could only be guessed and that the military would never admit to.

"I'm going to call home and let them know you're in the hospital," Dustin told Russ as the nurses fussed over him.

Russ groaned and dropped his head, earning a sympathetic pat on the shoulder from one of the nurses. "Mom's gonna be so mad."

Dustin found an available phone in the waiting room and dialed the number for the family ranch, hoping it would go through. There were no phone lines out to the ranch, and no cellphone network in Nahanni, so the only contact points the family had with town were a single satellite phone and an old ham radio. The phone was hit or miss on getting an answer. There were plenty of people there *to* answer, but the battery in the phone had been dying quicker and quicker of late. As for the radio, you never knew who might be listening when you used it.

The phone rang twice and Dustin let out a sigh of relief when Tessa's voice greeted him. She was his sister-in-law, Keaun's wife, and probably the most level-headed in the family next to his mother.

"Hello?"

"Tessa, it's Dustin."

"Dustin? I can count the times you've called on half a hand. Do I want to know why you're calling now?"

"Russ is in the hospital in Watson Lake. His arm was broken in an attack on the border today. It isn't too bad, but he might need surgery."

Tessa was silent for a moment. "Okay. So... what are you doing with Russ? You've been gone two months and then just happen to come back now?"

"I was visiting a friend in the town that got attacked. Russ and I ran into one another during the fight."

"Battery low," an electronic voice cut in.

Tessa sighed. "Alright, we're on our way. Love you."

"Love you too."

Dustin hung up the phone and turned to find the waiting room empty. He took a chance and removed the paper from his waistband, no longer feeling it was safe to keep it there. The risk of it falling out as he walked was too high. Instead, he unlaced one of his boots and tucked the paper down inside, lacing the boot back up around it, thankful he hadn't had his short boots on.

An hour later his mother, Isabella, strode into the room, the smell of oil and grease coming with her, oil stains on her overalls. She no longer looked like a coven actress with her farm-tanned skin and salted brown hair thrown into a messy braid, but she still commanded the attention of everyone around her as she moved, head high and posture trained straight. Age had not yet dulled her features, leaving her cheeks sharp and pale brown eyes bright.

Tessa and Keaun were behind her. Tessa was dressed for work in a clean gray suit, her stomach-length straight black hair done up in a braided bun, bangs brushing her eyebrows. Keaun looked like he'd been helping their mother with whatever mechanical project was going on; his jeans were filthy and he had dirt in his mussed up wavy brown hair. Dustin had expected Tessa, but not his older brother. Keaun wasn't good with situations like this.

Injuries and hospitals tended to stress him out ever since what happened to his best friend.

"Where's Russ?" their mother said without preamble.

"They took him to surgery," Dustin told her. "He only needs a few pins put in his arm so it shouldn't take long."

"He shouldn't have even been there!" Isabella growled. "He was supposed to be home, but then he got a call from the base two weeks ago asking if he could come back to the border because they were shorthanded. There's supposed to be laws about how often soldiers can get called out!"

"There are only laws for often they can be required to go," Tessa said gently. "I helped try the case that established that law a few years ago. But if they choose to go, they can go as much as they want. Russell chose to go."

"He'll be okay, Mom. Russ is a tough kid," Keaun said.

Their mom huffed and said she was going to look for a nurse to get more information from.

"I don't envy that nurse," Keaun said once she left.

"The nurse will live. You didn't answer my question on the phone, Dustin," Tessa said, arms crossed. The people she faced off with in court were the ones Dustin didn't envy.

"What question?" Keaun said, looking between his wife and little brother.

"How he just *happened* to meet up with Russ after being gone for two months and it just *happened* to be during an attack."

Keaun shrugged. "I'm sure it was a coincidence."

Dustin nodded, relieved to have some backup in the

conversation. "I promise it was. I'd stopped in the town to visit a friend who runs the inn there. Russ was one of the responding soldiers and we ran into each other at the inn. We were both shocked to see one another."

"Well… I'm glad you're home, finally," Tessa said, uncrossing her arms and reaching out to pull Dustin into a hug. Dustin hugged her back and hugged Keaun as well, relieved that Tessa let the topic drop.

Their mother came back in, seeming somewhat happier than when she'd left.

"They said he should be fine with a couple months of healing, and he should be out of surgery soon," she announced.

"That's good," Tessa replied.

"What exactly happened, Dustin?" Keaun asked.

Dustin told them the story, careful about the parts that involved him. The paper pressed against his leg as he spoke, but he didn't mention it. It wasn't a good idea here. Too much risk of being overheard.

When the family first sought refuge in Nahanni nine years ago, it had taken months to be fully processed into the settlement. They were untrusted because they were famous, yes, but also because Shae had not been with them. She had only been twelve when she'd vanished, and would've been thirteen when the family arrived, but that was old enough to be a potential spy in Nahanni's eyes. They'd made it clear they thought the family might pass information to Shae, risking the safety of the settlement. Only after a therapist thoroughly examined all of them and concluded that their traumas were genuine did Nahanni allow them entrance.

Over the years the Lockwoods had gained most people's trust. They'd built up a thriving cattle ranch that provided meat and dairy to most of the southern half of the settlement, some of Dustin's siblings had gotten jobs in towns around the ranch, and Keaun and Rose each married locals and started families of their own. The younger kids and Dustin's nieces were all in school in Watson Lake and had scores of friends. But some rumors still persisted.

A short time later a nurse came in to tell them Russ was out of surgery and being taken to the post-surgical ward for observation. They met Russ in the hallway, finding him settled rather comfortably under several blankets on the stretcher the nurses were wheeling along. A thick blue cast went from the knuckles of his left hand up to the elbow. He was clearly coming off some very strong sedatives, giggling at the lights above him.

"Hey, Dusty," Russ said when he spotted Dustin. The nickname was one that usually only Keaun used, but Dustin let it slide.

"Hi, kiddo," Dustin said, patting his good shoulder as they walked.

"I think I get why you don't like cars now," Russ slurred.

"Well, maybe if you hadn't tried to be a badass by running the vamps over you wouldn't have that problem."

Russ looked rather put out. "There were too many of them and I *am* a badass."

This pulled a laugh out of everyone, including the two nurses who had wheeled him into an empty room and begun arranging his monitors and IV bag.

"Yes dear, you are a badass, we'll talk *all* about it later," their mother said, leaning down to kiss his forehead.

Russ looked incredibly pleased by the comment, clearly missing the fact that he was going to be in trouble later, and drifted off to sleep.

"Well. Good to know his sense of humor is uninjured," Tessa observed.

"Yeah, we've just gotta hope he doesn't remember Mom making it sound like it was a good thing or he'll go and do it again," Keaun teased their mother.

She crossed her arms, a look of oncoming lecture on her face. "Oh, don't worry, he won't ever consider doing it again."

Two hours later Russ was still sleeping off the sedatives when his C.O. knocked on the door of the room.

"Anthony," Isabella said icily. "Care to tell me what happened to my son?"

"My apologies, Ma'am. Things got slightly out of hand," Anthony stated. Anthony was a broad shouldered man twice Isabella's size, but he had the good sense to look a little afraid of her. Dustin's mother never outright objected to anything Anthony did in his position as a high-ranking military officer, but ever since he'd been one of the strongest voices against allowing the family into Nahanni, Isabella had been quick to set herself opposite the man. He seemed to get that having her son lying in a hospital bed was doing nothing to improve things.

Dustin could see his mother swelling up with indignation at the answer and stepped between the two of them to prevent a shouting match over Russ' sedated form. "It happens, especially with the state of things at the border and in the coven. There were casualties, but Russ and Mike lived," Dustin placated. "Nahanni is still finding its feet after not engaging with the coven for so long, after all."

Anthony nodded, the harsh fluorescent lights bouncing off his dark skin. "Used to be we kept to ourselves and Wood's kept to themselves. But in the last decade that has changed. We're scrambling to keep up."

"I have offered, many times, to help catch this settlement up on what they have missed by cutting themselves off since the wars," Isabella said stiffly. "Not once have I been taken up on that."

"And it is time for that to change," Anthony agreed. "Clearly your family has more to offer than we originally believed." At this he glanced at Dustin, causing him to stiffen. "But right now your son is understandably your biggest concern. Take him home, and we can set up some sort of meeting to decide the best path forward in a week or so, once things have settled somewhat."

Isabella softened somewhat and nodded. "I appreciate

that, Anthony."

Anthony thanked them and left, the silence heavy once he was gone. Dustin was desperately hoping none of the others had noticed Anthony's glance at him.

"Do you think they'll listen to us?" Keaun asked into the silence.

"I'll make them listen," Isabella proclaimed.

Dustin didn't doubt the truth of this statement, but his mother's intensity was a bit much for him at the moment. He excused himself, saying he needed to use the restroom and clean himself up to get a reprieve from the weight of the secret he was carrying in his boot.

Once in the restroom, he locked himself in the largest stall, extracting the newspaper and opening it on the changing table. May as well fully understand what he was lying about, even if he did intend to tell them once they were all safe and unwatched at home.

He studied the picture again, taking in every little detail. Shae had grown up beautifully, the same confidence to her she'd always had. The more he stared at the photo, the more Dustin missed his spitfire little sister like crazy. Finally, he flipped to the article about her tour, reading every word.

> The actress Anastasia Derringer, who has now revealed her true identity to be that of Shae Lockwood, one of the missing children of Isabella and Christian Lockwood, will be touring Wood's Coven to promote her newest

movie throughout August, flying between the variety of stops. Since the revelation of her identity, Lockwood's popularity has skyrocketed with copies of her first and second movies, a period drama set during the Plague Wars and a period drama about the 1960s music festival Woodstock, selling out around the world. Her new movie, a drama centered around a plane crash on a remote island, is sure to be a hit with Lockwood at the helm along with seasoned actor Ariane Cordova.

Over a decade ago the Lockwood parents were beloved worldwide. Isabella and Christian, both orphans turned childhood actors, attracted the attention of people everywhere. Their love story was movie worthy in its own right; a beautiful romance from the ashes of war and seven wonderful children with an eighth on the way. But then it turned into a horror movie when their oldest son murdered his best friend Clayton Kitzes, son of Mendez Coven's senator Malcom Kitzes. Isabella and Christian reacted without thought and stole away in the night with their children, endangering the children's lives in the process.

Three years later, Shae, showing incredible bravery for a child of only twelve-years-old, managed to slip away after much of the family died of disease. According to her, all but two members of the family had passed before she made her bid for freedom. However, fearing the repercussions of what her parents had done, she lived on the streets for nearly a year before going to a shelter under the assumed name of Anastasia Derringer, after which she was adopted. Only recently, and on the advice of many close friends, did Shae Lockwood feel safe coming forward with the truth.

Her bravery and status as one of the missing children of Isabella and Christian have made her the darling of London, England, which she now calls home, with the rest of the world growing excited as well. All stops on her tour are expected to sell out, and many have been moved to bigger venues since the conformation of her true identity. The stops are as follows and tickets can be purchased at local box offices or over the phone. Internet sales are not available at this time.

Miami, Florida..............August 1st

<pre>
Jacksonville, Florida.........August 2nd
Richmond, Virgina...........August 4th
Boston, Massachusetts.......August 5th
Chicago, Illinois...........August 7th
Denver, Colorado............August 9th
Salt Lake City, Utah........August 11th
San Francisco, California....August 13th
Los Angeles, California......August 15th
Tucson, Arizona.............August 17th
San Antonio, Texas..........August 19th
</pre>

Dustin read the story through twice, working to make sense of it. So many parts of it confused him that his mind couldn't even figure out which one to focus on. He sort of understood the fake name, but why had she lied about so much else? Said they were dead? Why had she become an actress? How had she gotten away from whoever had taken her out of their camp?

Really, though, it was the tour dates that caught him the most. The tour had started today in Miami, but the Denver stop wasn't for another eight days, and Denver... Denver he could get to.

Folding up the paper and tucking it back in his boot, he left the bathroom stall and headed back to Russ' hospital room. Russ was sitting up, sipping on a glass of water, and was the only one there.

"Where'd everyone go?" Dustin asked.

"I made them go downstairs to get breakfast," Russ replied, his voice a touch slurred by drugs. "They said they'd bring you something back."

"How long ago did they leave?"

"Couple minutes. Why?"

Dustin turned and shut the door to the room, then turned back to Russ. "Did you actually read the article about...her?"

Russ stiffened, glancing at the door, then back at his brother. "What happened to waiting until we got home?"

"Did you?"

"Of course I did."

"And?"

Russ threw up his good hand. "And it's confusing as hell. I mean, I get it's a short newspaper blurb, from a coven paper at that, and not the whole story, but it raises so many questions. What's this brave twelve-year-old crap? And why are we all dead?"

"She's protecting us," Dustin said, unable to hold back a bit of a smile as the answer came to him. "She got taken, couldn't get back, and lied to keep the rest of us safe."

Russ stared at him, eyebrows tilted in skepticism. "That...is a very large leap."

"Do you have a better answer?"

"Well, no, but—"

"*She protected us.*"

"Dustin—"

"We have to get her back, Russ. And now we finally can. She'll be in Colorado in less than a week. I can get there in time."

They were cut off by the door opening behind them. Keaun, Tessa, and Isabella entered, each carrying a tray of food.

"Clearly we've walked in on a heated topic of discussion," Tessa observed.

"Oh, no, just teasing Russ a bit," Dustin scrambled for a lie. "I told him that, since he has pins in his arm now, I'm going to tell all the kids he's been turned into a robot."

Russ smoothly joined the story, voice deceptively light; "I will fully encourage the robot story, but pins aren't enough to sell it. They're too smart for that. We've got to say my whole bone was replaced or something. Since you're going to be home for a while now we can really play it up."

"You're going to be home for a while?" Keaun asked.

Dustin cursed Russ internally, knowing exactly what he was doing.

"Well, maybe," Dustin said slowly, wishing there was a way to glare at Russ without anyone else seeing. "I might have to leave again, just for a little bit, but it won't be nearly as long."

"Well, that's good. We've missed having you home," Isabella said.

"Yeah... it'll be good to have the family back together."

7: Start of the Train Tour

"I still think the plane would've been a better way to do this tour," Helen grumbled.

She perched on the edge of the bench running along one side of Shae's greenroom, fidgeting with her collar. Miami did not agree with her. Shae had tried to wrangle her into some shorts and a tank top but had only managed a t-shirt, Helen refusing to part with her suit pants and flats. She'd even tried to put her suit jacket back on several times until Shae sent it off with an assistant so Helen couldn't get at it.

"This is more intimate," Shae replied. "We do it this way and we get to make lots of little unofficial stops, wave out the windows, that sort of thing. More people to love us."

"More people to try and eat you," Helen grouched. Her shirt collar would be unsalvageable by the end of the day.

"Aren't you the one who is always advocating for the lack of danger the Turned present?" Shae dabbed some light blush across her cheeks. Just enough to add color without covering her veins.

"To regular people, yes. But regular people don't flaunt themselves the way you actors do. You all *try* to make yourselves look appetizing."

"How's that any different from what actors have always done?"

"Actors were sex objects before, not dinner."

"Oh, I'm pretty sure multiple actors were thought of as dinner by a select bit of the population even before the wars."

Helen kicked out at Shae's chair, the impact causing Shae to stab her scalp with the bobby pin she'd been manipulating. She shot an exasperated look over her shoulder at her girlfriend.

"Sorry," Helen said, getting up and grabbing Shae's comb to help with her hair. "I just worry about you. I trust the Turned, and I trust you, but I... I guess I'm still adjusting to how much they love you."

Shae hummed in response, enjoying the feeling of having her hair combed. "Nothing will happen. There's plenty of security for the tour. Besides, the Turned have even less access to me now than they did before. I don't even have to donate blood every two weeks now."

"Personally, I think that's a rather unfair policy. There's no reason you shouldn't still have to contribute just because you act. It all gets mixed together during processing anyway."

"We're too tempting," Shae replied.

"And thus we are back to our original problem," Helen

announced. "You look like a snack."

Shae threw up her hands. "Me looking like a snack got us a fancy new apartment and an all expenses paid tour around North America. Besides, you clearly don't mind all that much if you're still dating me."

"I didn't say you aren't beautiful, just that you've chosen to accent that beauty in a way that is mildly alarming and possibly detrimental to your safety."

Helen finished what she'd been doing with Shae's hair; a messy off-center bun resting at the nape of her neck. Shae twisted this way and that, examining her reflection.

"It's the way things are," Shae said. "The Turned can't make their own movies, so humans have to. We're creating something they want but can't have. They crave us, and we have to appeal to that."

Helen hummed noncommittally as Shae stood from the dressing table and turned to examine her reflection in the full-length mirror hanging on the back of the door.

"What do you think of the outfit? The late 1900s are the popular fashion in this area right now; most of their influential Turned were turned then."

"Well, I wish you'd wear something with straps," Helen said, tugging lightly at Shae's bright blue and white patterned tube-top that left her shoulders and stomach exposed. "I keep picturing this thing getting pulled off by a rowdy fan. But it does look cute on you."

"What about the shorts?" They were bleached white cut-offs with frayed edges, a little butterfly keychain clipped to one belt loop.

"I'm certainly not objecting to what they're doing for your figure," Helen said, a blush creeping up her cheeks.

Shae made sure to set her legs in a way that accented her butt as she turned back to the dressing table. "Still, I feel like it's missing something."

Shae pawed around in her jewelry case. She'd spent over a week researching the fashions of all the areas they'd be traveling to and ordering clothes and jewelry that fit each place. Designers around the world had been happy to help her, and she'd hardly spent a pound on any of it.

At last she found what she was looking for; a thin maroon choker made of braided stretchy string with red beads woven in. Every good outfit needed a dash of blood, after all.

A loud thudding on the door interrupted Helen's complaints about the bloody choker. "Are you done primping yet, Lockwood?" Ariane's voice came through the wood. "We can't wait forever for your tiny ass to get out here."

Shae leaned over and opened the door, finding Ariane leaning on the frame on the other side. He had on a tight black t-shirt and slim, acid-washed jeans.

"Helen and I were just discussing the fact that my ass is anything but tiny, especially in these shorts, Cordova," Shae returned.

"Don't involve me in this," Helen warned. She hadn't liked Ariane even before the night Shae had gotten drunk at his apartment, but now she loathed him. However, she was too kind and nonconfrontational of a person to do much more than glare and refuse to speak with him.

"Sorry. I'll see you in a bit," Shae told her, stretching up to give her a quick kiss before splitting off with Ariane to go on stage.

"Your girlfriend is rather icy," Ariane remarked as they waited off stage with the rest of the main cast and several crew members who would be on the panel.

"Actually, she's quite sweet. She just doesn't like you."

"I don't see why not. She's a primary teacher, after all."

Shae's face screwed up in confusion. "What in the world does that have to do with anything?"

"She works with children, I am an overgrown child according to our esteemed director. The correlation's there."

Shae laughed. "I don't think it works that way, Ariane. You drink far too much to be a child."

"Two minutes!" The event coordinator barked over everyone's conversations. "You've got an audience of three-hundred confirmed. We think more snuck in, though, because it looks like more. They're five feet from the stage and you're just above eye level. We're showing a new trailer, then a press Q&A, then audience Q&A, then autographs for the VIPs. Ten seconds." He counted down on his fingers and everyone trailed out on stage, waving as they took their seats to the cheers of the crowd.

Shae was on the far right end, then Ariane, then the director, followed by the head costume designer and finishing with two of the supporting stars. The whole group waved and smiled as the coordinators tried to tone down the crowd enough to play the new trailer, the glaring stage lights dimming so it could be seen. Shae didn't bother to turn around and see what bits of the movie had been cut up for this one, more interested in the crowd and their reactions. Her eyes scanned across the people packed into the room, taking in their shifting expressions.

"I spy with my little eye, an idiot with a bird on his head," Ariane whispered in her ear.

"What in the world are you talking about?" Shae asked, eyes sweeping the crowd again.

"About twenty feet back, eight feet from the right edge of the crowd."

He was right. There was indeed a man who appeared to be in his late thirties with a large, motley bird perched on his head.

"Is that alive or is it stuffed...?" Shae whispered to Ariane, watching the man while trying to appear not to. It was never good to get caught paying too much attention to one particular fan. You'd either end up with a stalker or a riot made up of other fans who got envious.

"Er... no idea. Stuffed. I think? It doesn't look like it's moving...."

"Maybe it's just petrified that it has been forced to perch on that man's head," Shae suggested.

The trailer ended and the stage lights came back up, hiding the bird man and everyone in the crowd from view due to their brightness. The crowd was cheering and clapping, shouting their praise.

"Let's play a game, Shae-Shae," Ariane said to her over the noise of the crowd. "Whoever spots the weird fans first gets a point. Whoever has the most points at the end of the tour owes the other a favor. Any favor."

This could be interesting, Shae thought. She had no idea what she might want from Ariane, nor did she believe he would follow through on his promise of *any* favor, but it would be fun to see what happened.

"Aren't I already doing you a favor by playing along with your game against your father?" Shae asked.

"You are so far," Ariane answered cryptically.

Shae eyed him for a moment before shrugging, figuring that this didn't change much. "Alright. But the bird man doesn't count. We weren't playing yet."

Once again it took some effort to get the crowd quieted down, but they did and the moderator stepped up to her stand at the end of the table opposite Shae.

"I'll hazard a guess and say you're all a wee bit excited for this movie!" she said. Shae didn't know who she was, nor did she care. "We'll be starting with a press Q&A." She indicated a line of reporters along one wall, and the first stepped forward into a spotlight.

The reporter was a timid looking human girl, probably a first-timer or a student that had somehow wrangled a press pass. "Um, hello. Ms. Lockwood, this is your third movie, and it's quite different from your first two, which were a historical biopic and a historical drama, respectively. What made you want to do a survival movie?"

Shae smiled at her. "It wasn't so much that I wanted to do a survival movie as I wanted to be sure to branch out early in my career so I didn't get typecast into the same parts over and over again."

The girl nodded, said thank you, and bumbled back into the crowd of reporters as another stepped forward. This one was a tall and slightly grizzled Turned man who, based on the silvery pallor of his skin, had not fed recently.

"For all of you; there's been three survival movies released in the last year, none with the best reviews. Why should viewers think any different of this one?"

"Simple," Ariane spoke, "I'm in it. And with a legendary Lockwood, no less." He flashed a smirk at the crowd and the shouts this time had a distinctly female edge to them.

A third reporter stepped forward; a Turned woman who appeared to be in her mid-twenties. There was something about the set of her shoulders that seemed determined, but she paused to take a deep breath before launching into her question.

"For Ariane and Shae; Ms. Lockwood, the world now knows your true identity as the younger sister of the murderer, Keaun Lockwood. Yet, somehow, no one seems to have noticed that you are now working side by side with the murder victim's younger step-brother: Ariane Cordova." At this the crowd broke into astonished whispers, forcing the woman to raise her voice since she had no microphone to amplify it, as they didn't work for the Turned. "We all know the public story of Keaun blowing up Clayton, but we've never heard it from either of you. So, tell us, what is the *real* story and why have you kept your connection hidden?"

Ariane answered her, voice raised over the building whispers of the crowd, "You are right. It is rather strange that the papers haven't picked up on that connection until now, darling, though I would like to clarify that neither Shae nor myself made any attempt to hide it. I'm not close with my family and haven't been for so long, it just isn't something people look at in relation to me. Even Shae herself was not aware of it until a week ago. As for what happened between our older brothers, well," he smirked knowingly at Shae, "you'll have to ask my stepfather if you want new information on that whole scandal."

The crowd roared up into a tumult of sound, every reporter now shouting questions and the whole audience yelling amongst themselves. Their director stood up, trying to help get the crowd back under control, but they refused to quiet down this time. This revelation was too juicy to be dropped so quickly.

"Are you enjoying making this go to hell?" The director asked Ariane, exasperation clear in her voice.

"I answered the question I was asked, and it hasn't gone to hell until they break the barriers," he responded, flashing another smirk at the crowd.

The director shook her head, her lips quirking in a poorly suppressed smile. As long as Ariane's antics didn't get anyone killed, she let them slide. She was of the mind that any press was good press, chaotic or otherwise.

"Want to make it go to hell?" Shae whispered to Ariane, enjoying the chaos of it all and curious as to how far she could push it.

"What are you thinking?" He asked, blowing a kiss to the crowd.

Shae responded by slipping a pocketknife out of her cleavage, the only place she'd been able to keep it in this outfit. She'd had the knife since she was seven-years-old and kept it with her everywhere. In a world revolving around blood, it was good to always have a way to get at it.

The thing was small, one blade she kept razor sharp, the handle decorated with an enameled cameo of a Victorian woman. She flicked it open beneath the table and slid it across the pointer finger of her left hand, giving the flesh a squeeze to cause the blood to well. Ariane grinned and shifted so the director and the rest of the table couldn't see what she was doing. Shae handed him the knife and stood, leaning over the table while supporting herself with her good hand. The other people at the table now knew something was up and were watching warily as Ariane stood to join her. Several of the Turned in the front row had clearly scented the blood, heads tilted back and noses searching out the source of the scent.

"Hey lovelies!" Shae shouted to the crowd. "We've got a treat for you!"

And with that Shae and Ariane flicked their hands out towards the crowd, sending droplets of blood out across the front row. The effect was instantaneous. The crowd surged forward against the rather useless metal barriers and security rushed to shove them back while two guards whisked everyone off stage to safety.

"That… was brilliant," the director said after a moment of contemplation. "Don't ever do it again. We don't need an actual riot on our hands. Should bring in the crowds for future stops, though."

"Yeah, that's what our intent was," Ariane grinned.

"What, *precisely*, *was* your intent, then?" An angry voice cut through the noise and Shae turned to see Helen standing several feet away, hands on her hips and eyes glaring through her glasses.

"Mom's home," Ariane sing-songed.

"Quiet," Shae said, smacking him before walking over to Helen. "I'll be back in a minute, everyone."

She prodded Helen out of the room and into the hall. Up close she looked livid.

"I'm in trouble, I'm guessing?"

"You. Are. In. So. Much. Trouble," Helen growled.

"Security had it under control," Shae pointed out.

"Security… *security had it under control*?! Shae, there's twenty guards and hundreds of Turned! And who knows how long since they last fed! All it would take is one blood-deprived one to slip past a guard and you'd be dead. Not turned, dead. It doesn't matter if only one in five of them are infectious anymore, every single one of them could drain you dry!" She was starting to flail her arms, even stomping her foot once. Sometimes Shae wondered if she spent too much time around her students.

"I won't do it again, Helen. Promise. I'm sorry I scared you," Shae said softly, dropping her voice in a way she knew Helen liked while reaching up a hand to stroke her cheek.

Helen continued to glare and didn't respond.

"Ariane and I just wanted to rile them up a bit, that's all. Get more people to come to the rest of the stops. We did it, now we're done." Done with flicking their blood on the crowd, anyway. Maybe. It had been rather fun, after all.

"You better be," Helen muttered, still glaring.

She slipped a hand into her pocket and pulled out a bandaid, reaching out and wrapping it around Shae's injured finger. Leave it to a primary teacher to always have bandaids on her person.

Shae assured her she would be better behaved before giving her a kiss that wasn't returned and going back to join everyone else. The organizers had decided that they would cut the remainder of the Q&A with the press and the fans, but the autograph signing was still a go—though they were waiting for some local police who were being brought in as extra security.

"Of course you two get the car on the end. Don't have to deal with anyone walking through all day," Ariane grumbled, eying the train they'd be living on for the duration of the tour.

Shae and Helen had the last car all to themselves, Ariane had the one after that, then came two cars split between the rest of the cast and various crew members, a lounge car, a dining car, and then the gleaming silver engine.

"I'll admit, I'm surprised they didn't put you on the end, Ariane. Apparently they felt Shae and I will enjoy having to walk through a haze of drug smoke to get to the rest of the train," Helen said briskly as she stepped up onto the platform at the back of her and Shae's car. She'd spent the walk from the venue down the street well ahead of Shae, her continued anger clear.

"You should join me sometime, Helen. Might make you interesting to have around for once."

Shae quickly stepped between them, reaching around Helen to open the door. "Time to all go our separate ways, I think."

"I don't know how you can stand him," Helen said as Shae closed the door behind them.

"*I* don't provoke him. Besides, he's a lot more fun than you give him credit for."

"He's a druggie and rude and pretentious and a bunch of other such things," she huffed.

"You refer to me as rude and pretentious quite often," Shae pointed out.

"That's different! With you it's an act. With him it's just his personality."

"Sure," Shae replied, taking in the train car.

They had entered from the open-air boarding platform at the back and before them was spread out a beautiful lounge full of plump brown leather couches and chairs along with a high-end entertainment center. Each side of the lounge was solid windows from the ceiling down to about two feet off the richly carpeted floor, though heavy velvet drapes were drawn across most of the glass. At the back of the lounge was a small staircase to the upper level of the car, a little bar tucked in between the stairs and the wall on the right side and a narrow hallway to the back of the car on the left.

"It smells like rich people in here," Helen announced. "Old rich people. The oak and whiskey and cigars kind."

"We'll open the windows and air it out once we get going," Shae told her. "Now come on, let's go see what the rest is like."

Shae strode off, passing the stairs, passing the door to a lavish bathroom, and coming out in a lavish dining room. A long, over polished wood table took up most of the room and a stiff chandelier that wouldn't swing with the movement of the train hung over it, faceted crystals sparkling in the chinks of light coming between the curtains.

Uninterested in a large table that would serve her no purpose on this tour, Shae continued on, walking through a doorway at the end of the room to enter the kitchen. It had the newest everything in it; smooth black stainless steel appliances, deep reddish brown cabinets, a gleaming black countertop that sparkled with veins of muted gold. Shae spotted a touchpad on the counter next to the oven and was sure that if she poked at it various things would open to up to reveal further amenities.

She glanced back at Helen, amused but unsurprised to see that her jaw had gone slack, anger seemingly forgotten for the moment. Helen had always loved cooking, since even before she could stand according to her mother. Shae had picked their new apartment not just because of the bookstore, but also because she knew Helen would love the kitchen in it.

"What is all this stuff?" Helen asked, fingers brushing along one of the unfamiliar appliances.

The kitchen had the standard things; an oven and a fridge and a stove and a coffee maker. All things a good kitchen in any coven would have, because they had all been things good kitchens had before the wars. However, after the wars, some covens had recovered and moved forward much faster and better than others. Mendez hadn't, though it made sense that Ariane's stepfather would still have the best of everything on his train. Helen, meanwhile, had grown up in the Coven of D'Cruz, which was one of the poorest covens in the world and it had barely advanced at all. She'd never experienced all that kitchens had become. Even their one at home was rather basic compared to most.

"That would be a dessert printer, Love."

Helen eyed it suspiciously. "A dessert… printer?"

"Yes. Most models print candies and the like, but some are fancier and will make you a whole cake or pie."

"You can't be serious."

"Why not?"

"Well… how does it do it?"

"Do I look like an engineer to you?"

Helen prodded at it, still looking dubious. Shae wrapped an arm around her waist and pulled her back towards the door. "Come on, we've still got to see what the upstairs is like."

"But kitchen!" Helen whined, letting Shae pull her out anyway.

They walked back to the lounge and up the stairs, coming out into a beautiful glass domed bedroom.

"I'd say this was worth leaving the kitchen," Shae said.

Helen nodded, eyes wide.

It was a rather spectacular room. The bed was huge, custom built to take up one whole end of the room and piled high with pillows and blankets. Several more plush chairs and a nice desk took up the center area, and at the top of the stairs were two decently sized closets, one on either side. All their luggage had been brought into the room and stacked neatly along the walls.

"Won't people be able to see us, though?" Helen asked, stepping out to brush her hand across the glass.

"Nah, the director told us earlier that the dome has one way glass for during the day, and retractable shades for at night. There's a remote for them somewhere," Shae said as she walked over to the first of her trunks and flipped open the latch.

"What are you doing?" Helen asked as Shae pulled

out various garment bags.

"Unpacking. The less time my clothes spend in these trunks, the less ironing I will have to do."

"How about, instead of unpacking, we discuss what happened today?" Helen said.

Shae turned to see Helen had crossed her arms and was frowning at her.

"I apologized," Shae pointed out.

"You did," Helen admitted, "but I'm not all that sure you meant it."

Shae remained silent, unable to come up with anything to the contrary. Seeing Helen staring at her like that, Shae felt a slow realization creeping up on her that she was no longer quite sure what she liked about Helen. When they'd met she'd found Helen funny, felt charmed by her determination to become something better than what she'd been born into. But now... well, there was still something there, Shae just couldn't pin down what it was, nor if it was enough to matter.

As Shae's silence stretched out between them Helen's shoulders dropped and she tilted her head back, speaking to the ceiling. "Just tell me *why*, please?"

"Because... I have to," Shae said, picking her words carefully. "I have to make them love me. Make them want me. Fame is so tenuous. Just look at my parents. I gave up *everything* to get here. You know that more than anyone. If I don't manage to hold on to it now, I'll never get it back."

Helen tilted her face back down, eyes searching Shae's.

"I know... but... what's the point of fame if you're dead?"

"I don't intend to end up dead for quite a while."

"Nobody does," Helen said, frustration back in her tone.

Shae sighed, sitting on the edge of a trunk to think over her answer. She didn't think she had one that would make Helen feel any better, and Helen seemed to sense it, tears starting to leak from her eyes.

"I love you, Shae, as much as you do things that I hate I do love you."

"I'm sorry," Shae said softly without thinking. She wasn't sure if she meant that she was sorry for what had happened, or sorry that Helen loved her. Maybe it was both.

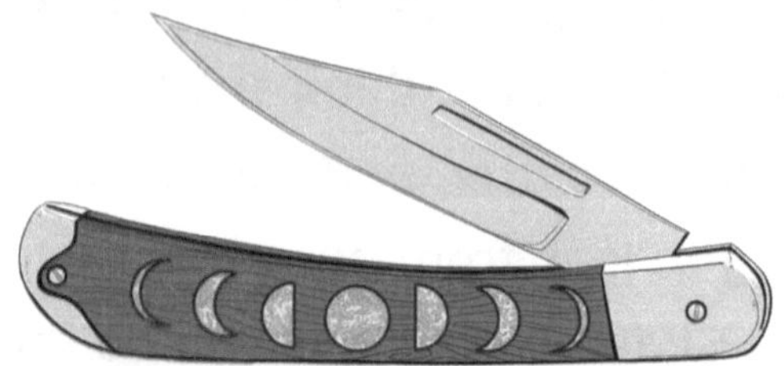

8: Out of the Hospital

Russ was released from the hospital several hours later and packed into the family truck to drive home. The nurses had given him more pain medication before his release, and he had gotten a bit loopy on it, so getting him in the vehicle took some convincing. Eventually he'd been lured in with a candy bar offered to him by Tessa, and he was now munching on it in the back seat, framed by Dustin on one side and Keaun on the other. They'd figured it was safer having him the middle in case he ran out of candy and decided this meant he could leave the truck despite it being in motion.

Tessa was in the shotgun seat and Isabella was driving, the window rolled down and her arm resting on the open frame, stray strands of hair whipping in the wind. The smell of several BBQs blew in as they twisted through the suburbs, replaced by the heady scent of pine as they left the town limits and wound their way up into the mountains towards home. The highway was smooth under the tires. Repaved just a year ago, the long winter had not torn it up yet.

Despite the chaos of the last twenty-four hours, and being trapped in another vehicle, Dustin felt himself relaxing. This was home. Even with all the tension and guilt being here sometimes brought him, it was home. This was still his family.

Forty-five minutes later they reached the family property, the entrance hand-carved out of old pine tree trunks with the words "Lockwood Ranch" burned into the top beam. Rose and her husband Robert had made the gate three years earlier as a birthday present for Isabella. The gate itself was never closed, though. Too many people coming and going for that to be practical. Isabella pulled them right up to the front porch of their two-story house and shut off the truck. Rose was standing, alone, on the wraparound porch. She'd dyed the underlayer of her chestnut hair evergreen since Dustin had last seen her, but otherwise she looked the same as always; like a second mother who was just as apt to interrogate him about what happened as their actual mother was. Though, where Isabella would instill a sense of disappointment and "I raised you better than this" with her lecture, Rose would probably short-sheet his bed and tie his favorite reins in knots.

"Kids are all at school and everyone else is at work," Rose announced as Dustin helped a giggling Russ out of the truck. "How are you, kiddo?"

"Delightful," Russ grinned, attempting to give her a thumbs-up with his bad hand.

"He's very medicated," Isabella said, patting Russ' back as Dustin and Tessa herded him up the five steps to the porch and towards the entrance.

"I was beginning to pick up on that, yeah," Rose said with a hint of laughter as she held open the door.

The livingroom was open and airy, a soaring ceiling and large windows keeping it from feeling cluttered by the excess of chairs and couches stuffed everywhere they could fit. Fourteen people lived in this house, and it showed. They took Russ to the largest couch, the sectional in front of the old flat-screen TV that didn't serve much purpose beyond watching DVDs, and cajoled him into sitting down on it. With a little more effort, and by turning on his favorite movie—some old western Dustin thought was called *She Wore a Yellow Ribbon*, they got Russ to lie down and rest.

As Dustin moved to stand from where he'd crouched next to the couch, Russ reached out and snagged his arm.

"Don't do anything stupid, Dustin," he mumbled before promptly falling asleep and starting to snore.

"What does he mean by that?" Rose asked, eyes narrowed.

"Who knows with how much medication he's on," Dustin shrugged, hoping he looked as nonchalant as he was trying to be. "He saw one of the Mickinnons' horses in their field on the way here and told us, very loudly, that he was going to steal it and name it Clip-Clop."

"Or, maybe, he's referring to you taking on a pack of Turned on your own," his mother observed, her eyes narrowing as well. It was amazing how alike she and Rose looked when suspicious.

"I'm exhausted," Dustin announced before they could corner him. "I'm gonna take a shower and go crash."

He slipped around them and through the back hallway into the bathroom. Really, though, it was more of a locker room. There were five shower stalls, five toilet stalls, and six sinks. When they'd first been accepted into Nahanni, there hadn't been an available property big enough for all of them, so the Nahanni officials had put them up in a hotel until, six months later, this ranch had come on the market. The previous owners had gotten too old to run it and were happy to pass it on to a young family, even staying in a trailer on the grounds for a while to help the Lockwoods learn how to run everything. However, the house had still been much too small back then. Only one level—not counting the cellar. Three bedrooms, the livingroom, the kitchen, and one bathroom. Isabella had immediately drawn up plans to expand the house and traded some of the best cattle to pay for it. They'd re-arranged the first level, expanding it to include a fourth bedroom and double the size of the bathroom, as well as extending the kitchen. As the years went on more additions had been made; the second level with four more bedrooms, a real laundry room to replace the laundry closet, an office/library area, doubling the size of the bathroom again, expanding the kitchen even more to make room for a second fridge and third oven. The house grew with the family, no one willing to split up after all they'd been through. Not even Keaun and Rose had left when they'd gotten married and started having children of their own, just moved their spouses in.

Dustin's shower was quick, and he was careful to keep the paper hidden in his boot as he left the room, a towel wrapped around his waist and old clothes balled up in his arms. He'd meant it when he said he wanted to tell the family about Shae, but he'd also said that before he'd read the article. Now that he knew he had a chance to get her, to rescue her, he was hesitant. He wasn't sure how the family would react to his plan. The only way to convince them about any of it would be to tell them every secret he'd been keeping, and he was sure they wouldn't react well to most of it. It would be so much easier to just keep them in the dark for now, get Shae in the limited time he had to do so, then explain everything once they were both home and safe.

The house was silent save for the sounds of Russ' movie, the volume low, as Dustin padded up the stairs to the room he and Russ shared. Lately they were hardly ever home at the same time for long, though, so sharing was a bit strong of a word. It was a small room towards the front side of the house, just two single beds, two small closets, and a little stove. Dustin's bed was under the window, which looked out at the craggy mountains surrounding the valley the ranch was nestled in. The only sign that he lived there was a small single shelf of his favorite books, screwed into the wall above the foot of his bed, next to the door. Russ' side of the room looked somewhat more lived in. There was a movie poster of a beautiful blond woman hung above his headboard, an empty holster hanging on a bedpost, his favorite coffee mug on the floor next to the bed, forgotten there when he'd last left.

As Dustin dropped his clothes on the floor next to his bed someone knocked on the door. Dustin turned to see Keaun stepping into the room. Keaun said nothing as he came and flopped back on Russ' bed. Dustin, used to Keaun's silence, got dressed in sweats and a t-shirt from his closet. Since the death of his best friend, Keaun had developed an interesting relationship with talking. He rarely spoke to anyone outside the family and when he spoke to the family he almost never started the conversation. Once someone else started it, though, you'd never realize he had a problem with talking.

Part of Dustin yearned to open up to his older brother, to show him the paper and tell him everything. Even if Keaun hadn't been much of a typical big brother figure in a long time, he still understood better than most of the family what it was like to lose someone you cared deeply for. Sure, the rest of the family loved Shae, but she and Dustin had always been closer to one another than to anyone else in the family. What stopped him, though, was not knowing how Keaun would react. Would it be too upsetting for him to talk about a sister he thought dead? To bring up anything connected to the death of his best friend? Dustin had never tried either before.

Dustin only remembered bits and pieces about

Clayton. He'd been Keaun's best friend until he'd died when Keaun was seventeen. Keaun had been accused of the murder, throwing the world upside-down for the entire family. One of the clearest memories Dustin had of Clayton was him showing up one day to take Keaun out sailing, as was usual for them, and not being at all annoyed as Dustin peppered him with questions about what they were doing. He'd died less than a month later, and Keaun hadn't been the same since.

Keaun's PTSD manifested mostly in nightmares and loss of speech, both at their worst in the years following the accident. He'd gotten better as time passed, but when Shae vanished he'd regressed and stopped talking at all for over two years. Once he'd met Tessa, he'd gotten much better. Something about her, and eventually their three children, had helped ground him in a way he hadn't been able to manage since Clayton's death. Dustin would be forever grateful to Tessa for that, however, he was well aware that PTSD was not something that ever went away entirely, so he avoided bringing up hard subjects like Clayton and Shae.

Maybe there was a way to frame this without delving too deep into uncomfortable territory, Dustin thought. He laid back on his creaky bed, staring up at the horsehair plaster ceiling.

"Yesterday was… a lot." Dustin started. "If it had just been me, I would've been fine, but seeing Russ in danger, seeing him get hurt… it… brought up a lot of memories."

Keaun was silent for several seconds, staring up at

the ceiling as well. "Are you referring to Shae?"

Dustin noticed with a start that this was the first time he could remember Keaun saying her name since she'd disappeared.

"Yeah. It… made me think about her. About losing her. It doesn't ever really get better, does it, losing someone you love? People say it stops hurting, but it doesn't."

Keaun went silent again for several minutes and Dustin worried he'd pushed too far before Keaun spoke again. "I've lost two people I love. Clayton and Shae. Shae was kidnapped from us and could be dead for all we know. Clayton… Clayton died in my arms. Honestly, I'm not sure which is worse anymore. At least with Clayton, I know he's gone. I know what happened. I know we'd been on his boat at the dock. I know he'd left his phone on the hood of his car and I ran back to get it when it rang. I know that as soon as I reached the car there was an explosion. I know I ran back and found him unconscious and bleeding, trapped under the mast on the sinking boat. I know I pulled him out. I know I held him until he stopped breathing."

Dustin was frozen in his own bed. Keaun had *never* talked about the accident before. He rarely even talked about times with Clayton before that. Dustin wanted to stop him, tell him that he didn't need to share all of this if he didn't want to. But, at the same time, he didn't want his brother to stop. He wanted to know what had happened to him. He wanted to know how Keaun had kept going, even though he'd faltered a few times on the way.

Keaun took a deep breath and kept talking. "But with Shae, we don't know anything. We don't know who took her or why or even exactly when they did. We don't know if she's alive or dead or worse. All we know is that when we went to bed she was there and the next morning she was gone. I've never been able to stop thinking about either of them, and neither has ever hurt any less than it did the day it happened. I guess... my point is that you're right. It doesn't get better in the sense of going away. That pain will always be that pain. You just find different ways of dealing with it as time goes on. I've got Tess and my girls. Sometimes they aren't quite enough, but they still help just by being around."

"You saying I need a girlfriend?" Dustin asked weakly, not having the faintest idea what else to say.

Keaun chuckled before responding, his voice sounding a bit tired, "Or a boyfriend. Running off into the woods won't be the best answer forever."

"Not into guys, but thanks."

"Nothing wrong with it if you were."

When he said that something occurred to Dustin, and he asked before he could think better of it. "Were you and Clayton together?"

Keaun stretched out on the bed, humming as he did. "Sort of, I suppose. We really were just friends but... right before what happened, we were sort of... encroaching on being more than that. Never got the chance to see what would come of it, though."

"I'm sorry," Dustin whispered, regretting having asked.

"Don't be," Keaun said, smiling softly. "It's not that hard to talk about anymore, as long as I focus more on before he was killed."

"Tell me what he was like, then?"

Keaun smiled more. "He was a dreamer. Always scheming. His life goal was to become a treasure hunter. Half the time we were on his boat we were looking for old wreaks. It never really worked since neither of us knew how to dive, but it was fun."

"Did you guys ever find anything?"

"Well, we found a few gold coins in a lagoon once. I always suspected his dad paid someone to hide them for Clayton to find, though, but I never said anything. The coins made him so damn happy."

Keaun sat up on the bed, tugging on a leather cord hanging around his neck and inside his shirt. He'd had it for as long as Dustin could remember, and for as long as Dustin could remember he'd never seen what was on the end of it. Once the cord was free from Keaun's shirt a gold coin about an inch across swung out. It did look old, but not quite old enough to count as treasure.

"He had two strung into necklaces, and we each kept one. The rest he put in a little display case in his room," Keaun explained. He ran his thumb around the coin a few times before tucking it back in his shirt and standing up. "I'll let you get some sleep."

With that he left, closing the door behind him. Dustin felt more wound up than before, and he still had no idea what he was going to do now.

Dustin had eventually fallen asleep out of sheer exhaustion and woke that night, stomach growling, images of bleeding children still lingering on the edges of his brain. This was the first time they didn't have Shae's face, though, so that was something. He made his way quietly downstairs, finding Russ still asleep on the couch and Isabella in an armchair with one of his nieces, Tessa and Keaun's four-year-old daughter Mariah, on her lap.

"She alright?" Dustin asked, keeping his voice low to avoid waking Russ.

"Ear infection," Isabella said. "I gave her something for it, but it hasn't quite kicked in yet."

Mariah peaked her head out from where she'd buried it against Isabella's chest, her eyes lighting up when she saw her uncle.

"Dustin!"

"Hi, Munchkin," Dustin smiled, coming over to ruffle her hair. "Want me to take her for a while, Mom?"

"Depends. Is 'want me to take her' code for 'let me free up your hands so you'll go cook me something because I've been off in the woods for months'?" Isabella smiled wryly.

"I eat just fine out in the woods, thank you."

"Mmmhm." She stood up, passing Mariah to him. "I'll get started on that meal. Also, are you aware that you still smell like dirt?"

"I took a shower!" Dustin said, following her through the glass paneled French doors and into the kitchen, Mariah nestled happily in his arms.

"Clearly not a long enough one. And your hair!" She gave him a scathing look. "You're lucky I'm not going after you with a pair of scissors, letting it get down to your shoulders like that."

"I'm sure Rose or Tessa will get to the scissors before you can," Dustin chuckled. Tessa, at least, would give him a good hair cut. Rose was liable to either cut it all off or give him something ridiculous, like a mohawk.

"Well, I wish them luck. Trying to get you to tame that bramble is much harder than it should be." She pulled out a cutting board, knife, and a selection of vegetables.

Shrugging, he shifted Mariah a bit so he could sit down at the huge kitchen table that took up half the room. "Do you know how hard it is to cut your hair with just a knife and no mirror?"

"Well, maybe if you spent more time among us civilized people instead of running off into the wilderness at every turn, it wouldn't be such a problem," she teased, sliding the vegetables she'd been dicing into a pan to simmer along with a slab of chicken.

"I live in a house with an average of six children under the age of thirteen. It's nice to go somewhere quiet sometimes."

She and Dustin both knew this wasn't really the reason he left. He loved his youngest sister and all his nieces too much to ever get annoyed by them, but they both also knew better than to delve into the real reasons. After all, the first time Dustin had ever gone off into the woods was because he'd hated Lockwood Ranch when they'd first moved in, feeling it was a further sign that Isabella had given up on ever finding her missing daughter. Things had gotten better between them since then, but they still avoided the subject.

Logically, Dustin understood his mother's decision to leave after Shae had vanished. It had been too dangerous to stay put. Even if they were in an uninhabited area, it was still technically claimed, and thus patrolled, by Wood's Coven. Almost two years had passed since they'd left Mendez, but they'd still been wanted, still been well known even if only Dustin's parents and Keaun would be recognizable as the rest of the kids had never been in the public eye. None of that made the decision any easier to accept, though. He'd started to forgive her a couple years after that when he'd come home to find she'd commissioned a local artist to paint a portrait of Shae in her late teens. It hung in the livingroom now, on a wall of family photos. But a bit of blame still lingered in the back of his mind.

"An *average* of six children?" Isabella said. "What do you mean by average? Do I have more grandkids I don't know about, Dustin Johnathan Lockwood?"

Dustin laughed. "No! No! I just meant the kids are always having friends over."

"Good." She leveled a spoon threateningly at him. "I'd

never forgive you if you didn't tell me you had children for me to spoil."

"Trust me, if I had kids you'd know and would be given full spoiling rights and abilities."

She nodded in satisfaction and continued shuffling around the kitchen as Dustin rocked a dozing Mariah. Soon enough Isabella finished the meal and slid it out onto a plate, bringing it over with a bottle of beer. Dustin handed Mariah back, trying not to wake her, before digging into his roasted chicken and vegetables. As much as he loved cooking over a fire he always missed his mother's cooking. Simple and delicious.

"Where's dad?" Dustin asked as he finished up his food. Not seeing his father around wasn't unusual, but with Russ injured Dustin was curious.

"He was out in the garden when we got back from town. He's on the porch now."

"How long has he been out on the porch?" Dustin asked. He was well aware that, left to his own devices, his father would lose track of time and sit out there for hours, days if they'd let him, without even remembering to eat. Keaun hadn't been the only one deeply affected by Shae's disappearance.

"A few hours now."

"It's two in the morning," Dustin pointed out.

Isabella sighed. "It's a nice enough night. He ate dinner so we'll leave him be."

"Are you sure? I don't mind convincing him to come in."

Isabella shook her head. "It's alright. But if you want

to help... I was meaning to run into town today to pick up some things. I know you hate driving, but with Russ... I'd prefer to stay here and keep an eye on him."

"Of course. What do we need?"

She pointed to the list stuck to one of the fridges and Dustin went over to get it, depositing his empty plate in the over-large sink on the way. He hated driving the truck enough that normally he would've wrangled Rose or Tessa into going with him and doing the driving, but with sleep had come clarity about what he was going to do about the paper, and for that he needed supplies. Supplies that would raise too many questions from his sisters. An excuse to go into town alone was exactly what he'd needed.

"Dustin...."

Dustin turned back to his mother, folding the list and tucking it into his pocket.

"What happened yesterday, is there something you aren't tell me about it?"

Dustin looked away, dreading what was coming.

When he didn't answer his mother continued, "I've never tried to stop you going into the woods. I know it helps you, as much as I might tease you about it. But... I need you to understand how dangerous things are right now."

"Mom—"

She held up a hand. "I'm not done. I know I've made decisions you don't agree with, and I can't blame you for that. You didn't grow up in the covens the way I did, and you don't understand what they're like from the inside. I was *theirs* from the time I was four-years-old, the same age Mariah is now. Think about that, Dustin. They took a child and formed her into a tiny little actress decked out in ribbons and blood. They did the same to your father. The things we had to do to stay alive, to stay in their good graces…" Isabella shook her head, going silent for a moment. "Just… whatever you're doing, and after today I'm sure I don't know about most of it, please be careful."

Dustin nodded, going over to wrap his mother in a hug. "I am careful, Mom, I promise."

9: Richmond Stop

"Time to strut," Ariane said. He was dressed in ripped and burned clothing, makeup bruises marring his skin and a fake cut stretching across his forehead with stage blood poured artistically down his face.

He and Shae were going to be performing a live rendition of a scene from the movie for the tour stop in Richmond, the third stop of the tour, and both had gotten completely done up for it. Shae's outfit was much the same as Ariane's, but with more stage blood from a large abdominal wound, and a wig of long black hair. Performing a scene on stage was an idea concocted by Nadia during their last stop in Jacksonville. She'd told them she wasn't sure how it would go over, but was hoping playing on the popularity of live theater among the Turned—since it was the only way they could act without being recorded—would push attendance even higher. The crew had scrambled to go all out, flying ahead of the rest of the tour to set up the stage to look just like the setting of the movie. They'd built a whole beach and somehow secured bits of what could be considered plane wreckage as long as you didn't look too close.

"Completely ready," Shae replied, doing one last check of her wig in a mirror next to the stage entrance. She would've given Helen a kiss on the cheek before going on, but Helen had a weird thing about not liking Shae in costume, so she'd decided to spend the day exploring the city around the venue instead. Given that things were still somewhat tense between them, Shae hadn't objected to the arrangement. Besides, once Helen learned the town had a museum dedicated to the history of the Turned prior to the Plague Wars there'd been no stopping her.

Ariane and Shae waited for their cue, listening to the announcer rev up the crowd before moving offstage. Ariane rolled his head on his shoulders, his whole posture melting into his character. As much as he drank and drugged, Ariane was easily the best actor Shae had worked with so far. He never just said the words, he became them.

A second later he stumbled out onto the sand, screaming Shae's name from the movie, "Evelyn! Evelyn!"

Shae watched as he collapsed in the sand, gripping his "injured" leg, using the other to scoot up the beach as he looked around frantically.

She waited until he screamed her name for the third time before stumbling out after him and screaming his name. "Ashley!"

Arm wrapped tightly around the fake wound to her

abdomen, Shae lurched over to him, falling into the sand at his feet. He grabbed her and pulled her close, clinging to her and pressing his face into her hair.

"Oh my god, I thought I'd lost you," he gasped.

Shae sobbed, making sure the movements were dramatic enough for the audience to see them. It had been a few years since she'd been in a stage play, having gotten her start in them, but she still remembered how to play up her actions more than she would for cameras.

"What, what do we do now?" Shae hiccupped. "The plane turned around, I felt it. What if they don't know where to look for us?"

"I'm sure they know where to look," he assured, kissing her forehead before startling when he noticed the wound to her stomach. "Evelyn! How bad is that?"

He pried her arms away, hissing as he saw the wound.

"I saw a medical kit down the beach a little way," Shae offered meekly.

He nodded and got up, shuffling to it while trying not to put weight on his bad leg. When he came back, he gently pushed her down into the sand and began going through the motions of treating the wound. In the actual movie Shae would've been staring up at the stars. Here it was just the beams of the ceiling.

"I'm scared," Shae whispered as Ariane finished.

He grimaced. "Me too, but we'll be okay."

Ariane leaned down, pressing his lips to Shae's as the stage lights clicked off, signaling the end of the scene. The crowd roared as he rolled off, grinning and slipping out of character.

"Does your girlfriend know you've been smoking, Lockwood?" He whispered, hand clasped over the tiny microphone clipped to his shirt.

Shae smirked, covering her own microphone. "Nope. That's our little secret."

She could barely see his grin in the dark.

"This movie is horridly cheesy, you know," Shae whispered as she sat up.

Ariane laughed. "Doesn't matter. We're in it so it will do gloriously in the box office and that's all that matters."

Shae nodded and held out a hand to help him up before the lights clicked back on. They both bowed before stepping up to the edge of the stage to wave at the crowd while the stage crew came and set up a table right on the sand. As soon as it was ready, she and Ariane sat on one end while the director and a few other people joined them. They took questions for about twenty minutes, though none were about her and Ariane's background, as those had been banned due to the commotion they caused. After the Q&A everyone but the people who had purchased autographs left the theater.

"What's that?" Ariane asked, pointing at the sleek wooden box a crew member brought over at Shae's request.

"My pen," Shae told him, pulling out the slim dip pen and blacked out inkwell.

"Well then! Little Miss Lockwood needs a fancy pen all to herself? It would be such a travesty if she were forced to use a regular pen like the rest of us commoners," Ariane said dramatically.

Shae rolled her eyes, unscrewing the lid on the inkwell. "It isn't the pen that's fancy. It's the ink. Helen said I wasn't allowed to fling my blood on the crowd anymore. She said nothing about signing my autographs with my blood."

Ariane blinked a couple times before barking out a laugh. "You never cease to be interesting, Shae-Shae. Where'd you get the pen and well?"

"Planning on stealing my idea?" Shae scratched out a few test lines on a scrap of paper, happy to see she wouldn't need to water-down the blood to get it to flow well. The anti-coagulation agent had been easy enough to get hold of, so the blood would stay good for the day. She'd refill it before each event so that it would always be fresh.

"Of course. Oh! Look, lady with a cat on a leash riding on her shoulder. My point. It's four to three now. I'll have you owing me a favor yet."

"The tour is young."

The fans began filing up, the first a Turned boy who looked a bit younger than Shae. When he caught a whiff of Shae's blood his eyes widened so much Shae had a split second of wondering if they were going to pop out. His lips twitched in a way that made Shae suspect his fangs had just slid out.

"Is... is that *yours*?" He stuttered out, voice thick around his spindly fangs.

Shae smiled demurely. "Of course it is, darling."

She dipped the pen and looped out "Shae Lockwood" across the bottom of a glossy portrait of herself, sliding it to the boy. He picked it up with the reverence of a priest touching a saintly relic, eyes fastened on the still wet signature. He was so focused on the letters as he walked away, he nearly fell off the stage, saved only by an attentive security guard.

"Twenty bucks says at least one of them licks it," Ariane whispered in Shae's ear as he signed something for a middle-aged human woman.

"Bets only work if we each think something different will happen," Shae answered.

"Oh, so you agree that someone will lick it?"

"Of course they will." Shae smiled sweetly at the human man standing in front of her. She'd used a regular pen for him. No point in wasting blood on someone who wouldn't be affected by it.

It only took three more autographs for their prediction to come true. A doe-eyed seemingly twenty-something Turned girl took one look at Shae's signature, shuffled away a few steps, looked back over her shoulder, then brought the photo to her face and licked at the blood. Ariane burst out laughing and had to turn away so he could compose himself.

"There is no way I'm not stealing your idea now," he informed Shae, still choking on a few laughs.

"Have at it. And that girl totally earns me a point so we're back to being tied."

He nodded, still grinning as he went back to signing things.

Thirty minutes later the signing finished and there had been a total of six Turned who licked Shae's signature off of their photos. One even tore off the whole corner where the large "S" had been and popped it into his mouth.

"I propose an addendum to our game," Ariane stated as they walked back to the train station down the road, trailed by security. "We each get a point for the Turned that lick off our signatures, two if they try to eat them."

"In that case I've now got twelve points and you've still only got four so I'm hardly going to say no," Shae replied, looping her arm through his.

The August evening was warm, a gentle breeze filled with the scents of a nearby bakery wafting around them. Shae found it quite pleasant, her skin still tingly from scrubbing off all the makeup and stage blood.

Ariane grinned. "Don't worry, Shae-Shae. I'll catch up."

"Are you coming to dinner tonight?" Ariane asked as they reached the train.

"No, I think Helen and I will cook for ourselves. We'll come for breakfast though," Shae told him.

He nodded and pecked her cheek before striding off to his own car while Shae climbed the stairs to hers. She found Helen curled up on the sofa, hard at work on the journal she was keeping for her students back home. She looked up and smiled when Shae stepped inside.

"How'd the performance go?"

"Great. Nadia wants to do it again at a couple more stops. Farther down the line, though, so we have more time to prepare," Shae told her. She ran through the whole thing, leaving out the bloody autographs, as she slipped out of her shoes and went to sit with Helen.

"Sounds like it was fun. Your dinner is on the stove, by the way. I stopped at a cute little restaurant I found, so I've already eaten."

"Traitor," Shae teased, standing up and kissing Helen's forehead, relieved that the tension between them seemed to have vanished.

In the kitchen she found a pot of simmering soup and scooped out a bowl of it, grabbing a roll to dip in it, before going back to the lounge. She settled herself on a cushy chair next to a window, pulling the string to open the curtains so she could wave at any fans who saw the train as it pulled out of the city. There was already a crowd at the station, behind the eight-foot cast-iron fence that separated the platform from the street. Their screams were muffled by the thick glass, but as soon as they saw Shae they got even louder. Arms slid through the bars and waved frantically. Shae waggled her fingers at them, blowing a few kisses.

With a slight jerk the train started to move. Once the big station crowd was out of sight she started in on her soup, delighted by the rich taste of it; sage and rosemary and beef with a heavy dose of red potatoes. As the train sped out of the city the sky darkened, fading through shades of pink and into purple.

"How was the museum?" Shae asked.

Helen lit up at the question, and Shae knew she was now in for at least an hour of Helen babbling happily while all Shae would have to do was nod in the right places.

"It was amazing! This lovely woman, Alaina, gave me a full tour. The way they structured the covens back then was so fascinating. Did you know they had immigration policies to help Turned fake their deaths in one coven and move to another coven with a new identity once people started noticing their lack of aging? It was like a whole secret system of countries!"

Shae nodded, continuing to eat her soup.

"And there was this actress just before the wars, Elizabeth Blank, that accidentally got turned so, of course, she couldn't act any more. But she refused to leave her friends and family behind. Know what her coven did? They faked the murder of her *whole* family and moved *all* of them to a new coven with new identities! No one knows what happened to them, though. The wars started the next year and they were never heard from again."

Helen kept on, enumerating on different famous Turned from before the wars and how the covens had functioned in secrecy. Shae continued to nod and ooo in all the right places, though she didn't really care about much of it. Helen started to lose steam after about an hour and a half, letting out a large yawn.

"I think I'm going to head to bed," Helen said, voice still caught in the yawn. "Join me?"

"Sure."

Shae walked her empty bowl into the kitchen before following Helen upstairs, unsurprised to find that she had already drawn the shades of the dome. Shae snagged a baggy t-shirt to sleep in, changing by the desk before joining Helen in bed. Helen was studiously brushing her hair before twisting it back up into a loose ponytail at the nape of her neck. She never wore it down for more than a few minutes at a time, even at night, but for some reason Shae didn't understand she also refused to cut it off.

"Shae… I've been wanting to ask you something," she said tentatively, setting her brush down on a nightstand.

"Ask away," Shae told her, snuggling down under the silk covers.

"How long have you really known about your connection to Ariane from when you were children?"

Shae quirked an eyebrow, propping her head up on her hand, wondering why this mattered. "I found out right before the tour, like Ariane said. Ariane suspected it for a while before that, but he wasn't sure I was actually me, so he didn't bring it up until he was. Why?"

Helen shrugged. "Just… trying to understand you better, I suppose. Can I ask you something else?" She waited for Shae's nod before continuing on. "Part of this tour is taking us through the south of the United States, and into Mexico. We'll be going through some of the same places your family crossed through on the run from the Mendez Coven, right? And near your childhood home?"

"Yeah, so?"

"So isn't that sort of weird for you? Being back there a decade later, I mean? I feel like it would be weird. I remember I once went back and visited my childhood home when I was a teenager and it was such a strange feeling being there. Ethereal almost."

"I never *lived* in the southern U.S., Helen. We pitched tents in the countryside. And they weren't even tents most of the time, they were ratty tarps strung between trees. And if there weren't any trees we had to hope like hell it wouldn't rain because there was no way to put the tarps up. As for my 'childhood home', even that wasn't what you seem to be picturing. It was a compound full of nannies and servants. I left that place *once* before we were on the run. I was even born there; my parents didn't go to the hospital. That's not a home, that's a prison."

"I know, I know. But you were there with your family. Your brothers and sisters. You have to have some good memories of it, don't you?"

"Do you think I would've left if I had good memories, Helen?" Helen gave her such a forlorn look that Shae couldn't help but sigh and continue on. "Okay. Maybe there were a few. But not enough to matter."

"Tell me about them?"

"You're very persistent this evening."

"I'm very curious this evening."

Shae was silent for a while, thinking about what she could tell her girlfriend that would make her feel better.

There wasn't much.

"My older brother, Dustin, and I liked to read stories to our younger siblings when we were on the run. We'd each take different characters and use different voices. It made the little ones so happy. One time our parents even joined in. I think it was hard for them, because of how much they missed acting. But then they got really into it and it was one of the best nights we ever had. And then the next morning we almost got caught and things got even harder. Our parents became even more paranoid, and we never stayed anywhere longer than one night. That's how it always was, though. Something good would happen and then everything would go wrong right after. The universe never let us have anything good. I'm glad I left."

"Don't you miss them, though?"

Shae flopped on her back, staring up at the stars through the still unshaded top of the dome. "Honestly? Not really. I've got a better life now than I ever could have had if I'd stayed. And I'm sure things were easier for them with one less kid around to feed and watch."

Helen huffed and Shae could picture the dubious look on her face to go with the sound.

"I may be an only child from a family that has technically led a relatively easy life," she said, "but I don't think that's how it works."

"That's how it works for me. They were my family, I loved them, I left, I moved on. No point lingering."

"I just don't understand how you could ever stop loving someone, let alone your family. It's not like they were abusive or anything."

"Because I needed to move on, and they were holding me back."

"You just drop anyone who holds you back, then?"

"When I need to, yes."

Helen stood up, shaking her head. "I'm going to sleep on the couch.

Shae looked up at her, eyebrows knitted in confusion. "What? Why?"

"I wouldn't want to hold you back," she snapped before disappearing down the stairs.

Shae groaned, wondering if she should go down and try to fix this or leave Helen to her own space for a while. The problem was, she wasn't sure how to fix it. Nothing she'd said was untrue.

10: On the Road

"Why couldn't the apocalypse have destroyed the gas industry?" Dustin grumbled, staring at the family truck. Someone had taken it from the front of the house and put back into the vehicle barn where it lived with their tractor, a vintage sports car one of his younger brothers, Darius, was restoring, three ATVs, and various attachments for the tractor. The truck, a battered old mostly periwinkle blue amalgamation of several ancient Fords, seemed to stare at him out of the shadows of the old structure, dappled with dawn light filtering between the slatted walls.

Though, the access to natural gas was one reason Nahanni had managed to grow to the size it had, and remain stable, so Dustin couldn't really fault it. He was, however, rethinking his old plan of smuggling some sort of old horse wagon into the settlement. Or making one. That he could live with driving.

There was nothing to be done now, though. He'd promised to go into town for the family, and he needed to go for himself as well. Getting in, he rolled down all the windows and put the truck in neutral, easing it down the short road to their gas pump, which was getting low. Once the truck was full, he took off down the road, trying to balance the need to get there—and thus out of this thing—as quickly as possible, and not going so far over the speed-limit he risked getting pulled over by some eager military officer.

Parking was easy enough to find as the day's market hadn't really gotten started yet. Most of the hodgepodge stands were set up, scattered haphazardly in the old parking lot designated for such events, but there were still a few vendors frantically weighting down tents and arranging their produce as the first customers wandered in. It was that rare time of year in the Yukon where the weather was warm enough and calm enough at the same time for the market to set up outside. Otherwise they tended to set themselves up in the high school and the library across the street. It seemed everyone was taking advantage of the warm weather and open space, and Dustin didn't doubt that the town officials would look the other way when it came to sellers permits today. Sometimes they just had to let that sort of thing slide.

Dustin's first goal was to find someone in the mess of little shops who had two jackets that were the right size for his twin nieces, Rose and Robert's daughters Elizabeth and Maia, but beyond size they had to be different. If they received jackets that were even remotely alike there would be a fight. Generally, finding a matching set of anything in the chaotic Watson Lake Market was a rare occurrence, but somehow whenever the family shopped for the twins they couldn't find anything different, at least not different enough.

Dustin wove through the stalls, following the cinnamony scent of baking coffee cake as he glanced at each stall, making a plan for when he was ready to start trading. The market had a bit of everything, all of it traded and traded again. Hardcover books that had been read so many times they were now as soft as paperbacks, board games with half the pieces hand carved out of wood, engagement rings that had graced half a dozen fingers. Other stalls sold fresh food; oranges and bananas and apples grown in geothermally heated greenhouses, wild berries that were just coming into season, jerky from a dozen different kinds of animals. They were isolated here, sure, but they didn't want for much.

Little by the little the market filled up with a scramble of people. Dustin didn't mind them. It was interesting to listen to their chatter, everyone trading and bartering their way into a chance to survive the Yukon winter in comfort. None of them paid him any mind, save a few quickly averted glances. He assumed, with gritted teeth, that they were among those who still didn't trust his family.

After his first round through the stalls he began again, bartering for things on the list, arranging it all in a wooden cart he'd borrowed. He'd brought elk and deer hides to trade, the scent of tanning chemicals not quite faded out of them yet. His mother had given him some money as well, little paper bills that resembled old Canadian currency from before the war, but he was doing his best not to use it. That's what he tanned the pelts for, after all. Anything to make his family's life a little easier.

Eventually he had everything but the jackets. He'd even gotten peanut butter for Rose, something she'd raced out to demand he get as he'd been pulling away from the house. He'd nearly hit her. Now he was suspicious that she might be pregnant again given she'd been absolutely addicted to the stuff last time.

Some time later he found the stall with the coffee cake and bought two to take home, plus a fresh warm slice for himself. He'd given up on the jackets for now. It would be at least another month before they really needed them, so someone would have to try again another day. Worse came to worse, he could make them himself, but he doubted that elk skin brown would be an acceptable alternative to his nieces' favorite colors of yellow and lilac. That left only the stuff he needed for himself. He had no doubt Ramona would be keeping his pack safe at her inn, so he could just swing by to get it. He still needed food for the journey, though, because Colorado was a long way away.

His three youngest siblings, Darius, Corman, and Arabella, were messing around on the porch when Dustin pulled back up that afternoon. He roped them into helping take everything from the market inside, climbing into the bed and handing the coolers and bags to them.

"What are you doing skulking around in the truck?" Rose said. Dustin looked up and saw her standing on the top step of the porch, fists on her hips. She was smiling a bit, but wasn't a nice smile. It was a "give me my stuff or I'm putting you in a headlock" sort of smile.

"I'm not skulking. We're unloading," Dustin said, eying her warily.

"Did you get my peanut butter?"

"Yes, I did get it. And I was able to get you three jars instead of two." Dustin dug the jars out of one of the two remaining bags, handing them down to Rose once she skipped down the stairs and over to the truck.

She took all of them, tucking two under one arm while she unscrewed the top of the other. "Well, at least you did something right while you were down in town."

"Did I do something *wrong* while I was down in town?"

"You didn't get a haircut," she said, promptly sticking her finger into the peanut butter and pulling out a large dollop and popping it in her mouth.

"Why would I get a haircut in town? It would deprive you, Mom, and Tess the opportunity to chase me around with scissors, and that's your favorite pastime."

"Don't test me, kiddo. I only need two of these jars. I'll sacrifice the third if you make me." She waved the open jar threateningly towards Dustin before turning to go back in the house.

"How exactly is a jar of peanut butter a threat?" Keaun asked from where he stood in the open doorway.

"Grow your own hair to your shoulders and you'll find out," Rose replied as she passed him.

"I'm assuming she'll try to suffocate me with it by shoving it down my throat," Dustin told Keaun. "Help me unload the last couple coolers so I can take the truck back to the barn?"

"Either that or she's planning to coat your hair in it and let the mice cut your hair for her," Keaun said as he came down the steps.

"My hair is not that bad!"

Keaun chuckled.

When Keaun disappeared into the house with one of the coolers Dustin jumped down and slipped his own bag of supplies out from under the driver's seat. Glancing around to make sure no one was outside, he walked across the road to the horse barn, a movie-perfect faded red building with white trim. The tack room inside was where he kept all his rough living supplies, tucked in a locked cabinet at the back to keep the kids from getting at any of his guns.

His horse, a three-year-old gray mare named Echo, stretched her head out of her stall to nudge at him with whiskery lips. Dustin smiled softly and gave her an affectionate rub under her chin, laying his forehead against hers.

"Missed you too. I'll get you a treat in a minute." He gave her another pat and continued on to the tack room at the back, lifting the door as he swung it open so it wouldn't drag on the stone floor.

He knew he needed to be careful about how he left. The family was ripe to be asking too many questions, and there wasn't time for that. His best bet was to slip away at night, gone before anyone could notice. Getting to the border would be tricky, though. He could take Echo and leave her in Ramona's care until he got back, but that might raise questions given the amount of attention on the town after the attack.

He was interrupted in his planning by Russ slipping into the room, closing the door loudly, and leaning against it, arms crossed as best he could with a cast up to his left elbow.

"How'd you get away from everyone?" Dustin asked, not even trying to hide what he was doing. It must have been a recent escape, as Russ was still in sweats and a t-shirt, the hair on the left side of his head sticking up in wild spikes from where he'd slept on it.

"Not important. You're going to try and go get her, aren't you?"

Dustin remained silent, not braking his gaze from Russ'.

"I could go in the house right now and tell everyone what you're doing, find wherever you've stashed that paper. They'd lock you in the cellar until it was too late for you to go, and you know it. Otherwise you wouldn't be hiding this."

"She's family, Russell. And you guys... you couldn't keep me in that cellar."

Dustin could practically hear the muscles in Russ' jaw clench.

"Who the fuck *are you*, Dustin? What would you do, knock out your whole family just so you could run off and get yourself killed trying to find a sister who probably wants nothing to do with us?"

"Of course not!" Dustin said, louder than he'd intended. "Of course not. I just... I just want to find her, Russ. I have to find her."

"Why?"

Dustin spluttered, unable to fathom having to explain this. "She's our sis—"

"*No*," Russ interrupted. "You haven't held onto this for ten years, turned yourself into whatever the hell you are, just because she's our sister. There's something else."

Dustin went silent for a moment, staring at his little brother. He wasn't used to having anyone in the family mad at him, let alone this angry. Dustin was content staying in the background, silently supporting everyone with tanned pelts and scavenged artifacts and babysitting. He didn't get in the thick of things, and he was fine with that. If everyone in the family was loud, no one would be heard.

"Dad," Dustin said finally, hoping it would be enough of an answer for Russ. "Dad's tried to kill himself twice now."

Russ broke eye contact, dropping his gaze to the floor as his shoulders tightened under his shirt. "I know... I remember when you found him hanging in here...."

Dustin nodded. "And Keaun. I know he's better than he used to be, but he still misses her. And Mom. And Rose. Arabella doesn't even *remember* Shae. She was only a *toddler* when her big sister vanished."

Russ blew out a breath, hand tightening on his bicep. "Families lose people all the time, Dustin, especially now."

"I know," Dustin said. "But we have a chance to *get her back*. What family wouldn't take that?"

Russ stared at him for what felt like ages before thunking his head back against the wooden door, letting out a long sigh.

"Do you really, honestly, think you can make it to Colorado safely? That you can actually get to her without getting yourself seen and arrested? Killed?"

"Without a doubt," Dustin said quickly. "There's no better place for me to get to her. I know it better than I know home."

"That's not as comforting as you seem to think it is, given that as far as I was aware until two days ago you never left the settlement at all."

Dustin winced, aware that he had said too much in his eagerness to get Russ to let him go without a fight.

"Fine," Russ said after several moments of contemplating the ceiling. "We'll go to fucking Colorado."

"... we?"

"Yes, asshole, we," Russ said, leveling a hard stare at him. "It's 'we' or I handcuff you to your bed and tell Mom."

Dustin didn't point out that he could get out of that arrangement even easier than the cellar.

"You'll slow me down," Dustin tried. "You don't know how to travel the back roads the way I do, let alone train hop."

"Screw the back roads. I've got fake identities in the coven. We'll rent a car and take the Alaska Highway."

Great. More cars.

As much as Dustin hated to admit it, though, it could help. He would be cutting it far too close getting there by jumping trains. Even taking a car would be cutting it close, but not as close.

"Fine," Dustin grumbled. "But. I would like to know why exactly you have fake identities, plural, in the coven."

Russ shrugged. "Everyone who does border patrols has them. Gives us a better chance to stay out of trouble if things get dicey. We can dump our gear and pretend we're lost hikers. I've never had to use mine, but I've got them."

Dustin contemplated for a few moments, working out how Russ coming along would change things.

"We leave tonight, once everyone is asleep," Dustin told him. "Pack light. We're stopping at Ramona's to get my gear on the way."

They arrived at Ramona's at three in the morning. Russ had insisted they leave a note so the family wouldn't worry, then they'd walked the five miles to a military fueling station, borrowing a military truck to take to the border. Dustin didn't enjoy the idea, unsettled by leaving a trail, but Russ had insisted. Dustin suspected his brother might intentionally be trying to make him uncomfortable to make him change his mind.

Dustin was unsurprised to find Ramona at the bar.

She was old enough that sleep didn't seem to be much of a priority anymore. The broken front windows were boarded up now, the bits of glass swept away, and the pool table righted, but the pieces of the shattered mirror were still hanging behind the bar and there were plenty of gaps where now broken bottles had stood. Ramona was cleaning glasses by lantern light and seemed to have been expecting the boys.

"Dragging your brother into your trouble now?" She asked Dustin.

"He dragged himself into it by threatening to put me under house arrest," Dustin said, voice a little harsher than he'd intended.

"Not in the mood to listen to your family squabbles," Ramona remarked. "You leaving the settlement?"

Dustin nodded.

"Going far?"

Dustin nodded.

"Want to smuggle a car out for me?"

Dustin blinked, taken aback. Ramona had never asked him for something like that before. He took letters across for her all the time, dropping them in random coven postboxes, but a car?

"You aren't the only person I smuggle through here," Ramona replied to his obvious confusion. "Told this idiot to leave his car behind, but he didn't listen. I need it gone. Taking it off my hands is the least you can do for me after all these years. Dump it far from here so no one will suspect he made it to Nahanni."

"Of course," Dustin said. "I'm happy to do it, I just wasn't expecting it. Can we get out with a car tonight?"

Ramona eyed an antique clock on one of the bookshelves that adorned the south wall. "If you leave now, take route three, and cross the border between 4:15 and 4:25 you should make it just fine. Keep the lights off, though."

Russ, looking as though he was beginning to regret all of this, asked a question of his own; "Who is gonna be looking for this car?"

"Hard to say."

Russ groaned and muttered something that sounded like, "I should've stayed on the couch."

As they turned to leave Dustin stopped, looking back at Ramona. "Landen...."

"The funeral is in the morning," Ramona said, expression turning sad.

"Leave a rose for me?" Dustin asked.

Ramona nodded.

Five minutes later Dustin had his pack and a set of keys, which he handed off to Russ, and they were away.

"I hate all of this," Russ ground out once they'd crossed the border. "If we get caught in a vehicle belonging to a missing person—"

"Relax. We'll drive an hour and dump it."

"In a lake," Russ stated.

"Whatever makes you feel better."

"Are you incapable of sitting still?" Russ asked, glancing over at Dustin from the driver's seat of their newly rented car. They'd dumped the car Ramona had given them two hours ago, in a lake as Russ demanded, then walked four miles to a little coven truck-stop town. Between that and the distance they'd gone from Nahanni, Russ had started to relax. Dustin, meanwhile, was not happy.

"I don't think I've ever been in a car this long before," Dustin grumbled. "Cars suck."

Dustin slouched down in his seat, knowing it made him look childish but having no better way to show his dissatisfaction. Cars were loud and complicated and hardly had enough room to breathe in most of them, even less in this stupid little two-door thing Russ had rented. Dustin preferred to be outside, moving under his own power, feeling his muscles work as they carried him wherever he wanted to go. Horses were fine too, at least then you were outside and working with a fellow creature rather than a machine. Trains were alright because they were big. Though, he'd never actually properly ridden on a train.

Russ rolled his eyes and pulled the car over onto the shoulder, tires bumping along in the dirt as the car slowed.

"What are you doing?" Dustin asked as Russ fiddled around with something on the dash.

"You're terrible at hiding the fact that you're claustrophobic."

"I am not!"

"You totally are." He hit a button on the dash and the roof of the car shuddered before lifting up and folding back to rest behind them. Russ waited until it stopped moving before getting out and snapping a cover over the folded top using his good arm.

Dustin didn't want to admit how much better it felt having the car opened up. His little brother had won enough arguments for the day.

The wind brought in the scent of a wildfire and Dustin could see the column of smoke off in the east, maybe a few dozen miles away. No one would come to fight it. Not all the way out here. The nearest town of any consequence was the coven town of New Liard, and it was fifty miles away in the opposite direction.

"So," Russ climbed back into the driver's seat, "what is the plan beyond getting to Colorado?"

"Nothing during the daytime," Dustin said as Russ pulled back onto the road, raising his voice to be heard over the wind. "It'll have to be after her show. We'll just have to follow her and wait for a good opportunity."

"Do you hear yourself when you speak? Because you sound like an idiot. This is not something you do on a wing and a prayer, Dustin."

"A wing and a prayer has worked out fine for me so far," Dustin replied.

Russ once again looked like he regretted every decision that had brought him to this moment. It was becoming his most common expression.

They pulled off at a gas station around sunset on their second day of driving because Russ wanted a hot meal and refused Dustin's plan to pull onto a backroad so they could cook over a fire. Dustin tried to point out a fire-cooked meal from the food he'd packed would be a thousand times better than any gas station meal, but Russ wasn't having it. So now they were standing in some podunk little Canadian highway station trying not to gag while two vamps drizzled a blood sauce over hot dogs that had probably been spinning in the rollercase since the war.

Dustin wasn't good at guessing the age of vampires, but he assumed that these ones had to have a higher turn-age as they seemed to be suffering little effect of the sunlight shining on them through the windows. The lower turn-age a vampire had, the closer they were to the vampires of legend. That's what Dustin had been taught.

He forced himself to ignore the two men and grabbed a soda from the cold case and a bag of chips from the racks, checking the ingredients on both to be sure they had no blood in them. Russ, seemingly unfazed by the grubby station, was ladling something falsely qualified as cheese into a plastic cup in the corner of a tray of nachos. He, at least, seemed like he belonged out here in his red flannel, worn jeans, and cowboy boots. A rancher out on an errand. Dustin, though, knew he stood out. His dark brown shirt was patched in four places and stitched back together in eight more, splotches of dirt staining his canvass pants, beard and hair wild from the wind. A man who didn't belong indoors.

Dustin grabbed a local paper to go with his food, ignoring the few glances he was getting. Russ paid for everything with coven money Dustin wasn't sure how he got, both of them heading back out to the car, parked in a far corner of the lot. They lounged in the seats as Russ ate his nachos.

"I don't get it," Russ said between chips. "How the hell can some vamps stand in the sun like those two, and others start burning the second they step outside?"

"It's their turn-age," Dustin said off-handedly.

"Their what now?"

Dustin glanced over at his brother and saw that he was actually as confused as he sounded. "Their... turn-age? Like, how many turns from the original vampires they are?"

Russ' face remained blank.

"The Nahanni military doesn't know what turn-ages are? I mean, I figured you might have a different term for them, but...." Dustin had learned about them in a rather unconventional way, after all, but once he had it seemed so obvious. Other people in Nahanni had to have noticed.

"I have no idea what the hell you're talking about."

"Okay, well, you know how vampirism is kinda like a virus?" Dustin said. Russ nodded. "It evolves like a virus does, too. As it passes from person A to person B, it changes a little bit every time. A turn-age is how many turns a vampire is from the original vampires. So the first vampire that bit someone, that next person had a turn-age of one. Then when they bit the next person, that third person had a turn-age of two. The lower the number, the closer they are to the original vampires. The higher the number, the more recently they were turned, usually. It gets a little muddy since none of it is a direct line and some vampires change more people than others."

"What does that have to do with the sun, though?" Russ pressed.

"Lower the turn-age, the more like mythical vampires they are. Higher the turn-age, the more human they are, even though they're still monsters. Lower is more affected by the sun, needs more blood, more feral."

Russ groaned and pinched the bridge of his nose. "Nahanni doesn't know anything, dammit. Most of the people who live there have been there for generations. They've never interacted directly with vampires. And the damn military has kept us so cut off that they don't know anything either. And they refuse to listen to refugees like Mom."

"Mom may have made some progress on that front when you were in the hospital," Dustin offered.

"Think she knows about turn-ages?" Russ asked.

"I'd think she has some idea about it, as famous as she was. The covens have got to know to be able to feed their populations properly."

Russ was silent, finishing up his nachos.

"What's the next step in evolution if you're a monster?" He said eventually.

Dustin shrugged. "Don't some animals evolve themselves to death? They pick up traits that aren't sustainable, then they die off. With how much human blood vamps need, I can see that happening to them."

"They'd take us with them, though," Russ said grimly.

Once the sun set completely it grew too cold to keep the top down, so Russ pulled over again to close it up. He and Dustin had ridden in silence since their conversation about turn-ages. Needing to stretch his legs a little, Dustin got out while Russ was unsnapping the cover. The stretch of pavement they'd been driving on had been so poorly maintained people had begun driving in the scrub on the side, wearing it down to a new dirt road that ran parallel to the highway. It was not much better than the pavement had been, though, and Dustin felt a bit like his bones were still vibrating. Up until now the road had been decent enough that he and Russ had been able to trade off napping and driving, but Dustin doubted that would be happening tonight. Sleeping inside a rock tumbler just wasn't going to work out.

Russ stuffed the cover in the trunk and pulled out one of their extra gas cans to top off the car. Once the can was put away, he paused to look at Dustin.

"If you tell Mom about this, I'm going to kill you," Russ informed him before pulling a cigarette and a lighter out of his inner jacket pocket.

"You'd be dead before you could get to me."

"I'd haunt your sorry ass then." He took a long drag, showing off a bit as he exhaled smoke in a perfect ring, the ambient glow from the taillights painting it a faint red.

Dustin chuckled and pulled out the paper he'd bought earlier but had yet to flip through. He was only interested to see if it contained more information about Shae's tour, so he flipped to the entertainment section and started scanning, tilting the paper towards the light.

"Fuck! Wait, no, not fuck. Hang on," he said, looking closer at the paper.

Russ came around the car, peering over Dustin's shoulder. Dustin muttered the words to himself as he read and re-read the article, his grin steadily growing with each pass.

"What?" Russ asked, not seeming to get what Dustin was so excited about.

"Her tour was originally scheduled to fly between stops, that's what it said in the paper you found. But this says that, due to fuel costs skyrocketing, they switched to an electric train."

"So?"

"So we don't have to go to Denver anymore. Things just got ten times easier."

"I don't follow."

"She's got a stop in Denver, and then a stop in Salt Lake two days later. There's only one way left to get from Denver to Salt Lake by train in two days."

Russ waved his hand in a circle, encouraging Dustin to elaborate more.

"This country has increased its rail systems tenfold since the war, it's the most cost-effective way to travel across a mostly empty continent at any useful speed," Dustin explained.

"I'm aware of that," Russ said.

"This is through the Rockies, though. There's only so many places you can lay tracks, even if you're willing to dynamite your way through a mountain. The line I'm talking about, there's half a dozen places where it is forced to narrow down to a single track. We can get it stopped at one of them and get Shae off of it from there. The whole stretch of the Rockies in Colorado is abandoned territory that has never been officially claimed by Wood's Coven since the war. There won't be anyone around but the people on the train, and we can handle them."

Russ looked dubious.

"It's that or walking around in a city of over a million people who are all clamoring for the latest news on the Lockwoods since Shae is in town," Dustin told him.

"Oh, *now* you're worried about that!"

"I wasn't not worried about it before, there just wasn't a better option. Now there is."

"I hate you."

"I'm aware."

Russ groaned. "I'd ask if you honestly think you can pull this off, but I'm starting to think you don't have a realistic idea of what is and isn't possible."

11: Rebel Flowers

Shae had not yet had occasion to pass through Ariane's car very often. However, each time she had it was clear that Ariane was slowly and systematically destroying his stepfather's property. It had been subtle at first; a distinct lack of pillows, then the expensive crystal wine glasses vanished. Today it seemed he had gotten to work on the molding. As Shae crossed from her and Helen's car she could see strips of the intricately carved ebony wood were stacked in one corner and there was a screwdriver sticking out from the edge of a piece along the ceiling.

"I see you've lost your wife," Ariane drawled from a couch. It dipped a bit in the middle as if one of its supporting struts was broken.

"I see you've lost the fan you picked up," Shae returned, flopping down onto an armchair. Her light and swishy black skirt spread out around her like a puddle of ink, pooling across the cushion and dripping onto the floor. It was a good skirt for lounging, though not one she'd wear in public. Too simple.

They'd been stopped in a small town outside of Chicago for over an hour now due to a protest about unfair distribution of blood resources that was occurring up the tracks. Shae had seen some fringes of the protest outside their Chicago venue earlier in the day; a little knot of people waving signs and chanting as geared up police offers eyed them. She supposed she understood their frustration. Everyone deserved to be able to eat, after all. Her understanding was growing short, however, as sitting still on the tracks for so long was grating against her nerves. This tour was about motion, fans, people. Not sitting still. Besides, Helen was still upset with her about their fight from several days earlier, which was its own kind of grating. Shae's attempt to cheer her up with the gift of a fancy e-reader half-an-hour ago had just resulted in a lot of huffing on Helen's part. Shae had given up and left to visit Ariane instead.

"Oh, no, my fan is still here. Puking in the bathroom, I think."

"How classy." Shae snagged the cup dangling from his hand over the edge of the armrest, taking a swig. Rum and Coke. Mostly rum.

"Better than on the floor." He reached out and took the cup back, taking a swig as well.

"Still. What's the point of having a fan in your car if you can't even make-out with him?"

Ariane contemplated a moment. "Absolutely nothing." He twisted and shouted down the hall, "Finish up and get gone! Party's over."

There was an angry screech and a flash of unnaturally red hair before the door at the other end of the car slammed. Shae and Ariane both snickered, continuing to pass the cup back and forth.

"How'd you lose the wife?"

Shae sighed theatrically. "Bought her an e-reader. She got mad at me for it. I'd be surprised if she ever looks at me again."

"Nice fake tear," Ariane commented.

"Thanks. I've been working on the fake crying thing. It's so damn hard to time it right."

"Think about dying puppies."

"Puppies die, what's so sad about that? It's life. Do *you* think about dying puppies?"

"No. Can't really explain my process, actually."

"Emotions are weird," Shae replied, finishing their shared drink.

"Useful when you understand them in others, though."

Shae shrugged, knowing it was true but not caring at the moment. She was content to stew in her annoyance at Helen.

They talked for a while, conversation shifting through various topics until they settled on exchanging stories about weird fans they'd encountered over the years. Ariane had one that changed her last name to his and started telling everyone they had gotten married. Apparently she'd been arrested trying to break into his hotel room in Barcelona where he'd been filming a pirate movie.

Shae didn't have any major weird fan encounters yet, not in person ones, but she'd started collecting the weirdest fan-mail she got. Her favorite was one that had assured her it was okay to seek help for the trauma of getting abducted by aliens, as that was obviously the truth of what happened to her as a child. Another claimed she would help her "escape the governmental forces holding her back from her true destiny." It didn't clarify what that true destiny was, though.

"Have you been bitten by a fan yet?" Ariane asked with a smile worthy of a trickster god. He was looking at her over the rim of the cup, which he'd refilled, not bothering with the Coke at all this time.

"Not so far, no," Shae said. "You?"

"Once," Ariane admitted. "When I was sixteen. Middle of a premier, some woman broke through the line and sunk her teeth into my shoulder. My security beheaded her on the spot and whisked me off. I didn't turn, obviously, and my agent had me flown to San Francisco to see a plastic surgeon who specialized in eliminating scars from Turned bites. Not a trace of it left."

"What did it feel like, those moments before you knew if you would turn or not?" Shae asked, voice soft. It must have been exhilarating. The chaos, the uncertainty, the feeling of the entire audience focusing in on one intense moment that he was the center of.

Ariane swirled the cup, watching her without answering. Shae did not break her gaze from his.

"It made my career," Ariane said eventually. "I'd had

roles before that, but I got my first big one right after because a producer saw the footage and liked how I looked."

"All covered in blood?" Shae said, voice still low.

"All covered in blood," Ariane echoed, lips curling into a much more wicked smile.

The story didn't surprise Shae at all. She'd known her whole life that acting was a cutthroat business in a very literal sense. She had yet to cut any throats herself, but she'd cut plenty of ties and was finding more and more that she wasn't all that bothered by the concept of cutting a few throats as well. Perhaps she'd still change her mind in the moment, but it was hard to say.

Inevitably the conversation shifted to the fact that they were now nearing their third hour of sitting still due to the issue with the blood protest up the tracks. The conversation so far had kept Shae occupied enough not to mind the delay, but it still lingered in the back of her mind.

"I don't think they're being honest with us," Ariane said. "A little blood protest? We wouldn't be sitting here for so long. They'd kick them off the tracks and we'd be on our way. Any thoughts, Shae-Shae? You spent a couple years as a naughty little rebel."

Shae hesitated, watching him closely. There was a gleam to his eyes, a purposeful languidity to his body, that Shae had come to learn meant he was looking for a deeper answer than what the simple question implied.

"Well, first of all, they aren't rebels. Pissed off about blood allocation or not, they're coven citizens. Rebels don't protest against the covens, they kill anyone involved with them. Secondly, I was never a rebel. I was a child taken away from her home by her parents," Shae said, keeping her tone even.

"Touchy subject today?" Ariane asked.

Shae bristled at this, annoyed that he was learning to read her through her acting. Deciding to move past the comment without response, she turned the conversation back to their stoppage. "I agree with you; it wouldn't take this long to clear the tracks of a protest."

"What if there are rebels involved, though?" Ariane asked. "Stirring up some chaos in the covens can only benefit them. Make it easier for them to do their own thing."

Shae shrugged. "I still don't see why it would have us stopped this long. It isn't worth it for the coven police to chase down a few rebels, not out here. These aren't the kind that have gone off to live in some quiet settlement. They're still fighting. They'll bite their tongues off before ever allowing themselves to be captured."

Ariane grinned. "Not the protest, not the rebels... what do you think it could be, then?"

Before Shae could respond, the door at the end of the lounge slammed open, revealing a furious looking Helen. She stalked in, holding a large bouquet of flowers, pink ones in poofy little bundles, as far from her as she possibly could. She looked as if she thought they were going to come to life and attempt to shorten hers.

"Someone left these on the back porch of our car, Ariane. They're addressed to you. And I swear to god, if there are drugs hidden in these things somehow I will kill you in your sleep and toss your body off the train." She shoved the flowers at him, spinning on her heel and heading back to her and Shae's car.

Ariane was looking at the bouquet through narrowed eyes and before Helen could make it to the door he leaped up and took a few quick steps to block it. Not the wisest move, Shae thought, since she had just threatened to kill him. Shae didn't think Helen was capable of murder in general, but Ariane aggravated her enough that Shae wouldn't be surprised if she snapped. However, Ariane was also quick and scrappy and completely okay with fighting dirty. Something interesting was bound to happen, so Shae settled in to watch, sipping on the glass of rum.

"Move," Helen growled, looming over him.

Ariane didn't look concerned. "You said this was on your back porch? Did you see who left it? When they left it?"

Helen looked exasperated. "No. I was reading, then Steven—the head of security on the train you idiot—came around to do a check of the train and he found them on the back porch. He checked them for anything dangerous and then asked me to bring them to you so he could finish his inspection."

"They couldn't have been there long," Shae reasoned. "Security would've noticed."

"Who *cares*? They're just flowers." Helen sidestepped Ariane, reaching for the door when he didn't move into her path again.

"Not just flowers," Ariane murmured, eying the bouquet. This pulled Helen up short, her previous wonderings about concealed drugs probably crossing her mind. "Shae, you got your pocket-knife on you?"

Shae pulled it out of her right ankle-high boot and tossed it at him. He caught it, flicked open the blade with his thumb, and slipped it under the string binding the bundle shut, pulling away the wrapping and dropping it to the floor. Inside the stems were tied again, bound by a dark green string.

"Just flowers…" Helen muttered, but still didn't leave.

"Your mother is a florist, isn't she, Helen?" Ariane said, pulling one flower out of the bundle. Helen looked at Shae, her face livid, likely over the fact that Shae had dared to share this bit of information with Ariane. "And you live in Riddelsdale, a coven popular with Turned from the 1800s, so I'm guessing if you think about it you'll realize that these mean something."

Helen's face twisted up in confused disbelief. "Are you *honestly* trying to tell me you have received a *coded* bouquet? In case your drug addled brain has forgotten, Ariane, you *make* movies, you don't *live* in one."

"Ahh, but I do date a strange collection of people which happens to make my life quite movie-like at times. These flowers come from an ex-girlfriend named Dalton." Ariane snagged a beer bottle off the coffee table, dumped out the dregs at the bottom onto the carpet, and dropped the single flower into it before setting the impromptu vase on an end-table in front of a windowsill. He did the same with another flower on the other side of the car.

"And?" Shae prompted as he worked.

"And she's a rebel who lives among the Turned to gather information to bring the covens down. One of the few real rebels left, as you said. Dalton started a relationship with me to get close to my stepfather, since he's such a powerful political figure. She was new to espionage then, however, and easy to figure out. But, as I have no particular respect for my stepfather, nor many of his policies, I let things continue. The relationship lasted about three months, at which point Dalton was given a different assignment by her commander and we broke up. However, we've kept in touch and she'll pass me information when I get curious in exchange for updates on my father."

Now *this* was interesting, Shae thought. But why tell her, let alone Helen?

Helen scoffed. "Wait. *You* are a rebel? Mr. Sell-jars-of-his-blood-to-the-highest-bidder is a rebel?"

"I really don't give a damn what the world does or doesn't do, nor who rules it. I just want a front-row seat to whatever happens, and Dalton's information is quite handy in getting that seat." Ariane remarked. He was standing in the middle of the room now, eyes roving across all the windows. In contrast to Shae's simple lounging outfit, and to the old-world elegance of his stepfather's train car, Ariane was a riot of noticeable things all brought into sharp detail by the artfully dim lighting of the car. Tight acid-green pants, skull-sharp features, a few glittering rings, ribbed black tank-top tight over light muscles still sculpted from filming related workouts. He didn't look like a man waiting for a front-row seat, but one who belonged in the emperor's box. Not as the emperor, but as someone whispering silky words into the emperor's ear.

"And how do I get a seat?" Shae asked, swirling the glass.

Helen started, looking down at Shae, then glancing back at Ariane whose smile had transformed once more, this time into something feral. "I hate what you've done to her."

"He didn't do anything, Helen."

The most Ariane had done was provide her with a like-minded individual who didn't think it was insane to put oneself first.

Helen looked sad and shook her head, pulling the door open and finally leaving. Shae contemplated for a moment, searching her feelings to see if she was upset about what had occurred, and found that she wasn't.

"What's with the flowers then?" Shae asked Ariane as he rejoined her on the couch, though his eyes continued to rove the windows.

"Small confession, first. I'm the reason the train has been stopped. Paid off some people. I was supposed to meet with Dalton after the event—she lives near there. However, she got a message to me a couple weeks ago saying that plans needed to change as she suspected she was being watched."

The little shit. Shae honestly wasn't at all surprised. Ariane's lack of hesitation when it came to getting things done was one of her favorite things about him.

"Where's Dalton, then?"

"No idea. She just said she'd be here, that was all. But the woman is a florist, hence the flowers. As she puts it, 'no one would ever suspect an actor getting flowers.' Geraniums stand for an expected meeting. I am assuming that if I leave them in the windows long enough she'll show up and find her way on the train."

"Sounds overdramatic," Shae replied.

Ariane sighed loudly. "It is. Exhausting woman. I've told her multiple times to just call me, but she doesn't want to 'leave a trail.' Never date a spy, Shae. It is dreadful."

They were interrupted by the sound of footsteps in the bedroom above them.

"Dreadful," Ariane muttered.

Shae followed him up the stairs to his room to find a woman sitting on the bed in the dark. Shae couldn't make out much beyond the fact that she was broad shouldered.

"Who's this?" An attractively rough voice said from the darkness.

"An interested party," Ariane said, loudly flicking the switch to turn on the lights. "You could've knocked. Come in through the door. Accosted me outside the venue like a sex-crazed fan. Kept to our original plan at your apartment. Lotta options that don't involve whatever it is you did to get into the second level of this car. You got the flowers to the porch, you climbed onto the top of the car, you crawled through a window; you could've just come to my door."

Dalton seemed to be ignoring him in favor of appraising Shae, and Shae appraised her right back. She had light blue eyes ringed with elegant eye-liner and a form-fitting, expensive looking dark green blouse. Not what Shae expected from someone who just snuck onto a private train in the middle of the night.

Without looking at Ariane she gave him a clipped answer, "You're parked at a station full of witnesses who can't know I was here. I threw the flowers down from the roof of the station, then jumped from there onto the roof of your car. Too much security on the actual platform."

"Do you intend to fly back when you leave, then?" Ariane asked.

She ignored him. "You're the Lockwood."

Shae lifted an eyebrow, crossing her arms. "Oh, do go on. I love being referred to like I'm a piece of furniture."

Dalton glanced between her and Ariane. "This is one hell of a friendship."

Ariane snapped his fingers. "Important information, Dalton?"

Dalton looked at Shae one last time before fully shifting her attention to Ariane. "You know how much Mendez has been struggling for blood, your father has made more than one abhorrent policy to attempt to deal with it. It isn't working, though. The vampires are still starving. However, in the last couple months something has changed. It is just a few cities near the border with Wood's Coven, but they aren't struggling for blood nearly as much. We aren't sure what it is. No new policies have gone through."

Ariane shrugged. "My money is on mass kidnapping or incarceration. Have you checked the prisoner numbers? Inflating crime rates is one of his favorite methods for getting blood."

"High but stable," Dalton replied. "He is up to something, Ariane. Something new."

"That isn't useful to me, Dalton. I need concrete facts to hold against him. I need a lion I can throw into a ring of gladiators," Ariane said.

Dalton eyed him for a moment, glancing at Shae, an internal debate clear in her eyes. "There have been... a few strange shipments from Wood's Coven to Mendez. Trains coming from the Northern California Cryogenic Studies facility, and the Manhattan Institute of Cryogenics."

Shae kept her expression neutral, as interesting as this bit of information was. Cryogenics had been a big fad at the start of the plagues. Advancements in the technology coincided perfectly with the start of mass deaths. Problem was, the advancements had only been in the freezing process. No one had yet to figure out the whole waking them up part, and Shae felt it was unlikely they ever would. Things that died stayed dead. And, currently, millions of those things were frozen in cryogenics facilities around the world.

"I imagine there's a few arteries in the human body that are large enough to make a nice little popsicle snack for a few vamps, but it is hardly going to eliminate the blood shortages in Mendez."

"We think they're being wo—" Dalton was interrupted by the sound of a door opening downstairs.

After a second of pronounced silence someone shouted "Security, Mr. Cordova!" from below.

Dalton's eyes widened and she moved to the open window Shae assumed she'd come through.

"They'll see you," Ariane said offhandedly. He strode over to the bed and slid his hand under the center of the mattress and rooted around for a moment. There was a clicking sound and then the whole mattress rose up on a hinged board, revealing a large area of empty storage underneath.

"Do all the beds do that?" Shae asked.

"Lots of things do that. Must have plenty of places to hide things when you're as corrupt as Malcom is."

Dalton climbed in and Ariane shut the lid on her, throwing himself down on the mattress just as their head of security came up the stairs. Shae turned and smiled at the man, surprised to see a regular cop behind him. He was Turned, stopped aging somewhere in his fifties, and, based on the grayish pallor of his skin, he hadn't fed recently. Their security guard was Turned as well, but much better fed; his skin didn't quite have the rosy hue of someone alive, but neither did it go so far as to have the lack of color of someone dead.

"What can we do for you?" Ariane asked, sprawled out like he'd been there for hours.

"We got a report of an unidentified man leaving this train. We need to ascertain that he was not a rebel or one of the protesters from up the tracks," the cop spoke, his voice sounding deeper than it seemed like it should be for a man of his slim stature.

It seemed the local cops were not among the people Ariane had paid off. Or maybe this one just hadn't gotten the message.

"That was a fan," Ariane grinned mischievously. "Manuel? Or maybe his name was Miguel. We didn't talk much. I promise he was not a rebel, though. At least not in the way you're thinking."

The security guard for the train looked rather put-upon, and Shae suppressed a snicker.

"He left over two hours ago," Shae said. "I saw him go."

"Nonetheless, I will need to search this car. The head of security has given me permission," the officer said firmly.

Ariane looked amused, waving his hand lazily in the air. "Search away."

Shae waved sweetly and sat down in one of the armchairs, stretching out her pale legs in front of her, letting the waist-high slit of her skirt fall open to reveal the skin of her thigh, the tracery of veins stretched across her skin. The cop swallowed heavily and turned to check the closets, as it seemed clear to him there was no one else in the room.

"Nice skirt," Ariane mouthed at her while the cop was

distracted by his search.

Shae winked back at him.

Finding nothing of interest in the closets, the cop headed down the stairs to search the rest of the car, leaving Ariane and Shae with their security guard.

"How bad is this going to be?" He asked, looking between Ariane and Shae. "I know what you keep in here, Cordova."

"Easy," Ariane murmured, getting up from the bed. "Nothing says guilt like overreacting. And if you think I don't know how to handle cops...."

Shae watched as he walked by, going to the desk on her other side. He rustled around in the top drawer for a moment and came back out with an empty little glass vial, which he set on the desktop, and a leather satchel which he unrolled to reveal several capped needles. The security guard groaned as Ariane uncapped one and expertly slid it into a vein in his inner arm. The guard was well fed enough to not be overly tempted by the blood, but Shae could see his jaw clench as his fangs slid out over his regular teeth. Once the syringe was filled, Ariane extracted the needle and injected the blood into the vial, dropping the empty syringe in the waste basket under the desk.

"No. Whatever you're doing, no," their guard said, eyes flicking from the vial to the stairs as the cop stomped back up them, holding out a baggy of assorted pills for everyone to see. Shae was delighted, looking between everyone.

"That certainly isn't a rebel man," Ariane said into the silence.

The security guard let out a frustrated sound.

"Trade you," Ariane said, holding up the vial with the needle hole in his arm visible, a tiny, bright bead of blood forming there.

The cop's eyes went wide, carefully tracking the vial, his hand holding the baggie faltering a bit. His fangs slid out so quickly they cut his bottom lip, the pale flesh peeling open without bleeding, and he took a halting step forward towards Ariane. Shae guessed only his training as an officer kept him from lunging. The security guard opened his mouth to intervene, but Shae jumped up and clasped her hand over his mouth before he could speak.

"Shhhh. Let the man work," she whispered. She could feel the guard tensing against her, trying to pull his mouth back from her hand, could feel his fangs under his lips where her hand pressed against them. Too bad there wasn't an audience, because this was turning into a hell of a show.

The cop took a halting step forward, then back again, eyes tracking the vial and jaw grinding. It was easy to see that his instincts were going to win out. Fresh blood was a rarity for even the rich, let alone some nobody cop. And the blood of someone famous? If he managed not to drink it himself, he could probably sell it and never have to work again. Slowly his hand holding the baggy of pills lowered, dropping the pills to the floor.

"I...I suppose I should be on my way," he mumbled, a

new lisp to his voice from his fangs.

"Good man." Ariane smiled, handing him the vial. "Thank you for your service."

The cop gave a tiny nod and headed back down the stairs, vial clasped in his hand. A moment later the sound of a door closing echoed through the car.

"You… you… have you ever been in trouble in your *life*?" Their security guard spluttered. As soon as the cop left he'd shaken Shae off and taken several quick steps away from her.

"Only when I needed to be," Ariane replied.

Their security guard mumbled something about needing a raise, retreating down the stairs and slamming the door on his way out.

Ariane waited a moment before returning to the bed and opening the compartment, only to find it empty. "She found the trapdoor, then."

Ten minutes later they were back in the lounge, the train moving again. Another shared drink had been poured, but not much had been said. Shae had struggled to understand Ariane before, but tonight made it even harder. His loathing of his stepfather seemed to be the only solid thing about him, but even that Shae couldn't quite wrap her head around. When she'd grown tired of her family, she'd left. Why spend years wallowing in hatred? Why dance the line between beloved actor and rebel? And, most importantly, as far as Shae was concerned, why let her in on any of it?

Then there was Dalton's information... Shae wasn't sure, but when Dalton had been interrupted, it sounded like she was about to say that the corpses were being woken up. An interesting concept, if it was really what she'd been about to say, but Shae couldn't see how it warranted being stopped outside of Chicago for as long as they had. She felt like she'd gotten a few more pieces of the puzzle that Ariane presented, but she still hadn't figured out how to start assembling them. There was still time, though. Two days until the Denver event, four until Salt Lake, and fifteen days left on the rest of the tour, all locked on this little train every night. Plenty of time to figure him out.

"I'm going to tell you a secret," Shae said, mentally re-shuffling her cards based on the events of the night. "What I told the press about nearly the whole rest of the family being dead, that was a lie. When I left everyone was alive and perfectly healthy. Well, physically healthy anyway."

"Why tell me?" Ariane asked, eyebrows lifted in suspicion.

"Because I know you can't tell anyone, not after tonight. Mutually assured destruction and all that."

It was still a risk, telling him this, Shae knew that. He'd been at this game longer than she had, but that was exactly why she'd needed to make this play. They needed to be on even ground to move forward. She couldn't just be his cannon fodder in whatever game he was playing.

A predatory grin flashed across Ariane's face. "You're the most interesting friend I have ever had, Shae-Shae."

Shae tilted the glass towards him. "To friendship, and mutually assured destruction."

12: Granby

They were on their third day of driving now, and Dustin was ready to jump out of the car and walk. The road had been so bad in stretches they'd barely been able to go at a crawl for fear of the car shaking itself apart. At one point Russ pulled them over and went at the shocks with several tools and a lot of creative cuss words. It had only improved things for about ten miles. Russ had been popping pain pills the whole time, and Dustin couldn't imagine how uncomfortable the drive was with a broken arm. Part of him wanted to be petty and bring up the fact that his original plan of hitching a ride on a train would have been more comfortable—he never would have agreed to the car if he'd known how bad the roads were, and faster, but there was nothing to be done about it now so Dustin kept the thought to himself.

They'd only made it about two-thirds of the way so far, which was making Dustin antsy. They were cutting it so close. If they missed her... well, they could find her again down the line, but it would be harder. Her being on a train through northern Colorado had been a gift.

"Dustin?" Russ asked after a lengthy silence.

They were on a somewhat better maintained stretch of road now, but Dustin was still alert for bad potholes as he'd offered to take a turn driving. The headlights on the car weren't helping much, though, and it was hard to make out the holes until it was almost too late much of the time.

"Yeah?"

"What do you want to happen here? I mean. How do you picture this going?"

Dustin glanced at his little brother, eyes drawn in confusion. "What do you mean?" It was obvious how Dustin wanted this to go, he thought. Rescue Shae, take her home.

Russ shuffled around, starting to answer but stopping several times. He looked frustrated, like he couldn't come up with the right words to express what he was thinking. "I dunno, it just... it seems like... well, you've clearly got this all planned out, somehow. You've got this... idea in your head, and you've kind of got blinders on to anything but that idea."

"I don't have blinders on," Dustin huffed.

"... sure," Russ replied. "But either way, you've got an idea and you're set on it."

"And that idea is getting Shae back and getting her home. Beyond that I am, like you keep pointing out, winging it. We don't know enough not to," Dustin told him.

"But why?" Russ pressed. "Why is this your

responsibility? And don't say because she's our sister, or because of dad and Keaun. I *know* she's our sister. I *know* the pain her being gone has caused."

"Aren't those things enough?" Dustin asked. "If Darius or Corman or Arabella went missing tomorrow, or one of our nieces, wouldn't you raise hell to find them?"

"Well, yeah," Russ admitted.

"There's your answer. Tomorrow or ten years ago, we protect our family."

They lapsed back into silence cut only by the sound of the tires bumping along over the smaller pot holes. Dustin couldn't figure out why Russ kept bringing up his reasons behind this. Why did he find it so hard to believe that Dustin wanted to rescue Shae? He wasn't like Arabella, who had been a toddler when Shae had been taken. Russ had plenty of memories of their missing sister. Good memories. So what if Shae had become famous in the last ten years? She'd done what she had to. Shae always had.

"She'll be different," Russ said miles later.

"And?"

Russ shrugged, staring determinedly out the bug-splattered windshield.

"We're all different," Dustin said eventually. "We're still family."

"What are the chances I could convince you to go through Yellowstone?" Russ asked.

"Slim. It's too touristy," Dustin told him from the passenger seat. "We'd get slowed down by a bunch of tourists who've never seen a deer before and throw their car into park in the middle of the road to coo at it."

They'd made it back onto better maintained roads now that they were nearing the Canada-US border, so they'd been able to pick up speed for the first time in ages, but they'd still lost precious time with how long they'd had to go slow.

"Always wanted to see Yellowstone," Russ muttered, casted arm resting on the open window frame of the car.

"We can see Yellowstone any other time you want," Dustin told him. "After we get Shae."

"Look, breaking the law about leaving the settlement to rescue a sibling is one thing, but just to go on vacation," Russ trailed off with a shake of his head.

"They really don't notice," Dustin said. He'd never even come close to being caught, and that included the times before he'd had Ramona to help him. The borders of Nahanni ran through thousands of miles of wilderness. No military could ever hope to patrol them all.

"No one notices *you*," Russ said. "Don't take this the wrong way, but you're kind of... in the background in the settlement. You don't go into any of the towns much, you don't have friends, you don't have a job."

"No wrong way to take it," Dustin replied. "It's all true. And intentional."

"Well, I'm not like that," Russ said. "I have friends. I'm in the military. I spend nights in the towns all the time. People know me and notice me. I'm banking on the fact I was injured being a good excuse for no one *to* notice me being gone this time."

Russ had a point, and Dustin mulled it over for a bit.

"Well," Dustin said. "They may notice you being gone, but that doesn't mean they'd know you left Nahanni. Maybe I just took you hunting with me within the settlement."

"Still, you do realize the risk, right?" Russ said. "What they'd do if they caught you? Not only the risk to you, but to the rest of the family? We've worked so fucking hard to get people to trust us, Dustin."

"I know," Dustin admitted.

This was the only thing that ever worried him about crossing the border. Once he was out, and once he was in, the worry went away. Like he'd told Russ, they'd never find proof of where he'd actually been. As long as he made it across he was in the clear.

"Why, then?" Russ asked.

"You keep asking that," Dustin pointed out.

"They maybe you should answer for once," Russ muttered, barely loud enough to be heard over the wind.

Dustin didn't answer. There was still so much Russ didn't understand about what Dustin had done over the years, and he wasn't sure where to start with any of it. Yes, Shae was at the core of all of it, but things had gotten more complicated since then. He had other reasons to leave the settlement now, to go to Colorado again and again.

"Granby Colorado, population 'unyielding.'" Russ read off a faded sign as they crawled into the abandoned town, their little car struggling over the crumbled road. There wasn't much pavement left at all. What remained was twisted and turned to create a minefield of tire-popping risk. It was the worst stretch of road they'd been on so far. It hadn't seen true upkeep in decades, maybe over a century. The path Dustin led them in through was one of the only stretches still passable by vehicle, others long ago taken out by rockslides and intentional bombings. He'd never driven it before, but he'd seen it marked on maps.

"There used to be a rebel settlement out here," Dustin told him. "They dwindled a long time ago, though." As soon as he'd seen the sign he'd felt his shoulders unknot. They'd made it in time, though with only a handful of hours to spare.

The original population number on the town sign had been replaced during the wars to show that the residents would not cave to the newly coven controlled country. That's what Dustin had been told by the single surviving resident of the area. They had never surrendered, but had fallen to ruin anyway as their population slowly dwindled over the years. Some couldn't stand living like fugitives anymore, some got sick, and many didn't have children for fear of bringing them into such a terrible world. It had all led to a slow decline until all but the one were dead or gone.

"Where are we headed?" Russ asked, white-knuckling

the steering wheel.

"That garage," Dustin said, pointing to a large brown house built into the side of a hill about a hundred yards ahead.

Russ glanced over at his brother. "Why that garage?"

"It has things we need inside."

"You've been here before? I mean, I know you said you've been to Colorado before, but you were actually *here*?"

Dustin nodded, then nearly smacked his head into the dashboard when Russ slammed on the brakes.

"Enough," Russ snapped as dust billowed around the car. "I'm done with this no communication bullshit you've been pulling. I just crossed a continent for you, and I want some answers."

Dustin blinked a few times, taken aback by the harsh tone in Russ' voice. He supposed he deserved it, though. Ever since Russ had brought up the risks Dustin was taking leaving the settlement again and again, he'd been mulling over how to explain everything.

"You're right," Dustin admitted and Russ visibly deflated, seeming glad there wouldn't be an argument this time. "Pull us into the garage and I'll answer your questions, whatever questions you have."

Russ nodded and took his foot off the brake, trundling up to the faded green door which Dustin got out to open. The hinges screeched, the loudest thing in the dead town, and the air inside was choked with dust, but the floor was clear. Russ pulled in and shut off the car as Dustin retrieved a suspiciously clean box from a crooked metal rack in the corner. He dug through it, pulling out a hand-held radio about the size and shape of a brick with a six-inch antenna. Popping open a compartment in the back he flipped out a handle and wound so it would charge, then fiddled with the channels until he found the one for train traffic, clicking a few more buttons and flipping switches until the encryption on the channel was broken. He clipped it to his belt and turned back to Russ, who was watching him from his position leaning against the trunk of the car.

"Okay, first, Shae should be starting her event in Denver right about now. It's scheduled to be about two hours, which means her train should come through here between eleven and midnight, if they leave on time. This radio will let us know when the train is coming. Now..." Dustin took a deep breath, "ask away, but we've got some work to do while we talk."

Russ nodded and followed Dustin out onto what had once been a beautiful main street. Even through all the decay you could picture what it had once been, the bright, unobstructed Colorado sun bringing some life back to the faded ruins. Little shops dotted each side and aspens had been planted at intervals along the sidewalk. People must have bustled in and out of the stores, chattering happily. Faded but still colorful murals adorned many of the walls. It had all fallen into disrepair, however. Roofs sagged, buildings swayed to one side or the other, old aspens had fallen across the street while new ones pushed up through the concrete and asphalt. Everything was cracked and faded, flecks of old paint littering the ground like confetti.

"Are we looking for something?" Russ asked as Dustin scrutinized each shop.

"Explosives. The buildings with satellite dishes are rigged to explode when the doors open."

"*Why*?"

"So that if people who don't belong here go in them they won't make the mistake of doing it again."

"They'd be *dead*, Dustin. I don't think they'd be doing it again no matter what."

Dustin shrugged. "They're tiny bombs. They'd probably live. And it's only the doors that are rigged."

He stepped up to an old antique shop with a satellite dish and tested the lock with his thumb without opening the door. Producing a knife from a sheath on his hip, he opened the door a crack, sliding the knife in along the top until he felt it slice cleanly through the trigger cord, allowing him to open the door all the way. Russ hesitated before following him inside, matching his steps like a good little soldier going into a rigged building.

"Why were you here before?" Russ asked.

"The first time was kind of on accident. When dad hung himself...." Dustin glanced back to find Russ grimacing, fists clenching and unclenching. "Well, that was the first time I ever went outside the settlement. I thought if I could just find Shae, bring her home, it would fix dad. I wasn't thinking and didn't really know what I was doing, and I'd gone in winter, which was the dumbest thing I could have done. I fell through the ice into a lake. Woke up naked a few hours later next to a roaring fire in an abandoned house."

Dustin glanced back again to see that Russ had gone pale, his eyes wide. "Fuck, Dustin. You nearly died and you never thought to mention that to anyone? I mean... if you had actually died out there... just slipped into the lake and never came out... we never would've known. We wouldn't have even known you were dead. It would've been Shae all over again."

Dustin winced, guilt creeping up his spine. "I know, and I'm sorry. It was a mistake. But I learned my lesson, and quite a few more afterwards. I've made sure I'll never disappear on you guys. If something happened to me, you'd know. Ramona would let you know if I didn't come back when I said I would."

They stopped talking for a moment as the radio crackled to life, an electronic voice reading out mile-post and weather information before going silent.

"Who saved you?" Russ asked.

"A woman named Vivian," Dustin told him. He wished he had time to go get her, to get her help, but it was too far to her house and there was no guarantee she'd even be there. He'd sent out a few of their coded clicks through the radio, but gotten no response. She never carried one unless she was planning a robbery, and sometimes not even then if he wasn't with her. "Though, to be fair, she only saved me because Coal, who was still a puppy, was upset and she felt sorry for him. She didn't feel sorry for me in the slightest."

"Sounds like a great person," Russ muttered.

"She is," Dustin said, a bit forcefully. As they'd been talking, he'd removed the package of plastic explosives from above the door, carefully tucking it in a canvass bag he'd taken from the box in the garage. "She's just... not a people person."

Russ eyed the bag warily but didn't comment, instead pushing on with more questions about Dustin. "So she saved you, then what?"

"She hardly spoke to me for a while, but when I told her about Shae, that I was looking for my little sister, she started to warm up to me. She offered to help me get to Nevada where we last saw her, and she started training me how to be safer out in the wilderness. We didn't find anything about Shae when we got there, so I left and went home."

"But you came back?"

"Many times."

"Why?"

Dustin shrugged. "I like her. I like being here."

Russ fell silent after that, following Dustin around the town as they gathered further supplies. They procured a couple rusted shovels from an old hardware shop, a bright but slightly faded orange hat from a hunting store, and a very nice looking rifle from a case hidden under a porch. Russ whistled when he saw it, taking and examining the gun, balancing it as best he could with one arm in a cast.

"Yours?" Russ asked, looking down the scope, aimed away down the road.

Dustin nodded. "Stole it a few years ago."

Russ glanced at him without lowering the gun. "From where?"

"Some military supply train that came through," Dustin told him.

This time Russ did lower the rifle, tilting his head like he didn't quite believe his brother. "Are you... telling me you rob trains?"

"Well," Dustin felt himself grinning a little, despite the tension still hanging between them, "this is a good place for it. And there's not exactly a store around here. Nearest occupied town is over a hundred miles away, and nearly all the roads in and out of here have been blown up or buried by rockslides."

Dustin knew full well that Russ' love of dramatic westerns was now warring with his need to be mad at him for lying all these years. Russ had wanted to be a cowboy ever since he was five. Lockwood Ranch had been a dream come true for him, but it did not offer the more exciting cowboy adventures like train robberies and general outlawing.

"How?" Russ said after a minute.

"A lot of ways. You'll see one tonight, come on," Dustin said, leading the way down to the tracks.

The tracks, a single line, ran below the hill the town sat on. There'd been two lines at one point, but the other one had been purposely destroyed over and over until the coven stopped repairing it. The coven tended to leave most track maintenance to the last moment as much as possible in this area. Even then, multiple dead workers had at least trained them into only sending humans. An old one-room station had sat along the tracks in the past as well, but it was now a lumpy pile of rotting, moss-covered wood. To their left they could see the tracks winding away through the valley towards Denver, to their right they went straight for a bit before disappearing between low hills at the base of the ridges surrounding the valley, ridges which gave way to towering peaks all around. Dustin set everything down and held one of the shovels out to Russ.

"Put the pretty gun down and start digging," Dustin told him.

"... for?"

"Dirt. We need a good pile of it about five feet to the left of the tracks," Dustin told him. He paused for a minute, but decided he needed to continue since Russ had been pressing him for honesty. "We'll put the explosives in the dirt and when we see Shae's train approaching we'll trigger them with the rifle, throwing up a huge cloud of debris. The train will be too far to see if the tracks have been damaged, so they'll have to stop or risk derailing. We'll get on the train, get Shae, and get out before anyone knows we were there."

"The first part of that makes sense," Russ admitted, "but the getting Shae part... there's a lot of ways that could go wrong, Dustin. We don't know where on the train she'll be, for one."

"A problem to consider while we dig."

"Gimpy arm," Russ reminded Dustin, waving the cast around.

"Ah, yeah, true," Dustin said. He contemplated Russ a moment, trying to figure out another way he could help, but came up short.

"Sucks for you," Russ said, flopping down against the sun warmed beams of the collapsed station.

Dustin rolled his eyes and started digging and scrapping at the hard-packed dirt, forming it into a nice mound. As he worked the radio continued to crackle with electronic readouts of the track conditions. With each drive of the blade into the earth Dustin's mind turned more and more to Shae, to what was going to happen tonight. He had no doubts about being able to pull it off, but still, standing here next to the tracks and setting up this distraction made it all so much more real. Shae was so *close*. He let himself soak in the imagined feelings of having her back, something he rarely allowed himself to do because of the ache it caused. Would her laugh sound the same? Would she still wrinkle up her nose when someone tried to make her eat something she didn't like? Would she still like staying up late and telling stories?

While Dustin worked Russ played with the rifle, resting it on the beams of the collapsed station so he didn't have to use his bad arm, messing with the scope as he looked out across the field.

"So, say we get on the train and she's not alone," Russ said. "Plan?"

"Kill any vampires, knock out any humans," Dustin replied. Sweat had built up under his shirt, trickling unpleasantly down his back.

"I'm fine with killing vampires under normal circumstances, but in front of Shae... maybe it isn't a good idea this time around," Russ returned.

Dustin had to admit this was true. They didn't know how Shae would react, how anyone else would react. Problem was, you couldn't just knock out a vampire the way you could a human. Taking them out of the equation looked much the same as killing them, the only difference being keeping their head away from their body and burning everything at the end.

"I guess... we just have to wing it," Dustin said.

Russ groaned and rolled over to flop on his back, arms thrown towards the sky. "Stop saying we're going to wing it!"

"You're the one who insisted on coming with me," Dustin pointed out. "But fine. Since you're so determined to have a solid plan, *you* make the plan. We've got about five hours until the train gets here, explosives—more if you want them, guns, knives, and probably most anything else you can think of. Plan away."

Russ blinked, then screwed up his face in concentration, going silent for a good ten minutes.

"Ski-masks?" Russ asked. "Better we're not recognized, considering Shae said we were dead."

Dustin contemplated for a moment. "There's probably some in the same store we got the hat. If not, there are other ways we can mask our faces. I was going to use a bandanna."

Russ nodded and went back to being silent for another few minutes.

"Okay, so, first of all, no killing," Russ said. Dustin rolled his eyes but agreed. "We get the train stopped your way, and then…"

"Then?" Dustin prompted.

Russ groaned. "Fuck, I don't know. There's so many things that could happen."

"Exactly. *We don't know enough to plan*. Not for being on the train, anyway. We get on through the last car, and we work our way up until we find her."

"Can we at least make an exit plan?" Russ asked.

"The exit plan is run like hell and stick to me," Dustin told him. "Once we're out in the open things'll be easier anyway. More room to maneuver. Going back up into town will be our best bet. Plenty of places to hide."

"What about telling Shae who we are, since we'll be masked?"

Dustin took a break to think about this one, leaning on the handle of the shovel. He didn't want to scare Shae by just grabbing her and running for it, but if there were witnesses they couldn't exactly shout their identity to her. The Shae he knew didn't scare easy, though, so if they did have to just grab her it wouldn't be the worst thing.

Russ watched him thinking, eyes narrowed. "I swear,

if you are about to use the words 'wing it'...."

"We're gonna wing it."

Russ muttered a few choice words under his breath and got up, saying he was going to look for masks so he didn't punch Dustin.

Three times they had to hide in the brush to let shipping trains go by, but as the sun settled lower into the sky a new, human voice sounded over the radio; "All parties: the bus has left town. Unclaimed territory will be entered within the hour and exited via Grand Junction within ten hours. We have had reports of rebel activity in the UT over the last week, so extra security has been added to the bus."

The line was silent for a moment before another voice responded, "How much extra security?"

The first voice sounded, punched through by static, "—four Denver cops will be patrolling the bus. Occupants have been instructed to keep all curtains drawn and lights off. Speeds will be randomly varied to prevent arrival at any particular point being timed."

"Let's hope the local banshee is busy for the night," the second voice said.

"Spreading unfounded rumors is grounds for disciplinary action," the first voice said.

The apology was drowned out in static.

"Banshee?" Russ said from the ground.

"Vivian," Dustin said offhandedly, missing Russ' look

of confusion.

They were so close. So damn close. He dug into the ground with renewed fervor, finishing an hour later with a mound roughly four feet tall and four feet across. It would be enough. He hollowed out a divot in the center and placed the explosives, wrapped in the orange hat, in it. Producing a tin of gunpowder from the gun case, he sprinkled the whole thing around the explosives for a little extra sparkle in the dark.

The sun painted the sky in burning oranges and pinks before lazily sliding behind the peaks a couple hours earlier. Some light still lingered, though, just enough to trick a person's eyes into thinking they could see well when the reality was that they were unlikely to tell a bush from a bear until it bit them. With the sun gone the heat had broken, but the August evening was still warm. The train would be here any time now, and its approach had settled a different ache in Dustin's soul than the usual one. It was an itchy, anticipatory ache, rather than a sorrowful one.

Russ demanded he be the one to take the shot that would set off the explosives, so he found himself a perch on an old collapsed crane about thirty yards from the explosives. Dustin situated himself farther down behind some overgrown sage, guesstimating where the train would stop and where the end of it would be.

Dustin found it hard to stand still as he looked off into

the distance, waiting for the train to appear. Ten years. It had been ten years, and he was finally going to see his little sister again. He was going to be able to bring her home, make the family whole again.

He straightened when he saw a gleam of metal in the distance, moonlight glinting off a silvery engine. It had to be Shae's train. It was the only passenger train that had been mentioned on the radio, and only passenger trains had silver engines. He whistled to Russ, holding his hand up in the air as the train approached. Almost there. It wasn't close enough yet. The timing had to be just right.

There.

Dustin dropped his hand and heard the rifle fire behind him, felt the reverberation of the explosion and saw the glow light the surrounding fields. At first there was no visible reaction until the screech of brakes echoed out and the train began to slow, the engine sliding past Dustin's hiding spot.

13: Kidnapping

"Helen, Helen, come back here! Please!" Shae jogged to keep up with her as she stomped up the stairs to their bedroom.

Helen spun, glaring from several stairs up, tears sparkling in the corners of her eyes. "*This* is why I told you to stop messing with your blood at these stops, Shae! That 'fan' broke through the line and tackled you before security could even start moving! He could've bitten you or who knows what else! And you... you just laughed! You act like it isn't a big deal that you, or anyone else at that table, nearly died! I don't get it!"

"Of course I care!" Shae spluttered. "I'm just... not wired in a way that involves freaking out. It wouldn't have changed anything if I had, would it? I didn't die, I didn't get hurt, so why waste energy over something that didn't happen?"

The argument reminded Shae of an old saying about relationships; that you shouldn't marry someone until you'd traveled with them. She was beginning to understand the wisdom in it. Helen could be so sweet and attentive, and Shae had liked that for a long time, but lately it had become grating. What was the point of being upset over what happened in Denver? Sure, a scrawny little Turned had broken through the controlled autograph line, yes it had probably had something to do with Shae and Ariane signing autographs in their blood, and yes, he had tackled Shae. But Ariane had been right there and yanked the brat off before anything happened, so what was the problem?

Helen looked exasperated, tilting her head back as a couple tears fell. "You don't *get it*. Sure, you didn't die. But you could have. And if you keep bringing your blood to signings or flicking it on the crowd or whatever scheme you and Ariane cook up next, you *will* eventually get yourself or someone else killed. Yes, I'm glad you didn't get killed this time, but it isn't this time I'm worried about!"

Shae closed her eyes and took a deep breath before looking back up at Helen, softening her voice as she responded, "Alright. I won't lie and say I completely get it, but you're my girlfriend and if it really bothers you this much, I'll stop."

Helen shook her head, curling a finger under her glasses to wipe away a tear. "I don't think I believe that anymore."

With that she pushed past Shae to go back downstairs. Shae stayed on the stairs for a few moments. She knew she should go try to make up with Helen, come up with a believable apology, but she also felt that was a lot of effort for a relationship she was beginning to realize wasn't going to last. Perhaps it would be better to suggest to Helen that she catch a flight home from Utah, give both of them a little breathing room while Shae continued the tour alone.

Eventually she finished climbing the stairs, intending to try on clothes for the next stops while she mulled things over. Grabbing an armful of garment bags and depositing them on the bed, she went to work. The next stop was Salt Lake, which didn't really have a fashion trend beyond "conservative," but that still left a lot of room to play. Besides, a conservative outfit would probably help placate Helen. Shae pulled out a lacy white top and a pale pink undershirt, putting them together on a single hanger to examine the effect, twisting it back and forth in the light. The sleeves of the white shirt went down to her elbows but still showed plenty of skin in all the little gaps of the lace, while the undershirt had a nice rosy color that would accent the color in her cheeks.

Acceptable.

Still needed to see it on, though. Shae stripped off her shirt, not worried about being seen as Helen had tightly closed all the curtains and the shutters of the dome at the bequest of security. She'd even found a tin of clothespins somewhere to make sure the curtains downstairs were extra closed. Shae thought it was ridiculous. What would curtains do, anyway? There were obviously people on the train.

Putting the shirts on, Shae turned about to look at

herself in the full-length mirror she'd had brought onto the train back in Boston. Deeming the combination good, she dug around for a skirt, finding a perfect, gauzy white one that went to her ankles but had a slit up to the hip. A slight breeze and it would billow beautifully, revealing her legs as it did. A few bobby-pins to pull her hair back from her face in a simple, demure style helped complete the look.

This continued for several more hours, Shae working her way through potential outfits for the next handful of stops. Some proved trickier than others. LA ended up the hardest to choose for, as it was such a melting pot. No one style reigned there. There was a lovely, skin-tight mauve dress Shae thought might work, but she hadn't settled on it yet. Currently, she was trying on a summery blue dress instead. It had three silver rings going from below her breasts down to her navel, giving little peeks of her skin as they went, and three more doing the same down her back. Along the mid-thigh length hem more silver rings were spaced, the fabric of the dress hanging artfully between them. It was pretty, but the dress required accessories for her to judge its potential. Silver bangles, and perhaps some strappy sandals.

She went back to the closet, her bare feet sinking into the plush carpet. There was a specific pair of silvery gladiator sandals she had in mind. The soles were the wrong shade of brown for the dress, but if the style worked Shae would send an assistant to a store in Salt Lake to get a similar pair in the right color.

The shoes proved tricky to find, buried beneath and behind ten other shoe boxes. Slipping them on and doing up all the buckles, Shae stood back up just in time to feel the train begin to rapidly slow. She heard Helen call out from downstairs, a note of panic in her voice.

"Relax," Shae soothed. She came down the stairs to find Helen standing in the middle of the car, a piece of paper clutched tightly in her hands and soft instrumental music playing. "We're probably coming up on a big curve. They have to slow down so we don't derail, that's all."

"We aren't slowing down, Shae, we're stopping."

So they were.

The train gave one final shudder and stopped moving, though it remained running. This didn't seem to comfort Helen much. She had frozen in the middle of the room and looked like she was trying to figure out what the most weapon-like object within her reach.

"Relax," Shae repeated, going over to peek out the curtains as Helen quickly stuffed the paper down into the couch cushions.

It was hard to see much in the limited gap between the clothespins. The full moon lit up the area rather well, but all Shae could make out was a sprawling valley surrounded by black mountains. There was some sort of animal off in the distance, a herd of them, too far for Shae to make out what they were. Before she made it over to look out the other side of the train Helen snatched her and held her tightly, Shae's back to Helen's front, berating her about being dumb enough to open the curtains.

"They're *curtains*, Helen. Not magical warding."

"I don't care, Shae! We don't want the rebels to know we're in here! One of the security people we picked up in Denver said that this stretch of tracks is one of the most dangerous in the country, that it gets attacked all the time by some evil spirit."

Shae scoffed. "A, who said anything about rebels? The train may have just broken down on its own, or there could have been a rockslide up the tracks, or a hundred other things that don't involve rebels. B, I'm pretty sure if there *were* rebels they'd know we're here without us opening the curtains. It's a passenger train. What else would be in here? C, evil spirit? Really? There's no such thing."

Helen relinquished her hold enough for Shae to twist around and see that she was on the verge of tears again.

"There didn't use to be such thing as Turned, either! Just myths about vampires! Look where we are now!"

Shae sighed. "Want to go wait in Ariane's car? If anyone breaks in we can sacrifice him to them to give us time to get away."

Helen managed a small smile at the teasing. "It would be nice to finally be rid of him."

"You don't hate him *that* much," Shae laughed.

"I might. He's a pretentious brat. If he ruins my chances of ever getting tu—" The sound of the back door being jimmied cut her off abruptly.

Both of them froze, eying the door. Helen screamed as the knob turned, stooping to grab a large hardcover book off the coffee table, holding it aloft with one hand as she dragged Shae back with the other. Before they had even made it out of the lounge, the door burst open, slamming against the wall with a loud crack, and two masked men stormed in. One was slimly built and had a cast around his lower left arm, a rifle strapped around his abdomen. The other was stockier and a bit shorter with no visible weapons.

Helen screeched and leaped at the slimmer one, book swinging around in a wide arc until it connected with the man's cheek. Shae thought she saw a flash of blood as the man ducked down to tackle Helen back, sending her book flying, but she didn't have much time to observe her girlfriend's plight as she was busy dealing with the other man, backing away from him as he advanced.

"I'm a bit busy at the moment, darling, however if you'd like a private party I'd be happy to give you the number of my agent so you can set something up," Shae told him. She wished she still had on the outfit for Salt Lake. *That* she could fight in. She could probably fight in the blue dress, but it was so tight around the thighs it limited her range of movement. At least her shoes were flat.

She saw the man roll his eyes as he advanced forward, feigning left. Shae moved in time to prevent him from grabbing her. It looked like his mouth was moving under his mask, but at some point Helen or the guy she was grappling with had kicked the stereo and it was blasting full volume now. Helen may have even done it on purpose, Shae thought, to draw attention and thus help. Where was all their security, anyway? They'd picked up all those extra people in Denver, after all, and gotten a whole lecture about listening to them.

The guy Shae was dealing with moved again, and this time she didn't move quick enough to avoid him. He ducked down and scooped her up over his shoulder, one arm wrapped tightly around her legs to keep her there. She caught an awkward, upside-down look at the slim man picking Helen up and locking her in the bathroom. The man carrying Shae spun to race back out the door. Leaping off the train, he kept a secure grip around her thighs, racing off towards something she couldn't see. The slim man was quick behind them.

Shae slammed her fists against the stocky man's back only to be met with muscle so rigid it made her fingers sting. He seemed unfazed, and Shae realized she wasn't getting down until he put her down. As they scrabbled up the hill over broken concrete steps her annoyance gave way to curiosity. This wasn't some big group of rebels coming to rob the train. This was two men who had come on, grabbed her, and left without anything else. Shae was what they wanted, and she wanted to know why.

They ducked into a dark building, Shae still draped over the stocky one's shoulder. Shae found this a bit confusing. They were in abandoned territory, so what sort of building were they in? The darkness prevented her from making anything out, not to mention she was upside down and her hair was in her face.

"What the fucking hell was that?!" The slim man growled as they crouched behind a counter.

The stocky one gently deposited Shae on the floor. She smoothed out her dress, eying both of them, and eventually acquiesced to the stocky one's gestures to kneel next to them and stay quiet. Before she knelt she'd been able to make out a bit more of the shop from the moonlight filtering through the dusty glass. There were racks of what appeared to be clothing, many of them empty and a few fallen over.

The stocky one remained silent, taking the rifle from the slim one and resting it on the counter, looking over the scope and out the front window. Shae slid her eyes back and forth between the men, a creeping sense of familiarity she couldn't place beginning to tickle at her. She hadn't been able to see much of their faces through the masks when they'd been on the well lit train, and even less now in the dark, but the stocky one's eyes….

The faint sound of voices coming down the street interrupted the heavy silence. Shae saw both men stiffen, attention wholly focused on the windows. This was her chance. They didn't seem to have any other weapons. But she wanted to know what was going on even more now that something seemed familiar about the men.

She remained put but lifted herself up on her knees to see over the counter as well. The noises from the street were almost deafening in the silence. A whole crowd of voices tumbled through the air, crystal clear in the still, empty town.

"I'm sure they went this way, saw 'em running. Probably hiding in one of the buildings," an unfamiliar voice said. "We'll have to search 'em all."

"That'll take a while," another unfamiliar voice stated. Shae assumed they were guards.

"Why the fuck weren't any of you with her?" Nadia snapped.

No one answered at first, until Nadia snapped again, demanding an answer.

"She… requested we leave, ma'am. The train was in motion, so we figured it was fine."

"Well it fucking wasn't!" Nadia said.

"We were fighting with them for two minutes!" Helen said, tears in her voice. "And the train was stopped for at least three! Why didn't any of you come back?"

The group came into view and stopped outside the shop Shae and her captors were hiding in. Helen, Nadia, and Ariane were all there, along with four guards. Ariane. Could he be behind this? Part of whatever game he was playing with his stepfather? Shae glanced between Ariane and the men next to her, trying to catch any sign of recognition on the part of her kidnappers and finding none that were obvious. For his part, Ariane remained quiet, eyes scanning the buildings and thumbs through his belt-loops.

One guard, a tough looking woman, seemed to be in charge, her uniform a touch more ornate than the ones worn by the others. All the guards had pistols in hand. The slim man next to Shae tensed even more upon seeing the guns, but the stocky one didn't flinch, his cheek resting on the stock of his gun.

"There… must have been a communication error," a guard said. "Someone was sent, but clearly they didn't get that order in time."

"Mis—miscommunication?! We have to find Shae before they kill her!" Helen shouted, quickly being shushed by another guard.

"That's my star actress, and you will find her," Nadia demanded.

The guards looked between one another, not saying anything for nearly a minute.

"You three need to go back to the train," the tough looking woman said, tone firm. "Morgan will escort you back. The rest of us will begin searching."

Helen argued with the woman as two of the guards crossed to a shop across the street and tested the door, guns raised. This time the stocky man did tense, and within a second Shae knew why. As soon as they opened the door the whole building exploded. Fire bloomed out into the night, sound racing behind it. Bits of debris splattered against the building Shae was in, but the dusty display windows held against the barrage. Shouts rang back and forth and as the smoke and dust cleared Shae realized it hadn't really been the whole building. It had actually been a rather small blast. Only enough to blow out the windows and set a few things on fire inside.

As everyone outside straightened up from the protective crouches they'd assumed one of the guards stumbled back from the gaping doorway, screaming and clutching at his wrist. When he turned around Shae realized there was no longer a hand attached to that wrist, at least not any useful amount of one. The other guard, who seemed less injured, whipped off his jacket and grabbed his companion, wrapping the jacket around the wound. Shae assumed that it was more to hide the gruesome injury from its owner than to stop blood loss, as that wasn't an issue for the Turned. Even for a Turned, though, Shae knew the injury had to hurt like hell. At the sight of the maimed limb Helen seemed to have started hyperventilating, hands fluttering uselessly through the air, while Ariane looked around in silent interest. Nadia instantly began berating the guards.

"Back on the fucking train!" The head guard said over Nadia, helping support her injured comrade. "We need to get out of here. We don't have the resources to handle this on our own."

"We are not leaving!" Helen shouted.

"Yes, yes we are. I can't risk anyone else under my care getting hurt or taken. Everyone is getting back on the train and we are leaving. That damn explosion earlier didn't damage the tracks, it was a diversion. They lured us into stopping. We need to go. We'll radio for a full search team, and they will find Ms. Lockwood."

"But, Shae—" Helen started, only to be interrupted by Ariane.

"Shae will be fine. She's stubborn and quick witted. She'll manage until help comes," Ariane said.

Shae could've sworn she saw Ariane look directly at her through the windows, but there was no way he would've been able to see her in the dark.

Helen looked around, eyes wide and mouth drawn. Not finding any backup, her shoulders slumped. She turned with the others and walked away down the street, their steps fading quickly.

The stocky man let out a slow breath and flipped the safety on the gun. He let himself fall back behind the counter, slouching against the wall as a quiet laugh escaped him.

"Not so bad," he whispered.

"Not so bad?!" The other snapped.

Shae looked between them, wondering what the stocky man *would* consider bad, and wondering if she'd made the right decision staying with them. Only one way to find out.

14: New Plans

Dustin's reply to Russ turned into an exclamation of surprise as Shae snatched his balaclava off his head. She spun and pulled Russ' off as well. After a moment of hesitation her eyes widened she shouted, "Dustin! Russell! You assholes!"

Her voice! She sound almost exactly like she had when they were kids, though it had gotten a bit deeper with a slight hint of smoke to it.

"Who did you think it was? Your favorite football players?" Russ grumbled, hand coming up to probe his cheek where a shallow cut was dripping a bit of blood.

Dustin pulled out a small pocket flashlight to get a better look at the injury.

"I haven't seen you in ten years and you had masks on! You were a kid last time I saw you, Russ. Not a twenty-year-old man! And Dustin!" She gestured at his whole body. "You were *not* this built when you were a teenager."

"Living in the wilderness and wrestling bears does

tend to make a person bulk up," Russ grumbled as Dustin prodded at his cheek.

"I do not wrestle bears," Dustin said, grinning so hard it hurt. "And sorry, Shae, I tried to tell you who we were on the train, but I guess you couldn't hear me over the radio."

Shae took the flashlight when Dustin offered it, keeping it on Russ' face. "Is the rest of the family here?"

"No, just us," Dustin told her. "Everyone else is back home in the Nahanni Settlement. We'll have to lie low for a few days since they're sending a search party, but after that we'll be home and you can see everyone. They'll be thrilled. We never knew what happened after you got kidnapped."

The light bounced and Dustin glanced at Shae just in time to see her expression shift into a smile. For a second he thought she had looked confused, but he brushed it off as a trick of the light.

"Why didn't you show who you were when you got on the train?" Shae asked as Dustin pulled a tiny bag of medical supplies out of one of the cargo pockets in his pants to treat Russ' cut.

"We didn't know who would be with you," Russ said. "You're the one who said we were all dead. Figured we shouldn't break that story."

Shae agreed that was fair. "But still. Dramatic, much?"

"He's good at dramatics," Russ muttered. "And where are we going to be lying low, hmm? You didn't mention that part of the plan. With that Vivian woman?"

"Russ," Dustin laughed, "can you be happy for five

minutes? Please? It worked! We've got our sister back!"

"And a search party coming for our asses!"

Dustin swatted off the words, rolling his eyes. "We're in the middle of the wilderness, there's more places to hide than you can imagine and I know quite a few of them. Now, you two wait here. I'm going to go see if they've left yet. Russ, see if you can find Shae some better clothes. There's a cache of stuff hidden in a box in the old supply closet. I'll be back."

"Dustin!" Russ hissed as he walked away.

Dustin ignored him and slipped out onto the street. The fire in the shop opposite them had mostly extinguished itself, though a few stray embers still smoldered, casting faint dancing shadows across the walls. He slipped between two buildings, staying in the alley as he looked down the hill towards the train. He was about level with the top of the domed cars. The group of people from before stood outside the train, along with a few others. The blond woman who Russ had fought with and who had insisted they stay and look for Shae was gesturing wildly at the security officers, saying something about how she'd changed her mind about leaving. The black man who had earlier assured the blond woman that Shae would be fine looked bored and annoyed by the blond. Dustin recognized the man as Shae's co-star, but couldn't remember his name.

When they didn't seem to be moving after a few minutes Dustin pulled his rifle around and took aim above the dome of the last car, letting off a single shot.

Everyone ducked and made for the train, though the security guards had to haul the blond woman inside when she tried to refuse. Shae's co-star was the last one, standing on the little open porch at the back of the second to last car, looking around with narrowed eyes before turning and entering the car.

With the close of his door the train jerked into motion, gaining speed slowly. Once it vanished into the distance Dustin strolled back to the shop where he'd left his little brother and sister, humming a happy but tuneless melody. As far as he was concerned, this couldn't have gone better. The search party was an unwelcome but not unexpected hiccupp, though an easy one to deal with.

In a week, maybe even less, they'd be at home. The whole family together. Shae could meet her nieces, her sister- and brother-in-law. Nahanni would take some convincing to let Shae in legally, sure, but her not being with the family when they arrived had been the biggest reason Nahanni hadn't trusted the Lockwoods. Now she was back, the whole family together. No suspected channel of information between them. How could they say no to letting her in?

All they had to do was have Shae tell them she'd come in on her own, desperate to finally escape the covens and hopefully find her family. Russ and Dustin would give her the car, send her to the main gates of the settlement, then sneak back across the border on foot. No one would ever know they'd been gone, and Shae would go through the usual process of immigrating into the settlement.

"What was the gunshot?" Russ said immediately as Dustin reentered the store.

"Just a little encouragement to get them going," Dustin replied. "Air shot above the train."

Shae had changed in the time he'd been gone. Her blue dress and sandals were laying on the counter and in place of them she was wearing a pair of jeans, some hiking boots, and a thick flannel shirt, all from the cache. The leather of the boots looked cracked and dusty, left too long without a good conditioning and waxing, and the clothes were big on her, but the outfit would suffice. Dustin couldn't resist the urge to pull her into a tight hug. His little sister was here. She was alive. She was okay.

Shae chuckled and hugged back after a second. "Russ has been filling me in on how you two found me. Risky, but you seem to be managing, as exasperated as he seems about all of it."

Dustin stepped back, ignoring Russ rolling his eyes, and grinned, hands resting on her shoulders. "Yeah, he's had a hard week. Sorry we couldn't get you back sooner. I've been trying, but I could never find anything about what happened to you."

Shae seemed to smile, her expression hard to make out in the dim light.

"How about we get going before any search parties get here, hmm? Helicopters could be here in under an hour," Russ interrupted.

Dustin shared an amused look with Shae, pleased they could still silently communicate as easily as when they were teenagers. He finally dropped his hands from Shae's shoulders and nodded at Russ.

"It's a decent trek to where we're going. The only way there is on foot or on horseback, and once there the closest place a helicopter could land is about a mile away. And they won't even have any reason to look in that area anyway." Dustin led them out of the shop and down the hill, crossing the tracks and heading towards a half collapsed fence. He stepped over it, offering a hand that Shae didn't take, and they continued on across the field.

"We're not walking this decent trek, are we?" Shae asked. As they made their way across the field she'd been fussing with the flannel shirt, first rolling up the sleeves, then unbuttoning the front and winding up the ends to tie into a knot at her stomach.

"No, that would take too long with the terrain we're crossing. We're getting some horses." Dustin pointed off into the distance at several grazing figures.

Shae groaned. "I take it back. Let's walk."

"Oh, is someone a little city girl now?" Dustin teased. "Scared of the big bad horsies?"

She socked him hard on the shoulder, but smiled anyway. Russ let a small smile slip out as well, though he quickly dropped it in favor of his previous expression of annoyance.

"These are tame horses, right?" Russ asked.

"No, I'm just going to throw you two on the back of a couple mustangs and hope," Dustin said, stopping them at a mostly collapsed shack near the horses.

Up close it was clear that, though the horses had appeared free from afar, they were actually well contained. Parts of an old fence kept them in on one side, cleverly disguised ropes between a few aspen trees on the other. The shack on one side gave them a place to get out of the weather, sturdy despite its age and dishevelment. A few new beams had been lashed to the inside to hold it up against the wind and the years.

The horses raised their heads at the group's approach and Dustin whistled to them, prompting a little buckskin to trot over to the fence.

"Hey, Kodiak," Dustin said, reaching out and patting the horse's neck. Kodiak was his favorite of Vivian's horses. He'd been a foal when Dustin had first met Vivian, and he'd grown into a fine horse. Stout and stubborn, not prone to startling over any strange movement of his own shadow.

The horses, now aware that it was someone they knew at their paddock, came over to join Kodiak. Dustin had Russ and Shae come up one at a time, offering their hands for the horses to smell before patting them. Russ was good with horses, but these ones had never known anyone but Dustin and Vivian, so Dustin was being careful. The horses seemed unperturbed, allowing Dustin to leave his siblings with them as he went into the shack. There were a few trunks stacked in one corner and inside would be sets of tack, kept here for emergencies.

"Alright, so," Dustin said, emerging from the shack. "There's enough bridles and blankets, but only two saddles. I'll take Kodiak, he's fine for bareback riding. Russ, you can take Ghost, the white one. She's good, but she can startle a bit. She's usually content to follow Kodiak, though. Shae, you'll take Pinenut, the gray one. He's... well, he's about as dumb as a box of rocks. But he rides well."

Fifteen minutes later they were under way. Despite her earlier protests, Shae seemed to have a good grasp on the basics of riding. When asked she said she'd learned the basics for one of her movies.

"Which way, fearless leader?" Shae asked, trotting her horse in circles around her brothers. Pinenut seemed to find the strange riding pattern rather exciting, his eyes a little less crossed than usual.

"Don't encourage him, Shae. He's bad enough already," Russ warned.

"Well, I think he's just fine," Shae replied, managing to lean over in her saddle and kiss Dustin's cheek.

Dustin's face was starting to hurt from smiling so much.

"We're going to cross the fields until we reach Eight Mile Creek, then follow the creek up over the Blue Ridge, then down Cub Creek and back up Timber—" he paused at the lost looks on his siblings' faces, "nevermind. We're going to cross a couple small ridges, then go part way up a mountain, riding through parts of the creeks to conceal our hoofprints."

"Lead the way then." Shae swung her arm out

dramatically, having settled Pinenut into a steady walk on Dustin's left side.

Dustin nodded and turned them up towards the first creek, taking the chance to sit and really look at Shae. Pictures could never compare to the real thing, after all. Even in the moonlight she looked beautiful. Her hair was down and perfectly straight, reaching just below her collarbones. Dustin remembered her with a head full of soft waves, but supposed she had straightened it. Her face had filled out nicely since they were kids, but she was incredibly pale. Dustin almost wondered if she was sick, his heart tripping over the thought, before he remembered that all actors did whatever they could to stay pale and show their veins. It was a sick habit, one Dustin had vague memories of their parents doing as well, but now that Shae was safe with them she'd be able to get out and get some sun so she looked healthier.

As they approached the first creek he found a trail of elk prints and walked them through it for a while before doubling back to head up the creek, hoping it would help throw off any pursuers.

"Who was that blond chick, anyway? I'm going to have a scar because of her," Russ pouted, prodding his bandaged cheek.

"My girlfriend, Helen. And it's your own fault for breaking into our car when she's all paranoid about rebels coming to kill everyone."

"Wait... girlfriend?" Russ asked, eyebrows raised, shooting Dustin a meaningful glance. A girlfriend complicated things, and Dustin could see Russ knew it too.

"Yes, girlfriend. She's a teacher and we've been dating for about two years. You're lucky all she had was her regular copy of Poe's collected works. If she'd had the analysis copy she probably would've killed you."

"You don't... seem upset by not being with her," Russ said, his tone careful.

Shae shrugged and sighed. "This tour has... well, it has been a good two years, but perhaps two is enough."

Wanting to take the conversation away from anything that upset Shae, Dustin asked, "What kind of person goes for a book as a weapon, anyway?"

"Well, we didn't exactly have many options. The only actual weapon we had in the room was that pocket knife Keaun gave me when I was seven, and three inches of antique steel is hardly better than a hardcover book."

Dustin felt his eyes widen. "You still have that?"

"Yes." She stuck a hand down her shirt and rummaged around in her bra, pulling the small knife out and handing it to Dustin.

It was exactly as he remembered it. Silvery stainless steel blade with an intricate cameo decorating one side of the polished brass handle. Keaun had given it to her for her seventh birthday, behind their parents' backs, just like he had for the rest of their siblings on their seventh birthdays. He'd missed a couple, after he lost Clayton, but he'd made up for it later. All their siblings had them now. Dustin's looked much the same as Shae's, but with fire opals inlaid in a pattern of moon phases. Rose's was a slimmer knife with an intricately engraved pattern of feathers on it. Russ' was similar to Rose's, but with a picture of a galloping horse. Dustin couldn't quite recall what the rest of them looked like, but he knew everyone in the family held on tight to theirs.

Dustin handed it back. "Did you manage to hang on to anything else?"

She took it and tucked it back in her bra. "I have that family photo we all took that day we went to the beach, but it's back in London. Other than that, no."

Before Dustin could ask another question Russ held up his hand and indicated for everyone to be quiet, pointing off into the trees. They were about halfway up the second ridge now, and the trees were thick enough that the moonlight was relatively obscured, making it difficult to see. Dustin did see *something,* though. Just a hint of shifting in the blackness.

"What sort of furry creatures can be found in these woods?" Shae asked, voice low and eyes trained on the same spot.

"I'm guessing you aren't referring to the nice ones," Dustin whispered back, pulling his rifle around and holding it loosely.

"No," Shae answered. Out of the corner of his eye Dustin saw her leaning towards him, then felt as she slid out the pistol he'd tucked into his mid-calf-height boots before they mounted up.

"Bears, but they'll generally run off as long as there's no cubs involved. Wolves that'll do the same. Mountain lions, however…"

Mountain lions were something Dustin considered to be on the same level as vampires when it came to the level of threat they posed. They had similar strength, similar speed. The key difference, though, was that vampires were still human enough to be predictable in their attack patterns. Mountain lions were not.

The horses were getting agitated, kicking and scraping at the ground and snorting. Dustin knew aiming from a frightened horse would be difficult, though Kodiak was the calmest of the three. He didn't need to hit the unseen animal, though, he just needed to scare it. Whatever *it* was, though, mountain lion or otherwise, Dustin could no longer discern in the shadows.

"Stick close and walk slow. I'm going to try to lead us around. If, somehow, we get split up head for the top of the ridge and wait there," Dustin told them. They both nodded and gently knocked their heels into their horses to get them going again.

Dustin pulled them out of the creek and off into the woods, keeping his eyes on the shadows around them and his rifle in his hands, directing Kodiak with his knees. Shae had his pistol resting on her thigh, finger away from the trigger. Dustin hoped she actually knew how to use it.

They walked in silence for about fifteen minutes until they came back out to the creek and stopped to listen. It was too quiet.

"It's following us," Russ whispered.

Shae nodded and moved her horse around behind

Dustin's, positioning herself so that Russ, the only one without a gun, was between her and Dustin. It had been a smart move, and one made just in time. As soon as Shae's horse stopped moving there was a streak of movement out of the shadows. She didn't hesitate, taking quick aim and shooting, the sound cracking the night air. Dustin wasn't sure if she'd gotten a hit, but the animal still stumbled and made to circle around a different direction.

By now the horses were going wild, Russ struggling to control Ghost and Pinenut panicking more because the others were panicking than the actual threat. Kodiak was tossing his head, hopping up onto his back legs over and over, kicking out at the air. Knowing he couldn't stay on without a saddle and shoot at the same time, Dustin let himself slide off, leaping away from Kodiak and pulling his rifle up in the same movement. He let off two quick shots as the cat charged again.

The echo of the gun died away and the forest went silent. Several feet away was the corpse of a mountain lion, a bloody hole in its head and another in its shoulder. Dustin let out a slow breath as he straightened up, flipping the safety back on his gun.

"Everyone okay?" he asked, turning to look at his brother and sister. Shae had grabbed Kodiak's reins to keep him from bolting, and Dustin was grateful. Ghost and Pinenut were not built for carrying two full-grown humans.

Russ and Shae answered at the same time.

"We are *not* staying here," Russ said matter-of-factly.

"You guys should've kidnapped me sooner, that was delightful," Shae said, her grin clear even in the darkness.

Dustin gave her a quizzical look and she shrugged, tucking the pistol into the back of her jeans.

"Sorry, Russ," Dustin said after a second. "We need to keep out of sight until the search party passes. We'll be inside somewhere, mostly, if that makes you feel better."

Dustin pulled out his flashlight, kneeling by the cat. It looked around seventy pounds, maybe a touch more, and was a female. She looked healthy and showed no signs of anything that would keep her meat from being good. Likely she'd gotten over-aggressive as summer wound down towards winter and had thought the horses would make a good meal to bulk up.

"Does mountain lion taste good?" Shae asked as Dustin pulled out a hunting knife and slit the abdomen open.

"Depends how you cook it," Dustin said, reaching in to pull out the guts, trying not to get anything on his boots. "Hold my horse still?"

Shae did as asked, sticking her tongue out at Russell who still looked put out. Dustin moved one of the saddle blankets so it covered Kodiak's rump, draping the mountain lion over it. He washed his hands in the creek before climbing back onto Kodiak in front of the lion. As they started walking again Dustin glanced at Shae, mind playing back her statement after the attack. Delightful. What had she meant by delightful?

15: Vivian's House

They had been riding for so long the sun had begun to lighten the sky, lending a rosy hue to the scruffy sage covering the low hills around them. They'd crossed both ridges Dustin mentioned and were now working their way up a softly slopped mountain, heading towards a thick pine forest. Shae was starting to wonder if she'd ever be able to get her legs back into their normal position once she dismounted, wishing she was back on the cozy train. It was good to see her brothers, though, now that the surprise of their appearance had worn off a bit. Neither had changed much, it seemed. Russell was still acting like the world was his responsibility, and Dustin was still single-minded enough to drive Russell insane. Their bickering made for a familiar background noise to her own thoughts, thoughts currently centered around what was going to happen now. She tuned in and out of their conversation as she mulled over her options.

Shae gathered that Russ was a soldier of some sort, his sandy-brown hair shorn short, posture upright and disciplined. He was also sporting a pair of rather spectacularly tacky deep red cowboy boots which Shae had, so far, managed not to tease him about. Dustin, meanwhile, was—and Shae couldn't quite wrap her head around it—a mountain man, complete with buckskin jacket. Russ being a soldier made sense. Soldiers had orders and routine and chains of command, things Russ had thrived on since he'd gotten his first chore-chart from the nannies. Dustin, though... Shae remembered him hating the outdoors. He had always been the first to advocate breaking into an abandoned building for shelter, rather than staying out in elements, when the family had been on the run.

They seemed like good people, at least, but they were rough around the edges in a way Shae didn't quite know what to do with. The cowboy boots may have been nicely embroidered, but they were also faded and scuffed. And the buckskin jacket looked homemade, nothing fancy about it, just pure function. Whatever their lives were now, they didn't look comfortable. Not her kind of comfortable, anyway.

As time passed Shae's thoughts drifted more towards sleep than anything else.

"We're almost there," Dustin said into the silence as they came around a small bluff. Their conversation had died off about an hour ago, everyone too exhausted to continue catching up.

Several minutes later Pinenut stopped walking and refused to continue any farther. Dustin sighed and swung off the buckskin, waving Russ and Shae off their horses as well. Shae groaned as her legs took her weight, stomping her feet to get the blood flowing. She looked around and saw an old and fading sign on a crooked post off to their left, the red words "Caution! Mountain lions in the area!" barely visible at the top of the sign. If she wasn't so exhausted it would have made her laugh.

She glanced at Dustin, the mountain lion from the night before still hanging across the back of his horse. The horse—she'd already forgotten its name—nuzzled Dustin, nibbling on the end of the half top-knot Dustin had left his hair in. What she remembered of her brother did not fit what she saw; a man grinning at a horse with a dead mountain lion on the back after pulling off a train robbery and kidnapping. However, the man standing before her now seemed to fit the scene perfectly. If his actual features hadn't matched her brother, she wouldn't believe this was him.

"It isn't much farther," Dustin told them. "About a mile. We'll walk and lead the horses."

Russ nodded, looking as displeased by standing as Shae. Everyone took their reins and followed Dustin along what had probably been a dirt road at some point, but was now a flat, grassy area with a footpath winding down the center and leading up the mountain. Among the grasses Shae saw lots of sharp rocks that didn't quite look like they belonged. If anyone tried to drive this old road now their tires would be shredded, she realized. Several houses were spaced relatively far apart along the track, some mostly hidden by trees and others closer to the old road. All were in different states of collapse, one even lost to a pile of rotted wood.

Shae took a deep breath of the crisp morning air, taking in all the mingling notes of pine and dirt and sage and horses. With the light increasing she turned, eyes sweeping the mountains spread out behind them. There were more peaks than she had time to count, some more jagged than others. It made her want to film a movie out here. Maybe she'd try for a western next.

They passed through a grove of aspens growing wild and thick on both sides of the path, some of them stretching up fifty, sixty, seventy feet. Morning sunlight filtering through their leaves bathed everything in a hazy green. As they cleared the trees another house became visible. The dawn light hadn't quite reached it yet, rendering it hard to make out many details, but Shae thought it looked to be in much better condition than the other houses they'd passed. Two rectangular levels made up the building with a huge, wrap-around porch on the first level, stuccoed walls an off-white color and speckled with moss. Several more large aspens seemed incredibly close to the house, but as they got closer Shae realized they weren't just close to it, they were growing *through* the structure. Some grew around the edges while at least one seemed to be sprouting directly through the left side, its wide branches shading a third of the roof.

Closer still, Shae realized the house was not as intact as it had looked at first, even with the trees. A whole corner seemed to have been carved away, though there weren't any visible debris, and several windows were cracked, some empty of any glass at all. The damage didn't seem intentional, the edges of the missing corner jagged and crumbling, but it did look as if whatever happened had been cleaned up. Shae could just make out ropes lashing two of the aspens to the place the second floor now jutted out into open air, as if they held it up. It gave the whole thing a strange, unsettling feeling. Who would prop up a collapsing house with trees? Why stay there at all? And what had held the house up before the trees grew?

She glanced at her brothers, gauging their reaction to the strange building. Russ looked equal parts amazed and confused, his expression shifting between the two as he took in all the details. Dustin looked uninterested, as if such a strange house was no big deal. Russ had explained that, though he himself didn't know about it until recently, Dustin had been to this area a lot. She wondered if he'd found the house shocking when he'd first seen it.

They reached a path to the house and Dustin turned up it. Shae and Russ glanced at one another, then back at the structure. Shae tried to fathom what the hell Dustin was thinking taking them here. A house being held up by trees couldn't be structurally sound, could it?

As they approached the porch a woman came out through the double front doors. Shae stopped dead and stared up at this unexpected person, Pinenut bumping into her back. The woman was a lot to take in at once. Shae couldn't figure out if she was supposed to look at her waist length blue-black hair, her shirtlessness, the fact that she could probably bench-press a bear, or the fact that she had more scars than skin. One scar traced up the right side of her chin, ending below a prominent cheekbone, and another slashed from above her left eyebrow to her hairline. Others were layered down her arms, some across her chest and abdomen. The only thing she had on was a dark, ashy purple skirt that looked rather nice against her light brown skin. She turned her head slowly, surveying all three of them with coal-black eyes. Shae realized she must live in the house. Not because she had just walked out the front door, but because she had the same feeling to her as the building; something that had fallen hard before being built back up with a few pieces missing, and a few replaced with something other than what had originally been there.

After a moment she spoke, directing her words to Dustin, "First, you stop a train near my home and kidnap a famous person off it, guaranteeing the place is going to be swarmed with officials soon. Then, you blow up one of my buildings. Now, you show up here having killed my cat."

"This isn't your cat," Dustin defended, grabbing the scruff of the lion to pull its head up. "Yours is missing its left ear. This one has both of her ears. And I didn't blow up the building, someone else did."

He shifted his weight back and forth as the woman assessed him. Eventually she sighed, shoulders dropping and a slight smile gracing her face. "I didn't expect you back so soon, but I'm glad you came. Go hang the cat in the barn and put the horses away while I get your brother and sister breakfast." She stepped aside, gesturing to the open door.

"Why do I have to do all that myself?" Dustin asked, though he'd already taken Shae and Russ' reins.

The woman slowly raised an eyebrow, giving him a stern look. "Because you are an impatient man who didn't think things through and has now landed himself in a situation where he requires my help, so you had best listen to me. Hang the cat and put the horses away. Breakfast will be waiting."

Dustin nodded and led the horses around the broken corner. Shae glanced at Russ once and shrugged slightly, heading up the steps and following the woman into the house. The mossy boards of the porch creaked under-foot, loud enough to drown out the birdsong twittering down from the trees.

Once over the threshold Shae stopped, even more taken aback by the inside of the house than she had been by the outside. To their left, in the center of what had probably been a dining room, was the large tree Shae had seen shading the house. From its thick trunk were strung three green canvas hammocks, each with the rope on its other end leading out a broken window to be lashed to trees and posts on the porch. Behind that seemed to be a kitchen, but she couldn't make out much of it from here. Directly in front of them, in the center of the house, was a huge fireplace, open on all four sides with coiled steel netting hanging across each opening. To the right at the back was a set of faded, mismatched couches and chairs, some sagging, overcrowded bookshelves, and a set of stairs leading up. And, to the right, at the front of the house, was the missing corner. It was completely open to the air, the two aspen trees supporting the area cutting the view of the mountains into three slices. Everything in the house was faded and worn, the plaster of the walls and ceiling cracked and chipped. A large orange cat lounged on the stone ledge of the fireplace, its fur the newest looking thing here.

She felt Russ stop behind her and lean close.

"What the hell is going on?" Russ whispered in her ear.

"This is your kidnapping, shouldn't you know who you're hiding out with?"

"It was Dustin's idea. I'm just along for the ride."

"Hell of a ride," Shae muttered, turning to contemplate the still open front door. Did she need to close it? An entire corner of the house was gone, what difference did an open door make? After a moment of deliberation she decided that, since it had been closed when they arrived, it would be best to close it now.

"Please explain this place to me, Shae," Russ said.

"Obviously, Dustin is friends with a crazy woman," Shae surmised. "A crazy woman with a strange taste for living arrangements."

The woman appeared out of the kitchen then. "The house has been in the family for generations, long before the plagues started."

Shae got the sense that she and Russ had not been whispering quietly enough in the big house. The woman didn't seem annoyed, though, and was busying herself setting platters of food and empty plates out on a dining table set between the fireplace and the kitchen. She was laying out quite the spread for living in the middle of nowhere, Shae thought. And for not knowing they were coming. Sausages, scrambled eggs, piles of berries, toast, a large pitcher of orange juice, and a little jar of butter. There was even a tin of cinnamon.

The woman gestured to the food. "Eat. And stay out of the kitchen, or I will shoot you."

With that alarming statement she crossed the house and went up the stairs. Neither Russ nor Shae moved towards the food.

"Dustin has never mentioned this woman to you?" Shae asked Russ.

"Well, he told me yesterday there's someone out here that saved his life once, a woman named Vivian. Guess this is her?"

"What the hell happened to our big brother?" Shae muttered.

Russ gave her a sidelong glance and didn't say anything for a moment. "You vanished... life changed."

He left Shae standing by the door, going over to the table and grabbing one of the chipped and mismatched plates, filling it up with food. Shae joined him after a moment, making her own plate and spooning more berries onto his plate to balance out the meat and eggs. He rolled his eyes at her but didn't put them back.

Before their conversation could continue the woman came back downstairs, now dressed in tan cargo pants and a gray-green button up. She'd rolled up the sleeves and tied the ends of the front together at her navel, the same as Shae had done to Dustin's borrowed flannel. The woman's clothes were as faded as everything else in the house, the edges frayed and hand-stitching holding several larger holes closed.

"Vivian... right?" Russ asked tentatively.

She nodded and pulled out the chair at the head of the table, loading up a plate of her own, pausing to glance at Russ. "Wait... he didn't tell you who I am before bringing you here?"

Russ shook his head. "Not really, no."

She threw up her hands. "And he calls me cryptic."

Shae thought cryptic was a very generous description for this woman.

When Vivian didn't offer anything else Russ continued, "He said you saved his life once. Taught him how to survive in the woods."

She chewed on some eggs, contemplating Russ. "Regretted it for a while, but yeah. He grew on me eventually."

"Why did you regret it?" Shae asked.

Vivian took longer to answer Shae, staring at her the whole time. Shae could tell she wasn't Turned—her lips were too pink and her skin too warmly toned—but there was still something strange about her. She wouldn't have been able to guess the woman's age if she tried. Older than Dustin, probably, but younger than thirty, maybe.

Eventually Vivian answered, "I don't like people."

Just then Dustin came through the back door behind Vivian, stopping to hang his jacket on a hook by the door.

"Horses are away and brushed, cat is hung," Dustin told Vivian.

She nodded and slid a plate over to the empty chair next to her. He sat down and piled it up with food without another word. Shae noted a hint of fondness in the way Vivian looked at Dustin.

Setting her fork down, Vivian surveyed everyone. "Now that everyone is here, we need to discuss Dustin's boneheaded move of kidnapping Shae in the manner in which he did." Dustin mumbled something into his eggs that sounded very affronted, but Vivian shushed him with a wave of her hand and continued on. "I have been listening to the radios all night. The coven is not pleased. Someone leaked what happened to the press and half the world is up in arms about their precious Lockwood going missing. It is a political nightmare for Wood's. It happened on their watch in territory they've long known to be dangerous and never claimed."

Dustin sank down in his chair a, now only poking at his food.

Vivian gave him a gentle pat on the arm. "They've sent fifteen soldiers, all vampires, by train. They arrived in Granby just before you got here. A helicopter is being brought in by noon."

Dustin perked up a little. "Only fifteen?"

"'Only fifteen?'" Russ spluttered.

"Only fifteen?" Shae said, unable to keep incredulity from leaking into her tone. She was worth way more than fifteen.

"The fact that it's only fifteen means they're likely specialists," Vivian replied to all of them. "Better skilled, and better trained."

Russ groaned, dropping his head into his hands.

Vivian shrugged. "Specialists or not, they don't know this terrain like Dustin and I do. They aren't specialists for *here*. We are. I've handled fifteen on my own before, though they were only here for me. They didn't have someone to find, as they do now. They'll be determined."

"I just wanted my sister back," Dustin mumbled.

Vivian nodded, patting his arm again. "I know. And from what I've picked up over the radios, your plan really wasn't a bad one. However, you failed to take into account how famous your sister has become, and how hard people would try to get her back."

"Yes, people are rather attached to me," Shae said, leaning back and twirling her fork between her fingers.

"But you're *our* family, not theirs. They took you from *us* first. Russell and I are just trying to bring you home," Dustin said vehemently.

Shae's fingers froze, fork halting in place. She'd completely forgotten what she'd learned last night in the shop, too caught up in that moment and all the ones since then. Her family thought she'd been kidnapped, not that she'd run away. It had never even occurred to her that kidnapping would seem a more likely option. They'd been in the middle of nowhere, her parents, Rose, and Dustin taking rotating watches that Shae had slipped out between. Who would've even been there to take her? And how could they have done it if they *had* been there, with so many on edge people to notice? She'd thought about leaving a note, but they hadn't had anything to write with. It should've been obvious that she'd left, anyway. Especially to Dustin.

Now here she was in the middle of the wilderness with two brothers who thought she had been kidnapped and they'd rescued her. How the hell was she supposed to explain that she'd left of her own free will and, really, they were the ones who'd done the kidnapping? She didn't think her brothers were any danger to her, but they were still her only line back to civilization.

Everyone seemed to have noticed Shae's frozen silence after Dustin's statement, but before anyone said anything Vivian stood up and said, "You all look exhausted. Shae, let me show you upstairs to a bedroom and get you something more comfortable to sleep in. Russ can stay down here in the hammocks. There's no reason to worry about the soldiers yet, they need time to organize. The horses won't go near vamps, so it will take them a while to find their way here, if they even can. The tree cover is thick enough that this place is difficult to spot even from the air. We can discuss further plans after some rest."

She set off towards the stairs and Shae followed her without stopping to look at her brothers.

Upstairs the house looked much more intact. The walls of a room off to the left hid the missing corner, and the windows Shae could see remained intact. It was rather dusty, though, with cobwebs all over, and the floor felt uneven under her feet. Vivian led Shae past a small brick fireplace mounted against a center wall of the house, the opening facing a large sitting room, and opened up a door just beyond it. Inside was a cramped bedroom with nothing but a full sized bed and a single nightstand. Vivian went over to a little closet, rooting around inside for a moment before coming back with a set of fleece pajamas.

"Thanks," Shae told her, reaching out to take them.

Vivian's hands lingered on the clothing for a moment and Shae was once again struck with the impression that Vivian seemed a lot like the Turned without actually being one. Something about the way she held herself, the way she moved. Almost like one of the Turned who had a high turn age.

She spoke, her tone even, "Dustin is a good man, if a bit naïve. He doesn't like when people are gentle with him, though. It's better to be honest and let what happens happen."

With that, she turned and left Shae in the room, closing the door behind her.

"You are officially creepy," Shae said to the closed door.

She unfolded the pajamas to see if they would fit and

decided they would. They were a touch large, but Shae realized they would not fit Vivian as she was a fair bit taller than Shae and much more lithely built. Who's were they, then? Or, rather, who's had they been? Had they belonged to some dead family member of Vivian's, this being a family home as she'd said? How morbid.

Shae slipped them on and, despite having been awake for going on twenty-four hours, found herself too restless to sleep. Too many thoughts raced through her head as she tried to formulate a plan. Rather than climbing into the bed she went over to the window and pushed aside the rough, moth-eaten red drapes. The view took her breath away. It went on for ages, bathed in bright, low hung daylight that sent shadows racing out for miles. There was a hint of a body of water between two low hills a few miles away, glistening white under the morning sun.

After a few more moments she pulled her eyes away and looked down at the backyard. A multi-leveled patio took up more square footage than the house, circular levels set at different heights and overlapping randomly. Each part looked like it was made from a different material, as if they'd been built at different times with whatever the builders had at hand. There was a full outdoor kitchen on one, little stone alcoves with built-in benches on many, tables and chairs scattered everywhere, and flowers pouring out of planters. Off to the right was a barn surrounded by a multitude of pens. Shae could make out pigs, chickens, horses, goats, sheep, even a few cattle. So that was where breakfast had come from. Beyond the barn and patio was forest on all sides, sloping down away from the house.

Shae let the curtain fall and walked back to the bed, laying down on top of the covers. The thing was as hard as a slab of bricks.

Her mind drifted back to what Vivian said before she left the room. Perhaps she thought it would be better to tell Dustin the truth, but she wasn't the long lost family member out in the middle of nowhere with him. The truth wasn't an option here. Shae needed a story.

Maybe sticking with the kidnapping one would be the best way to go. Say her hesitation earlier was because of the trauma or something. That would settle things with her brothers for now, then she'd just have to find a way to slip back to civilization at some point. Details needed to be shorn up first, though. No more getting caught off guard.

Her mind was too wrung out for details, though. Rolling over she started counting forward and backward from ten until she managed to drift off.

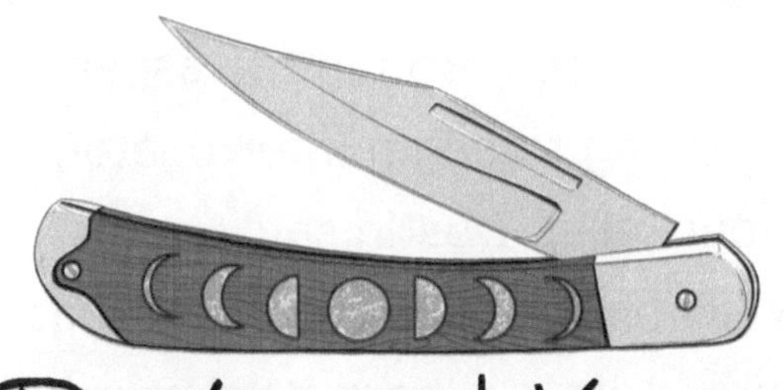

16: Dustin and Vivian Talk

Dustin watched as Vivian led Shae away, his mind stuck on Shae's hesitation at the mention of her kidnapping. She'd looked surprised. Cornered. But Shae wasn't the sort of person to get cornered.

"Well, uh…" Russ mumbled, drumming his fingers on the table and avoiding Dustin's eyes. "I'm just gonna… hit the sack, I guess."

"You saw her hesitate, right?" Dustin pressed.

Russ shrugged, looking between his empty plate and the sink in the kitchen behind him. It didn't have a faucet. The house hadn't had plumbing nor electricity in decades. Vivian got water from a well and from rain barrels, bringing in pitchers of it to wash things with, the water draining out the side of the house.

"Leave it," Dustin said impatiently. "Vivian doesn't like people going in her kitchen. She'll stab you if you try. I'll get it later."

Russ nodded and stood up, stretching before walking over and examining the hammocks. He made no indication that he was going to answer Dustin's earlier question.

"Russ. You saw her hesitate?" Dustin repeated.

Russ sighed and grumbled without actually saying anything, pulling on one of the hammock ropes, checking the knots where it looped around the aspen tree.

"For a guy training to be an interrogator, you're horrid at controlling your tells," Dustin said.

Russ threw his hands up and spun around. "You're my brother! Of course I have a hard time controlling my tells around you. For one, you know me better. For two, unlike you, I haven't spent the last decade lying to my family. And for three, I don't enjoy keeping things from you!"

Dustin ignored the jab about his lies. They'd had that fight enough times over the last several days. But the third point....

"And what exactly are you keeping from me?" Dustin asked.

"I...." Russ' eyes widened slightly, and Dustin could tell he was biting the inside of his cheek.

"Russell."

"It's... probably Stockholm Syndrome or something," Russ muttered, turning away from Dustin.

Dustin followed him around, making sure he stayed in Russ' line of sight. Russ ignored him, but Dustin kept it up. He knew there was more that Russ wasn't saying. Their awkward, silent dance lasted about twenty minutes, during which Russ took off his boots and belt, set them under his chosen hammock, grabbed a couple more bits of sausage, paced a bit, and sat down in the hammock.

"Stop staring at me like that," he grumbled in Dustin's direction.

"Give me a straight answer, then."

Finally Russ made eye contact and Dustin's shoulders tightened at the look, suddenly worried about what Russ was going to say.

"I don't like you'll like my straight answer, Dustin."

"Tell me anyway."

"I…" he sighed, running his good hand back and forth over his knee. "Sometimes I've wondered if… if Shae wasn't kidnapped. I wondered if maybe she just… left on her own…."

Dustin frowned, his stomach sinking with familiar, long buried guilt. "Why?"

Russ took a long breath, breaking eye contact to look down at the warped wood floor. When he spoke his voice was barely above a whisper, "I saw her leaving, Dustin. That night. I was half asleep, and I didn't really think it was weird. I was a kid. I figured she was going to the bathroom or something. Then we all woke up and she was gone and I just… I figured she'd been taken while she was away from the camp, before she could come back. That's what I told myself over and over again over the years. But…."

Dustin felt frozen, guilt having settled firmly at the base of his stomach. Memories he didn't want pushed at the edges of his mind.

"But *what*?" Dustin ground out, shoving the memories back down.

"But all this stuff with her using a fake name, then suddenly revealing who she really is which conveniently rocketed her career up the ladder, making her famous worldwide almost over night…. What kidnapper would've taken Shae, then let her live to adulthood? Let her reveal the truth about who she is? Let her spin that story to the papers?"

Dustin spluttered, clinging to the truth he'd spent ten years convincing himself of. "She was *twelve*, Russ! Do you really think a twelve-year-old could've run away and spun a whole new identity for herself? Just walked out of the deserts of Nevada and never get questioned on who she was? Never had a DNA test run on her that revealed who she was?"

Russ looked almost sad when he looked at Dustin again. "I don't know Dustin. But I've met people kidnapped by vampires before, even rescued a couple with my unit. None of them have acted like Shae has."

"Who says a vampire took her?!" Dustin spat, ignoring the feeling of grasping at straws. "There's plenty of human creeps in the world too!"

Russ sighed, closing his eyes and pinching the bridge of his nose. "I don't know, Dustin. I don't. There's so much that doesn't add up with things she's said and things we think we know. Maybe she didn't leave on her own, I hope she didn't. But she isn't being honest with us either."

Dustin spluttered for a moment before spinning and striding out through the back door, resisting the urge to slam it.

Russell was wrong.

Shae wouldn't leave.

She loved them.

They loved her.

Russell was wrong.

He nearly collided with a slim aspen growing on the edge of one of the lower sections of the patio. Without thinking he punched it, fist coming away covered in the white powder that coated the bark. After a moment he punched it again, trying to force his frustration out through the action. When his fists got sore he pulled out a hunting knife from his boot and went at the tree again, hacking bits of it away with each swing without caring how much it damaged the blade. He needed a new one anyway.

"I thought I taught you better knife work than that."

Dustin jolted, turning to find Vivian sitting on one of the benches that ran around the base of another level of the patio. He had no idea how long she'd been there. It could've been the whole time for all he knew. Vivian was like that. Weirdly silent and almost eerie. She also had an incredible talent for sitting so still that, if she had the right clothes on compared to her surroundings, you wouldn't notice she was there even if she was only feet away. Right now her tan pants melted into the sun-warmed stones around her and the green of her shirt matched the tumble of vines coming from the planter above her head, her hair mingling in with the leafy shadows.

"I'm not in the mood for proper knife work, Vivian," he told her, turning back to the tree and swinging out with the knife again.

Before he could swing it a second time Vivian came up and deftly twisted his arm down and behind his back, one hand on Dustin's shoulder to force him into an almost crouch. Dustin had no option but to drop the knife, Vivian having stolen all control from him. She bent down and picked up the weapon, gripping it by the dull side of the blade, and tapped the hilt against Dustin's chest, pressing close enough to remind him that she was a good six inches taller.

"You are using a knife, thus you are in the mood for proper knife work. If you don't agree, I'll happily hold on to this for you until you're in a better mood. This is a weapon. You need to respect it, no matter what mood you're in. If you're going to destroy the blade going after a hunk of wood, at least do it right."

Dustin fumed, still too caught up in his anger not to lash out even if Vivian wasn't the source of it. He wondered if he could get the knife back from her by force. Probably not. She'd taught him everything he knew about fighting, and Dustin also knew she wasn't above inflicting a small stab wound to prove her point. Or a large one.

"Fine."

"Fine what?" She asked.

"I'll use it properly."

She contemplated him before stepping back and holding the knife out. Dustin took it and she went back to her bench, making it clear she was going to stay and make sure he did as he said. Dustin gripped the hilt, making sure his hold was exactly right, before turning back to the tree and going at it again. This time he treated it as if he were attacking a living target, slashing out a couple Xs for eyes and a crude heart shape a foot below them. He was careful with every strike, highly aware of Vivian's eyes on his back. His steps were measured and thought out, strikes quick and planned.

After several minutes Vivian came up behind him silently and started nudging his feet and arms around to her liking. Apparently she thought he was rusty. This continued for fifteen minutes until the tree looked decrepit, the knife chipped beyond repair, and Dustin felt frustrated enough to explode again. It had felt good to go after the tree without thought, but now that it had turned into a refresher course on knives it had become grating.

He stopped, turning to glare at Vivian. "What's with the knife lesson? I thought you were upstairs comforting my sister."

She shrugged. "I've been meaning to cut that tree down for a while. I was hoping you'd end up doing it for me if I left you at it."

"That doesn't answer my question."

"It answers the first one."

"And what about the second one?"

"I have no reason to comfort Shae. I took her upstairs to get some rest. Comforting her is your job, though I don't think comforting is what she needs. Now, finish off that tree. I don't want it falling on my smoker."

With that she stepped away and walked off towards the barn, disappearing inside. Dustin watched her go, shoulders sagging under the weight of exhaustion and frustration and confusion. This wasn't how this was supposed to be, how any of this was supposed to be.

Retrieving an axe from next to the firewood stack that spanned the whole length of the back porch, tucked under the roof to keep it dry, Dustin set to work on chopping down the tree. It was small, only about thirty feet tall and maybe six inches thick at the base, but it would still cause damage if it fell the wrong way. It was in a somewhat awkward position between the patio, the corner of the house, and the fence of the paddock that surrounded the barn. There was only about a ten-foot gap between the fence and the house that Dustin could lay the tree down in without hitting anything. Vivian had been letting it grow to help camouflage the porch, but it had gotten too big for where it was.

A few careful swings and he had a large chunk taken out of the base of the tree on the side he wanted it to fall towards. The tree swayed menacingly, but remained upright as he'd intended. Stepping around to the other side, he took a few practice swings to get his placement right, then drove the blade into the wood opposite the point of the chunk he'd taken out. Acting quick he balanced on the exposed end of the axe-head with one foot, letting it take all his weight as he pushed the tree in the right direction. His weight levered the blade enough to crack through the rest of the wood, pushing the tree down in the direction of the opening he'd aimed for as he took a rapid step back out of the way. The branches whooshed through the air, cushioning the sound of the impact as the tree landed on the grass and clover.

Dustin took a moment to enjoy the little rush of pride at how perfectly it had fallen, right in the center of where he'd wanted it. Vivian hadn't asked him to cut it up once he cut it down, but he figured it was implied so he picked the axe back up and set to work, hacking off the branches first. After a few branches the heat became too much, so he stripped out of his shirt, tossing it back onto the patio.

The work was strenuous enough that thoughts of Shae slipped from his mind. Mostly. Sometimes between swings they'd still creep in. There was no way Russ could be right. Shae wouldn't have left them. She couldn't have. But... she *had* hesitated.

No.

She was just scared to talk about what had happened to her. That had to be it.

Dustin got so lost in his head, his thoughts wrestling with the conundrum that was his sister, that he nearly swung the axe into his leg. He let out a low curse and glanced over at the barn to see if Vivian might have been outside to see him do it. He didn't see her, but that didn't mean much. A better indication that she hadn't seen his screwup was that he couldn't hear her laughing or see her striding out to scold him.

When he was sure she wasn't coming, Dustin looked back down at his work so far. All but a couple of the topmost branches were cut, piled to the side and ready to be chopped down further into kindling, and the trunk was ready to be sawed into larger logs. It wasn't like any of it would rot in the time it took for him to get some rest, he decided. It wasn't just his focus on Shae that had caused him to almost maim himself.

Setting the axe down on the pile of branches, he walked over to one of the stone patio benches in the house's shade. He didn't even bother to take his boots off before laying down, feeling it was too much effort. He could've gone back inside—it would've been cooler—but going upstairs to the room he and Vivian shared would've meant going by where Shae was sleeping, and staying downstairs would've meant being near Russ.

He hovered on the edge of sleep, time slipping sideways and backwards as bugs buzzed and the midday sun cooked the plant life, its warm scent settling around him. The hazy rest was interrupted by something prodding his shoulder and he cracked open one eye to see Vivian silhouetted above him. After he decided she wasn't a dream he wiggled down on the bench to make room for her, resting his head on her thigh.

"You didn't bring Coal," she remarked, fingers lightly running through his hair.

He hmmed softly, eyes closing once more. "Sorry. Your love affair with my dog will have to continue another time."

She chuckled and lapsed into silence.

"This doesn't seem to be going how you expected," she stated after a moment. She didn't press for a response, still running her fingers through his hair.

"If you expect me to participate in this conversation you're going to have to stop doing that," he said with a yawn.

She didn't stop. "You don't seem too keen on participating no matter what I do or don't do involving your hair."

"I missed you," Dustin told her, hoping to take the conversation in a different direction."

"You haven't even been gone a month," she said.

"Still missed you."

They lapsed back into silence until Vivian broke it a few minutes later.

"I found out Shae was alive eight days after you left."

Dustin frowned and sat up, turning to face her. "What?"

She nodded, her gaze steady. "I was getting some supplies off a train and they had a big shipment of *Time* magazines. Her story was on the cover. Not the headline, just a little blurb. I almost went after you, but I figured you'd be back soon anyway, or you'd find out on your own on your way home."

Dustin groaned, resting his head in his hands. "I'm sorry I didn't come to you last night. There just—there wasn't *time*. Whenever I come here, I just come to the house and figure you'll be home eventually. I've never had to actually *find you* out here."

He should've tried harder. Driven faster. Insisted they dump the car and take a train once they found that second paper at the gas station. Something. Vivian knew more about his search for Shae than anyone did. She'd been helping him almost since they first met. Sure, she'd made it clear she never really thought Shae was alive like Dustin did, but she'd always been willing to help him find answers.

"Hey," she said softly, looping an arm around his shoulders and pulling him in to kiss his forehead. "Stop spiraling. Mistakes were made, but your exhaustion is making them seem worse than they are. Even if you hadn't gotten Shae last night, I would have."

Dustin pulled back a little, but not enough to make her let go of him. "Wait, you were there last night?"

She nodded. "After I found the magazine, I kept my eye out for more news. When I found out about her tour, found out it would come right along the tracks we know and rob so well, I wasn't going to let her go by."

Dustin huffed out laugh, curling an arm around Vivian's waist and leaning into her.

"I was in Byers Canyon, waiting for her train. I had no intention of taking her off it, I was just going to talk to her. Tell her you were looking for her. Though, if she'd asked me to take her off the train and to you I would have."

Dustin had thought about going to the canyon. It was only a few miles up the tracks from Granby, and it was the main point he and Vivian used to get on the trains they robbed. Problem was, getting on the trains there involved rappelling down the canyon walls and with Russ' broken arm that hadn't been an option.

"Thanks," Dustin said. "Sorry for being an ass earlier."

"Welcome. And apology accepted."

He rested his head in the crook of her neck and shoulder, letting her take his weight.

"I miss my little sister," Dustin whispered. "I miss my family being together. I miss not being on the brink of a war with Wood's Coven."

"Yes, the coven is getting restless." She sighed. "I've heard a lot of strange things. Seen some strange things as well."

"How long do we have until we need to worry about the soldiers?" Dustin asked.

"According to the radio chatter they found a trail of hoofprints heading north, and they're following those for now. Obviously they weren't yours, since you went south. Must've been some of the mustangs."

Dustin felt himself relax a little at this. "Good."

She continued to talk idly about whatever seemed to come to her mind. Dustin laid back down, head in her lap, ignoring her actual words in favor for enjoying their cadence and tone. He'd always found it easy to fall asleep here, to fall asleep with Vivian. At home there was always something else going on, something that kept him on edge. Was Russ okay, or had something happened that the family hadn't gotten word of yet? Had his dad wandered off when no one was paying attention? Was Keaun going to have another nightmare that kept him up for days afterward? Were wolves going to get into one of the barns again? Was it going to be the night the coven finally pulled off the veil of playing nice and attacked Nahanni full force?

All those thoughts and dozens more raced around his head every night back home. But here, here was peaceful. It was almost like the rest of the world didn't matter here in this little slice of the Rockies. Even if the covens did try to wage a full attack on the area, Vivian was a force to be reckoned with. She had been raised a solider from the moment she was born, she'd told Dustin. Over the years he'd cobbled together bits and pieces of her life before she'd lost her family. Her father had given her her first rifle at the age of nine, though she'd learned to shoot long before that. Her mother had taught her how to use knives to fight. One of her uncles taught her how to use explosives, an aunt had taught her archery, a cousin how to camouflage herself, an older brother how to work radios, another older brother how to farm. They'd been a family of soldiers and survivors, rejecting everything the covens stood for. Vivian carried on their legacy with her shoulders held high.

Dustin had asked her once what happened to all of them. How was she the only one left when they'd all been just as trained, just as capable in a fight? She hadn't answered and Dustin had decided to never ask again, knowing the answer couldn't be a good one.

"Your mind is wandering," Vivian observed.

"I haven't slept in over thirty hours, of course it's wandering," Dustin mumbled.

She bent down and kissed his forehead. "I'll let you sleep then. I have some things to take care of anyway."

She gently extracted herself from underneath Dustin, walking back to the barn. Dustin watched her go before rolling on his stomach and using his arms as a pillow, finally drifting off into real sleep.

17: Exploring

Shae peered out the door of the room Vivian had taken her to sleep in. Judging by the light she guessed it was the middle of the afternoon, but the house was silent so she assumed everyone was asleep. She had a strong urge to look around, but the idea of opening a door to find Vivian—or a hole in the floor that dropped into some strange pit—wasn't appealing. The outside of the house, though, that seemed like a safer bet. It would require something other than borrowed dead-person pajamas, however, so she stepped back into the room and changed into her clothes from before.

The shirt fit well enough but the jeans were tight around her hips and the boots were half a size too big. It amazed her they hadn't given her blisters yesterday. Country-chic was not her idea of a good look, and she was glad there weren't any mirrors around.

Downstairs she found Russ snoring away in one of the hammocks, one leg hanging off the side, and no sign of Dustin nor Vivian. Turning away from her little brother, she went out the back door, taking a deep breath of the summery air. It was quite beautiful out here, the property buried in the trees with all manner of birds zipping about. Maybe when she got home to England she'd move out of London to somewhere with a forest—because she was going home to England. She loved her brothers, but this couldn't last. It was one thing to enjoy the aesthetic of the wilderness and live in a beautiful house that sat on the edge of it yet still provided all the amenities, and another thing entirely to live in the Yukon and freeze to death every day while doing whatever it was they did up there.

Glancing to the side she saw hundreds of pieces of firewood stacked two layers deep all along the side of the house, up to the base of the windows and up to her shoulders in the areas between the windows. Shae made a displeased face at the thought of how much effort it must have taken to cut them all. The rails of the porch were battered and sun-worn, most of their white paint chipped and scratched away. Many of the posts were missing entirely. A single wide step led down to the first level of the patio, which was half filled with barrels. Shae lightly kicked one, listening to the echoey glugging sound of what she guessed was water. Out of curiosity she kicked another and was met with a different, heavier thud, as if this one contained something solid.

Padding down another couple of levels, she looked around the outdoor kitchen, marveling at the good condition of it. The stone counters were clean, the grill unrusted, the fireplace oven swept of ashes. Turning, she caught sight of Dustin out of the corner of her eye, laying face down on a shaded bench, breathing softly. His shirt was off and Shae couldn't help but stare. He'd changed so much from the wiry teenager he'd been when she left. He still hadn't grown into himself back then, but he had now. All broad shoulders and muscles and scars from who knew what, though nowhere near as many as Vivian had. And he was positively *covered* in freckles. He even had a few tattoos; bands of geometric animal designs around his upper arms, a simple linework mountainscape below the base of his neck, three crossed and tied arrows on his left shoulder-blade, and a stylistic wolf's face on his right shoulder-blade. He looked nothing like what she would've pictured him growing up to be. She wasn't sure what that was, exactly, but it wasn't this.

She left him to sleep in the cool shade and wandered off towards the trees. There was a twisting path between the pines and she wanted to see where it led. Once into the trees snatches of a babbling creek drifted through the air, the sound becoming steadier as she got closer. Eventually she came to a tumble of boulders through which the creek—bigger than it had sounded—had carved a path. A set of steps hewn into the stone led down to the water and she followed them, only to find Vivian wading in the center with a large net on a metal pole, her pants rolled up to her knees but still getting wet.

She spared Shae a quick glance before going back to what she'd been doing. "I'm assuming your brothers are still asleep?"

Shae contemplated a moment before sitting down on the edge of a boulder, deciding now was a good time to try to get some answers out of this woman. "They are. Russell's snoring away and Dustin is working on a nice sunburn."

Shae pulled off her boots and socks, letting her feet dangle in the chilly water. It created a nice contrast against the sunlight filtering through the trees to dapple across her back, but mostly she'd done it to seem more settled. Less like she considered Vivian a threat. She wasn't sure she did consider the other woman a threat, but she definitely didn't consider her a friend.

Vivian chuckled, taking a quick swipe with the net and scooping a fish out of the water. "Poor man's so pale he's more likely to burn up than some of the vamps I've come across."

She pulled the fish out of the net by its tail and waded over to a boulder a couple yards from Shae. With one deft movement she smacked the fish against the rock. It went still and she dropped it into a shaded pool next to the boulder that it couldn't float out of, returning to the center of the creek with her net.

"You come across a lot of Turned?" Shae asked.

Vivian's eyes swept the creek and she answered in between tracking different fish that went by. "A fair few. This is the biggest fully abandoned area left in North America. No coven lays claim to it, but it is no longer a rebel outpost, so there's no one to stop the coven from coming through. It's quicker, and cheaper, for their trains to cut through the area rather than go around and so they do. I quite enjoy liberating supplies from those trains, and many of them are staffed by vampires."

She caught another fish.

"And Dustin, when he was here with you before, did he help you liberate those supplies?"

She paused, fish still thrashing in her net. "He's been here many times, actually. And yes, he helps me liberate those supplies. He's very good at it. Quick. Smart. Intuitive."

So, not only was Dustin a mountain man then, he was an outlaw. A train robbing outlaw. Last night hadn't been a one off. He'd known exactly what he was doing. Fascinating. Seemed Shae wasn't the only one who didn't like the idea of a quiet life in the Yukon. That in and of itself didn't surprise Shae, just his method of going about it.

"What else is he like?" Shae asked.

Vivian killed her fish, dropping it into the pool with the other. "Loyal. Stubborn. Loving."

"Loving?" Shae felt her eyebrows raise, smiling despite herself. "Have experience with him being loving, do you?"

Vivian smirked, glancing over. "A fair bit. Though not in a sexual way, if that's what you're implying. Neither of us are interested in that aspect of relationships."

"I think the term for that is asexual," Shae said offhandedly. It was weird picturing the dorky brother from her memory dating this strange woman from the mountains. It must be a fascinating relationship where your go to night out involved robbing a train.

Vivian made a bemused face and gestured to everything around them. "Terms are for society. Does this look like society to you?"

"Unfortunately, no."

Vivian paused, watching Shae from her place back in the middle of the creek. Shae's skin itched under her gaze, under the stillness of her form. "Dustin is a good man, one of the best I've met. He has a hard time letting himself be happy, which I think is why he's always on the move. But when he loves someone, he does it with all he has."

"You're a very bizarre woman, Vivian," Shae said after a moment.

This startled a laugh out of her and she shrugged. "You're the bizarre one from my perspective. Not just living with the vamps, but sauntering through their society with that translucent skin flashing everywhere. I'd rather taunt a bear with a steak."

"From those bite marks on your arms it looks like you've done exactly that."

Vivian glanced down at her arms, each of which had a set of scars from different decent sized bites laced in among other scars. "Eh, the right arm was a wolf and it was my fault. Left arm was a guard dog. Technically, I probably deserved that one too."

Shae shook her head, unable to comprehend Vivian's calm tone. Who got attacked by multiple animals in their life and just went with it? Before she could respond she heard footsteps behind her and turned to see Russ walking down the path, thumbs hanging from his front belt loops and a cigarette between his lips. He looked startled to see Shae sitting there and snatched the cigarette out of his mouth, attempting to hide it behind his back.

Vivian gathered her fish and sloshed out of the creek, pausing next to Russ on the path. "If you burn down my forest with that thing I will feed you to a pack of vamps."

Russ looked alarmed by this proposition and stepped out of Vivian's way as she continued up the path. Once she was out of earshot he turned back to Shae, cigarette still held behind his back.

"That woman scares me," he stated.

Shae laughed and waved her brother over, patting the rock next to her. "She's certainly something else."

"Yeah, but what? I mean, her house has clearly been bombed. I can't think of anything else that would cause damage like that. But the coven hasn't bombed this area in nearly a century, and the damage doesn't look that old."

"How do you know they haven't bombed here in that long?" Shae questioned.

Russ folded himself down next to her, crossing his legs. "The Nahanni military does its best to keep records of Wood's Coven's military actions. What they do, when they do it, how they do it, what they use. We have to study them as part of joining up."

"Maybe the records are wrong."

"Yeah... maybe," Russ admitted. "It's just weird. She's just weird."

"No, well yes, but what's actually weird," Shae reached out and snatched the smoldering cigarette from between his fingers and took a long drag, "is that you think I'd give a damn about you smoking."

He grinned sheepishly. "Sorry. Mom caught Darius smoking last year and tore him a new one for it. Kind of habit to keep it hidden from everyone now."

"How is Darius?" Shae asked, handing the cigarette back. "How is everyone? Do they know you're here?"

She wanted to know how the rest of the family had taken her disappearance. Were they all under the same impressions as Dustin? Did they all really believe she'd been kidnapped? She'd begun to formulate a plan in her mind for how to get back to her life, but that didn't mean she wasn't curious about what had become of her old one.

Russ squirmed, his expression pinched. "No, they... don't know. Coming to get you happened kind of fast."

"You couldn't have left a letter?"

"We did, it just wasn't... specific. We didn't, *I* didn't, want to implicate them in anything illegal."

Shae frowned. "Illegal?"

Russ glanced at her, head tilted slightly. "You've got no idea what it's really like in Nahanni, do you?"

Shae shrugged, leaning back on her arms. "My only experience with rebel camps was living in the tent city in the Baja camp right after we left Mendez Coven."

"Baja is over-crowded," Russ admitted. "A lot of people flee there because of how bad conditions are in Mendez. Nahanni, though... it's different. Very different.

Open and laid back. Organized. Like the world was before the vamps."

Shae glanced over and saw a soft, homesick smile on her little brother's face. "I'm still not seeing the illegal aspect."

Russ sighed, stubbing out his cigarette on the heel of his boot and tucking the butt in his shirt pocket.

"Nahanni is a great place, and I love it there. But they're scared, and rightfully so. Wood's Coven is… restless. There's been attacks along the border, more and more. It's illegal to leave the boundaries of the settlement without proper documentation. Same for entering it. They're just being careful, trying to protect what we have."

"And you didn't leave with that proper documentation?"

"No."

"How does Dustin spend so much time in Colorado then?"

Russ' expression darkened for a moment. "Dustin… exists in his own world a lot of the time. Which I knew, we all knew. We just never assumed he took it this far."

Shae watched him for a moment, struggling to fit all the pieces together. "Why are *you* here, Russell? Just. Lay this out for me. A to B."

He nodded slowly a few times, eyes roving over the water. "What are you considering point A?"

Shae thought about it for a while, not really sure of the answer.

"Maybe you mean what brought Dustin and I here," Russ said, "maybe you mean what made Dustin and I the way we are now, maybe you mean something else…. I kind of suspect what that something else might be, but…."

"Maybe I mean all of that," Shae said. "None of us are who we were as children."

"But Dustin wants us to be," Russ replied.

The silence between them stretched much longer this time.

"Is Nahanni really like what you say?" Shae asked eventually.

Russ managed a small smile, though it seemed forced. "Yes. It's half a dozen little towns plus farms and ranches. We have a government and hospitals and libraries and schools, even a college."

"You're cut off, though. You said as much yourself. It can't be exactly the same."

"We're cut off because we want to be. Because the covens are abhorrent. And really, we don't lack much." He smiled a bit. "We even make movies."

Shae digested all of this, reformatting her picture of what had happened to her family. It had always been a picture of struggle before, of barely getting by.

"Do Mom and Dad still make movies?" Shae wondered.

"No. Mom runs Lockwood Ranch and Dad… Dad mostly keeps to himself. Does a bit of woodworking."

Shae blinked, waiting for her brother to say he was joking.

"What?" He asked.

"Mom... runs a ranch?"

Russ laughed, the sound genuine. "Well, we all kind of run it together. But yeah. Mostly we raise beef cattle."

Out of all the things Shae had struggled to wrap her head around in the last twenty-four hours, this one blew her away the most. She remembered her mother as a woman who would throw out a pair of shoes for having a speck of dirt on them. Even when they'd been on the run, she'd somehow kept herself looking clean and proper. Shae had envied how well she did it.

"Mom runs a ranch, Dustin is an outlaw, you're a soldier. That's just.... Damn."

Russ glanced at her, the corners of his mouth quirking up. "Not what you were expecting?"

"Not even a little."

Russ chuckled, looking wistfully up through the trees at the thin white clouds racing by. "A to B... we lost you, Shae, and it changed things. Different changes for each of us, but changes across the board. For Dustin, he never gave up on you and that led him down a path I still don't quite understand. A path I didn't even really know about until a few days ago."

"Did the rest of you give up on me?" Shae asked, unsure about how the different answers he could give would make her feel. She cared about her family, that had never changed, she just hadn't wanted to be with them anymore. Hadn't wanted to be a part of the direction they were heading.

"Of course not," Russ said. "But we did... move on. We

had to, even though it hurt like hell."

"I'm sorry," Shae said, a little surprised by how much she meant it. Her family's feelings after all this time weren't her responsibility, but she did get that her actions were at least a catalyst for causing some of this.

Russ didn't respond, and they lapsed back into silence.

As much as the other information shocked her, what confused her most of all was Dustin. His vehement belief in her kidnapping. If anyone were to have guessed that she left, to have figured it out, she would've thought it would be him. It had been his idea, after all.

She thought back over all the times she and Dustin had hung back as they walked across the desert as kids, talking about how much they missed their old life and wanted it back. Spending all their time dreaming and scheming about things being different, about their childhood of excess and comfort. Every need met, every want catered to. She'd even considered asking him to come with her when she'd left. The person he'd been back then would've come, probably. He'd hated their life on the run. She hadn't asked him to come, though, part of her too worried he'd say no and tell their parents what was going on, preventing her from going.

"I wish I'd known," Shae paused, choosing her words carefully, "I wish I'd known how hard he took me not being there. How hard you all did."

"Would the guilt have changed anything?" Russ asked.

Guilt. Shae didn't think that was the right word, but she was more caught on the fact that it was the one Russ had picked. Guilt seemed to imply that she had some responsibility in it, which she wouldn't if he believed that she had been kidnapped. He did believe that, didn't he?

She watched him as he played with a leaf that had fallen in his lap, feeling like the puzzle she was trying to put together kept getting shoved back in the box and shaken up.

"Russell—"

"I know you don't want to be here, Shae," Russ interrupted. "It's obvious. You've got a life out there, back in the covens. A girlfriend, fame, comfort."

Shae didn't contradict him.

He sighed and slowly pulled himself up from the rock, dusting his pants off and looking down at Shae.

"I'll take you back, Shae, if that's what you want. All I ask is that you say goodbye before you leave this time." With that, he turned and walked back up the path, leaving Shae alone at the creek.

Before you *leave*.

This time.

He knew.

A big part of her wasn't surprised that Russ knew, that he'd put it together. He was much more logical than Dustin, and clearly more level-headed about what was going on. To Dustin Shae was still a part of the family, a missing piece that needed to be found and protected. To Russ... well, maybe he still considered her family, but

Shae was getting the impression she was not the one he'd step in front of a bus for.

She didn't know what to do with this information. He had offered to take her back, but could he? It was clear he'd been dragged rather unwillingly on this adventure. Did he know enough about where they were to get them back to civilization alive? She wasn't sure that he did, which left Dustin, and Dustin was clearly going to be difficult to convince.

She needed a way to calm the waters. To drain away the tension radiating between all of them. Her eyes strayed to a small frog as it hopped up into a divot in the boulder just above the water. That would work.

18: Frog Hunting

Dustin woke up to something cold, round, and metal being dropped on his back. Cracking an eye open, he looked up to see Shae standing next to the bench, hands on her hips and a grin on her face. It took him a moment to get his bearings enough to realize she'd dropped an empty tin bucket on his back.

"Get up, lazy. We're going frog hunting."

"Why?" Dustin muttered, still not totally convinced he was awake. He sat up and scrubbed a hand over his face, still eying Shae. He couldn't decide if it was his sleep dazed state that was making this all seem so strange, or if it was actually strange.

"Because I want to see if we can trick Russ into eating one again like when we were little," Shae answered, turning and walking away towards the creek that ran behind the house. Dustin couldn't help but notice that she walked like she was on a runway, even on the uneven forest ground. All swaying hips and perfect posture.

Still a little asleep, Dustin grabbed the bucket and

trotted after her, catching up as she hit the treeline.

"Russ is a soldier now, I'm sure he's been tricked and dared into eating stuff a lot worse than frogs," Dustin pointed out.

Shae laughed, the sound light and bubbly. "That may be so, but we're going to try it anyway. Remember the look on his face last time?"

"Yeah," Dustin grinned, falling into the rhythm of happy memories. "He freaked. Doesn't top the time we handed Rose a piece of deer brain, though, and told her it was jello. She *flipped*. I thought we were done for." She'd filled their sleeping bags with rocks that night, and he and Shae's food tasted funny for a week.

"I thought she was going to murder us!" Shae said.

All the tension that had been knotting between Dustin's shoulders was melting away. *This* was Shae, *this* was his little sister. Pranks and laughs and easy conversation. She must've been tired before, like they all were. It seemed obvious now. Shae had always been a bit short with people when she was tired. Less likely to filter herself.

They made it down to the creek, taking off their boots and socks and rolling up their pants before wading in. Cold mountain water bit at his calves, numbed his toes. They left the bucket on the bank, waiting to be filled with frogs.

"So, tell me about this wild outlaw romance of yours with the crazy mountain woman," Shae prompted, grinning mischievously.

"What?" Dustin laughed. "Wild outlaw romance?"

"You and Vivian rob trains together and then come back and live in an old bombed-out house. That's not even a little what I expected for adult-you."

Dustin shrugged. "Not much to tell. Vivian saved my life years ago, proclaimed she regretted it for a time, then I saved a bunch of her animals when her barn caught fire and she decided that meant I was at least likeable. When I told her about you, she offered to help me find out what happened to you. She taught me how to survive in the wilderness, how to fight if I needed to. It eventually turned into more than a friendship."

Now that he thought about it, he couldn't pinpoint the exact moment it had shifted from a friendship to something more. It just sort of had. He did know the moment he'd realized he loved her, though. He'd caught her quoting Hamlet to one of her horses when she thought he wasn't around. Something about it had been very sweet, very soft. It had made him realize how much she'd come to mean to him.

"She's... interesting," Shae said, stepping toward a half-submerged log to try to grab the frog that had hopped onto it.

Dustin stepped with her, trying to corner it.

"Very," Dustin replied.

"Russ doesn't trust her."

Shae snatched for the frog, managing to grab it between her fingers. She kept a careful grip on it as it wriggled, taking it over and depositing it in the bucket.

"Russ doesn't trust anyone," Dustin said as she came

back. "Part of being a soldier, I think."

"Makes sense. Honestly, him being a soldier makes the most sense out of anything you two have told me." She was scanning the water for more frogs as they talked. They could hear them, but none were in sight.

"Why?" Dustin asked.

"Chore-charts," Shae snickered.

"Oh, yeah," Dustin laughed. Damn, it felt good to laugh like this with her. "He's always been rather... orderly."

"Just a bit."

An easy silence settled between them.

"Everyone will be so glad to see you, Shae," Dustin said, already picturing it. "We'll have to be careful getting you home, but we can manage."

"And how is everyone?" Shae asked. "Russ mentioned you guys run a *ranch* now?"

"Yeah," Dustin said brightly. "You'll love it."

He launched into an explanation of everything, telling her about the house, cobbled together and full to the brim with family, everyone with their own rhythms. How Keaun had an amazing wife and three kids, Rose had a husband and twin daughters, how their younger siblings were in school—even though Darius was struggling and much preferred to be tinkering with cars. Shae listened attentively to all of it, frogs forgotten as they went to sit on the bank.

"What about you...?" Dustin asked after he finished. Shae did seem more like herself now that she'd slept, but she had a girlfriend, she had a life out in the world. She hadn't been some prisoner this whole time. Dustin was glad for that, relieved to know that many of the scenarios that had tormented him over the years weren't true, but it didn't make sense. If she had gotten away from her kidnappers, why hadn't she tried to come home at any point in the last ten years? She had known where they were going, mostly.

Shae responded slowly, "Well... after what happened, I got away a few weeks later. There was no way to get back to you guys, so I lived on the streets for a while. Dyed my hair, cut it, kept my head down. I was scared of what they'd do to me if anyone found out I was a Lockwood. I went into the foster system after about ten months, they just assumed I was a regular street kid, then a few months later I got adopted by a couple who lived in Seattle. Barbra and Devon Thomas. We lived there until I was fifteen, then Devon got a job in London and we moved there. Been in London ever since."

Dustin watched her closely as she spoke, comforted by the honesty in her eyes.

"You did reveal who you are, though..." Dustin said.

"When I thought it was safe, yeah." She glanced at him and smiled sadly. "The covens are a hard way to live, Dustin. It seemed like the Lockwood name would do more to protect me than hurt me once I was old enough to be in control of the situation."

"Has it?"

"It helped you find me, didn't it?"

Dustin smiled. "Yeah, but before that?"

Shae hummed, tilting her head back to examine the spiky pine branches above them.

"It did. And it led to some... interesting things as well."

"Like your girlfriend? What did you say her name was?" Dustin asked. This was one thing that worried him the most. Shae had made the comment that their relationship wasn't great last night, but still. If Shae loved this woman....

"Helen, and no, I met her before I revealed my identity. No, actually, what I was referring to was, well, something about Clayton."

Dustin frowned, opening and closing his mouth a few times as he tried to formulate a response. "Like... the guy Keaun was accused of murdering? That Clayton?"

"Mmhm. Let me ask you, did you know he had a younger step-brother?"

Dustin thought back, digging through the old memories. He'd only talked to Clayton a few times, but he'd talked to Keaun *about* Clayton a lot back then. He'd been at that age where his older brother was cool and suave and awesome, and by extension so were all his friends.

"Maybe?" Dustin said after a minute. "I kind of think Keaun might have mentioned that at some point."

"His name is Ariane Cordova," Shae said.

It took Dustin a minute, but when he got it his eyes went wide. "Your *co-star*?"

Shae nodded slowly, lips in a pursed smile. "I didn't know either until he told me."

"That's…." Dustin didn't know what that was, but he was glad he'd gotten Shae to safety before anything could come of it.

A distant clanging sound coming from the direction of the house interrupted them.

"Dinner," Dustin said, getting up and reaching out to give Shae a hand.

They put their socks and boots back on, Shae grabbing their bucket with their single frog. Together they walked back up the path, the smell of grilling fish wafting down to them.

Vivian and Russ were both on the patio at the outdoor kitchen, Russ standing over one of the grills and poking at some fish. Dustin was shocked to see him doing it. Even though Vivian was less protective of the outdoor kitchen than the indoor one, she still hadn't let him use it until a year after they met. The indoor kitchen had taken three years. Dustin did notice that she was watching Russ rather closely while spreading other food out on one of the tables, though.

As they stepped up onto the patio Shae paused, bucket in hand, and stared at Russ with a calculative expression. When he noticed and turned to look back at her, his expression became suspicious, having enough practice in sibling related nonsense to know something was up. The moment broke when Shae grinned and held up the bucket in his direction.

"Hungry, Russ?"

Russ eyed the bucket suspiciously. "Yes. But probably

not in whatever way you mean."

"Oh, come on, you thought it was so delicious last time!" Shae returned, tilting the bucket so Russ could see the frog inside.

"No, no, no!" Russ said, waving his hands around and taking a few quick steps back. Dustin could see he was fighting a laugh. Russ lost the fight when Shae started to chase him around with the bucket.

Dustin grinned and put his shirt back on before taking Russ' position at the grill as he watched his younger siblings chase one another. Vivian came over and stood with him, leaning against the counter.

"Feeling better?"

"Yeah," Dustin said.

"The soldiers have given up on the northern path. They're heading back to Granby to regroup," Vivian told him.

"Do we need to worry yet?"

She shook her head. "The fish is slow cooking, go finish the tree."

Dustin nodded and handed her the spatula. Vivian had already brought out her hardiest handsaw and laid it on the trunk, as well as marked the proper lengths along the trunk with one of her red-clay crayons. She'd brought her homemade log-lifter too, a triangular metal contraption designed to leverage tree trunks off the ground for easier cutting.

Thinking he should've left his shirt off Dustin clamped the end of the contraption around the trunk several feet from the end and used his bodyweight to pull the long metal bar to the ground, lifting the end of the trunk about two feet in the air. It took some wiggling of both the tree and the lifter, but eventually he had it situated right and he set to sawing his way through the green wood. Part of him missed his chainsaw back home, there wasn't a way to get gas for one out here, but the other part did enjoy the physicality of the task, even if it took much longer this way.

After a few logs were sawed off, he turned to see Russ looking at him with a bemused smile.

"You know, I don't think I've ever seen you listen to anyone as well as you listen to Vivian," he remarked.

Dustin shrugged. "Love does that."

"Awwwww," Russ chuckled. "How cute."

"Stick with a girlfriend for more than a month and maybe you'll see what it's like," Dustin teased. "How many have you had this year? Six? Seven? And it's only August!"

Russ flipped Dustin off as Vivian and Shae laughed. Dustin went back to work and half listened between pulls of the saw as Shae teased and interrogated Russ about his girlfriends. The last logs fell to the ground as Vivian lay the fish out on the table. The branches still needed done, and the logs would need to be stacked up on the porch, but it could wait until after dinner.

Vivian had once again laid out a good meal. The fish—grilled with lemon and sage, corn on the cob, mashed potatoes, biscuits, and stolen beer. A good old fashioned country dinner.

"I can't believe you have all this out here," Russ said, loading up his plate with an absurd amount of food.

Vivian shrugged, loading hers up as well. "The growing season is short at this altitude, but the soil is good. It's enough for the basics, and a lot of good herbs. I have some greenhouses up the hill a ways, with fruit trees and other things that don't do well out in the open. Plenty of deer, elk, and antelope for hunting, plus smaller game like coyotes and birds, and the fish. Lots of wild food, too. Dry air's good for preserving the food. The rest I get off the trains that pass through."

"And you do all that yourself? The farming and the robbing and everything else? How the hell do you have time?" Russ asked.

Vivian shrugged again. "Time is different when you're alone."

Shae and Dustin had filled their plates as well and begun eating, listening to the conversation as they did.

"What about robbing the trains, though?" Russ asked. "Dustin and I barely got away and that was with two of us."

Vivian smirked. "Well, they care a lot less about groceries compared to a living, breathing woman half the world knows and loves. That, and they're absolutely terrified of me."

"We don't exactly rob them in street clothes," Dustin clarified. "There's a reason they think she's a witch or a banshee or a ghost or whatever they're calling her right now."

"You play it up then?" Shae asked as she used her knife to get the kernels of corn off of the cob and mix them in with her potatoes. Dustin grinned, remembering how she'd always done the same thing when they were kids. Shae caught the look and rolled her eyes, flicking a stray kernel of corn across the table at him.

Vivian grinned around her fork. "Of course."

There was a hint of danger in the look that reminded Dustin of how deadly she was capable of being. She'd blow up a mountain if it suited her.

She continued, "Some well placed and well timed pyrotechnics, some creepy face paint or a mask, some nonsense words. They're horrified. They may be monsters themselves, but they can still feel fear as if they were human, especially the civilians. I may not be able to wage full-scale assaults like my family could, but I can certainly remind the coven of the terror they felt when we were at our height."

Shae's eyes gleamed and she leaned forward, looking eager. She had the same dangerous look in her eyes as Vivian did, though it took Dustin a moment of looking back and forth between them to realize it. Russ was watching them as well, lips pursed.

"So you rob their trains for supplies, but do you monitor what they're up to outside their trains?" Shae asked.

Vivian contemplated her a moment. Dustin got the sense she'd seen something she didn't like. A little bit of the tension he'd thought was gone settled back between his shoulders.

Eventually Vivian nodded. "To an extent. It's surprising how much a couple of lone train conductors will tell you when they're terrified you're going to put a curse on them. Or cut off a couple limbs. Besides, a lot of them think I'm a myth right up until they see me on their trains. I don't give them time to be anything other than scared, and when people are confronted by a myth, they have some interesting reactions."

"Have you heard anything about cryogenic corpses?" Shae asked.

Vivian did not answer her question, but neither did she break eye contact. Shae didn't seem to care, holding her gaze. Dustin looked between them, chest tight at the excitement on Shae's face. He was forcibly reminded of something that had happened in the Baja rebel camp just before they'd gone on the run for the second time.

They, along with their younger siblings, had been playing under the trees outside their tent one evening when their mother came up with a grim look on her face. She'd told them, haltingly, that they couldn't stay here. They were too well known, and still too close to Mendez. Dustin learned years later that some people in the camp had been talking about turning the family in for the reward money from Mendez.

Their mother had told them they each got one backpack, and most of the space would be for food. They could only take a few personal things. They hadn't had many personal things left at that point, but a lot was still left behind. Dustin's favorite book, Russ' stuffed tiger that he'd had since was born, their mother's journals where she liked to write scripts. But Shae... Dustin remembered that, after their mother had left to start her own packing, Shae had laughed. She'd looked excited. Dustin realized he'd never asked her why.

Russ ended up being the one to break the silence. "What do cryo-corpses have to do with anything? They're part of an unproven fad from during the wars."

"Maybe," Shae shrugged, breaking her gaze from Vivian and going back to her food. "I've just heard some things lately, that maybe they haven't woken them up, but they could be trying."

"You can't wake up a corpse," Russ said.

"I agree that you can't bring one back to life," Shae admitted. "But you don't need to be all that alive for your body to make blood."

The silence this time was heavy, so when Vivian spoke it rang out clear despite the low tone of her voice, "Blood farming cryo-corpses. That's your theory?"

Shae nodded. "The dots connect. Starving covens, thousands of preserved centuries old bodies with no one to miss them. Why wouldn't they give it a shot?"

"Because that's *abhorrent*," Russ said, voice hard. "I get they're vampires, but that—" he trailed off, shaking his head.

Vivian picked up the conversation, her words slow and careful, "I've seen cryo tanks on two trains in the last month. I've never seen them before."

"How do you know what they are, then?" Russ asked.

Vivian's tone was matter-of-fact in her response, "They're labeled."

"Abhorrent," Russ said again.

"Is it?" Shae said. "It's no worse than the women in Mendez being required to have two children, or that blood donations start at twelve there. In fact, it's probably better."

"Better?" Dustin spluttered. How had things gone so wrong when twenty minutes ago they were all laughing and teasing one another? "They're people, Shae!"

"Didn't we just establish that they're not?" Shae said. "They're corpses that will never wake up. Frozen in facilities where they'll never see the light of day and just suck up energy and money. Why not use them?"

"Enough," Vivian said, voice cutting through the fight.

Dustin glanced at her, throat tight and world spinning. He looked back at Shae and noticed she didn't have the good sense to look afraid of Vivian, which Dustin very much thought she should.

Vivian's tone remained quiet and firm as she spoke, with a distinct undercurrent of threat. "I do not trust you, Shae. I trust Dustin, I even trust Russell a bit. But not you. I tried, for Dustin's sake, but it is clear, at least to me, that you are not a good person."

"Vivian," Dustin said weakly.

She pressed on as if he hadn't spoken. "Maybe you've been brainwashed by the covens, maybe you've just been with them for too long, maybe there was something wrong with you all along. It doesn't particularly matter to me. You are going to leave my home, and you aren't going to come back. Should you try, I will shoot you."

A wounded sound escaped Dustin's lips and Vivian glanced at him, an apologetic look on her face.

"I'm sorry," she said, her voice softer now. "I've helped you search for her, and I always hoped it would end with some peace for you, that you'd find out she was dead and be able to mourn and move on. But she's not who you want her to be."

"Is this where you call me a monster?" Shae interjected.

Vivian turned back to her, expression passive. "No. Vampires are monsters. They are dangerous because of what they've become. You are dangerous because of what you've chosen to be. I'd take a monster over a dangerous human any day."

Shae stood up, putting her weight on her splayed fingers as she leaned on the table. "Says the woman who slits people's throats."

Vivian shrugged, going back to her food. "At least I admit it."

Shae watched her for a moment before turning and walking away, vanishing back into the house. The table was silent with her gone, the only sound Vivian's fork scraping on her plate. Russ' eyes were wide, and he kept glancing up at the house, then back to Dustin. Dustin felt like he couldn't breathe. Things had been so good down at the creek. She'd been so happy, so much like they were as kids. He stood up without a word and followed her into the house, not having any idea what would happen when he got inside.

19: The Coven Arrives

Shae slammed the door behind her, cursing herself for getting so caught up in the conversation about the cryo-corpses. She'd thought Vivian might tell her something useful for her game with Ariane. Her excitement had caused her facade to slip, and she was aware that it might have slipped too much to fix this time.

Once inside she wasn't sure where to go. If she had the faintest idea how to do it, she would've run for it and tried to find the soldiers out looking for her. But she knew Dustin would come after her and, given his skills, would find her easily. That could put he and Russ in reach of the soldiers, and she didn't want them getting seen or hurt. They were still her brothers. Her supposedly dead brothers, according to her.

As she stood in the middle of the house debating, the back door opened behind her and she turned to see Dustin standing there, a wounded look on his face. He closed the door softly and leaned against it, watching her. Shae watched him back, gauging her options.

"I'm sorry," Dustin said eventually. "I'm sorry I couldn't save you sooner, couldn't protect you from the covens."

Fuck. Did he really still believe her? Did he really still believe she'd been kidnapped? Brainwashed, even? There was no way. Dustin wasn't that naïve.

But maybe he *was* that desperate.

"Your girlfriend doesn't seem to care," Shae said.

"She's just being protective," Dustin replied, taking a few steps forward but not coming close. "Can we just… talk? Please?"

Shae sighed and nodded, following Dustin to the ratty couches and chairs. She settled herself in a patchwork armchair that had the back towards the opening in the side of the house, tucking her legs up under her. Dustin perched on the edge of a faded red couch across from her, elbows on his knees.

Shae didn't say anything, choosing to let Dustin lead the conversation.

"I don't know what you went through," Dustin started. "But you're family, and I'll always protect you. Once you get to Nahanni, things will be better. I promise. It won't matter what the covens are up to, what schemes they've got going."

Shae ached to come clean. To tell him to stop deluding himself because it was painful to watch. But it all circled back to being trapped out in the wilderness with him. Maybe she *could* walk out to the soldiers, but she knew her chances were slim even if Dustin didn't catch up with her. She didn't know this wilderness, how to navigate, what to eat, or even where she was supposed to go aside from sort of to the north. She didn't think for a moment Dustin would abandon her out here if she told him the truth, but the prospect of telling him still seemed complicated without a solid escape plan.

"Do you remember our home in Mendez?" Shae asked, voice soft.

He frowned but nodded.

"We had everything we ever wanted, but we never left home. We lived in a compound. Walls all the way around, topped with broken glass and barbed wire. We never even learned Spanish, despite living in Mexico."

"What does that have to do with anything, Shae?"

Shae took a slow breath, buying herself time to think. "Because that was all we knew. Then, all we knew was being on the run. Being wanted for something our parents did in reaction to a crime Keaun didn't even commit. We were never *kids*, Dustin. We were never *people*. Maybe things are better in Nahanni, I hope they are. But you've got to let the past go. Please. Let *us* go."

Dustin's eyes searched hers, his expression open and sad. "I miss you, Shae."

She smiled sadly. "You miss a memory, one you've sculpted and polished into something it... never was. If this is going to work, you have to let that go."

He would have to let her go too, but he didn't need to know that yet. She'd keep up the lie of going home with him until they were back among some sort of coven civilization, then she'd slip away. This time, though, she would leave a note. Doing it that way gave Russ and Dustin a better chance of getting away safely, and hopefully more closure than she'd left them with last time.

Dustin dropped his head into his hands and didn't respond. Shae sighed and got up, moving to sit next to him. She rested her head on his shoulder and let the silence remain.

After a few minutes he raised his head and turned to pull her into a tight hug. She let him, hugging back lightly.

"Nahanni will be better," Dustin muttered like it was a mantra.

Shae took a deep breath, exhausted by Dustin's inability to admit what was going on right in front of him.

"Will it?" Shae asked without thinking. "You and Russ told me about what it's like for the family there, but Russ also told me the coven has been lately. That you might be on the brink of war."

Dustin pulled back and shrugged. "Yeah, but Nahanni realizes that now. Before we left Russ' Commanding Officer finally agreed to sit down with Mom and talk about what she knows about the covens. They never would before. They just liked to pretend things weren't getting bad."

"So now Mom is a rancher *and* a spy. What the hell," Shae huffed.

Dustin laughed, but it sounded tired. "I guess so, yeah. Maybe you could help too. You'd have more up-to-date information than Mom."

Shae contemplated him, pulling hard on her feelings, trying to sort them out. She wasn't sure if love was the right word for any of those feelings, but loving them didn't have to be connected to keeping them safe. Really, keeping them safe was just as much a benefit to her as it was to them. Safety meant no one discovering that they were alive. If Nahanni was really at war, or about to be, then the picturesque story Russ and Dustin believed they had might not last.

"What would you want to know?" She asked.

"Well, anything, I guess. The Nahanni military doesn't seem to actually know much about vampires beyond the general stuff. Needs blood, incredible healing abilities, behead and burn to kill, etc.."

"Beheading doesn't kill them," Shae pointed out.

"Well, no, but it sure slows them down," Dustin said.

Shae conceded this point. "I honestly don't know that much about them beyond the basics either. If you wanted a breakdown of the weaknesses and strengths of the Turned, you should've brought my girlfriend with instead of locking her in the bathroom. She's the one who's obsessed with that stuff. Reads about it constantly."

Dustin blinked, head tilted in contemplation. "Would she help us? If we could find a way to contact her, would she come with and help us?"

Laughter burst out of Shae. "No! Not for a second. She loves everything about living in the covens, in London. She'd never want to be so cut off from the rest of the world."

Picturing Helen in the Yukon was comical. All Shae could see was a bundle of twenty sets of coats and hats and snow pants with a pair of grumpy blue eyes glaring out from their midst. No, that would never happen.

Before Dustin could say anything else, a distant whooping sound broke through the air. Dustin frowned and got up, walking to the opening in the side of the house and leaning against one of the aspen trees, eyes scanning the horizon. Shae joined him and in seconds picked out the shape of a helicopter in the distance. It was barely bigger than a pinhead from so far away, and heading south-west. Shae guessed that it wouldn't come anywhere near the house if it stayed on that heading, but if they were doing a search they'd make more passes in other directions.

"Vivian! Russ!" Dustin shouted, spinning around and grabbing Shae's hand. He pulled her with him as he raced back to the patio. Shae felt her heart racing, excitement buzzing in her veins. She couldn't help it, as much as she wanted her brothers safe.

Vivian met them right outside the door. "Into the barn. If they get any closer and they've got thermal cameras we should be able to hide among the animals."

They all followed her, Russ hesitating for a moment as he stared at Shae. Dustin broke him out of his hesitation by grabbing him with his free hand, the other still clasped with Shae's, and spinning him around.

The barn was dark as they dived inside, Vivian slamming the door behind them. Inside was dimly lit by evening light filtering through cracks in the walls. A large pen of sheep and pigs took up the left side and horse paddocks took up the right. Vivian ordered everyone to kneel in the sheep pen and to stay quiet.

Shae thought the request for quiet was excessive. It wasn't like the people in the helicopter could hear them with all the noise of the machine. But she did as Vivian said, crouching on her toes to keep her knees out of the muck on the floor. The sheep smelled disgusting. Wet and musty and something else she didn't have a name for.

"They'll see the house," Russ whispered.

Vivian raised an eyebrow. "Do you think I have an aspen tree growing through my dining room for fun?"

"Your animals, though," Russ pressed. "No specialist is going to ignore animals in pens, in a barn, in an area that's supposed to be abandoned."

Vivian shrugged. "Let them come. I have no qualms taking out a helicopter."

She gave Dustin a look and pointed over to a corner of the barn where there was a large, green metal cabinet. Dustin stayed crouched as he ran over, gingerly opening the door and slipping a hand inside. He came back holding a very modern looking sniper rifle. A gun wouldn't do much to a Turned, unless it was a headshot, but a helicopter explosion would get the job done.

Russ socked Dustin on the arm, whispering angrily, "Bad idea. They crash here and the rest of their group know exactly where we are."

Dustin whispered back, "Relax. I'm not going to do anything unless they spot us. Now shut up."

Russ clenched his jaw but stayed quiet. The helicopter

was hard to hear over the animals at first, the noise rising and falling as the machine moved. Shae wasn't sure how close they passed, but didn't think it had been very close as it never got all that loud. Vivian was the first to move once the sound had faded and stayed gone, striding over to the cabinet Dustin had retrieved the gun from. She pulled out a large handheld radio and fiddled with the dials until a strange series of beeps came over it. It took Shae a minute, but she realized it was Morse code, the only way the Turned could use radios.

"Finished grid 14. No activity. Return for fuel," Dustin interpreted.

Vivian clicked the radio off. "Time to go. Russ, Dustin, take care of my animals and get everything tied down out here. Shae, you're helping me pack up inside. We're out in half-an-hour."

Everyone looked equally confused at the division of labor Vivian had proposed, and none of them moved.

Vivian rolled her eyes. "I promise I will not kill Shae in the next thirty minutes. Let's go."

She turned and left, Shae following after a moment. Vivian only said she'd kill Shae if Shae ever came *back* here, after all. And Shae sort of doubted she'd even do that, given how much she seemed to care about Dustin.

They walked inside and as soon as they were through the door Vivian turned to look at Shae. Shae could barely see her. The sun had set enough while they were in the barn to send the house into darkness. Only a trace of ambient light made it in through the opening in the side of the house. Just enough to accent the curve of Vivian's cheek and the long, thin scar on the right side of her chin, a tiny bit of the light glinting in her near-black eyes.

"I thought we were on a timetable?" Shae said.

Vivian didn't answer at first. Shae was growing tired of how often she seemed to pause before she spoke.

Finally, she said, "You're trying so hard to convince your brothers you're a good person, but you aren't. I think you break anyone who comes too close to you, and I don't think you care."

"Good for you," Shae said, crossing her arms.

The last of the light faded from her face as she answered, voice soft, "If you break Dustin, I will do worse than killing you."

Shae eyed the place Vivian had been, willing her eyes to adjust faster. It didn't matter though, as she heard Vivian turn and walk away. A moment later a light flared up in the kitchen and Shae saw Vivian closing the glass on a lantern on the wooden island.

Shae stepped up to the threshold of the cluttered kitchen, not crossing into it, and looked around. She hadn't really gotten a chance to examine it before. The homemade wooden plank island sat at the center of a U of cabinets and counters. A battered fridge was against one wall and Shae watched as Vivian pulled one of its doors open, revealing a sawdust covered block of ice at the bottom and containers stacked on the shelves. Vivian grabbed an armful and tossed them onto the island, shutting the door again.

Next she moved to the cabinets, pine with the same flat mountain scene chiseled into each door. Some doors were missing and all the handles were mismatched or missing as well. As Vivian opened doors Shae caught sight of stacks of canned food, jars of preserves, and dozens of eclectic sets of dishes and other kitchenwares.

Once Vivian had a good sized stack of food she produced several leather bags from under the island and began to strategically pack the food into them, tetrising it all together. From what Shae could make out, it was a lot of jerky, dried fruit, oatmeal, and rice.

Knotting the bags closed, she blew out the lantern and slung the bags over her shoulder. Walking out of the kitchen, she grabbed a couple masks Shae hadn't noticed off of pegs on the wall between the kitchen and dining room. One looked like a large piece of tree bark with two holes for the eyes and no other features. The other was glossy black and looked sort of like the top half of a short beaked bird skull.

You didn't bring masks unless you thought you'd be seen by someone you didn't want to see you, Shae realized. Vivian wasn't planning on avoiding the soldiers.

20: Leaving

Dustin secured the last saddle as Vivian came out of the house, Shae behind her. He tried to convince himself he wasn't relieved that Shae had come back out. He didn't really think Vivian would hurt her, but there was still a twinge of that relief anyway. Dustin reached out and took one of the bags of food from Vivian, turning to secure it to Pinenut's saddle.

Vivian stopped and stared at the gray horse as he slowly chewed on some nice grass he'd found. "We're gonna need to switch horses...."

Dustin glanced at Pinenut's vacant expression and couldn't help but agree. Pinenut was not a long distance horse. Nor was he a good horse for much of anything else. In fact, of the horses at the house, only Kodiak was good for a longer trip.

"Who do you have at the lower paddock?" Dustin asked. Vivian had about twenty rideable horses total, and she had them spread out across six or seven paddocks in the area. She kept roughly thirty other horses as well.

Some were too old to ride, some had never been broken for riding but didn't mind Vivian and Dustin being around, and a few would happily murder any human who looked at them.

Vivian secured her bag to the back of an older mare named Arrow as she spoke, "Rails and Digger, they're good for a trip. Maybe Mudcake. He's still young, though. I've never taken him out far."

"I'll take him then," Dustin volunteered.

Vivian nodded and swung up into her saddle. Russ and Shae had already mounted up on Ghost and Pinenut. The last rays of the sun had vanished, revealing a moonless night. With no electric light to dilute them, the stars blazed bright, the Milky Way swirling a clear path above them. Nights like this Dustin could see as well as he could in the daylight.

"Traps are set?" Vivian asked.

Dustin nodded. "The mines in the driveway and around the perimeter are primed, the spike pits opened and disguised. Vivian, I'm sorry. I didn't mean to bring this down on your home."

He hated knowing that he'd put this place in danger.

Vivian shrugged. "Relax. It isn't the first time they've figured out where I live. And they won't be coming near the house anyway."

"They went back to refuel, not give up looking," Russ pointed out.

Vivian smiled. "So we'll give them something better to look at."

With that she clucked her tongue and knocked her heels on Arrow's sides, leading the way along an unmined, winding path down the driveway. Everyone followed her, Dustin bringing up the rear. He spared one glance back at the house, the chipped white stucco bright in the starlight.

Once they passed the mined area Dustin urged Kodiak a little faster, reining him back in once they arrived next to Vivian and Arrow.

"What's your plan?" Dustin asked.

She glanced at him out of the corner of her eye. "What's yours?"

"Bring Shae home, same as always."

Vivian hummed and Dustin could tell she didn't agree, but she didn't press it. "Well, then I guess we'll have to get you three back to Nahanni. But first, we need to get the soldiers out of here. We're going to lay a false trail."

"How?" Russ asked. He'd trotted Ghost up on Vivian's other side, leaving Shae behind the three of them as they worked their way down the same path they'd come up so early that morning.

"They're here for Shae, so we let them see Shae," Vivian replied.

"No!" Dustin said vehemently. "We are not using my little sister as bait."

"I might be amenable to being bait," Shae said from behind them. "Depends on the exact plan."

Dustin turned and looked at Shae incredulously.

Vivian turned to look at her as well. "We're going to

let them see you from a distance. Let them radio back that they've seen you, let it slip that we are going to Baja. And then Dustin and I are going to kill all of them."

⁂

An hour later they'd switched horses and had stopped on the crest of a sage-covered hill looking across a small valley towards a bluff half-a-mile away. On the bluff was a buzz of activity from a cluster of soldiers. Vivian had brought along four of the more wild horses, and they weren't happy about it, stomping and yanking at their leads that Dustin had secured to a nearby tree.

"Why'd they move here from Granby?" Shae wondered.

Vivian shrugged. "Could be a million reasons."

Centuries ago there had been a tiny town of less than a hundred people perched there. Vivian had told Dustin its name once, but he couldn't remember it now. At the bottom of the valley the Colorado river wound through the fields, mellower here on the flat land than it was in the surrounding canyons. They'd be able to cross it without issue.

No ruins still stood in this town, Dustin knew. No cover. Just vague outlines of the footprints of buildings where the rotting wood had nourished the soil. You wouldn't have even noticed them unless you really looked.

The whole bluff was lit up like a stadium. The helicopter, a little five-seater, sat off to the west side, its blades still. To the east side stood a large brown canvass tent. A myriad of ATVs and dirt-bikes were parked around the perimeter, and there were over a dozen tiny figures striding back and forth in the light. The night carried the buzz of speech, but not the distinction of words. Russ was looking at it all and shaking his head.

"They're idiots! You can see them for miles, and they're completely exposed!" He grumbled.

Really, though, they didn't have many other options, Dustin thought. The old roads in the area weren't passable by car or even ATV, Vivian and her family had made sure of that over the years, and no one had ever successfully habituated horses to vampires. Their only efficient way through with all their gear was along the tracks, which ran at the back of the bluff along the contour of the hill behind it, and with their helicopter. Dustin suspected they'd set up camp here over Granby specifically because it *was* empty and open. No buildings to hide in, or get blown up in. They were exposed on three sides, yes, but they'd assume that would mean anyone trying to attack them would be exposed as well. The only cover they had, if it could be called that, was the hill to their north.

Vivian watched the camp through binoculars. "They're not bothering to be stealthy because they don't think they're in danger."

"I thought you attacked them constantly," Shae said.

"Yeah, but not *here*," Dustin told her. "We just quietly rob them here, and save the big attacks for random places miles to the west and east so they can't pin down where we are. Mostly."

"And, at best, they think we're only four or five people," Vivian added. "Even then, the biggest attack I've staged against them since I met Dustin was five years ago against twenty low level politicians on their way to some conference. They don't see us as a threat against a bunch of soldiers."

Vivian lowered the binoculars and handed them to Dustin. He scanned the camp, tallying up the soldiers. It looked to be just the fifteen Vivian had said they'd send, but it was hard to be sure without having a way to see into the tent. Quite a few more might be in there. He'd handled a lot with Vivian, but this many trained specialists....

Her plan was a good one, even if it was dangerous. A false trail would give them time to get away safely, would pull attention off of Vivian's home. He knew it was the right move, and he trusted her to get them all out alive. Russ had put up a fight about it, but Vivian had shot down all his worries, saying they didn't have time for them.

Dustin lowered the binoculars. "Let's go then."

Dustin swung his leg over Kodiak, stepping back onto solid ground. He'd broken off from the others, taking a wide path around the bluff and up the hill behind it. Knowing this was their only cover, and also the high ground, Dustin thought he would have met at least some resistance by now. He wasn't sure how he felt about the fact that he hadn't.

He secured Kodiak loosely to a sage bush fifteen yards further up the hill. Enough to let the horse know he needed to stay through all the noise, but easy to get away from if any vampires got too close. Dustin pulled the sniper rifle he'd brought around from behind his back and found a log to rest it on, peering through the scope at the camp a hundred and fifty yards down the hill. Several vampires had begun to mount up on ATVs and dirt-bikes, and he could hear them much clearer now. The ones heading out were part of a ground search team, sweeping under the trees where the helicopter couldn't see. The ATV riders each had a rifle strapped across their backs, and Dustin saw pistols on the hips of the others still walking around.

Taking a deep breath, he aimed and squeezed the trigger. A vampire in the middle of the group on ATVs slumped to the side, smacking into the ground next to his vehicle as the sound echoed through the hills. A frozen pause enveloped the camp, everyone staring at the downed soldier, before a roar of noise burst out, vampires streaming from the tent and looking up the hill towards him. The wind was on his side, so Dustin knew they couldn't smell him, but he also knew their hearing was good enough to eventually pinpoint the sound of his gun, even with the echo. That was the plan, though.

Swinging his gun to the right, he took several shots at the chopper, unsure where its gas tank was. When he saw a spray of fuel, he lifted his head and slid in a tracer round, aware of his limited time. Three vampires had begun to ascend the hill, stymied only momentarily by a crumbly ten-foot cliff. Dustin settled his gun on a spare gas can strapped to the back of the closest ATV, taking a final shot and igniting the little red container. The heat and power of the ATV gas exploding was enough to set off the more stable helicopter fuel and blow the chopper into the air. Shrapnel went in all directions, slicing through vampires as flames mushroomed up into the sky, bathing everything in orange.

The vampires screamed, running in all directions now, and the ones coming for him had just made it up the cliff. Dustin shoved the rifle under the log he'd been using as a stand and drew a pistol instead, taking two quick shots at the advancing pair of vampires, aware that the third seemed to have vanished. Both dropped and he waited, focused on the fight and ready to jog down the hill and into the thick of it. But it wasn't time yet.

He scanned the perimeter of the chaos, waiting for the planned moment.

And... there!

Russ was at the edge of the fray, face masked with tree bark. He had a pistol in one hand and Shae's reins tied to the pommel of his saddle. Shae's wrists were looped with rope and there was a gag in her mouth. It made Dustin sick to see, even though he knew it was fake. The rope around Shae's wrists wasn't tied, and they'd given her a small pistol to hide in her boot. Russ took quick, accurate shots at any vampires that made for him and Shae.

As Dustin stood to race down the hill the missing third vampire came up from his side, Dustin catching the movement in his peripheral vision just in time, falling on his back in a smooth motion to avoid them as they leaped. Rolling onto his knees, he sent two quick shots into its head as they spun back to face him, pistol raised. He'd felt something bite into his shoulder as he shot but ignored it. Another roll and he was back on his feet, racing into the fight. Vivian was already there, having come up from the valley. She had a sword in hand, the hilt a length of elk antler, and laid waste to any vampire who got close. Bits of flesh and a few whole limbs were scattered at her feet, several detached hands still clenched around guns. Dustin pulled out a matching short sword from the sheath on his back, wielding it with his right hand while he kept the pistol in his left.

"Baja promised us no interference!" Vivian screamed as Dustin worked his way closer. She had on her shiny black bird mask, one of her favorites. Dustin had settled for a smear of green face-paint covering the top half of his face and a scarf wound around the bottom. Easier to see down the scope that way.

"They promised us a lot of shit," Dustin ground out, slicing the throat of a vampire who got too close.

"I'll kill 'em for this when we get back!" Vivian growled over the noise, shoving her sword up into the gut of a vampire with so much force his feet momentarily lifted a few inches off the ground.

Dustin was in the rhythm of the fight now, shooting

and slicing with his back to Vivian's. The vampires had thinned out considerably, their bodies scattered on the ground. A young soldier made a grab for him and Dustin sliced cleanly through the tendons at the base of their wrist, feeling his blade stick in the bones. He yanked it back out and kicked the screeching monster away, shooting it in the head as it stumbled back.

The soldier distracted him enough that he missed another lunging up from his side, fangs bared. Dustin felt the pressure as the creature clamped down on his right forearm, the vampire looking shocked as its fangs caught in the thick leather bracer he had on. Dustin shot the soldier between the eyes. It dropped soundlessly, eyes rolled back.

The only sound left now was the crackling of flames, and occasional moaning. The chopper explosion had taken out most of the forces. Dustin and Vivian surveyed the scene, checking that none of the vampires were still moving in any effective manner, before turning their attention to the tent, and the frantic tapping coming from inside.

"Backup! Send backup! We're getting massacred! Baja rebels!"

Vivian slid her sword between the flaps of the opening, pushing one aside. The sole occupant was the radio operator. He spun and looked at them, dropping the handset in favor of raising his gun only to be met with Dustin's own, as well as Vivian's small backup pistol. She much preferred knives and swords, but she always kept a gun as a backup.

"You can only shoot one of us before the other shoots you," Vivian said. "Pick wisely."

"They know you have Shae Lockwood. They know who you are," he spat, gun switching back and forth between them.

"No, they don't," Vivian replied as Dustin shot him through the eye when the gun was between them.

Vivian dropped her sword, letting the tent fall shut. She had a gash on her lower right arm, but it seemed to already be clotting so Dustin didn't mention it. Bandages came later. He felt that he had a couple as well, though he didn't remember when or how he'd gotten them aside from the one on his left shoulder. He glanced at his arm, seeing blood soaking the leather. Peeling back the edges, he checked the wound, finding what looked like a graze from a gunshot just above his tattoo. There was still enough adrenalin in his system that he didn't feel it, but it had also started to clot enough that he wasn't worried. It might need stitches, but those came later as well.

"They'll send more backup," Vivian said. "We need to be well out of here before they do. Burn the bodies. Quickly."

Dustin nodded and turned to do as she asked, finding Russ and Shae standing a few feet away, surveying the destruction. They'd left their horses tied to sage outside the perimeter of the burning bluff.

"You actually did it," Russ said in awe. "You two took out fifteen fucking vampires, soldiers, on your own."

"You got in a couple takedowns too," Vivian said, voice distracted. "I saw you drop them."

Russ shook his head, eyes sweeping over the downed vampires.

"What?" Dustin asked Vivian.

"They sucked," she muttered, scanning the soldiers as well. "Those weren't specialists."

"I agree," Russ said, frowning. "Soldiers, yeah, but not specialists."

The three of them went silent for a moment, looking around the destroyed camp as Shae hung back. Some of the vampires were already burning.

"Doesn't change the plan," Vivian said eventually. "We laid one false trail, we're going to lay another as we leave. Those trails were the whole point of this."

Dustin nodded and grabbed a long stick from the ground, holding it over a flaming sage bush until it lit. The smell of the burning sage was strong, but not strong enough to drown out the gut-turning scent burning flesh. Vampires didn't quite smell like humans when they burned, but the scent came close enough. Sort of like meat gone bad. Dustin always found this to be the hardest part of their fights. He knew the vampires weren't human, that the world was better off without them, but once the fight ended it was hard not to feel uncomfortable at the destruction.

Shae had been quiet and Dustin avoided her gaze. He realized this couldn't have been pleasant for her to see, that it wouldn't have been pleasant even if Dustin hadn't been the one doing it. He had been, though.

Taking his burning stick, he began touching it to the clothes of the vampires who weren't already burning. Vivian did the same. Military uniforms didn't burn easy, though, so Vivian instructed Russ to grab a spare gas can off the back of an intact ATV and douse everything. He did, struggling to manipulate the heavy can with only one good hand.

"Aren't you worried this will start a forest fire?" Shae asked, not moving to help.

Vivian shook her head as she lit the tent on fire. "Without humans around this forest burns a little every few years, like it should, and it has been a wet summer. Big fires don't have what they need to get hold. This will burn through the sage for a while, then put itself out."

Dustin left them, taking a mostly empty gas can up the hill to the three he'd shot there and lighting them. Retrieving his rifle, he swung back up into Kodiak's saddle and trotted down the hill, Kodiak leaping down the short cliff without hesitation. Dustin met everyone else where Shae and Russ had tied their horses. They had Mudcake as well, Vivian having left him down in the valley since he'd never been around a fight before, and the four wilder horses.

Vivian tied a strip of cloth around her bleeding arm, tightening it with her teeth and waving away Russ' offer of help. Dustin knew she wouldn't treat the wound until they made it well away from here. The cloth was a stopgap to keep it clean. Dustin had done the same to his wounds.

Vivian took the wilder horses and, one by one, spooked them off towards the west along an old road. They galloped away and Dustin figured they'd probably join up with the mustangs in the area or form their own wild herd. As Vivian sent the horses off Dustin pulled out a series of interlocking poles covered in dangling chains from one of Kodiak's saddle bags. Linking them together, he assembled a contraption to drag along behind Mudcake and hide their own hoofprints, attaching it to Mudcake's saddle with lengths of sturdy rope.

"Now what?" Russ asked as Vivian and Dustin worked.

The heat of the fire beat into his back, turning his clothes uncomfortably hot where they touched his skin.

Dustin mounted Mudcake as Vivian swung up into Kodiak's saddle, looking back over the burning camp. "We head for Hayden," Vivian said. "It's a little coven town right on the border of the unclaimed territory. You guys can get a car there, take it home. As long as our trails worked, and Shae keeps her head down, you'll be fine."

Russ nodded, glancing over at Shae. Vivian knocked her heels on Kodiak's side, careful what path she took so that the trail from the wild horses wouldn't be messed up. Shae followed her on Rails, but Russ hung back.

Dustin looked at him, head tilted. "What?"

Russ glanced over at Vivian and Shae, who were now a good twenty yards away. The roar of the fire behind them drowned out his voice the first time he spoke, and Dustin moved closer to hear him better when he repeated himself.

"I'm not sure we should take her home, Dustin."

Dustin laughed, the laugh fading when he realized Russ was serious. "Why?"

"She's not right, Dustin. She's… she practically let us take her on the train, not knowing who we were. She's lied to us about what happened ten years ago. When the chopper came near Vivian's she looked elated. And just now, in the fight, even over the gunfire and through the gag, I heard her laughing, Dustin."

Dustin drew himself up, leveling a glare at his brother. "You heard wrong. We are not abandoning her."

"I didn't say we abandon her. I'm saying we get to Hayden and leave her there, let her walk into the police station and say she miraculously escaped. Stop shoving your head up your ass for two seconds because I know you think she's off too. We can't bring her home, Dustin. *She is dangerous*."

"She's our sister," Dustin spat.

"She abandoned us once, Dustin. There's nothing stopping her doing it again. She doesn't give a damn about this family, and I don't know that she ever has. She will *always* put herself and her own interests first. Right now running around in the woods playing hostage is fun for her, maybe it would be fun to go home and see everyone too, but the second she gets board she'll leave again to find something else she considers fun. What if that's giving away the secrets of our settlement just so she can see what happens? Because, honestly, her doing that wouldn't surprise me at this point."

Dustin's chest heaved, breaths rushing through his nose. "Fuck. You."

"Dustin—"

"*Go*," Dustin ordered, pointing toward Shae and Vivian.

Russ hesitated, then did as asked, following their exact path.

Dustin worked Mudcake forward, careful to obscure only their path and not the wild horses', looking back to check that the contraption hid their hoofprints well enough. It seemed to do the trick, the chains beating up the dirt as they rattled over it. A trained tracker would see the marks on the relatively open dirt of the bluff, Dustin knew, but it was only a couple yards to the sage where the marks would be better hidden. Hopefully it would be enough, along with the other precautions they'd take along the way.

Once in the sage he trotted Mudcake up closer to the others, though staying in the back to keep obscuring their tracks. With immense effort he tried to strip the anger from his face as he came up behind Shae. He examined his sister, wondering how Russ could be so wrong.

She almost glowed in the starlight with how pale her skin was. It wasn't the silvery pale of a vampire, there was still a flush of life there, but it was close enough. Even in the darkness the tracery of veins on her neck and exposed lower arms were easy to pick out, even a few on her face when she glanced back at him. Deep down he was aware a person didn't get that pale without trying. She barely even had the family freckles, only a few here and there along her nose and cheeks.

He thought back on the photos of her he'd seen in the two coven papers about her tour. In both of them she'd had on little makeup, her clothes showing as much skin as possible without stripping her nude. He'd seen plenty other famous humans in the coven papers over the years and thinking back he realized he couldn't recall any of them being as exposed as she was. It hadn't been some standard thing to look like that... it had been a choice she made. She had tried to display herself in a way that would most appeal to the vampires.

"What?" Shae asked, looking back at him again.

"... nothing," Dustin said.

She rolled her eyes, turning her attention back to the direction they were going.

Dustin spared a glance over at his brother, finding Russ watching him with a grim expression. Russ couldn't be right. Shae was their sister.

21: Breaktime

Three days. Three days on horseback. This time Shae was sure her legs would never be the same shape again. The ride had been smooth—mostly they'd been on old roads which helped them make good time—it had just also been relentless. They'd finally stopped for more than sleep or a quick break in the middle of the afternoon of the third day, tying up the horses along a lazy little river meandering through a valley full of late season wildflowers. Shae took in their heavy, dying scent with every inhale.

According to Vivian and Dustin the stop was to replenish their food and water, but Shae saw them wincing almost as much as she was and figured food and water was an excuse. Dustin stretched, cracking his back, and mumbled something about going to set traps. He cajoled Russ into coming with him so he could show Russ how to do it. The two had been icy with one another for the first couple days, and Shae wasn't sure why, but they seemed to have made amends some time in the last twenty-four hours.

As soon as Dustin and Russ vanished over a small rise Vivian stripped off all her clothes and flopped into the shallow edge of the river. She sighed contentedly as her long black hair fanned out and swayed in the water, mingling with the plants.

"That can't be very warm," Shae remarked, walking up to the edge of the water, boots squishing in the damp dirt.

Vivian shrugged. "It isn't. But it feels great after riding for so long."

With that she pushed away from the shallow edge and into deeper waters. It was barely more than a few feet deep at the most, but she ducked under the water and stayed under long enough to swim a few yards against the meager current before resurfacing. Shae watched as she repeated this a few more times, secretly hoping Vivian might drown.

Since the battle Vivian seemed to have taken a stance of pretending Shae didn't exist. Somehow it was more unnerving to be glossed over by Vivian than acknowledged by her. She spent most of her time chatting softly with Dustin, and with Russ, whom she seemed to have warmed up to considerably since the fight. He'd peppered her with questions about the way she'd fought, how she'd learned to fight like that, what she thought about the coven's fighting tactics. Vivian always kept her responses quiet and away from Shae during these conversations.

Vivian and Dustin had also started to train Russ in some of their techniques. He'd gotten rather good at turning around in the saddle while in motion, but held off learning to stand up in it given his broken arm and the high likelihood of falling. Vivian had also shown him how to toss knives in the air and make sure to always catch them by the handle—a technique taught with a crude wooden dummy knife she carved.

When Dustin and Russ came back over the hill Vivian stopped swimming and drifted back towards their camp. She didn't come out of the river, though, instead settling on a rock in the middle. She folded her legs under her and peered out of the water that came up to right below her eyes. Every minute or so she'd tilt her head back and take a few deep breaths before going back to being mostly underwater.

"Are you going for some sort of selkie now?" Dustin asked.

She tilted her head back and smiled sweetly. "Come over and find out."

"You two flirting scares me," Russ stated. He was eying Vivian's pile of clothes on the edge of the river, seeming to try to distract himself with the evidence of Vivian's nakedness rather than look at the nakedness itself.

"I'm pretty sure she's offering to drown me, not kiss me," Dustin replied. Vivian only answered with a devious smile.

"So, mighty hunters, what's for dinner?" Shae asked Dustin.

Dustin turned to rifle through their pile of saddle-bags.

"Depends what wanders into our traps," he said. "We

set some near what looks like a couple woodchuck dens, and along a few rabbit trails. Otherwise our choices are jerky and… jerky."

"Check the bottom of my left pack," Vivian told him as she wrung out her hair and redressed. "I've got some graham crackers in there somewhere, and there should be some dried fruit."

Dustin nodded and pulled Vivian's packs over, pulling out the battered box of crackers and a small leather satchel, which he opened to reveal a pile of dried apples and raspberries. Dustin divided everything up and Shae took her share, sitting down next to the campfire Russ was stoking to life. She sucked on one of the apple slices, watching her brothers.

Something had changed since the fight. Dustin had been quiet, hardly speaking at all, while Russ seemed excited to be here for the first time. Shae couldn't figure it out, at least with Dustin. Russ being excited about a battle made sense, as a soldier. But Dustin. He said he'd been in fights with Vivian before, though this had been the most serious, so what was there to be upset about? They'd won, and there'd been no sign that they'd been followed, so their false trails must have worked.

After about an hour Dustin got up and went back over the rise, returning with a dead woodchuck dangling from one hand. He set to work butchering it as Vivian sharpened four sticks, handing one to each of them. Shae took hers and watched as Vivian speared a slice of meat that Dustin handed her and held it over the fire to cook. Shae did the same, waiting until the meat was nice and crispy before taking a bite. It was a bit of a strange taste, a little greasy, though Shae wasn't sure if that was because of what it was or how it was cooked. No one else commented on it, though, so she didn't think much of it.

What she did think much of, though, was that her brothers both seemed to be watching her. Dustin was trying to be sly about it, glancing out of the corner of his eye when he thought Shae wouldn't notice while Russ wasn't bothering to hide his observation.

"What?" Shae asked, skewering another piece of meat from the pile Dustin had made on a scrap of leather.

"Why'd you come with us, Shae?" Russ asked. Dustin choked on his piece of meat and flailed a hand out in Russ' direction, but Russ pressed on. "You had no idea who we were when we grabbed you. You could've screamed, fought harder, anything. You had so many opportunities to get away from us in that first twenty minutes. Why didn't you try to take them?"

Shae sat back a little, rolling her cooking stick between her fingers as she regarded her little brother. He'd become hard, Shae realized. Maybe from life in general, maybe from being a soldier. Either way, his expression made it clear he didn't trust her nor anything she'd said and done up to this point, and he was done deferring to Dustin in this plan.

This was it, then.

Shae sighed. "I'm assuming 'I was afraid' isn't going to cut it?"

"No," Russ stated.

"It doesn't matter," Dustin cut in, looking between the two of them, eyes pleading for the conversation to be over.

Vivian watched it all with a blank face, gaze shifting between the three of them.

"It does matter," Shae said. "Russ obviously suspects me of some ulterior motive."

"He doesn't suspect you of anything!" Dustin said.

"I damn well do," Russ said, his voice remaining calm.

"What, then?" Shae asked, still rolling her stick between her fingers.

"I think you're acting," Russ said. "I think you let us take you because you thought it would get you attention, because you thought it would be fun. I think you left on your own when we were kids and spun the kidnapping story for attention. I think you would do anything to keep yourself in the limelight, even betraying the people you say you love. I think you're dangerous, and I don't want to bring you home."

Shae smiled softly, feeling almost relieved that the charade could be over. "You always were the most observant in the family, Russell."

"Am I right then?" He said lowly.

Everyone was silent. Dustin looked on the verge of tears.

"Mostly," Shae responded. "When you first grabbed me, and I realized you were there for *just* me, I wanted to know what was going on, so I didn't fight. Then something about you two seemed familiar, so I didn't try to leave the shop. Since then, well, I've been going along with it. I don't have the skills to walk out of the wilderness on my own. I did leave on my own when we were kids, because I didn't want to spend my life in the dirt. But I spun the kidnapping story to protect myself from the Lockwood name, not for attention. We were still wanted back then, and if it had come out who I was, I would've been immediately handed over to Mendez. Prisoner or bait for the rest of the family, things wouldn't have gone well."

"Were you ever really going to come home with us?" Russ asked.

She shook her head slowly. "No."

Things went quiet between all of them, the only sound the crackling of the flames. Shae's bit of meat had turned into a blackened hunk, but she didn't care. Dustin was staring at her, a few tears running down into his beard. She felt a small pang of regret at this, but knew it was for the best. No more lies. He opened and closed his mouth a few times before shaking his head and getting up to walk away, vanishing over the rise.

Vivian watched him go before turning to look at Shae. "If I didn't think it would hurt him more than he's already hurting, I would leave you to die out here. Alone and unremembered."

After Dustin left Russ tried to go after him. Vivian stopped him, saying Dustin would come back in his own time and if Russ wandered off to try to find him, he was liable to get lost. Russ went anyway and Vivian followed him, leaving Shae alone in their camp.

She pulled out her bedroll and laid back to watch the stars come out. As much as she'd wanted to avoid the truth coming out while they were still in the middle of nowhere, she was glad it had. The weight of Dustin's expectations had become exhausting. Things would be easier now. No false stories and plans she wasn't committed to. They'd split up and she could go back to her life and come up with a good story for the press while Dustin and Russ went back to theirs.

"Where's Russ and Vivian?" Dustin asked, appearing behind her head and looking down at her. His hair was out of its normal half ponytail and it looked like he'd been running his hands through it, sending it splaying wildly about his head. He looked rugged and exhausted.

"Russ went after you. Vivian went after Russ to make sure he didn't fall off a cliff or something."

"Oh," Dustin answered, still looking down at her without moving.

"This is not your best vantage point," Shae told him in an attempt to get him to move out of the way of the stars.

He sighed and came to sit next to her, not speaking.

"I don't get why you're so surprised," Shae said eventually. "You were the one who always talked about leaving when we were kids. Said you wanted to go to Italy, didn't you? See Rome?"

He made a small sound like she'd hit him. "But I

never *did it*, Shae. It was just talk."

"And what if I hadn't left? Would it have stayed just talk?"

Dustin didn't answer. Shae could see his shoulders tightening beneath his faded red shirt.

"It wasn't just talk," Shae continued. "You wanted to leave too, because you couldn't stand it either. You couldn't stand the hunger and the fear and the confusion. I remember the things you said back then, Dustin. How you blamed Mom and Dad and even Keaun."

Dustin winced and made another soft, unhappy noise. "I was a kid. I didn't understand. I didn't know how much it would break our family."

Shae sat up and rested her forearms on her knees. "The family isn't broken, Dustin. You're all alive. You're together. You have a home. Do you know how many families out there can't say the same? Let alone one as big as ours?"

"But you aren't with us," Dustin pleaded. "We aren't together if you aren't there."

Shae sighed and moved so she was crouching in front of Dustin, putting her hands on either side of his face.

"Stop lying to yourself," Shae said firmly. "You have a good life, you all do. Don't throw it away on a memory. I'm not coming back. I am never coming back. Now you know I'm alive, and I *am* sorry you ever suspected differently. Let that be enough."

His eyes searched hers, tears glistening in the corners again. "What happened to you, Shae? You used to be so sweet. Acting out stories for the kids so they'd laugh, collecting flowers to give Mom and Dad. What happened to that little girl?"

Shae smiled sadly, wiping away one of Dustin's tears with her thumb before dropping her hands. "She grew up."

"But how'd she grow up into you?" Dustin whispered.

"She needed to."

After an extended silence Dustin wandered over to their pile of stuff and grabbed his own bedroll, setting it up on the opposite side of the dying fire. A short time later Russ came back into camp, followed by Vivian. He looked relieved to see Dustin sitting there and went over to try to talk to him, voice quiet, but Dustin ignored Russ until he gave up.

"We need to decide what to do now," Russ stated loud enough for everyone to hear. No one answered him, so he turned his attention to Shae. "What was your plan?"

"Get to Hayden and tell you two the truth," Shae replied. "Then give you time to get out of town before going to the police station. Despite what you may assume, I don't want to see you two hurt or in danger."

"That's what we'll do, then," Russ said.

Dustin dropped his head into his hands. Vivian sat down next to him and started gently rubbing his back.

"I'll send something home with you for the rest of the family," Shae offered. "We'll find a store with a video camera or something."

Russ nodded, turning his attention to Dustin. "It *will* help everyone to know Shae is alive and safe, Dustin. Honestly, it might help them more than actually seeing her since she's...."

"A self-absorbed narcissist?" Shae supplied since that seemed to be what Russ was dancing around.

"That's a very technical way to say 'bitch,' but sure," Russ answered, seeming to miss Dustin's wince.

"This is the best outcome," Vivian said to Dustin. "Even if it hurts."

Dustin remained silent. Vivian wrapped her arm around him and he rested his head on her shoulder. After a while she coaxed him into his bedroll and ran her fingers through his hair until his breathing evened out into sleep. Russ went to sleep as well, snoring softly. Vivian, however, remained up, sitting at the head of Dustin's bedroll and watching Shae, her fingers drumming lightly on the hilt of a knife protruding from her boot.

Shae rolled her eyes and whispered, "You wouldn't kill me in front of my brothers."

Shae thought she detected a dark smile on Vivian's face in the dim light of the dying fire.

"Not in front of them, no," Vivian said.

"You going to ask me to take a walk?"

"No. Dustin would know I was responsible."

"Is there a purpose to your posturing then?"

She shrugged and pulled the knife out, idly playing with it.

"You seem quite ready to judge me for my choices but very unwilling to let anyone question yours," Shae pointed out.

Her movements with the knife halted. "What is that supposed to mean?"

Shae laid back on her bedroll, stretching out and looking up at the stars. "How *does* one end up the last of a rebel camp anyway? Did you sit back and watch the rest of them get murdered by the coven? You must have, or you wouldn't be here."

Before Shae could realize what was happening, and faster than it should have been able to happen, there was a knife at her throat and Vivian was straddled over her. Shae stared up into Vivian's dark eyes, saw the rage and pain in them.

"Says the woman who wasn't even worth fifteen good soldiers," Vivian hissed. "They sent two-hundred after me that day. Not my family, not my camp, *me*."

Shae's eyes narrowed. She'd been thinking about the lack of good soldiers a lot the last three days, and she fully intended to figure out why it had happened, but now her mind was firmly set on figuring out what about Vivian was worth two-hundred.

"You leave my life to me, and I'll leave yours to you," Shae said, putting just as much venom into her voice as Vivian had.

Vivian didn't move for a long time until suddenly she was up on her feet, glaring down at Shae. Without a word she turned and stalked off into the darkness.

22: Hayden

Vivian woke Dustin by lightly shaking his shoulder. The sun was not even up properly yet and he wished Vivian had left him be. His dreams had been much more pleasant than being awake was.

"Check the traps, I'll start packing up camp," Vivian whispered.

Dustin nodded, crawling out of his bedroll to face the bracing morning air. It woke him up as he yanked his boots on, clearing his senses bit by bit. He didn't remember taking the boots off and figured Vivian must have done it for him. Hauling his exhausted, aching form off the ground, he headed in the direction of the traps. Part of him wanted to keep walking. To get away. To pretend none of this had ever happened, especially last night.

He wanted to be mad at Russ, to blame him for bringing everything up, but he couldn't be mad at Russ for being right. Russ had said from the beginning this was a bad idea, that something was off with Shae's story. Dustin had equivocated and rationalized his way into believing that Russ was seeing it wrong, that Shae was just surviving however she could, that as soon as she was back with them, with family, she'd be the person he imagined her to be. Part of him, a big part, still wanted to believe that.

But she'd never planned on coming with them at all. She'd admitted to everything Russ accused her of. There was no going home with her anymore. His sister was gone.

Finding nothing in the traps Dustin dismantled them and headed back to camp, thoughts still running in circles. Shae was his sister. Shae didn't want anything to do with them. Shae was not the sister he thought she was. Shae was his sister.

He found Vivian saddling up the horses alone, Russ and Shae still asleep.

"Not waking them?" Dustin asked, grabbing a set of saddlebags to throw over Mudcake's back.

Vivian paused and glanced down at Shae. "The less time I have to listen to her speak, the better."

Dustin gritted his teeth and turned away, hearing Vivian sigh behind him. He felt her hand squeeze his shoulder.

"Sorry," she said. "I tried to give her a chance, but after last night...."

"I know," Dustin whispered, fidgeting with the saddlebags. After a moment he continued, "You've been helping me with this for so long, and you told me a long time ago that you didn't think she was alive. I should have listened."

"I always figured she got lost and died of exposure,

honestly," Vivian admitted. "I thought, maybe, if you were lucky, someone had found her body and given her a proper burial, something that there would be a record of, something that would give you closure."

"I wish…" Dustin hesitated. "I wish she'd never left London. That I'd never found out what happened to her."

"You would've kept hoping, though," Vivian said. "Hope hurts. So does truth, this time, but at least you know."

She gave his shoulder another gentle squeeze and stepped away, toeing lightly at Russ who tried to inchworm away in his bedroll, still half asleep. Vivian responded by bending down and yanking the zipper open, exposing Russ to the cold air. Chuckling at his cursing she went over to wake Shae, though rather than toeing at her bag she gave Shae a hard kick in the legs and walked off. Dustin wanted to chastise her but he couldn't bring himself to do it. Shae sat up, glaring blearily in Vivian's direction, and flipped her off behind her back.

⁂

An hour later they were on their way again. Vivian said they should reach Hayden by late afternoon and little else. She stayed in the lead, gaze forward and shoulders back. Dustin got the sense something more had happened, but he didn't have the energy to figure out what it was. He barely had the energy to stay in his saddle.

Deep in his gut was the familiar pull of wanting to go to Vivian's, like he always did when things got rough. To curl up on the ratty couches, dance to old Johnny

Cash records, hunt deer at the little ponds dotting the mountain, gallop through the sagebrush. To be somewhere quiet.

Now, though... would the memories of everything that happened in the last week taint the place forever? Would he think of hunting frogs with Shae in the creek, about how she'd probably been faking her enjoyment of it? Would he think of her smiling in the barn as the helicopter raced nearer and nearer? He hoped not.

"We walk from here," Vivian stated suddenly.

Dustin looked around, glancing at the sun, and was startled to realize how late it had gotten. They were standing in a clearing surrounded by young, spindly aspens quaking in a slight breeze.

"And how far is 'from here?'" Shae asked, not dismounting.

Vivian didn't answer, just got off Kodiak and dug a large coil of rope from one of her bags. Russ caught Dustin's eye and sent a confused glance between Vivian and Shae before looking back at Dustin. He shrugged at his little brother, still not sure what the new, crackling level of tension between Shae and Vivian was. It seemed too much for the fight that had occurred the night before, at least on Vivian's end. Eventually, after watching Vivian through narrowed eyes for several moments, Shae gave in and dismounted.

Looping the rope all the way around the clearing, Vivian made an impromptu paddock as Dustin removed the tack from the exhausted horses. He gave them all a good scratch before they wandered off to find something green to chew on. They set the tack outside the paddock to prevent it getting stepped on, Russ covering it in hacked off branches from several spruce trees, while Shae sat on a rock and watched.

Once Vivian was satisfied with her work, she grabbed a small pack and the group set off, Dustin grabbing his pack as well. Russ and Shae walked in front, heading the direction Vivian indicated, while she and Dustin hung back. Dustin wished she'd give him a little space, but after her interactions with Shae today maybe it was best she was back here with him. Vivian wasn't the best with impulse control, and if she got the impulse to stab Shae she might actually do it. Dustin was sort of surprised she hadn't already.

"This is the right thing to do, Dustin," Vivian said after nearly a mile of silence between them.

Dustin didn't answer.

"She's dangerous," Vivian continued. "Just take the video and make it seem like she's a happy little actress and your family will never know the difference."

"I'll know," Dustin whispered. "Russ will know. I don't want to have to keep that secret."

"You didn't really expect her to be the same, though, did you? After all this time."

"Of course not. But I didn't expect this."

"What do you intend to do then?"

Dustin shrugged. "Go home, I guess. Show everyone the video. Maybe tell Mom the truth. Or Keaun's wife,

Tessa. Someone."

"Then what? You've been focused on your sister for ten years."

Dustin thought about it for a long time, unable to come up with an answer. "I have no idea. Maybe I'll join the military with Russ or something, now that they're starting to admit how serious things are getting. Try to keep Russ out of trouble."

Vivian chuckled. "Oh yes, I'm sure he'd love having his big brother looking over his shoulder all the time."

Dustin felt his lips twitch in the slightest smile. "Guess he'll have to learn to live with it."

"The military might be interesting," Vivian mused. "It sounds like I've taught you to fight rather differently than them. Maybe they'll find that useful."

Dustin coughed out a surprised laugh. "Just a bit different, yeah."

They lapsed back into silence for about a hundred yards.

"What about you?" Dustin asked. "We may have distracted the soldiers for now, but they might still be poking around your place when you get back." Maybe he'd just go back with her. But no. Russ needed his help to get home safely, to tell the family what had happened.

"You know me. I'll be fine. Set a few traps. Throw some bombs. Put on some scary makeup. The usual."

"I wish there was a way for us to keep in touch," Dustin said wistfully.

"We'll find a way if we really need to," she answered.

"But if you're trying to get me to ask you to stay so you don't have to feel guilty about wanting to, I can do that."

Dustin sighed, watching Shae and Russ walking ahead of them. "I do want you to ask. But I can't stay. I need to get Russ home safe, help him explain what happened."

"Come back after, then. Stay longer this time."

"Remember what happened last time I showed up to your place in winter?" Dustin pointed out.

Vivian grinned. "I think I've smartened you up enough that you won't fall through the ice this time."

"This is where I leave you," Vivian said twenty minutes later.

They'd stopped on the edge of a forest looking down a gentle slope above the town of Hayden. It looked like something out of a storybook. Quaint, colorful little houses, treelined streets. Even from this far away Dustin could hear children laughing and a dog barking, could smell dinner barbecues being cooked. There were no train tracks here, but there was a modest regional airport on the east side of town and a highway twisting away to the flat horizon in the west.

Vivian pulled Dustin into a tight hug, giving him a quick kiss and telling him to be safe before she slipped back into the trees, vanishing from sight within moments. Dustin wished she'd stayed. He had no idea what to say to Shae right now, nor Russ. Their walk down into Hayden was silent, the only sound other than their footsteps coming from Shae adjusting the scarf she'd draped around her head to help hide her face. When they reached the edge of town Dustin told Shae and Russ to get the car while he went to buy the camera. Russ stopped him long enough to produce a small wad of coven bills, which Dustin took.

As he wandered the cutesy mainstreet he noticed the strange looks he was getting. Belatedly he realized he was still dressed for living rough; homemade buckskin jacket, worn and muddied cargo pants, long knife on his hip, heavy pack on his back. At least he'd taken the time to clean and sew up the gash in the sleeve of his jacket from where the bullet had grazed him in the fight. From the way they were wrinkling up their noses at him he guessed he still smelled like he'd been living rough too. Good. It would keep them the hell away from him.

He started to notice the decorations on the street had a theme. Yellow and blue bunting, banners with fountains depicted on them. It took him a few minutes before it clicked; Wood's Coven's Establishment Day was coming up. They'd been officially formed on August 20th, 2177. Dustin wasn't sure what day it was now, but he knew that soon the town would celebrate "the fountain of trust that secured the future." All bullshit, as far as he was concerned.

Nearing the end of the street Dustin wondered if he'd even be able to find a store with a good video camera. They weren't exactly a big seller since vampires couldn't be recorded. Mostly he was passing lots of small, touristy type shops with kitschy wood carvings and forgettable watercolor postcards. Lots of ice-cream shops as well, which sent a nostalgic pang through him. Once, just after they'd gone on the run the second time, Rose and Dustin had snuck out of camp and robbed an ice-cream shop of six gallons of various flavors of ice-cream. They'd taken it back and divided it up between all their siblings, having a grand, sticky party. Their mother chewed them out for the theft, but it had been worth it for how much it had made their siblings smile. Even their mother had come around eventually, though she'd warned them to never do it again.

At the very last building on the south side of the street Dustin found a shop that might carry what he was looking for. He ducked into the small electronics store and stopped just inside, looking at the five shoulder-high rows of shelves. Glancing at the bored looking vampire slouching behind the counter, Dustin gritted his teeth and went to look on his own.

The first row contained "non-photographic" security equipment; window and door opening sensors, mostly. The second was wildlife cameras, not useful for him. The third had a plethora of robotics kits for children. The fourth was musical equipment; electric keyboards and other stuff Dustin kind of recognized but couldn't name. Finally, in the fifth row at the very end, after a bunch of laptops, Dustin found a tiny display of six cameras. Only one had a video option, so he grabbed it, a memory card, and some batteries, taking it all up to the counter.

"Been out in the woods then?" The vampire asked. He

looked not much older than twenty, but that didn't mean much.

Dustin pushed his purchases closer, ignoring the man as he rolled his eyes, grumbling about rude customers. He scanned the items and took Dustin's money. Dustin didn't wait for the change, turning and walking back out to the street. Heading away from the touristy area, he unpacked the camera, sliding the batteries and memory card in, tucking the instructions in his pocket. The camera was a small thing. He could close his hand around it and only the corners peaked out. Shiny blue with silver accents and a few stickers detailing its various attributes. Hardly thicker than the slim batteries powering it.

This was it.

This would be the only part of his sister he got to take home to the family. A stupid little camera with a stupid little video on it.

He glared at the thing for a few moments before yanking his hand back and sending the camera hurling at a brick wall. It shattered into a handful of shiny pieces that tumbled to the ground. A few vamps and a couple humans stopped to stare warily. Dustin ignored them and strode away.

He was not bringing home some stupid video.

He was bringing home his sister.

Shae had thought of Nahanni as some boring little backwater, another tent city like Baja had been. If Dustin could convince her, really convince her, that it wasn't like that at all, then she wouldn't have reason to stay away. And if he got her home, even for one day, she'd see how much the family missed her and loved her and she'd stay. He knew she would.

It took him twenty minutes, but he found the little car rental shop a few streets over. He marched towards it, not seeing Russ and Shae anywhere, figuring they were still in the building. He was so focused on finding them, on coming up with a way to convince Shae to come with them, a way to convince Russ to let her, that he didn't see the cop cars until they were right on him. They'd spun around the corner, lights and sirens off, and parked at awkward angles in front of the rental shop, only a few yards from Dustin. Their doors were thrown open with force and left that way as the cops darted inside.

His initial instinct was to turn and get the hell out of the area. But that wasn't smart. They'd notice his abrupt departure, as would all the people who'd stopped to see what was going on. He needed to stay calm and act like everyone else, watch and wait and hope Shae and Russ were not what had brought the cops down on the shop.

A crowd began to grow, peering around in hopes of seeing something interesting. Dustin would put money on this being the most exciting thing to have happened in their town all year. Gossip was sure to fly. He attempted to nonchalantly slip off his pack and jacket so he'd blend in better, but before the pack had even dropped off his shoulders three cops burst back out of the building, along with a suited man. All four looked around and the suited man, a human, raised a finger and pointed at Dustin.

"That's not him, but he looks like him!" The man shouted.

Dustin tried to take off but there were too many people in the way and the three cops, all vampires, were too fast. One had raced around the crowd to cut Dustin off. The only gun he had right now as in his boot, and he was cursing himself for that. He had time to draw a knife, but the cop had a gun on him before it could matter. The crowd screamed, dashing to the opposite side of the street.

"Drop it!" The cop screamed.

Dustin glanced around and saw that the other two had drawn guns as well. Several vampires in the crowd were edging back over, looking like they would be willing to help the cops should Dustin try anything. Gritting his teeth, he dropped the knife and slowly raised his hands.

While two cops kept their guns on him, the third came over and roughly patted him down, removing his pack, the pistol in his boot, and the four other knives he had before cuffing him. They dragged him over to a cop car and slammed his face down on the hood. He didn't make a sound. Let them posture and overcompensate. As soon as they were away from the crowd he'd be back to having the advantage.

One of the cops leaned down, metallic-scented breath making Dustin pull his head back as much as he could. "Where is Shae Lockwood?"

23: Arrested

Russ jogged back over to Shae after giving Dustin the money, Shae wondering what Dustin had intended to do without it. A robbery was hardly advisable right now. He did seem a bit lost in his head at the moment, though, so perhaps he hadn't realized he didn't have money.

"Come on, let's find a couple cars," Russ said.

Shae adjusted the scarf she'd draped artfully around her head before they'd gotten into town and followed her brother. She doubted, and also hoped, no one would recognize her in this state. Disgustingly dirty were not the sort of pictures she wanted in the tabloids.

"Just get one for yourselves. I don't drive," Shae told him. "I'll lie low until tomorrow morning, then wander into a police station or something. No! A theater. Does this town even have a theater?"

Odds of Two wasn't out yet, but her previous movie might still be playing. Even if it wasn't someone in a theater was bound to recognize her.

Russ stared at her. "This is just a game to you, isn't it?

Don't you care at all how much you hurt Dustin? He loves you and this... crushed him."

Shae shrugged. "He'll be fine. He just needs time."

"I don't know that he will, Shae." Russ shook his head. "How can you be so cold?"

Shae sighed, snagging a pair of seemingly abandoned sunglasses off a sidewalk cafe table and sliding them on to further hide her face. "Is there anything I can say that would actually make you feel better about any of this?"

"Probably not, but why don't you give it a shot anyway."

"You and Dustin *chose* to come and get me. You *chose* to take me off that train. You *chose* to try and take me home. The results of those actions are on you. I'm not going to be upset over a decision someone else made just because they ended up unhappy to have made it."

"But you're the one who is acting in a way that means it isn't safe for us to take you home."

"Yeah, but I've been this way for a long time now. It's not like its something that happened just because you kidnapped me."

Russ frowned and stayed silent for a while. "Why are you like this then?"

"Why are you the way you are? Why is Dustin the way he is?" Shae returned. "It's just how I ended up. I don't bother thinking about it."

This time Russ stayed silent for much longer so Shae assumed he'd decided to drop it. They were on some little side street now, still no rental shop in sight. Around them were mostly odds and ends shops and one tattoo parlor.

Russ did a double take when they passed the parlor, eyes widening.

"What the hell is a 'blood wheel?'" He asked, stepping closer to look at a sign in the window advertising various blood wheel accessories.

"It's a little glass vial that sits on top of your skin, usually on your wrist or the back of your neck, and it's attached to your veins so it fills with blood and spins the little metallic wheel inside, then the blood goes back into your vein on the other side. Some of them are really intricate and expensive," Shae told him, coming up to examine the advertisement as well. Their prices were on the low end, and they only offered simpler versions of the accessory. Probably not the best quality either.

Russ looked horrified. "People *get these*?"

"All the time. They're huge right now, especially for people whose veins don't show well." She caught Russ eying her wrists warily and laughed. "I've never had one. Not really my style."

Russ shook his head. "The vamps are one thing, but the way the coven humans act around them. I don't get it. Why throw yourselves at the feet of predators?"

Shae chuckled and hooked her arm in his, pulling him away from the shop before he could see any evidence of the more extreme body modifications.

"They're well fed predators," Shae said. "And they're predators who pay our bills when we make them pretty pictures. The perks are worth it."

"But they aren't *all* well fed," Russ pointed out.

"That's our biggest problem in Nahanni right now. The surrounding coven towns are starving. Or being starved. So they come into the settlement, desperate for food, and kill anyone they find."

"Kill them first," Shae said lightly.

"I think I liked you better when you were acting," Russ muttered.

"Shouldn't have called me out, then," Shae told him.

Russ puffed out a breath between his lips and unhooked their arms, taking a couple steps away. They walked in silence until they found a tiny rental shop towards the edge of town opposite the one they'd come in from. There were barely ten cars in the lot next to the brick building that had been painted a horrendous shade of limeish-green. The paint was chipped and peeling, revealing the original red brick underneath, giving the building a sickly, speckled look.

Shae followed Russ inside and over to one of the two clerks, sliding down into a chair at the woman's desk while Russ took the other chair. The clerk was a young, human woman with strawberry blond hair in bob and bright blue eyes. The nameplate in front of Shae read Jessica McDermott. Shae roved her eyes around Jessica's desk, looking for something personal she could use as a way in. Before she could find anything Russ leaned forward, arms crossed on the desk and a cocky smile on his face.

"Evening, Jessica," Russ said, smiling as the woman blushed.

Well then. Apparently Russ could handle this just fine on his own. Shae leaned back to watch her little brother work.

"Evening, what can I do for you two, Mr....?"

"Davis. Eric Davis." Russell answered. "My cousin Eliza and I went hiking this morning and lost track of time. Now we've missed our bus back to Salt Lake, and we're on a bit of a tight schedule so we figured we'd get a car instead of waiting for the next one."

"We can do that, Mr. Davis."

Russ smiled. "Eric, please."

She giggled and nodded. "Alright, *Eric*. What sort of car can we get for you? I'm afraid we don't have the largest selection, but we'll do our best."

"I'm sure you will. What sort of trucks do you have?"

She giggled again and tapped away at her computer for a moment. "We've got a Ford-350 X8-Series ready to go out. Four doors, eighty miles to the gallon. Should give you a nice, comfortable ride to Salt Lake, and we've got a partner agency out there where you can drop it off."

"Wonderful!" Russ said.

"I'll print the paperwork, then," Jessica said. She got up and smoothed out her plain gray skirt, casting a little smile at Russ, then walked away to a back room.

"Men and their trucks," Shae teased.

Russ looked over at her, dropping his flirty expression in favor of one that looked very done. "Dustin is claustrophobic. I'm not sticking him in some little sedan. He's been through enough."

"Ah," Shae said. "And Eric Davis?"

"I'm not explaining my work as a soldier to you."

"Oh please," Shae whispered. "It's obviously some fake identity you've got, with paperwork to back it up, or this whole car rental plan wouldn't work. Can't rent a car without an ID."

Russ sighed, pinching the bridge of his nose. "Yes. It is one of two I have. I used the first one to get the car we took to get here, and I'm using this one now to avoid connection to the first one. Happy?"

"I do like having all the cards on the table."

She turned to watch Jessica through the metal meshed window to the printer room she'd gone in, looking in time to see her blush and turn away. She'd been watching Russ through the window.

"Someone thinks you're sexy," Shae snickered.

He frowned. "What?"

Shae looked bemused. "Jessica? The woman you just flirted into giving you a car?"

Russ looked genuinely confused. "I wasn't flirting with her."

"Wow. Well, I'm beginning to understand why you've had so many girlfriends," Shae laughed. "I'll leave you with blondie. Continue with your not-flirting."

With that she stood up to go look around. Jessica was still in the backroom, a sheaf of papers clutched to her chest as she talked with a scruffy guy. He had on an ill-fitting suit that screamed "underpaid-manager." Shae ignored them and wandered over to a bulletin board crammed full of fliers. There were advertisements for hiking tours of the surrounding area, whitewater rafting trips, a couple potlucks, the upcoming Establishment Day celebrations, and even one for some wolf-hybrid puppies someone had for sale. There were also advertisements for things people were selling, including one for sweaters made from dog hair. No one had torn any of the little contact info strips off of that one. And, right in the middle of the board, tacked over all the other fliers, was a huge sheet of bright white paper with Shae's picture right smack in the middle. Beneath it the words "MISSING/ABDUCTED" were spelled out in huge red letters. Under them was a short description in a blocky, all caps font:

SHAE LOCKWOOD WAS KIDNAPPED OFF THE TRAIN CARRYING HER AND THE COSTARS OF HER NEW MOVIE ON THE EVENING OF AUGUST 9th. SHE WAS TAKEN WHILE IN THE UNCLAIMED TERRITORY NEAR THE ABANDONED TOWN OF GRANBY COLORADO. TWO MASKED MEN WERE OBSERVED TAKING HER. IF YOU HAVE ANY INFORMATION PLEASE CONTACT YOUR LOCAL POLICE DEPARTMENT IMMEDIATELY. ANY INFORMATION LEADING TO THE SAFE RETURN OF SHAE LOCKWOOD WILL BE REWARDED.

Another piece of paper had been hastily stapled to the bottom of the flyer, the words in the same blocky font.

UPDATE: AUGUST 11th
SHAE LOCKWOOD HAS BEEN SPOTTED WITH A LARGE GROUP OF REBELS DURING AN ATTACK ON COVEN FORCES SENT TO RESCUE HER. THEY ESCAPED WITH SHAE LOCKWOOD AND MAY BE HEADING FOR THE BAJA CALIFORNIA REBEL CAMP. IF YOU SPOT ANYONE SUSPICIOUS DO NOT APPROACH AS THEY ARE CONSIDERED TO BE *EXTREMELY* DANGEROUS. REPORT THEM TO YOUR LOCAL POLICE IMMEDIATELY.

Interesting. Shae wondered what the reward was. How much was she worth to the world, aside from fifteen terrible soldiers? Perhaps they didn't put an actual amount to discourage false tips attempting to claim the money. She figured she should tell Russ about the poster. This town was obviously on high alert about her. She turned to get him only to find him right behind her.

"Come on," he hissed, putting an arm around her and steering her out the front door.

"I take it you saw the giant missing poster of me?" Shae said.

"What poster?" Russ asked, rushing her across the street. "Why the fuck didn't you tell me there was a poster?"

"Well I was about to, but you were already whisking

us out of the building."

"Whatever. I think the manager recognized you and called the cops," Russ said. He led them into an empty alley. "We'll find Dustin and get back to the woods. Find a place to hide out until we figure something out."

"*You'll* find a way back to the woods," Shae said. "No reason for me to leave."

Before Russ could respond they heard tires screeching and turned back to see cop cars pulling up at the shop. There were only two of them, and they rolled up without lights and sirens. The cops inside threw open their doors and charged into the shop. Russ was glancing up and down the alley, breathing fast. Shae could see there was nowhere for him to go. The cops were between him and the closest edge of town, and it was the wrong edge of town. It led to empty fields with nowhere to hide. And there was no way he could make it back through the whole town to the side they'd come from, to the forest. Even then, he'd never leave without Dustin.

"Fuck. Fuck. Fuck," Russ cursed, freezing and going pale, his eyes locked on something Shae couldn't see.

She took a step to the side and peered out of the alley. A large crowd had gathered, all watching the shop with their backs to Russ and Shae's hiding place. It took Shae a moment, but she saw what Russ had. Dustin.

Just as her eyes settled on him he twisted around in an attempt to run, only to be cornered by the cops. Shae couldn't hear what was said over the shouts and surprised screams of the crowd, but within a minute

Dustin was cuffed and slammed face-first down on the hood of one of the cop cars.

Russ continued to curse, hand floating back and forth towards and away from the gun hidden under his shirt.

"That won't do any good," Shae told him. "They'll kill Dustin before you get a second shot off."

"Well we have to do something!" Russ hissed, his eyes locked on Dustin.

"I am going to do something," Shae said, looking around the alley to see what she had to work with. There wasn't much.

"Like what?" Russ asked. He'd dropped his hand from the area of his gun, but he hadn't taken his eyes off of Dustin. "Do you have any idea what they'll do to him? Prison in general is bad enough in the covens, but for a rebel who kidnapped *you*? And if they find out he's a *Lockwood*?"

"I'll take care of it," Shae told him.

Dropping the scarf and sunglasses, she strode over to a spigot and turned it, getting only a dribble of water. It was enough. She swiped her hand through the mud it created on the dirt floor of the alley, rubbing some of it into her clothes and across her cheeks, tearing her clothes in a few places and mussing up her hair. Standing back up, Russ seemed to finally notice what she was doing.

"What...?" Russ said.

"Once their eyes are on me they won't be on you for long enough for you to get away. Go back to where we left Vivian's horses. I'll make sure Dustin gets there as soon as I can." She moved to stride out of the alley, but Russ grabbed her arm.

"I don't trust you," Russ growled.

"Trust that I'm a self-absorbed narcissist then," Shae told him. "You really think my big brother, my dead brother as far as the covens are concerned, you think him turning up is going to be good for me? Good for the story I've worked so hard to tell?"

Silence hung heavy between them. Slowly, finger by finger, Russ loosened his grip, dropping his hand. His gaze remained hard.

"If you don't get him out of this, I will hunt you down, Shae. I will blow your whole world apart with the truth, even if it kills me."

Shae smiled. "Love you too, little bro. Give my best to the family."

Russ stared at her for another moment before walking backwards out of the alley, keeping her in his sights. Once he reached the other end Shae turned, took a deep breath, and melted into the character she was about to play.

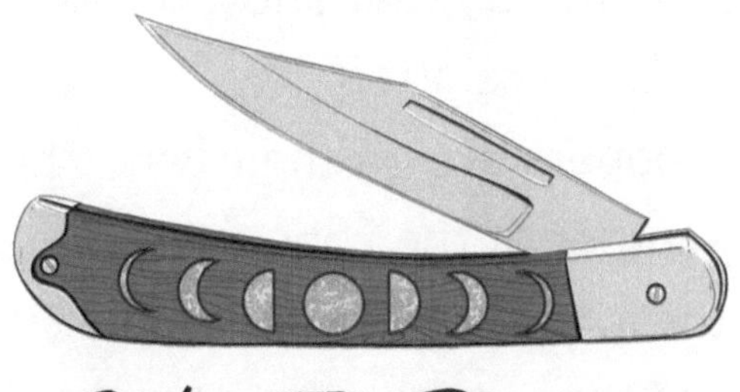

24: To Prison

"Where. Is. Shae. Lockwood?" the cop leaning close to Dustin's face growled again. It was the only question he'd asked, and he'd asked it several times now.

Dustin remained silent, waiting for the cops to take him away. He doubted they'd kill him with Shae still missing, not when he was their only lead. That meant an interrogation, likely at some sort of police station. The town didn't seem to be big enough to have a jail, just a few drunk tank type cells at the station. One cell. Escaping one cell would be easy.

The other option was getting out of the car on the way there. Maybe he could jam the door when they were putting him in. Something so it looked like it shut but didn't quite latch. Then, at the right moment, a solid kick would open the door for Dustin to roll out and sprint for somewhere safe, somewhere to regroup with Shae and Russ.

They did have his weapons, though, and there was still plenty of light. Plus, they knew this town. He didn't.

Dammit.

He wished Vivian were here.

The cop grit his teeth, grabbed Dustin's hair, and slammed his head against the hood. It wasn't enough to do more than sting, a great show of restraint on the vampire's part, Dustin realized.

"The state troopers are on their way. They're thirty minutes out," another of the cops said.

"Tell them they need to get here faster. There's at least one more of those bastards in town, and we don't know what he might do to her now that his partner has been captured!" The one who had been interrogating Dustin snapped.

"Should we put out a reverse 911 call?" The third cop suggested.

"Too dangerous."

The one who suggested the call scoffed. "It's one human man. He's hardly a threat."

"One that we know of, and you heard what they did to that deployment a few days ago."

Their bickering stopped, interrupted by a scream for help that came from behind the gathered crowd. The cops froze, looking in the direction of the sound, hands hovering above their pistols as the crowd parted to reveal a woman in dirty clothes with messy hair and a dirt-streaked face. She was leaning to one side, clutching one of her arms as if she was injured.

It was Shae.

What the fuck had happened to Shae?

Two of the cops darted forward and grabbed her as

she started to fall, wracked with sobs. Dustin was trying to hide his shocked and terrified expression, but he felt like he was failing. She had been *fine* thirty minutes ago. And where the hell was Russ? Was he hurt? Had they been attacked?

Dustin struggled against the cop still holding him against the car, trying to twist around enough to see the crowd better, hoping to catch sight of Russ. The cop holding him down slammed his head again, harder this time. Everything spun and the edges of his vision went fuzzy. With a lot of effort he won the fight for consciousness.

When things settled back into focus he saw Shae sitting on the hood of the other car, cops and concerned citizens clustered around her. They'd wrapped a blanket around her shoulders and handed her a paper cup of something steaming.

She sniffled and thanked an elderly woman, sipping the beverage. Something wasn't right here. Shae didn't act like this. Dustin couldn't remember her crying since she was a toddler, not unless she thought it would get her something.

"Tell us what happened, love," one of the cops asked, his hand running up and down Shae's back. Dustin wanted to snap his wrist.

"I, I..." She hiccupped. "They just came on the train and grabbed me! I don't know who they are, but they kept acting like they know me! Like I knew them."

Dustin stilled his efforts to see better, turning all his attention on Shae.

"What then, sweetie?" The cop pressed.

Shae sniffled again. "They kept me in this old abandoned house, in the basement. Then suddenly they dragged me into this big fight and it was awful! They hurt so many people!"

"Oh, you poor thing," the woman who had brought the beverage crooned. Dustin couldn't tell if she was a vampire or just so old she'd lost the color in her skin for some natural reason.

"They... they said they were going to take me home with them, to the Baja rebel camp. I don't know *why*!" Shae hiccupped. The cop cooed at her until she calmed down a little and continued. "When, when you captured that one," Shae waved a shaky hand in Dustin's direction, "the other one panicked and attacked me. I almost didn't get away."

"Was he the only other one? Which way did he go?" The other cop asked.

Shae shook her head. "There were eight of them. And he, I don't know, I think he went south? I just wanted to get away!"

South.

No way Russ had gone south. Dustin would have seen him. It was the one direction he *could* see from his position on the hood of the car.

Someone pulled Dustin roughly off the hood as one of the cops got into the car he'd been on and sped away, sirens blaring and wheels shrieking. Shae watched them go, still sniffling and hiccupping.

What was her plan here? Where was Russ? Fuck. Dustin couldn't take not understanding what was happening.

"Let's get this one down to lock up," the cop holding his wrists said, voice gruff.

The other cop nodded. "I'll remain with Ms. Lockwood until the troopers show up. Don't want to put this poor thing through a car ride with that bastard."

"Wait," Shae whispered. "I... I want to talk to him."

"Ms. Lockwood, I'm not sure that's a wise idea…"

Shae put on a firm-through-the-tears look and aimed it at the cop who had spoken. "I deserve to know why he did what he did."

The two cops looked between one another, then between Dustin and Shae.

"Alright," The one behind Dustin spoke. "But let us get him in the car first, and we'll crack the window for you to talk through."

Shae tucked her hair behind her ear and nodded, watching as they manhandled Dustin into the back of the car she was sitting on. The door slammed behind him before he had the chance to jam it slightly open. With the door closed, one of the cops opened the driver's door and pushed the button for Dustin's window.

Shae came over and leaned down, curling her fingers in through the crack as her eyes searched Dustin's. The cops were standing behind her, listening to every word.

"I'm not who you want me to be," she said. "What made you think I was?"

Dustin didn't answer, still unsure of what was going on.

Shae let out a little frustrated sob and straightened, fingers still in the window, and turned towards the cops. As soon as their attention was on her, she uncurled her fingers and two slim black pieces of metal dropped into the little plastic indent where the handle to open the door would be in a normal car.

Bobby-pins.

The cop drove Dustin to an empty station a few blocks from the rental shop, parking in a garage and making sure the door had shut completely before removing Dustin from the car and dragging him inside. He hadn't had enough time to slip the cuffs, but he'd managed to hide the bobby pins in his back pocket. There were four desks in the station, two on each side, and two cells behind them. The cop threw him into one cell without bothering to take the cuffs off. It was not the kind of cell Dustin had been hoping for. No bars, no window, only a solid metal door with a slim food slot well below the handle.

The cop slid open another hole in the door, this one the same size as the food slot but at eye-level.

"Look," he said through the opening. "If you just tell us where to find your partner, the rest of your gang, I might be able to convince them to go easier on you. Maybe get you sent to one of the nicer prisons down south where it's warm and you get a lot of yard time."

Dustin stared at him, not responding in any way.

"Come on, work with me," the cop said, trying to seem friendly. "My name's Rohn. What's yours?"

This startled a laugh out of Dustin. "Not a chance."

"What would it hurt?" Rohn asked.

"Quite a few things," Dustin replied as he fiddled with the cuffs and bobby-pins behind his back.

"How? We've captured you, rescued Ms. Lockwood, and we'll get the rest of your gang soon enough."

Dustin smiled and pulled the unlocked cuffs from behind his back, tossing them to the floor. "No, you won't."

Rohn shook his head, looking like he pitied Dustin. "If you rebels would just—just let us *help you*. Your lives would be so much better! All your settlements, full of people struggling to find food, shelter, anything, when they could be well taken care of with us. Don't you want that for your people? Comfort and safety?"

Dustin marveled at the level of brainwashing this man seemed to be under. Vampire or not, there was no way he was that willfully ignorant.

"You people can't keep this up," Rohn pressed. "Baja is barely hanging on, Stesse and Nahanni aren't doing much better. Soon you won't have anywhere to go. The coven is done playing your games."

Dustin kept his face neutral, fighting to even out his pulse that had begun racing at the mention of Nahanni. It wasn't enough, though. Dustin could see that Rohn had heard the uptick in his heartbeat. Why did the damn station have to be empty, silent?

"They're all going to fall," Rohn said, pressing his

advantage. "You must have heard the rumors of the preparations for a full attack. Tell me where your partners are, and maybe I let you send a letter home to warn your loved ones."

Dustin took a deep breath. He had to get out of here. He had to find Russ. "Bold talk for a small town cop who has clearly never dealt with anything worse than a feisty raccoon."

Rohn growled, the sound reverberating with an inhuman pitch. He slammed his hands against the metal hard enough that an ear-rattling clang echoed around the cell, then stalked off.

Dustin took one quick step up to the door and started running his fingers over it. It was just as thick and solid as he'd assumed. Neither opening provided enough room to get his arm through and to the exterior lock. Even if he did manage to reach the lock, it wouldn't be as simple as the ones on the cuffs. Bobby-pins wouldn't do the trick. Someone with a key would have to open it.

When Dustin heard Rohn stomping back over he stepped back to where he'd been. The vampire peered back through the top opening, looking a bit calmer.

"Here's the deal," he said. "The state troopers are nearly here. Turns out they have several federal coven agents with them. These federal coven agents have been given kill-on-sight orders for you and anyone working with you, so long as Ms. Lockwood is safe. Of course, now that you're in custody, that order only applies should you try to escape. But, well. Small towns and all. Not too many people around to see what happens."

"So... what? I tell you what you want to know and get taken to some prison where I die slowly as I'm repeatedly farmed for blood, or I keep my mouth shut and die quickly here and now. The second one sounds more enticing, I think," Dustin said, needling at Rohn's poorly hidden anger.

The vampire's nonchalant expression twitched slightly. "Perhaps we'll have to start farming you early, then. Have ourselves a nice little town banquet."

"Feeding straight from a human is against coven laws," Dustin chided.

Rohn's face turned icy and he let out another growl, keys jingling before he whipped the door open. Dustin dropped as Rohn lunged for him, ignoring the jolt that went through him as his knee hit the concrete floor. Rohn caught his arm and between their differing momentums they swung around to land in a heap. Rohn's fangs were bared as Dustin kicked out towards his face, making a grab for the dropped cuffs but missing.

They scuffled across the floor, punches flying. Dustin felt one connect with his abdomen, forced himself through the blurring that raced across his vision. Throwing a hand out he successfully grabbed the cuffs and hooked them through his fingers, slashing out across Rohn's chest. Rohn howled and lunged forward, biting down on Dustin's shoulder. His fangs caught in the fabric of Dustin's shirt and he pulled away without hitting flesh, allowing Dustin to slide a knee between them and lever it to throw Rohn off. The damn vampire wouldn't let go, though, hands tight on Dustin's upper arms, and pulled Dustin with him, going in for another bite.

This one hit home, fangs sinking into Dustin's exposed left wrist. He ignored it and slashed out again, catching Rohn in the eyebrow. Before Dustin could swing again another set of hands had grabbed his shoulders, yanking him back as Rohn was pulled up. There was a whirl of movement and police uniforms before the cell emptied and the door slammed, trapping Dustin once more and removing any opportunity of escape. He gasped for breath, cursing himself for losing his chance. No one would be opening his cell again. Not alone.

In the ringing silence Dustin glanced down at the bite on his wrist, watched the blood dribble out of it and splatter onto the floor next to where he was kneeling. He forced his breathing to calm, his pulse to slow, emptying the adrenalin from his system until he really felt the injury. It stung, but only like a cut. It didn't burn the way he'd always heard vampire bites that caused turns did. The only way to be sure, though, was time.

25: At the Hotel

Shae watched them taking Dustin away, hoping he wouldn't do anything stupid. He'd been lucky she still had bobby-pins in her hair after all this time, but she doubted that would be enough. She needed time and she wouldn't get it if he did something stupid.

"Ms. Lockwood?" The remaining cop said, his voice gentle. He was Turned, and young looking. Probably in his late teens when he'd been bitten. "We've arranged for you to have a room at the hotel so you can get cleaned up while you wait for your friends and the state troopers, they're on their way here. Is there anything else we can get you?"

"Some new clothes?" She sniffled, keeping up her character. The persona was obnoxious, but the temporary annoyance would be worth it. Shae had been developing her in the back of her mind all day. This pretty much was the original plan, after all. Russ and Dustin just hadn't quite made it out in time.

"Of course," he said.

He waved over the blond woman who Russ and Shae had spoken with in the rental agency. Jasmine? Jenifer? Shae had already forgotten. She came over slowly, arms crossed and hands on her elbows.

"This is my wife, Jessica," the cop said.

Shae struggled not to laugh, wondering if he knew how much his wife flirted with her customers.

"Honey, do you think you could run to the store and get some new clothes for Ms. Lockwood, and bring them to the hotel?" He handed her a credit card out of his wallet.

She hesitated, then took it. "Umm… sure. What would you like?"

Shae worked up a little smile. "Just… I don't know. Something clean. Comfortable. Thank you so much."

Jessica nodded and walked away as her husband helped Shae into a car the rental agency provided.

"We'll get you something to eat and send a doctor to the hotel as well," he said once they started to drive.

Shae shook her head. "I don't need a doctor, but thank you. Just a shower and a hot meal and I'm sure I'll be fine."

"Ma'am," he started.

She waved him off. "I'm alright."

He didn't look convinced but didn't press it. Within minutes they pulled up at the hotel. It seemed to be the largest building in town, and much newer and nicer than Shae would've expected for the area. It seemed like a bit of a tourist trap town, however, so she supposed it made sense they'd have a good hotel. The driveway curved up to a covered entrance supported by thick, decorative columns, and a human hotel worker stood waiting for them at the entrance.

The man reached out and opened the passenger door of the car for Shae, holding out a hand to help her out. She took it and followed him inside, the cop behind them.

"We are so glad to know you are safe, Ms. Lockwood," the hotel worker said. Shae suspected he was the manager, based on the quality of his clothes. He wasn't wearing a suit, but his dress pants were crisply pressed and his beige button-up shirt looked like silk.

"Thank you for letting me stay here," Shae told him as they got into an elevator that whisked them to the top floor.

"Of course, of course," he said, leading them down a long hallway to a door at the very end. Another worker was waiting and promptly opened the door, revealing a small suite.

The main room was cozy but not too small, containing several lush couches, an entertainment center, and a modest kitchenette. A door off to the right led to what Shae assumed to be the bedroom and bathroom. The last dregs of the sunset came in through the window at the opposite end of the room from the door, but the lights dangling in artful glass fixtures along the ceiling drowned them out.

"If there is anything you need, Ms. Lockwood, please just pick up the phone. It will give you a direct line to the front desk," the probably manager said.

"If you could bring me up some sandwiches that

would be wonderful," Shae told him. "Something light. Oh. And chocolate! God, I've missed chocolate."

"Of course. Right away. Would you like anything to drink?"

"Wine. Red. I think I deserve a drink, don't you?"

"You deserve several, I believe."

She smiled as he gave her a courteous nod before walking away down the hall. The cop came back up from where he'd stopped several feet away to examine something on his phone.

"Federal coven agents have chartered a flight for themselves and several of your friends, they should be here within a couple hours. The state troopers should be arriving any minute, but they have been instructed to wait for the feds before speaking with you."

"Thank you," Shae told him before arranging her face to look worried. "And... that man... where is he?"

"He's locked up in the station," the cop assured. "He won't be going anywhere. You are safe here, I promise."

Shae let out a deep breath. "Thank you."

He smiled. "You're welcome. My wife should be here any minute with some new clothes for you. If you like, I can stay until she gets here?"

"No, no. That's alright. I feel very safe here, thank you," Shae smiled.

He nodded. "The hotel staff are monitoring all the entrances to the hotel, and I will circle between them. Please let the front desk know if you need me."

"Thank you," Shae repeated, finally closing the door.

She couldn't believe she'd gotten away without any attempt at evidence gathering.

As soon as the lock clicked she flipped the cop off and rolled her eyes, shaking off her character. She hated acting like some weak scrap of meat. It was bad enough when she was playing a movie character, but to do it while she was pretending to be herself was infuriating. It had worked, though, so she couldn't complain too much. Now if only Jessica would hurry with her new clothes so she could take a damn shower.

In the meantime Shae kicked off her boots and peeled away her socks, grimacing at how dirty and smelly her feet had gotten. Dirt had caked into every crevice and her expensive pedicure was ruined. She dreaded seeing what hid under the rest of her clothes.

Jessica appeared several minutes later, knocking on the door so lightly Shae almost didn't hear her. When Shae swung open the door she found the shorter woman holding a couple bags and still looking wary.

"I don't bite," Shae said.

"Maybe. But I think you do lie," she whispered.

Shae quirked an eyebrow. "Oh?"

She nodded. "You sat at my desk with that man for several minutes... you walked away from him and he didn't even hardly notice. He wasn't holding you against your will."

Shae assessed the woman. She wasn't an inch over five-feet tall, her clothing was plain, her hair lank, and makeup badly done. A little silver cross adorned her neck.

"You could've told your husband that back at the rental agency," Shae said.

Jessica stared at her. "He loves your movies," she said eventually.

A slow smile built on Shae's face. "Most people do."

"Your lies are going to catch up to you, Ms. Lockwood," she said.

"Maybe," Shae shrugged. "But who's to say what parts of my story *are* lies? After all, the best lies are mostly truth."

"Maybe I *will* tell him," Jessica said, bravado that Shae saw right through forming on her face.

"Go ahead," Shae told her. "I'll claim Stockholm Syndrome. Say he threatened to mutilate me if I ran. Say the reason I got up in the first place *was* to try and escape, but I never got the chance because you and your manager did such a poor job of getting a hold of the authorities."

Jessica glared, then shoved the bags at Shae before turning and stalking off. Shae chuckled and closed the door again. She rooted through the bags, finding a beautiful strapless sundress in one. It had a simple gradient, cerulean at the top to almost white at the bottom, as the only decoration. There was also a set of pajamas patterned with smiling cartoon moose heads. Some underwear and socks rounded out the clothing options. In the other bag Shae found a simple pair of sandals, a hair brush, toothpaste, toothbrush, razor, and some shampoo, conditioner, and body-wash. For not trusting her, Jessica had gone all out. Small town hospitality really was something.

Entering the bedroom, Shae examined the master suite. A large cushy bed sat off to the left in front of a sliding glass door leading to a narrow patio. Lacy privacy curtains hung across the glass, and large gray velvet blackout curtains hung to either side, tied back with dull-gold rope. A plethora of pillows and a deep purple comforter adorned the bed. Shae longed to sink into it. To the right, separated from the rest of the room by a partial wall of warped glass bricks, stood a large walk-in shower and spa tub. Perfect.

Shae tossed the bags onto the sink counter and started the shower before stripping out of her clothing, cramming it all into the bin under the sink. She glanced in the mirror and made a face at what she saw. Streaks of sweat and dirt ran from her shoulders and along her hips, but the worst was her hair. It was going to take ages to salvage. The hot water would have to last a damn long time.

Stepping into the warm stream of droplets, she sighed in contentment. Warm showers were not something anyone should be forced to go without. She let the water from the multiple showerheads run over her skin for several minutes before sitting down on the floor of the shower and getting to work. Dousing the complimentary hotel loofa with a healthy amount of the lavender scented body-wash Jessica had provided she started to scrub, beginning with her feet and working up, making sure to get all the dirt from under her nails. Her hair took even more work, but eventually she finished up by using the razor to get rid of every stray body-hair that distracted from her veins. Once she'd given herself a last overall rinse Shae stepped out of the shower. She grabbed a fluffy towel with the hotel monogram and wrapped it around her, walking over to the mirror. Leaning in, she examined her reflection, muttering a curse under her breath. She'd gotten a tan. Dammit. It was faint, but there was a clear outline of her shirt collar around her neck and a V where the top couple of buttons had been open. She glanced at her arms and saw faint lines around her wrists as well. At least she'd had the foresight to unroll her sleeves on their ride to Hayden so only her hands had tanned. Nothing to do but wait for it to fade, though, so she moved on.

Letting the towel around her body drop, she pulled out the sundress, sliding it over her head. With a few twists she examined herself in the mirror. The dress didn't fit quite as well as she would've liked, but it was still nice enough. Needed more thigh, though. Shae reached down and grabbed both sides of the slit that only went up to her knee, yanking hard to rip it all the way up to just below her hip. Much better. She rolled the ripped edges in, pinning them in place with safety pins from a complimentary clothing repair kit she found in a drawer.

Wandering out of the bathroom she went over to the windows, pushing aside the gauzy lace curtains to look outside. The town sparkled around her in the evening light, plenty of people still milling around on the streets.

She hoped they were gossiping about her. The missing actress that their town had found, locked safely away in their tower until her friends came to whisk her away from the nightmare they believed she'd endured.

Stepping away she went back into the main room, finding a bottle of wine chilling in a bucket in the sink. On the counter was a tray with several kinds of sandwiches—turkey and cheddar, peanut butter and jelly, ham and Swiss—along with a large selection of chocolates. Stomach growling, Shae skipped over, scooping up two pieces of chocolate and popping them in her mouth. Mint burst across her tongue and she hummed with contentment.

She took a cup of chocolate pudding, stuck a chocolate chip cookie in the top, and poured herself a glass of wine. Taking everything to the couch, she turned the TV on and started flipping through the channels. Every news channel she found carried her story in some manner: direct coverage or a scrolling banner along the bottom or a promise to give updates after the next commercial break. After the incompetence of the soldiers, Shae had been worried that the scandal was not as big as she would've hoped, but it seemed that worry was unnecessary.

Some of the stations were messing up some of the details, but they were all covering it and that was all that she cared about. Trailers for *The Odds of Two* played every commercial break, the anchors frequently mentioning how ticket sales had sky-rocketed. She couldn't wait to tell them how Wood's coven had so utterly fallen short in their efforts to retrieve her. That would really rile things up.

Only one station seemed to have picked up the fact that she'd been found, a station out of Grand Junction Colorado, but before Shae could watch the coverage there was a rapid knocking on the door.

"Shae! Shae, open up!" A frantic voice said through the wood. Helen.

Shae puffed out a breath and walked over, wine still in hand, and opened the door. Before it was all the way open Helen had pounced and was giving her a suffocating hug. The action jolted Shae so much she almost dropped the wine. Ariane, who had been standing behind Helen, saved it.

"Good to see you again, Shae-Shae," he grinned. He looked good, wearing an artfully tattered neon-pink t-shirt under a silvery suit jacket. "Have a fun trip?"

Helen stopped her sobbing into Shae's shoulder to spin around and glare at him, though she kept one arm around Shae. Shae noticed she did not look nearly as good. There were bags under eyes and her normally crisp clothes were wrinkled.

"Did she *have a fun trip*?" Helen hissed.

Shae rolled her eyes. "Oh, don't start now you two."

"Oh, I'm sorry, Shae!" Helen said, looking a bit frantic with worry.

Shae rolled her eyes again. "Shut up and get in here, both of you. I need to talk to you."

Ariane stepped into the room, still holding the wineglass. Helen stayed glued to Shae's side as Shae slid the chain lock on the door.

"First off," Shae looked at Helen, "don't you dare start fussing over me because if you do I'm kicking you out."

Helen opened and closed her mouth a few times as Ariane laughed.

"You...you were kidnapped! I'm allowed to fuss!" Helen spluttered.

"Yeah, kidnapped by two of my idiot brothers. It was hardly traumatic," Shae told them.

"Ahhhhh," Ariane said, taking a sip of the wine. "That's who it was then. I did wonder why you didn't fight back. You're smart enough to have gotten away if you'd wanted to. I confess, though, I was entertaining the idea that Malcom might have been involved. As I've mentioned, he still loathes your family, even if he gave us this train in a show of support."

"Well, to be fair, I didn't know it was my brothers," Shae admitted. "Not at first. I just wanted to see what would happen, because I also suspected your stepfather might be involved. Or you yourself."

Helen was looking between the two of them, her face growing more and more livid. "Your *brothers* did this to you? And what do you mean *you thought Ariane might be involved?*"

"Yes, my brothers. Seems the whole family thinks I was kidnapped when I was twelve, not that I ran off of my own free will. Poor things thought they were saving me," Shae said, snagging the glass of wine back from Ariane.

He chuckled. "So, this was a dramatic and daring rescue of a lost loved one, then? Which two brothers?"

"That it was. And it was Dustin and Russell."

"I don't care if they were trying to rescue you! They had to right to… to…" Helen trailed off, gesturing wildly, failing to come up with what Dustin and Russ hadn't had the right to do. "*And what do you mean you thought Ariane might be involved?*"

Shae and Ariane both ignored her.

"Well, from what I heard at least one of your brothers is now in prison, though I'm guessing they don't know who he is. Either way, I would assume things haven't gone quite to whatever their plan was," Ariane said.

"Not quite, no. Their original plan was to bring me home with them, but Russ vetoed that when he decided I'm too dangerous," Shae said.

"What a sweet brother. Not that I think he's wrong." Ariane's eyes crinkled mischievously.

Shae grinned back at him over the rim of the glass. Helen huffed in exasperation, stalking over to the couch and turning off the TV before sitting down forcefully and crossing her arms.

"If it makes you feel any better, Russ will have a nice little scar on his cheek from where you hit him with your book," Shae told her.

Helen didn't answer, but Shae thought she might have detected a hint of a smile.

"Anyway, Ariane, I need your help with something," Shae told him.

"Oh? What sort of games would you like to play tonight, Shae-Shae?"

"Like you said, one person got captured. Dustin." She gave Ariane a brief rundown of everything that had happened that afternoon, promising to give him more details later when he pressed for more information.

"What do you need me to do?" Ariane asked.

"I was winning the weird-fan game when I was taken," Shae said. "You owe me a favor."

He smiled. "Who says the game is over?"

"If you do it, I'll tell you a secret, something that could be connected to what Dalton told us," Shae said, voice low.

A slow grin spread across Ariane's face. "Oh? This really *was* an interesting trip for you then."

"You have no idea." She finished off the glass of wine. "Go get my brother out of prison before they find out who he is, and I'll tell you all about it."

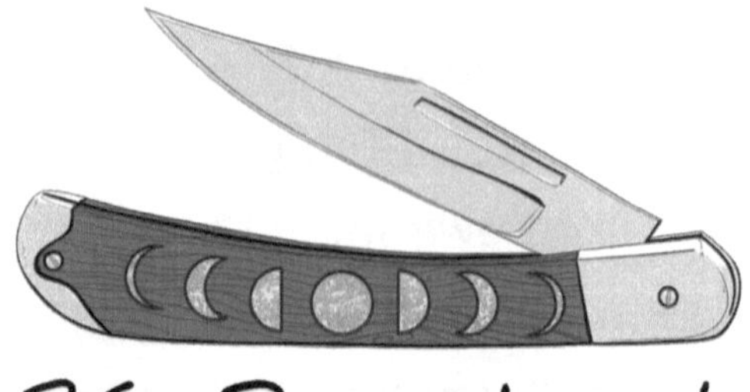

26: Prisonbreak

Without thinking, Dustin rolled over onto his side, hissing and rolling back as pain shot through him from presumably broken ribs. He took a little comfort in the fact that he'd heard Rohn get chewed out and put on leave by the other cops and state troopers who had come in. No one had bothered to come check on his injuries, though, leaving him to curl up on the cot and grit his teeth through the pain.

As far as he could tell none of the injuries were life threatening, nor were any of them that terrible on their own, but there were a fair amount of them adding up to a lot of discomfort. Several broken ribs, a black eye, a couple broken fingers, a lot of bruises, and the vamp bite. Several hours had passed and it still didn't burn, so Dustin figured he was in the clear. Vamp bites that could turn you were obvious, and the process started quickly. From what he knew the wound burned within minutes of the bite and soon the rest of you felt like it was burning as well.

A punch had broken open the healing bullet graze on his shoulder, which stung a fair amount, but the bleeding had stopped. He'd turned his right ankle funny, though he couldn't remember when. Light probing with unbroken fingers seemed to indicate the ankle wasn't broken, at least not seriously, but it had still swelled quite a bit. He'd folded back one end of the mattress to provide some of elevation, popped his fingers back into alignment, and now he waited.

The more time passed, the more certain he became Russ must have gotten away. He hadn't been brought into the station, which had filled with people. Dustin had been listening for any mention of another fugitive being captured. Or killed. So far everything was about looking for the second man and the other six Shae had made up, not about finding anyone. Dustin was grateful for her lie about their numbers, but also confused. Was she on their side or not? Was the lie for them, or for her?

Dustin pulled himself out of his own head, tuning back in to the conversations going on outside his cell. It sounded like there were supposed witnesses being questioned, as well as reporters questioning the cops, and it seemed a lot of false stories had spread. The feds were trying their best to get out of the station to go question Shae, but they kept getting held up by the crowds.

"The other guy was at least six and a half feet tall, and he was wearing a red shirt!" A woman's voice said.

"There were at least six of 'em! Stopped at the ice

cream parlor on Main and Pine Bough," an old man muttered.

"Sir, what *are* the actual suspect numbers?"

"I'm sure I saw him dumping something into the water supply! They're trying to kill us all!"

"Has a grid search of the woods been arranged?"

"They stole three of my chickens!"

"Ladies and gentlemen, please! We will take all your statements one at a time!"

The voices outside helped keep his mind off the tiny confines of his sell, but it still lingered in the back of his mind. Tiny. Isolated. No airflow. No way out. Dustin shuddered, trying to keep his breathing even so as not to aggravate his ribs. He would get out of this. They'd have to open the door again eventually. He just had to ride it out. He'd get out, he'd find Russ, he'd apologize profusely, and they'd go home. After stealing some pain meds.

Without warning a piercing wail interrupted the voices outside. The wail repeated seconds later and Dustin recognized the sound as a fire alarm. The cops, he assumed, started ushering everyone out. Ignoring the pain in his everything, Dustin pulled himself out of the bed, stumbling on his injured ankle, and yanked the mattress off the cot frame. He'd been hoping for slats that he could break off to form a crude knife, but wasn't lucky enough for that. Only a useless metal mesh had been strung across the frame.

He was starting to wonder if it mattered, though, as no one seemed to be coming to get him. No more voices were audible between the wails of the siren. Just as Dustin turned, contemplating looking through the food slot, he heard a key slide into the lock. The person opened the door a few inches, enough for Dustin to see a sliver of his face and police issue t-shirt. A human man stood there, his nametag reading "Josiah" with his job title of "Dispatcher" below the name. Why was the dispatcher of all people letting him out of his cell?

Josiah held the door mostly shut and turned away, talking to someone Dustin couldn't see. "We need you to leave the building, sir. There's a fire in the news station upstairs."

"I'd rather not," The man answered.

"Sir, it isn't an option," Josiah said, his voice firm. "You need to leave immediately."

Dustin stepped to the side, trying to get a better view out into the station. The cell door was only open about six inches, and Josiah still blocked most of the view, but Dustin saw enough to make out a man standing behind one of the desks. He was black and wearing a tight black turtle neck. Dustin recognized him, despite the limited view. Shae's co-star. The back of his neck prickled with apprehension, remembering the way the guy had lingered outside the train back in Granby, and what Shae had said about him being Clayton's brother.

"Aren't you... Ariane Cordova?" Josiah said.

Dustin realized this was likely his best chance at escape. A good slam against the door would send Josiah spinning, and a human was much easier to handle than a vampire. Knock him out, drag him out a back door so he wasn't trapped in the burning building, and run for it.

Except Shae's co-star was out there for some reason, and Dustin didn't think it was a coincidence. Besides. Running on a busted ankle didn't present the best odds of success.

"I am," Ariane said, leaning over the desk, weight on his slightly splayed, gloved fingers.

Josiah shifted uncomfortably in front of the door, opening up a bit more of Dustin's view into the station. "I need you to leave the building, sir."

Ariane didn't answer, just slid a leather gloved hand into his back pocket and produced a wad of cash. "You leave first, without him, and this is yours."

"It is illegal to bribe a police officer," Josiah said, voice stiff. "You need to leave so I can safely evacuate the prisoner."

Ariane sighed. "You're a good man, Josiah. Not even an officer, but you're the only one who came back to get the prisoner."

"No one deserves to burn. You need to leave. Now."

"Humans are much harder to bribe than vampires, did you know that? Vampires will always, always take blood. Some hold out for more than others, but they always take it. Humans, though, every human wants something different. That makes them tricky. I am a rich, well connected man, Josiah. I'll figure out what you want."

Dustin heard Ariane rifling around in the desk he stood behind, but could no longer see him due to Josiah's shifting.

This time Josiah didn't answer.

"Pawnable jewelry, medical treatment for a loved one, an expensive car or two, a mansion in the Hollywood Hills," Ariane listed. He came back into view, a bottle of what looked like whiskey in one hand, and sat on the closer side of the desk, only feet from Josiah.

The room had begun to fill with a haze of smoke, the alarm still wailing.

"Look," Ariane said, popping open the top of the bottle and taking a swig. "We really don't have an incredible amount of time here. The fire I lit is going to reach this room at any moment, and the firetrucks are only going to be distracted by the warehouse I set on fire for so long. Pick something. Your heart's desire."

The prickling on the back of Dustin's neck grew into a full blown spine chill. Even if he got past Josiah, Ariane was clearly the worse threat. Two fires set. People potentially killed. And he was Shae's co-star, he had to be here because of her. For her. Dustin didn't want to think about what that might mean.

He was running out of time, though. One opportunity to escape had already been wasted. Pushing away his pain, he went to the back of the cell and ran for the door shoulder first. The impact was hard, jarring across Dustin's chest and catching on the places his ribs were broken. Josiah went flying, not even having time to catch himself before he hit the floor. Dustin followed him down, slamming a fist into the side of his head. Josiah went limp and Dustin rolled off him, coughing.

"Well. That was interesting," Ariane said, looking down at Dustin. He hadn't moved from his position on the edge of the desk.

"Why the hell are you here?" Dustin groaned, struggling to his knees and grabbing a set of cuffs from next to Ariane's thigh. He snapped them around Josiah's wrists as the man started to come around with a moan.

Ariane ignored Dustin's question, posing his own instead; "I'm assuming you *are* Dustin? Your face is sort of... deformed at the moment, but you look mostly like Shae said you would."

"What exactly do you have to do with Shae?" Dustin asked, using the desk to pull himself up into a standing position. His ankle sent pain screaming up through his leg, combined with the pain in his ribs, and a wave of dizziness overtook him once he made it upright. There was no way he could run.

"She's a friend. I'm breaking you out for her. Too many eyes on her at the moment. I've been instructed to take you to the north-east edge of town so you can meet up with Russell in 'the clearing where you left the horses.'"

The smoke in the room was reaching eye-watering levels, curling in under a door on the right side of the room.

"You don't like me," Ariane surmised, taking another swig of whiskey. "Whatever. I have a car waiting out back. Take it to the edge of town yourself if you like. I'll give you the keys."

Dustin held out his hand, not getting any closer; he

didn't trust Ariane in the slightest. Everything about him screamed predator. The door the smoke was coming from had begun to glow around the edges, popping and crackling in the heat. Ariane dropped the keys into his palm, along with a crinkled envelope.

"It's the black four-door sedan with tinted windows in the alley on the east side of the building. The letter is from Shae. In summary, it states: don't come after me you idiot, Russ is waiting for you, get your ass home."

Dustin took the letter and stuffed it in his pocket, looped the keyring around a finger, and attempted to bend down to get Josiah.

"Leave him," Ariane said.

Dustin looked up with a frown. "Josiah's human. I'm not leaving him here to die."

"You can't carry him in the state you're in. Probably can't even drag him."

"And, what, you'll get him out?"

Ariane didn't answer so Dustin went back to attempting to bend over, only to be stopped by a familiar click. Looking up slowly he saw that Ariane had drawn a small, shiny, black pistol. His finger was off the trigger, but the barrel was pointed directly at Dustin's face.

"Shae would know," Dustin said, remaining still.

"How? Anyone could have shot you before I got here," Ariane replied. "Leave."

The door burst into flames, sending sparks in all directions. Several of them alighted on papers on the desks, starting half a dozen new fires. Dustin was out of time and out of options. He gave Josiah a last look, then started hobbling for the east exit door, feeling sick.

Looking back, he saw Ariane lower the gun to Josiah, aim, and shoot him once through the forehead. Dustin watched, unable to pull himself away from the sight. Ariane contemplated the body a moment, then poured the rest of the whiskey over his clothes. With a slim grin, he grabbed a burning piece of paper off of a desk and dropped it. The paper arced back and forth through the air until it brushed against Josiah's shirt, the flames jumping to the whiskey soaked fabric.

Ariane laughed.

Dustin tore out of the building, no longer feeling the pain from his injuries. The door led to the alley as promised, the black sedan parked just feet from the door. Without looking to see if there was anyone to notice him Dustin threw himself into the driver's seat, gasping in the cleaner air. Fumbling with the keys, he found the right one and slid it into the ignition, put the car in reverse, and slid out onto the street behind the station. A crowd of people stood there, staring up at the building. He couldn't tell if they noticed him and he didn't look back to see if Ariane got out. He didn't want him to.

No one tried to stop Dustin as he drove out of town, and a glance around the car made him suspect that it was an unmarked police vehicle. A large radio system took up most of the dashboard and there seemed to be a lot more buttons than a normal car. Pushing a few, he found the one that turned the radio on. A mix of human voices interspersed with Morse code clicks from the vampires that couldn't use the radios rattled out of the speakers.

"—... ..—.. .—.. —.. .. —. — ——. / —.—. ——— —. ... ..— ——. . —.."

"Evacuation ordered for the surrounding buildings."

"We don't have enough trucks for this, dammit. The warehouse one is starting to spread!"

".—.. . .—. ...— . / ..—"

"The warehouses can burn. The entire street could go up out here."

Dustin turned the radio back off, figuring the cops were distracted enough to not be looking for him for a while yet, especially in one of their own cars. He wondered if they even realized they had left him in the building.

Driving proved tricky with a bad right foot, broken fingers, and one eye swelled shut, but Dustin made it out of town. He would've abandoned the car, worried about a tracker in it, if not for how bad his injuries were. Finding a backroad heading the right direction he turned up the mountain, resolving to take the car a few miles before dumping it. That would put him far enough away that he could hobble to a place to hide for the night before making for the clearing in the morning.

As he drove higher and higher up the slope he caught glimpses of the twinkling town through the trees. Both fires, one on each end of town, still raged. Firetrucks had arrived at the one at the police station, though they didn't seem to be making much impact. Maybe, if it got bad enough, they'd think he died in it. That would be a good thing.

He wondered where Shae was. Was she watching the fires too? Did she know what Ariane had done to get him out? Mostly, he wished he gotten the chance to say goodbye, no matter how messy things had gotten. His heart still ached for the little sister he'd thought he was going to be bringing home.

Twenty minutes out of town the road was still going the direction Dustin wanted, so he kept going. Just a little longer. Just a little less walking. Without any sign of a problem from the car both headlights went out within seconds of one another. Dustin thought he'd heard gunshots over the sound of the engine, but he wasn't sure. Letting the car roll to a stop, he waited to see if his suspicions would be confirmed.

Nothing happened for several minutes, and then a figure slid out of the shadows, rifle raised and pointed at the car. Vivian's shiny black bird mask gleamed in the moonlight.

"Dustin?!" The glass muffled her voice, though that didn't stop it from sending a wave of comfort through him.

He cracked open the door so she could hear him. "Do me a favor and don't shoot me? I've had a shitty enough day."

She'd already lowered the rifle and jogged over to his

door, pulling it open. "I saw the smoke. What happened? Where's Russ? Shae?"

"Shae's back in town. Russ is supposed to meet me in the clearing where we left the horses."

"Supposed to?" She asked, leaning in to examine his injuries in the light of the car. Her hands were gentle as she probed the swelling around his eye. "What other injuries and what caused them?"

"Long story. Shae said he's meeting me there," Dustin told her. She frowned, but didn't comment. "Broken ribs, smoke inhalation, twisted ankle. Dry vamp bite on my arm. Broken fingers. Cop came at me in a tiny cell. No weapons, no armor, no time to react."

She examined his face, fingers on his chin to tilt his head back and forth. Still frowning she slid a hand under his shirt and pressed at his abdomen in a few areas.

"I'm glad you're here," Dustin whispered.

"Couldn't leave you with a psychopath," Vivian muttered. "Can you ride to the clearing?"

"Yeah," Dustin said, not sure if it was true.

"Wait here. I'll get the horses."

With that she slipped back into the shadows, reappearing several moments later with all four horses. She led Kodiak over and lured him into laying down next to the driver's side door, taking a moment to secure the contraption for eliminating hoofprints to his saddle. With Vivian's help Dustin got out and into the saddle, hanging onto the pommel as Kodiak stood up, managing to jar every injury Dustin had in the process. Vivian made sure he was steady before mounting up on Mudcake.

The ride to the clearing took about fifteen minutes, Vivian riding so close to Dustin their knees brushed. He suspected she thought he might pass out, and he wasn't sure she was wrong to think it. When they reached the clearing Dustin's heart dropped. It looked empty at first glance, until Russ stepped out from where he'd been crouched behind a large pine, a look of pure relief on his face that matched Dustin's own relief at seeing him.

"Dustin! You're ok— Fuck, you are not okay!"

"Nothing life threatening," Vivian said. "Help him off Kodiak while I find my med kit. We can't stay long, but I need to treat his wounds before we move on."

Russ nodded and did as told, taking all of Dustin's weight as he slid out of Kodiak's saddle. Dustin hissed as his ribs go jostled once again.

"What *happened*?" Russ asked as he settled Dustin on the ground.

"Got arrested. Cop attacked me when I wouldn't tell him about Shae. Shae got whisked off somewhere. Few hours passed. Her co-star, Ariane, showed up. He lit the building on fire. He tried to bribe the human dispatcher who was getting me out of my cell. Didn't work. Ariane killed him. Set him on fire," Dustin explained, having to stop to catch his breath a few times.

"He lit the guy on fire?" Russ asked slowly.

"The body," Dustin said. Not that that made it much better.

"How'd you get away?" Russ said.

"He gave me the keys to a stolen cop car. Drove it up here. Vivian found me," Dustin replied. "Gave me a letter from Shae, too. In my back pocket."

Dustin lifted his hip a bit to allow Russ to extract the letter as Vivian came back over with a lantern and her med kit. She kneeled down, setting the lantern in the dirt between all of them.

Russ sucked in a sharp breath, looking at the wound on Dustin's arm. "Is that...?"

"Yes," Vivian answered, pouring clean water over the wound before going at it with antiseptic that stung like hell. "No need to panic, however. If he was going to turn he'd have a raging fever by now, and his pulse would be all over the place."

"You're sure?" Russ pressed, eying the wound.

"Entirely. More worrying is that I think he has a bruised liver. His abdomen isn't ridged, so he isn't bleeding internally, but he's pale, his blood pressure seems low, his pulse is fast, and there's a large bruise forming over where the liver sits."

"Can you treat that?" Russ asked, looking a bit pale as well. Dustin wanted to comfort him, tell him Vivian was being overdramatic, but he couldn't call up the energy to do so.

"There isn't much of a treatment besides fluids and rest," Vivian said. She'd pulled out a suture kit and started sewing up the bite on Dustin's arm. She did just enough to hold the wound closed without bothering to make it pretty. Dustin didn't care. It wouldn't be his first scar. Wouldn't be his first vamp bite scar, for that matter. She finished by dabbing more antiseptic on the wound and wrapping it in a sterile bandage.

"What can I do?" Russ asked.

"There's some packs of electrolyte drink mix in the med kit. Mix one into a canteen," Vivian instructed.

Russ did as she asked, tucking Shae's letter into his own pocket. As he mixed the drink Vivian moved on to examining Dustin's ankle, peeling off his boot and setting it aside. The swelling had gone down somewhat, despite Dustin walking on it. She splinted and bandaged it to keep the swelling from getting worse now that his boot was off. She did the same to his three broken fingers while Dustin sipped from the canteen Russ handed over.

"Not much I can do for the rest of your injuries," Vivian said once she finished. "You'll have to tough it out for now. I've got willow-bark aspirin, but that's it. Sorry."

"I'll manage," Dustin told her.

"What now?" Russ asked. He'd started running a hand softly up and down Dustin's back. It felt strange, but Dustin suspected it was more to comfort himself than it was to comfort Dustin, so he didn't comment.

"We get farther back in the hills where we can lie low," Vivian said. "Dustin, what are the chances we get followed?"

Dustin shrugged, exhaustion creeping up on him.

"Dustin's not going to be able to stay on a horse," Russ said, worry in his voice.

"I'll ride with him," Vivian said. "Kodiak is exhausted,

but he's tough and strong. He can manage with both of us for a while."

Their voices faded as Dustin let himself give in to the exhaustion. He knew they still weren't safe, but he trusted that Vivian would fix it somehow.

27: The Game

Shae was lounging on the couch with her feet in Helen's lap when Ariane wandered back in using the keycard Shae had given him. He smelled of smoke and was swinging an empty whiskey bottle between the fingers of one hand.

"Your big brother is off and moderately well," Ariane said. "He was somewhat beat up. Wouldn't let me drive him, but I gave him the keys and he drove in the correct direction so I'd assume he's alright." He dropped the whiskey bottle in the trash in favor of pouring himself a glass of wine.

"Why do you smell like smoke?" Helen asked, suspicion in her voice and written out across her face.

Ariane shrugged, dropping into the armchair next to the couch. "There were a lot of people in the station. Cops. Reporters. Civilians. Lighting the place on fire seemed like the easiest way to get them all out quickly."

"*You lit that fire*?" Helen asked, tone incredulous.

"I lit both those fires. First one was to occupy the

firefighters. Second one was to get Dustin out."

"You couldn't have just pulled the damn alarm?" Helen asked.

"Of course not," Ariane said, shaking his head at Helen. "People would have come back in the station as soon as they realized there wasn't really a fire. I needed more time, so I disconnected the fire mitigation systems and lit the place."

"You could have killed someone!" Helen shouted.

Ariane quirked an eyebrow at her and took a slow sip of wine. "I did kill someone, Love."

This froze Helen mid rant buildup and she stared at him with her mouth hanging open. Shae could feel the tension in Helen's body where her legs were still on her girlfriend's lap.

"Oh? And who did you kill?" Shae asked.

"The 911 dispatcher. He was the only one who stayed to get your brother out, and the bastard just wouldn't take a bribe. Couldn't have a witness, so," Ariane finished with a shrug.

Shae grinned, holding up her wineglass and tilting it towards him in a distant toast. He'd certainly come through.

Helen had begun to shake her head, holding up her hands like she was trying to push away the knowledge of what transpired. Before anything more could be said there was a knock on the door which about sent Helen through the roof. Shae, rolling her eyes at Helen, got up and opened the door, finding the cop who was meant to be guarding her on the other side. He looked harried, eyes darting from side to side and one hand rubbing at the back of his neck.

"Officer?"

"Ma'am, I, I'm sorry, but there's been a fire," he stuttered.

Shae frowned, looking worried. "I know, I saw it from the window. Was it... was it the people who took me?"

He nodded. "We think so. They lit two fires, one as a distraction so they could... could help the captured rebel escape. I'm sorry. He's gone. We've posted multiple guards at the hotel and have started searching for him, though he did... get a bit of a head start due to the confusion. The federal coven agents have taken over everything.

Shae let her hand fly to her mouth, sagging against the doorframe. The officer looked like he was about to grab her and hold her up when Ariane appeared, wrapping an arm tightly around her waist and glaring at the officer.

She saw the cop's nose twitch and knew he could smell the smoke on Ariane.

"I think you need to leave, sir," Ariane said.

"You smell like smoke," the cop said, eyes giving Ariane a once over.

"Of course I do," Ariane snapped. "I'm a smoker. And the bloody smoke from those fires has been blowing this way since the damn things started. I get a face full of it every time I step out on the porch to have a cigarette."

The cop tried to speak again, but Shae spoke first,

making her voice meek, "He told you to leave."

"That I did," Ariane said, chest swelling. "You and your idiotic excuse for a police force have obviously proved incompetent, so your being here is just making things worse. Get lost. We will make sure those who we trust to actually do their jobs protect Shae as you are incapable of the task."

With that Ariane slammed the door in the cop's face. They could hear him spluttering on the other side before he turned and walked away, footsteps quiet in the carpeted hallway. As soon as they heard the elevator doors close Ariane and Shae both burst out laughing, hanging onto one another to stay upright.

"You two...." They turned to see Helen shaking her head before stalking into the bedroom, slamming the door behind her. This produced another round of laughter and the two of them slid to the floor, leaning against the door.

"Next time you go missing, Shae-Shae, take me with you. Life is so dull without you around," Ariane said through his laughter.

"Oh yes, positively drab I'm sure," Shae giggled.

He nodded and they leaned against each other as their laughter subsided.

"So, I believe you promised me a secret," Ariane said.

"Cryo-corpses," Shae said, still catching her breath. "The woman who helped my brothers, Vivian, she's seen them being transported on a couple trains she's robbed recently, the first time she's ever seen them. It confirms what Dalton said. My guess is that they're trying to wake them up enough for their bodies to start producing blood again. A ready made blood farm that no one will think to look for."

"Fascinating," Ariane murmured, head tilting back against the door. "Cryo-corpses being transported through Wood's Coven doesn't necessarily point to my father, but it does back up some of what Dalton said. I'll have to dig into it more."

"Your turn," Shae said. "What happened after my brothers took me and the guards blew up that building?"

Ariane smirked. "Well, the guards had to drag Helen back onto the train. Once they got her on we pulled out and raced out of the area, stopping in some town called Grand Junction. Been there ever since while everyone figured out what to do. Got put up in a nice little hotel. Helen was harping on the police every minute we were there. Lots of press came through, all wanting interviews with anyone who knew you. Demanding every little detail."

"And you gave them the juicy ones?"

"Of course. Do you really think I am the kind of friend to let you slip into obscurity? I alerted the news media before we ever even got to Grand Junction."

"Tell me this, then, why did Wood's Coven only send fifteen incompetent soldiers after me?" Shae asked.

"Did they?"

She nodded. "At least according to Vivian and Dustin. And I am hardly an expert in military tactics, but even I could tell they were woefully under skilled."

"Well, that's an interesting little mystery," Ariane

hummed. "Wood's Coven claimed they sent the best of the best. The fact that they were all killed blew the story up even more. Fifteen good soldiers lost, and you still missing. The politicians are having a dreadful time."

"More scandal to unleash, I suppose," Shae replied.

Ariane chuckled. "It will be fun to see them scramble to explain themselves. Though I am curious about the real reason."

"As am I, but enough on that for now." Shae grinned, hooking her arm through his. "What about the movie? I saw on the news the first few days of showings are selling out all over the place."

Ariane nodded. "Indeed. People love a scandal, and you've provided plenty lately."

"You've seen all the coverage. How do you think I should play it when the press gets to me?" Shae asked.

"Hmmm," Ariane contemplated, helping Shae up and keeping their arms linked as they wandered back to the couch. "Play it strong. Show people the rebels aren't worth worrying about. Play it off as some silly thing, that if a single actress can escape them, how dangerous can they really be?"

"Believably nonchalant, then."

"That's what people want to hear right now," Ariane said, settling into one end of the couch with his glass of wine. "Especially here in Wood's Coven. Take the side that they pose no real threat, at least against competent soldiers, and it will make you even more popular."

Shae took the other end of the couch, tangling their

legs together, and picked up her own glass. They continued to trade details of the last several days, emptying the bottle of wine little by little. Ariane told her all about every aspect of the news coverage and everything else that had happened. In turn Shae told him all the lurid details of her adventure with Dustin and Russ.

"Ugh. Horse riding," Ariane muttered. "I hate horses. They smell atrocious and are just generally unpleasant to be around."

"They aren't my favorite either," Shae admitted. "I'm still sore from all the riding."

"I would imagine so. That Vivian woman, though, she sounds rather interesting."

"Yes, well, she was about five seconds away from killing me when we parted ways, so I can't say I'll miss her."

"What did you do, piss in her breakfast?"

Shae laughed. "Nothing so mundane. I just pointed out some… inconsistencies in things she'd told us about herself. She didn't like that much. Now, what do you think my chances are of convincing the powers that be to finish up our tour?"

Ariane grinned. "Well, the people involved with the movie won't take much once they see that you're alright. They're seeing nothing but dollar signs right now. *Helen*, however…."

Shae sighed, throwing her head back. Helen. Always ruining the fun.

"Why do you put up with her?" Ariane asked idly, running a finger around the rim of his glass to make it sing.

Shae shrugged. "She's sweet. She's hot. The sex is good. She can cook."

"Delightful things to build a relationship on," he said, slowing his finger to bring out a different note.

"We were very different people when we met," Shae said, staring at the off-white ceiling. "I'm not surprised things are coming apart. If I'm being truthful, I *am* surprised she hasn't already left me. I do wonder what's keeping her around."

"Well, as I was saying, she doesn't seem particularly keen on doing anything other than going back to London," Ariane said.

Shae pulled her head back up and shrugged. "Then she can go back to London."

"Let me rephrase, she doesn't seem particularly keen on doing anything other than going back to London *with you*."

"She'll just have to deal with it or come along on the rest of the tour then. I'm not wasting this opportunity."

"As you shouldn't. We'll be filling stadiums at this rate."

Ariane and Shae talked for several more hours before Shae surrendered to exhaustion and left for the bedroom, leaving Ariane to sleep on the couch. Helen was bundled under the covers, looking long asleep, though her reading lamp was still on. Shae padded over to Helen's suitcase that had been brought up earlier and opened it, digging around until she found a t-shirt. She was not wearing those moose pajamas.

Slipping out of the sundress and into the shirt, she walked over to the patio door and pushed the curtains aside, peering out at the town. The fires seemed to be out now, and many of the lights in town had gone out as well. She couldn't make out the mountains from where she was, but she wondered where in them Dustin and Russ were. They should've met up by now. They'd have to stay hidden for a few days, but they'd be alright with just themselves to worry about. Shae would continue to misdirect the press and the police, pointing them towards a group of rebels from Baja.

She let the curtains fall and turned to watch Helen, who'd fallen asleep with a book clutched to her chest, a common occurrence. Shae carefully extracted the book, intending to set it on the nightstand, but her eyes caught on the title. "A Story of Turning: The Biography of Zahari Louise Slavik."

"Zahari Louise Slavik," Shae whispered. Even she knew that name. Everyone did. Zahari was the first human who was legally Turned in Riddlesdale Coven after the coven was established and unregulated turning was deemed illegal. Now it was a highly restricted process. Almost no one got turned anymore.

There was a piece of folded paper sticking out of the middle of the book, and Shae's curiosity got the better of her. She flipped the book open, holding the spot with her thumb, and unfolded the paper with her other hand. It was a printout of an email sent two days before Dustin and Russ had taken her.

<table>
<tr><td>To: Helen.Thibault.Personal@CMail.com</td></tr>
<tr><td>From: Applications@RDTurningInstitute.com</td></tr>
<tr><td>Subject: Congratulations!</td></tr>
</table>

Ms. Thibault,

I am elated to inform you that your application for turning has been accepted. We at the institute were blown away by your credentials, future plans, and connections. More info is forthcoming about next steps, but we wanted to send this short initial email to let you know you're in. We look forward to going through this process with you.

Sincerely,
Doctor Miriam J. Appletin, Director of Turning Studies

"Connections..." Shae murmured, tracing her finger over the word. "So that's why you've been putting up with me."

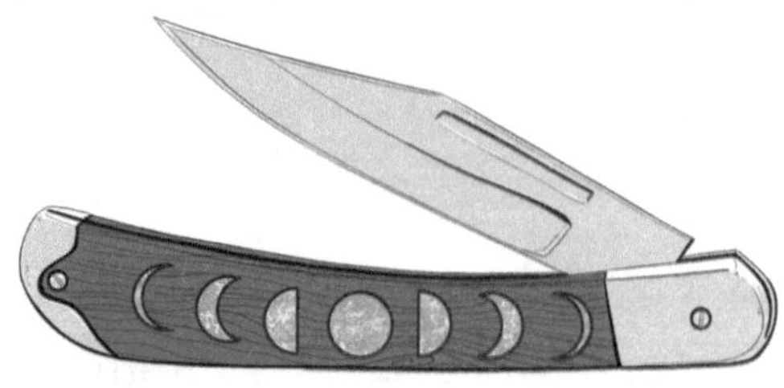

28: Going Home

Dustin woke up with a groan, blinking in the soft light. He was in a room, sort of. It looked half collapsed, wooden beams at a strange angle above him and sunlight coming in through sizeable holes in the walls. A bedroll was beneath him, and there was no sign of anyone else.

"Vivian?" He said, voice raspy.

She appeared in the crooked doorway, Russ behind her.

"Where are we?" Dustin asked as they came over. Vivian helped him sit up, leaning him back on the wall of the building. It creaked ominously but didn't move.

"Well out of Hayden," Vivian told him. "Some old cabin."

"How are you feeling?" Russ asked, handing him a canteen. The water tasted lemony, like the electrolyte water last night.

"I'm never getting in a fight without armor again," Dustin muttered.

"You didn't have armor when you charged that pack of vamps back in Nahanni," Russ pointed out.

"Yeah, but I did have a gun, several knives, more

room to maneuver, and backup. And a lot more sleep."

Vivian had pulled up his shirt and was examining the enormous bruise over his liver. "You're talking better now, at least. And you've got some color back in your skin."

"How long did I sleep?" Dustin asked.

"About eighteen hours. We've been at the cabin for about twelve," Russ told him.

"That's not far enough from Hayden," Dustin told them.

"You think they're coming after you?" Vivian asked.

Dustin thought about it. Really, he wasn't sure of anything. Everything had happened so fast. Shae had told so many lies.

"What does Shae's letter say?" He asked Russ.

Russ shrugged and pulled it out, starting to read the blocky print that Dustin suspected was not Shae's normal writing;

I'M SORRY THIS WENT SO WRONG. YOUR FRIEND WAS RIGHT WHEN SHE SAID YOU UNDERESTIMATED MY FAME. BY NOW YOU SHOULD HAVE GOTTEN OUT OF PRISON. TAKE THIS CHANCE AND GO. YOU'LL FIND YOUR PARTNERS WHERE YOU LEFT YOUR HORSES. GET HOME. LIVE YOUR LIVES. ACCEPT THAT I AM NOT WHO YOU WANTED ME TO BE.

"That's all it says," Russ said. "No greeting, no closing..."

"She didn't want it to be able to be connected to her,

or to who you and I really are," Dustin guessed.

He tilted his head back, resting it against the wall and closing his eyes as he played over everything that had happened the day before. Everything that happened over the last two weeks. All the stupid decisions he'd made. Somehow it all seemed so clear now, how much he'd let slide. Maybe it was because he was still exhausted, still in pain, but he didn't have the energy to lie to himself anymore. He'd fucked up. He'd trusted Shae, believed she was a good person even when it kept being thrown in his face that she wasn't.

He'd just wanted his little sister back. But that wasn't quite right either. He'd wanted it to not be his fault that she left. Because Shae had been right, he *had* talked about wanting to leave. Craved it. He'd missed the plush beds, the expensive food, the access to anything he could ever want, the dreams he'd had.

"Russ… I'm sorry. I never should've dragged you into this," Dustin whispered. The regret hurt more than the bruises. He opened his eyes to see Russ shrug.

"You didn't drag me into it, Dustin," Russ said, shuffling around a bit. "Well. Maybe you did. But if I'd really wanted to put a stop to this, I could have. I guess… deep down I've always wanted to know what happened to her too, even though I saw her leave and never told anyone."

"Still, I should've gone alon—"

Russ waved a hand to interrupt him, "Stop. We're not getting back on that merry-go-round. I came because you're my brother and because I wanted to. Did I have reservations? Yes. Did things go sideways? Yes. But we made it through, and we know the truth now. End of the day, I think that's better than I expected."

Dustin hesitated a moment before nodding, grimacing when it sent a spike of pain through his skull. Vivian wordlessly tapped the water bottle he was still holding and Dustin took a long swig.

"I can't travel like this, not all the way home," Dustin said, grimmacing as he jostled his injuries.

"We'll wait for you to get better," Russ told him. "We need to lie low anyway."

"No, Russ. Last night, the cop who was interrogating me about Shae, before he beat me up, he said Wood's Coven is planning a full-scale attack on all the rebel camps in their territory."

Vivian and Russ both tensed up, looking between one another, expressions grim.

"He could've been lying, trying to rile you up," Russ said, no real belief behind the words.

"Could have," Dustin admitted. "But what if he wasn't? It makes sense, with everything else that's happened lately."

"Dustin—" Russ started.

"Vivian's going to help you get some supplies together," Dustin interrupted. "She's going to get you a route home that takes you up through the rest of the unclaimed territory on horseback, following the old roads to make better time. That'll get you over the border into Canada. Then you're going to steal a car—not rent, steal—and you are going to take it a hundred miles. Then you're going to dump it and steal another. And you are going to get home, and you're going to warn them."

"What about you?" Russ asked.

"I'll stay with him here for a few days," Vivian said. "Then get him back to my place to finish recovering. We'll follow you when we can."

"We?" Dustin asked her.

She lightly flicked his shoulder. "Yes, we. I'm not letting you hobble off to war while I sit home drinking coco."

Dustin smiled and reached out to take her hand, squeezing it gently. She smiled and returned the squeeze.

"So... suddenly you've got enough faith in me to let me navigate home on my own?" Russ teased, though his eyes looked worried.

"I never didn't trust you, kiddo. I just...you're my little brother."

Russ nodded, looking almost as exhausted as Dustin felt. "I hope that cop was lying. But I guess we better get to work, Vivian."

Acknowledgements

Third time's (hopefully) the charm, right? My first attempt at this book needed a heavy rewrite, but when I tried to re-release it that annoying little thing called COVID slammed down onto the world. On top of that I got a new job at roughly the same time, and until I was able to move closer, I had a lovely hour-and-a-half commute each way. The last thing I had any energy for was promoting a book launch.

SO HERE WE GO AGAIN.

Thank you so much to all my awesome beta readers, critique partners, and friends who have managed not to strangle me as I rambled endlessly about this project over the last seven or so years. Nicole, Erica, you two are the best. Thanks for always letting me throw ideas at you until I figured them out, and for some fantastically weird late-night conversations about the similarities between vampires and various types of marine life. Swifty, thanks for being endlessly devoted to Vivian. And, of course, to everyone across my social media that has been letting me know how excited they've been for this book: you're fantastic! Book 2 is coming, I promise.

Visit Katy L. Wood on her website to learn more about
her other projects, and join her newsletter to be the first to hear
about the second book in the *Glory is Poison* series!

www.Katy-L-Wood.com

About Katy L. Wood

Katy L. Wood is a queer author and illustrator who lives in varying areas of Colorado with her two cats, Rumble and Rebel. The majority of her childhood was being handed a bear-whistle, pushed out the door into the forest, and told to be back for dinner. Occasionally she would have cousins with her, occasionally she'd be alone. There were many adventures to creepy abandoned trailers with bones in the front yard (which she learned as an adult were not actually abandoned, making them ten times creepier), up creeks while making rudimentary maps, and into old mineshafts. Honestly, it is probably a miracle she survived to adulthood. She is now taking bets on if she'll make it to middle-age, given that her habits have not changed the slightest.